"Walker builds her _____ ing romance, and fleshe_____ and a healthy dose of steamy, sensual interaction that's satisfying on an emotional and visceral level." —*Publishers Weekly*

"It was the perfect mix of angst and drama and sweet surrender . . . I think this is one of Walker's best series. Her characters are memorable, the setting vivid, and their struggles real without being all-consuming." —BookPushers

"*Razed* is a passionate story about family, betrayal, heartbreak, and moving on . . . Shiloh's characters will captivate your imagination and pull you in along their journeys of romance and love." —The Reading Cafe

"If you like the rock-type, strong, and supportive heroes, then look no further than Zane Barnes." —Under the Covers Book Blog

WRECKED

"The sexy surprises . . . send their comfortable relationship into uncharted (and utterly hot) territory . . . Walker ably demonstrates her skill with a contemporary scenario." —*Publishers Weekly*

"A touching romance about best friends finding out that love was right in front of them the whole time. It has plenty of sizzle . . . We get to see the interior feelings of both leads in this lovely little contained look at two people that any reader would love to call friends. A beautiful story!" —*RT Book Reviews* (★★★★½)

"A sweet and sexy story that . . . was charming and fun to read." —*Smart Bitches, Trashy Books*

continued . . .

"A successful romance and a good read . . . Sexy and poignant."
—*Kirkus Reviews*

"Made my heart beat out of my chest."
—*Fiction Vixen*

"Full of love, humor, and a passion that burns brightly."
—*Joyfully Reviewed*

PRAISE FOR THE PARANORMAL ROMANCES OF SHILOH WALKER

"Shiloh's books are sinfully good, wickedly sexy, and wildly imaginative!"
—Larissa Ione, *New York Times* bestselling author

"An action junkie's thrill ride that hits all the right notes. I recommend this series as a must read for those who love their paranormal romances to be wrapped in dark emotional suspense and intrigue."
—*Smexy Books*

"This story showcases Walker's talent . . . Her characters are complex . . . Her plots twist in very interesting ways . . . The sex is sizzling . . . This is a taut, beautifully written thriller readers won't want to miss."
—*RT Book Reviews* (★★★★½)

"An outstanding story fraught with sexual tension and a spine-tingling mystery. *The Departed* will keep readers turning pages faster than they think trying to put the pieces of the puzzle together."
—*Fresh Fiction*

"Chilling [and] heart-wrenching . . . A richly emotional and wildly imaginative story that grips the reader with genuine, vivacious characters and a sinuous, flowing plot."
—*Fallen Angel Reviews*

"Suspense that can rip your heart open and leave you raw . . . The characters are absolutely fantastic, from the leads to the side characters."
—*Errant Dreams Reviews*

BUSTED

Shiloh Walker

BERKLEY SENSATION, NEW YORK

THE BERKLEY PUBLISHING GROUP
Published by the Penguin Group
Penguin Random House LLC
375 Hudson Street, New York, New York 10014

USA • Canada • UK • Ireland • Australia • New Zealand • India • South Africa • China

penguin.com

A Penguin Random House Company

BUSTED

A Berkley Sensation Book / published by arrangement with Shiloh Walker, Inc.

For information, address: The Berkley Publishing Group,
a division of Penguin Random house LLC,
375 Hudson Street, New York, New York 10014.

ISBN: 978-0-425-27393-7

PUBLISHING HISTORY
Berkley Sensation mass-market edition / May 2015

PRINTED IN THE UNITED STATES OF AMERICA

10 9 8 7 6 5 4 3 2 1

Cover art: Young couple in embrace © Photodisc / Getty Images;
Architectural background © Joshua Haviv / Shutterstock.
Cover design by Rita Frangie.
Interior text design by Kristin del Rosario.

Thanks to all my readers.
I appreciate you all so much!

As always, to my family. I thank God for you.

To Ann M.

Thanks for the day in Norfolk . . . and library talk.

To Robin T. It's always good to have librarians
on hand. For lots of reasons.

Thanks to Cindy and Kristine and the team at Berkley.

Prologue

There was, at times, only one way to completely lose yourself.

This was a fact that Trey Barnes knew all too well.

He'd spent a great deal of time losing himself to books, for instance—first as a reader, and then, as he'd gotten older, as a writer. He found other ways to lose himself, too. He liked to dabble in photography, although he was a bumbling amateur compared to his oldest brother, Zane. Still, it was a good way to while away an afternoon.

And he had loved to lose himself in the arms of his wife, Aliesha.

Now, though, all he had of her were memories . . . and that small infant on the other side of the glass, struggling for every breath.

"Mr. Barnes?"

He didn't look at the nurse.

"Sir, why don't you go home and get some rest?"

It was creeping up on ten. He'd been here since . . . hell. He'd come straight here after the funeral. Yeah, it had been a while. He'd taken every precious moment he could to be as close to his baby as possible. Not that he could do much more than stroke one small, frail hand.

Clayton Barnes, a mere three days old, was a tiny, little miracle from God. He'd been born more than two months early. Without the ventilator that was doing the breathing for him, he wouldn't be alive.

"Mr. Barnes."

Slowly, he looked away from the window and met the compassionate gaze of the nurse. She was older, her round face softened by time, and her eyes held his steadily.

She reached out and rested a hand on his shoulder.

"You need rest," she said gently. "You have to take care of yourself now . . . for him, if nothing else. You're all he has."

A knot settled in his throat, then he nodded. "Can I have another few minutes with him?"

"Of course."

Once he left the neonatal intensive care unit and the hospital behind, he didn't go home. Not yet.

There was no way he could sleep in their bed.

Their bed.

Aliesha . . .

Tears burned his eyes and he blinked them away as the road blurred in front of him.

His phone buzzed—it was still on silent mode from the funeral. It had too many ignored phone calls, too many unanswered messages and he planned on letting them go ignored. Unanswered. The only people he'd care to talk to were his family, and all of them knew where to track him down. He'd be at the hospital sixteen to eighteen hours a day for the foreseeable future.

For now, he didn't want to be around anybody he knew. Anybody . . . or any place.

Taking the interstate downtown, he found a hotel. Somebody came out from behind the valet parking stand but Trey already had the door open. "Will you be checking in, sir?"

He gave a short nod and moved to the back, grabbing the bag his mother had packed so he could have clothes for after the funeral. He'd never changed. They'd come in handy now.

"Do you have any other luggage?"

"No." He turned his keys over and went to head inside, but then looked back at the man. "Where's the nearest bar?"

"There's the hotel lounge, although it closes at eleven."

"Aside from that?"

The man cocked his head and gestured west. "Take a left at the next block. You'll find quite a few. Plenty of places open til midnight, some even later."

Trey gave another nod and passed over a few of the bills he'd shoved inside his pocket earlier. He'd meant to get coffee, or something from the vending machines at the hospital. Meant to—forgot. Again.

Check-in was a short, silent affair. One thing about some of the more upscale hotels—they seemed to realize when somebody wasn't in a mood to chat.

The lady at check-in apologetically told him the hotel was rather full due to an upcoming convention, although she did have a single open for only one night. The word *convention* had his gut turning—

. . . *an accident . . . hospital as soon as possible . . .*

Shoving the memories aside, he said hoarsely, "I just need it for the night."

He'd figure something else out tomorrow.

Trey barely remembered the walk from the desk to the elevator to the room.

He barely remembered throwing his bag on the bed and stumbling back out.

It was all a blur, and then he was sitting down at the bar, his hand closed tightly around a glass.

It was a dive. He'd asked for whiskey, a double, neat, and it had come in a smudged glass, the fumes of whatever horse-piss they'd brought so strong, it might have doubled for rocket fuel.

He tossed it back and tapped his glass.

The bartender slid him a look but served him up another before disappearing to tend to everybody else jammed in at the bar, elbow deep.

"You look like you want to drink away your sorrows."

Sighing, Trey lifted the glass and pressed it to his head. He closed his eyes and said, "Go away."

"Aww . . ." A hand stroked down his arm. "Don't go being like that."

Jerking his arm away, he tugged his wallet out and fished out some bills—how much did whiskey cost in a dive like this? He didn't know. He caught the bartender's eye and held up two twenties.

"Get your change in a minute—"

"Keep it," Trey said sourly as the woman on his left leaned in closer. The feel of her breasts, the scent of her, had something inside him going cold.

Aliesha—

He half stumbled away as days of grief, of guilt, crashed into him. He found a bare space of wall near the back of the bar, a painted-over window tucked up over his head. He rested there, taking another drink of whiskey, slower this time, grimacing at the almost painful bite of the cheapest, shittiest whiskey he'd ever had the misery to experience. Appropriate, he decided. Today was the most miserable, shittiest day of his life.

A tear squeezed out of the corner of his eye. He swiped at it with the heel of his hand, not giving a damn if anybody saw it. Then he tipped back the glass and had another sip.

"Hey."

Cracking one eye open, he bit back a groan. It was the woman from the bar. At one time in the past, he would have given her a thorough look. Her hair was done in long, thick plaits that hung almost to her waist, while her hourglass curves were poured into a belly-baring shirt and a skirt that just barely skimmed the legal limit. A gold ring flashed from her navel and there was a piercing in her nose.

She looked like a woman capable of wicked things.

No doubt about it, she could make a man's cock stand on end.

Now, though, all she did was angle her head to the side. "Look, I'm sorry if I came on too strong. You . . . hell, you look like you're having a rough day. You want to talk about it?"

"No." He closed his eyes again and had another long, hard pull of his drink, realized it was empty.

His head was also starting to spin. Usually two drinks wouldn't do it, but he hadn't eaten since the toast his mother had forced on him that morning. Not exactly the ideal dietary intake.

Didn't matter. He could still think. If he could think, he wasn't drunk enough.

Shouldering up off the wall, he went to cut around her.

She caught his arm and when he tried to pull away, she just gripped him tighter. "Come on," she said, her voice firm. "If you're going to get plastered, at least do it sitting down."

He might have argued, except he was damn tired.

A few minutes later, he was in a booth.

She sat across from him and he watched listlessly as she picked up his glass and sniffed at it. "What is that, Old Grand-Dad? You trying to kill your stomach or what?" She flagged down one of the servers and Trey snorted.

She wasn't ever going —

Well, scratch that. Some sort of blurry amusement worked its way free in his mind as somebody sidetracked to their table, shooting the woman across from him a hard look. "Yeah?"

That look was meant with an equally hard smile. "Get him something that isn't going to kill his gut," she said, her tone all sugar. Sugar, but the gaze was steel.

Too many undertones there for him to process.

Trying to juggle his way through all of that and deal with the noise in his head was making his brain hurt. He still wasn't drunk enough. Maybe what he should do was hit that liquor store he'd passed . . . yeah.

He liked that idea. He could grab himself a bottle of whatever was closest to the door, lock himself in his room, and get plastered. The headache he'd have in the morning would keep him focused on something other than what he'd done today—

Something thunked down in front of him, hard.

Blinking, he stared at it.

He went to reach for it but before he could, a hand tugged it out of reach.

"Give me that," he demanded.

She kept her hand over it as she slid into the booth next to him. He'd settled in the middle and he wasn't exactly a small guy, so that didn't leave her a lot of room. She didn't seem to care.

Alarms started to screech in his head.

"You wanna talk now?" she said, managing to make that low purr of a voice audible over the din in the air. She stroked a finger down the glass.

"No." He took the glass and the scent of it hit his nose before he took the first swallow. He almost sighed in appreciation. That was more like it. He couldn't quite recognize it—some sort of bourbon, he thought, but a damn sight better than whatever swill he'd been tossing back. Slumping in the seat, he rested his head on the back of the booth.

The fog in his head crept in closer.

"So what has you looking so miserable today, handsome?" Her hand settled on his thigh, dangerously close to his crotch.

He picked it up and slowly, carefully, deliberately settled it on the table. That right there was enough to have the fog in his head clearing.

Even when she started to lean in closer, Trey found the energy to get his leaden legs moving, forcing his too-fogged brain to function. Her eyes—he studied her eyes through a haze of alcohol and realized something was off.

"I buried my wife," he said. His gut went slippery cold as he said it, and then, he said it again. "I buried my wife. She went into early labor and died during the emergency C-section. My son almost died, too."

She went to open her mouth and he leaned in, ignoring the absolutely lovely breasts she displayed as she reached out to touch his arm. "I'm not interested. You're better off looking elsewhere."

Something flashed in her eyes and then she inclined her head. "Pay for your own whiskey, then."

"I wouldn't have it any other way." He nodded toward her and looked around, tried to figure out where the fucking hell he'd *put* the damn whiskey. He'd had a drink, hadn't he?

"Son of a bitch," he mumbled, barely even noticing that he'd banged into the wall on his way out of the bar. Lights blurred together and shadows swayed in and out of the focus, coming alive on him.

There were voices.

Then a shout.

The one last clear thing he remembered was trying to remember where the hell he'd put his damn phone.

A harsh pounding noise split through his head, like a
cleaver striking through bone.

Trey jerked upright and immediately wished he hadn't so
much as moved.

Nausea churned inside and his belly revolted.

He shuddered, braced an arm over his gut as he looked
around.

No light.

Couldn't see—

"You awake there, sunshine?" Lights flashed on.

He flinched at the sound of that voice, as familiar to him as
his own. It was quiet—logically, he knew that, but it sounded
as loud and booming as a fucking gong.

He groaned and rolled over, grabbing for his pillow so he
could drown out the too loud sounds and the too bright lights.

Hearing his twin's sigh, he thought maybe Travis would
take pity on him and let him sleep off this hangover from hell.
Trey couldn't remember the last time he'd been this wasted.

"Come on, man," Travis said a moment later. "You need to
wake up."

The sound of his brother's voice was too loud, too harsh
and he groaned pitifully.

"Mr. Barnes?"

He jerked at the sound of the new voice.

A hand pressed down on his shoulder.

"Easy there, Trey. I'll take care of it. You just . . . try not to
fall out of the bed."

That made him crack open one eye—immediately, he
wished he hadn't, because the lights were harsh and bright and
unforgiving. Anybody who had ever painted hell as a dark and
smoky place was out of his mind. Hell was pure, unrelenting,
blinding light and there was no escape from it. Trey flinched
away from the searing brightness, feeling like his eyeballs had
been singed.

He heard low voices, a hushed, hurried argument and he

decided he was going to have to brave that hell. Cracking open his eye once more—just a slit—he looked around.

The place was disturbingly familiar.

Too bright. Yeah, he didn't like that. Aseptic smells—

That tugged at something—immediately, his mind went on a sideways lurch and he rolled into a seated position and found himself on the edge of a bed that was most certainly *not* his own. He was bare-chested but wearing pants that he thought probably were his, although they were torn at the knee and dirty. His knuckles were bandaged—bruised.

What the—

"You okay there?"

He flexed his hand as Travis came around to stand in front of him.

Looking up, he found himself looking face-to-face at a disheveled mirror of himself. Then he glanced down at his wrecked trousers, his bare chest and his torn-up fists. Maybe *he* was the disheveled reflection this time around. Swallowing the nasty taste in his mouth, he eyed the wrinkled button-down Travis was wearing with a pair of trousers. He looked like he'd slept in them.

Then he looked down at himself, eyed the identification bracelet on his wrist. His head was an endless void—nothing but black stretching back—an awful pain settled at the base of his head and he slid from the bed, half stumbled, half shoved his way past his twin.

"Why am I in the hospital?"

"You . . ." Travis paused, taking his time before he said anything else. "You were at a bar. There was a fight. The bartender ended up calling the cops—you were all but unconscious in the parking lot."

Trey ran his tongue across his teeth. "A bar."

"Yeah. Ah . . . you lost your wallet. Whatever cash you had. I already shut down the credit cards, although I think whoever had them might have already tried to use them—I heard some talk from the cops. You can . . . we can talk about this later."

"There was a woman," he muttered as he flexed his aching hands. "I . . . I almost remember."

"The doctors here, they ran a few blood tests. Ah . . .

nothing happened. Just so you know—apparently you defaulted to fight mode and some . . ."

"What aren't you telling me?" Trey asked, studying his brother's face.

Travis came to stand closer, only a couple of feet away. "It looks like somebody slipped you something in your drink, Trey."

"Slipped . . . what?"

He stared at Travis, confused.

"Somebody gave you drugs—you've got Xanax in your bloodstream." Travis's mouth went tight.

Trey's head continued to pound and it only got worse as he studied his brother. "You didn't need to come here for this, man. I can . . ." He swore and reached up to rub at his head, hoping it wouldn't fall away. A memory tried to work free.

Voices . . . shouting . . .

Misery.

Abruptly, his throat started to ache.

"Why are you here?" he asked, his voice rough. "You were working some stupid-ass case in Toledo, last I heard. Wouldn't be able to visit for a while."

"Trey . . ."

The compassion in his twin's voice almost shattered him.

"No." He shook his head and spun around. The movement almost sent his aching head crashing off his shoulders and he welcomed it. He banged into the bed, almost fell down—would have—if Travis hadn't steadied him.

He threw his twin's hands off. "Get out of here!" he shouted. "You got a fucking job to do! Ain't no reason for you to . . ."

He almost hit the floor when he tried to take a swing at Travis, his aim off. Just that movement had nausea pitching through him.

"Easy," Travis said, steadying him once more, ignoring the anger as if it had never existed. "Come on, Trey. Just sit down. Just sit down . . . and breathe. This . . . some of this, it's just the drugs. Once that shit is out of your system, you'll feel better."

"Drugs." He latched onto that, desperate to think of anything but the knowledge that had started to work free in the back of his head. "Why would somebody spike my drink?"

"Yeah." Travis eased him back onto the bed. "The bartender saw you talking to a woman, but he can't really describe her."

Trey's lids drooped down. There was an echo of a laugh, but even as he tried to grab that memory, something else snuck up, grabbed *him*.

Aliesha's memory. Warm and soft and wonderful. Out of the gaping void of his mind, something ugly crept up. He saw himself, gripping a phone.

"Mr. Barnes, I'm afraid there's been an accident . . ."

"Travis?" he whispered.

"Yeah?"

He swallowed, the words trembling on the tip of his tongue. He didn't want to say it—didn't want to think it.

No, what he wanted to do was go back to those few moments when he'd only had the hangover from hell to deal with.

Those few moments when he'd forgotten that his wife was dead.

Chapter One

Week One

The first time Trey Barnes saw her it caught him by surprise.

Not because he knew her.

Not because of anything she did.

But because it had been almost six years since a woman had caused this kind of reaction in him.

Six years.

So it was a punch in the gut when he walked into the main branch of the Norfolk library for the kid's reading program and saw *her*. His tongue all but glued itself to the roof of his mouth and his brain threatened to do a slow meltdown.

The woman was kneeling down in the middle of a circle of kids, a smile on her face. Her mouth was slicked wine red, and he suddenly found himself dying of thirst.

It had also been almost six years since he'd touched a drop of alcohol, but in that moment, he found himself imagining a glass of wine. Wine . . . wine red lips, wine red sheets and the two of them stretched out on a bed as he ran his hands over that warm, lovely brown skin.

"Come on, Daddy!" Clayton jerked on his hand. "Let's go! I want to go play."

His son's voice dragged him out of the fantasy, rich and lush as it was, and he shook his head a little to clear it. A heavy fullness lingered in his loins and he was glad he'd gotten used to looking like a bum. The untucked shirt had fit him well enough when he bought it years ago, but the weight he'd lost after Aliesha's death had stayed off, so the shirt hung loose on his rangy frame. Loose enough that he figured it would hide the hard-on that had yet to subside.

A few minutes surrounded by chattering preschoolers ought to do it.

Clayton let go of his hand as he got closer and Trey reached up, nudging his sunglasses firmly into place. As he'd retreated further and further into hermit mode, fewer people recognized him, but he rarely went anywhere without something to hide his face. Between the hair he rarely remembered to cut and the sunglasses, people often looked right past him these days.

A shrill shriek split the air as two kids started to fight over a book.

That's going to do it, he mused. Blood that had burned so hot a minute before dropped back into the normal zone.

Only to jump right back up into the danger zone.

Miz Sexy Librarian had crossed to the kids and now stood in front of them, her back to him.

And *fuck* . . . her voice was a wet dream.

"Now I *know* you two weren't raised to treat books that way. Do you do that at home?"

Two pint-sized little blond heads tipped back to stare up at her. Trey barely noticed them, because his gaze was riveted on the plump, round curve of her ass. How could he *not* notice that ass? She wore a long, skinny skirt that went down a few inches below her knees and her stockings were the kind with a seam that ran up the back of her legs.

He passed a hand over his mouth.

Hell of a way to realize he could still get aroused—in the middle of the children's section of the very public, very busy, Norfolk library. Gritting his teeth, he focused on the ceiling. Would counting sheep help?

"Hello."

That whiskey-smooth drawl was like a silken hand stroking down his back . . . or other things. He cleared his throat. *Speak, dumb-ass.*

"Hi!"

Saved by the Clayton-meister.

Mentally blowing out a breath, he watched as his son rocked back and forth on his heels, smiling up at the woman.

"Are you here for the program?" she asked.

"I am!" Clayton stuck out his hand. "I'm Clay. I love books. My dad tells me stories. All the time. Sometimes he even makes them up. He gets paid to do that, too."

Despite the total insanity of the moment, Trey found himself biting back a laugh.

That boy, in so many ways, had been a bright and strong light in what would have been nothing but a pit of misery for far too long.

Oh, honey . . . come to Mama.

Ressa Bliss would have been licking her chops if she had been anywhere remotely private.

Long, almost too lean, with a heavy growth of stubble and a mouth made for kissing, biting . . . other things . . .

He wore a dark pair of glasses that hid too much of his face and she wanted to reach up, pull them off.

Because she wanted so much to do that, she focused on the boy instead.

She shook his hand, much of what he'd just said running together in her head. She'd caught his name, though. "Well, hello, Clay. It's lovely to meet you."

He grinned at her, displaying a tooth that looked like it might fall out at any second—literally—she thought it might be hanging in there by luck alone.

Clay caught the man's hand in his and leaned against him. "This is my daddy."

She slid Mr. Beautiful a look. "Hello, Clay's daddy."

He gave her a one-sided smile. "Hi." Then he crouched in

front of his son. "So. Program lasts for fifty minutes. I'll be over in the grown-ups area if you need me."

"That area is boring." Clay wrinkled up his nose.

"Well, if I stay here, I'll just play." A real grin covered his face now and Ressa felt her heart melt. Since he was distracted, she shot a look at his hands—ring? Did he have one?

Crap. Some sort of gloves covered his hands from knuckle to well up over his wrists. No way to tell.

Clay leaned in and wrapped his arms around his father's neck. "Love you."

And her heart melted even more as he turned his face into his son's neck. "Love you, too, buddy. Have fun."

A man like that was most certainly *not* unattached.

But she still stole one last, quick glance as he walked away.

The back was every bit as fine as the front.

Chapter Two

Just breathe, man.

That had become his mantra any time he was even in the general area of the library.

Trey sometimes felt like Pavlov's dog or something, but instead of salivating every time he heard a damn bell, he got hard every time he was close to the library. Didn't matter if he went inside, didn't matter if he knew she was here.

Because he was used to *seeing* her here.

Which was why he was now in the condition he was in. He'd gone for a run, but not anywhere around home. No. He'd come downtown. Close to the library and as he crossed onto Ocean View, he caught sight of the sun shining off the glass and, right on cue, his gaze locked in on the second floor, the children's library, where she worked.

And predictably, his blood started to pump harder and hotter. It didn't have jack to do with the fact that he was two miles into his run, or that it was barely ten o'clock and it was already pushing up on ninety degrees out.

He found his feet slowing down, an idea spinning through his mind.

He could go inside.

The air conditioning would feel good.

No, he didn't have Clayton with him, but he could wander around. Maybe wander upstairs, say hi . . . let one thing lead to another.

If the opportunity presented itself, would it hurt to ask her out for coffee sometime? Maybe dinner?

If he had an hour or so alone with her, maybe he could take a chance and see if he could do the one thing he'd been dying to do for almost three months now.

Take that lush, sexy mouth with his, tug that amazing body close—

Feel her moving against him . . .

And then the same thing will happen that happens whenever a woman touches you. Your brain is going to lock down and your dick is going to play dead, just like always.

Closing his eyes, he turned away.

Yeah.

Better to just keep things in fantasy land.

But hey, at least he *had* fantasy land back.

That was better than nothing . . . right?

"That *is* him, right?"

All but pressing her nose to the glass, Ressa jabbed her elbow into Farrah's . . . err . . . boob? That's what happened when your best friend kept jabbering on in your ear and stood about four inches shorter than you. "Hush," she said irritably, watching as the muscled back, barely covered by a threadbare, heather gray tank top started to pound down the sidewalk, the runner moving at a sharp angle—*away* from the library.

"Ress!"

Heaving out a sigh, she looked over at her best friend.

"I couldn't see his face."

"Nobody can *ever* see his face. The man seems to have *two* looks. Either his hair is in his face or he's hiding behind those glasses." Farrah pursed her lips. "Maybe he's a criminal."

"Get out." Annoyed, Ressa nibbled on her lower lip and went back to looking out the window. Not that she could see him any longer. But man, what she wouldn't give for another few minutes to stare.

That man had a body on him, for real. Skin stretched tight over long, rangy muscles, and while she had a weird need to feed him a sandwich—or ten, that long and lean look fit him. And the tattoo . . . She hadn't been able to make out what it was, but it was something dark and dense and it appeared to cover his entire back.

Echoing her thoughts, Farrah murmured, "You saw the tattoo, right? I wonder what it is."

"Hmmm." Out of habit, Ressa traced the triquetra inked on her chest between her breasts. "Oh, yeah. I saw it."

Farrah snorted. "So, let me guess, you *still* haven't gotten his name, have you?"

Ressa moved away from the window. "Don't you work? You're the big gun around here. You should be doing whatever they pay you the big bucks for, not bugging me."

"How is it possible that you *still* haven't gotten his name?" Farrah ignored her completely.

"I don't know!" She winced as several of the kids in the area looked up at her. Lowering her voice, she shrugged. "I don't know. It's like he . . . he . . . he's *tormenting* me. I've tried every way *other* than just outright saying, *Buddy, just what is your name?* Nothing subtle works."

"Why *don't* you ask him outright?"

Ressa moved to the cart. "You know, even if *you* don't have work to do, *I* do. I *like* my job." She sniffed. It was summer and that meant more kids in the library, more kids reading . . . the summer reading program . . . man, if she survived another summer of it, she considered herself lucky.

"Obviously. That's the only reason you're *here*," Farrah said, lifting a brow. "It's not like you *have* to be."

Ressa ignored that comment.

"You didn't answer me. Why don't you ask him? And hey . . . just bite the bullet and ask him out on a date?"

It's too obvious. She kept that answer behind her teeth. Then, with a sidelong look at her boss, she lifted a shoulder. "I just . . ." She grabbed a couple of books and went to shelve them, pausing as she studied one. "I can't explain it. He's crazy hot. He's crazy sexy. But something is holding me back."

"You're not a timid woman, Ressa. What gives?"

Unable to explain, she displayed the book to Farrah. "Did you read these as a kid?"

"*Boxcar Children*." Farrah smiled. "Oh, yeah. That was more my speed than the crazy psycho bunny you love so much."

"I'll have you know that the psycho bunny is *very* popular with a lot of readers."

"Yeah." Farrah picked up a few books. "The weird ones. And you're in dodge-mode, girl."

"No. I'm in *I don't know what's up* mode. There's a difference. But since I haven't been able to find it in me to make a move, then I'm not going to push it." She slid the first two books in the series up on the shelf. They were probably only going to go out another few times before they had to be replaced. They were getting pretty worn. "If it ever feels right, I'll know."

"If you say so." Farrah heaved out a sigh. "I've been wondering . . . Mr. Hot and Sexy—"

"Mr. Hot and Sexy?" Ressa cut in, amused.

"He's gotta have a name," Farrah said, a smile curving her lips. She wore bronze lipstick today—a bronze that almost perfectly matched her silk shirt, and the color glowed warmly against toffee brown skin. "Tell me, does he look at all familiar to you?"

Ressa stopped and stared at Farrah. "You, too?"

Arching a black brow, Farrah pursed her lips. Then she nodded. "I'll take that as a yes."

"Yeah. That's a yes." She huffed out a breath and grabbed another book, slid it on the shelf below the *Boxcar* books. "I just can't figure out why. You?"

"Nope. I was kind of hoping you'd tell me he reminded you of some hot football player or something."

"As if." Ressa snorted out a laugh. "Like I know the Cowboys from the Orioles."

"You moron." Farrah bumped her with her hip. "The Orioles play baseball."

"See? That's just what I mean!"

"Hopeless. You're hopeless." Farrah sighed. Then she pushed away from the cart. "So . . . anyway. The main reason I came here?"

Ressa glanced over at her and then turned, recognizing that glint in her friend's eyes. "Yeah?"

"I just got this, right when I was getting ready to head to lunch." Farrah brandished her phone.

The name practically leaped from the screen. It was a book cover—she knew that because she recognized the author's name.

The cover was pale green. The woman on it was mostly naked, save for the miniscule panties that covered the important bits, and her breasts were covered by her arm.

She also wore a tie. One incongruously patterned with bright pink smile faces that matched the bright pink font of the author's name.

Exposing the Geek Billionaire.

Muffling a squeal, she tapped on it.

Nothing.

"What?"

Farrah chortled as she nabbed the phone back.

"It's just the cover . . . there was a big reveal on one of the romance blogs, Ress. It's due out in early fall. But I thought you'd wanna know. So you have something to check out on your lunch break. Maybe it will distract you from Mr. Tall, Dark, and Tattooed."

Ressa barely acknowledged the change in names, just giving Farrah a cursory scowl. *Mr. Hot, Sexy, and Tattooed* might work.

"You gotta call him something."

Ressa already *did* call him something. But she wasn't sharing her mental nickname for him with her boss.

Chapter Three

Week Twenty-six

"You look tired."

Trey jerked up his head, realizing he'd been *this* close to falling sleep. With his laptop open in his lap. In the middle of the children's area.

Ressa Bliss stood in front of him, Clayton holding her hand and swinging it back and forth.

"Did you bring it in, Dad? Did you bring it in?" He let go of her hand to launch himself toward Trey.

Habit had him catching the boy easily even as he looked up at Ressa through dark lenses. "Yeah," he said, wishing he had about a gallon of coffee to guzzle. "Have had a few late nights . . . trying to catch up on work before we fly out to California later this week."

"We're gonna see Grandma for Mother's Day!" Clayton chirped. Then he grabbed Trey's messenger bag and hauled it up, dumping it onto the low table. "Where is it, Dad? Where is it?"

It was a gift.

Mother's Day was on Sunday. It had been one rough week.

*She said we were making presents for our moms . . . Daddy,
I don't have a mommy anymore and I was making it for
Grandma and she said I wasn't listening, but I didn't want to
tell her what happened and she kept trying to make me start
all over . . .*

Well, she sure as *hell* had listened to Trey. Sometimes he
wondered what was wrong with people. It was very clearly
marked in Clayton's records that his mother had passed
away—if they weren't going to *look* at those records, why did
they ask?

They'd finished up their crafts with Clayton working on his
project that he'd give to Denise, his grandmother. He'd been
so pleased with it, they'd hit one of the local craft stores and
bought kits to make little clay paperweights for all of his
grandparents, but he'd wanted to make something special for
Ressa, too.

When Trey had pushed him on why, Clayton had just
shrugged.

*Everybody has a mommy who smells good and is pretty
and tells them stories . . .*

I tell you stories, man. Are you saying I stink?

Clayton had laughed. But then that sad look came back into
his eyes. *Miss Ressa read a book about a little girl who'd lost
her mama. There was a lady who lived next door who the girl
was friends with. Miss Ressa told us that sometimes people
don't have mamas . . . or daddies . . . but they still have people
who love them. Maybe . . . You think maybe she loves me?*

The kid could cut his heart out sometimes.

So there was another clay paperweight.

Trey rubbed the back of his neck as Clayton turned, clutching it in small hands as he looked up at Ressa. He opened his
mouth, nervous, then shut it. Then he shoved it out at her.
"Here!" he blurted. "I made it for you. I . . . I wanted you to
have it."

Ressa looked down, puzzled.

And then, as her face softened, Trey felt something wrench
inside his heart.

"Oh . . ."

She sank to her knees. A smile curved up her lips and he
was struck, straight to the heart, by how beautiful she was.

Something came over him and it wasn't that gut-twisting lust. It wasn't that blood-boiling need that would never end in anything but frustration and humiliation.

It was something . . . more.

Something maybe even better.

A weight he hadn't realized he still carried lifted inside him and he found he was smiling himself as she reached out, but instead of taking it from Clayton, she cupped her hands under his, steadying the oddly shaped heart the child had molded himself. "Wow," she said, her voice husky. "You made this, didn't you, handsome?"

Clayton nodded, chin tucked.

"My goodness." She bit her lip and then leaned in, angling her head until she caught Clayton's gaze. "Can I maybe hold it?"

"It's yours." Clayton dumped it into her hands and she caught it, handling it with the same care she might have shown had he just presented her with a Waterford crystal vase.

Judging by the light in her eyes, he might as well have done just that. "Clayton, that was really sweet of you," she said, stroking her thumb over the overly bright, glass "jewels" they'd found to push into the clay. "I don't think I've ever had a paperweight quite so beautiful in my life. But . . ." She looked up at him. "It's not my birthday or anything. Why'd you give me something so nice?"

"Cuz . . ." Clayton shrugged his skinny shoulders. "You are nice. And I can't give nothing to my mama."

He didn't say anything else, just turned and flung himself toward Trey, his face jammed against his thigh. "I wanna go. Daddy, can we go now?"

"Clayton—"

Trey looked at her and shook his head. "It's okay. He's okay." Or he would be. Scooping Clayton up, he went to scoop his laptop into his bag.

"Here." Ressa moved in. "Let me help."

He got a headful of her scent, felt her curls brush his cheek. All the while Clayton clung to his neck like a monkey. "Thanks," he said, his voice brusque. Things were coming to attention now—of course, and here he was juggling his son, her concerned gaze, his bag.

"I'm sorry if I—"

"You didn't." Trey shot her a look, almost explained then, but the last thing Clayton needed was to hear the blunt hard facts laid out just then. He lived with them every day of his life. "He's just had a rough week, haven't you, buddy?"

He gave her a smile—the practiced one he'd used when reporters had hunted him down over the years, whether it was because of his writing, his wife's death, or his connection to two famous actors. It was a blank smile, one that could say everything and nothing, one that could hide a million secrets or be as open as one could hope. "He needs a nap and maybe some pizza. In a few days, we hop on a plane and he'll be seeing all his cousins and his uncles. He's been looking forward to that. Don't worry, he's fine, aren't you, buddy?"

Voice muffled against his neck, Clayton said, "I'm gonna see 'Bastian this time, Daddy?"

"You bet." He rubbed his cheek against Clayton's curls. "Uncle Sebastian wouldn't dare miss Mother's Day."

"Is Aunt Abby making cake?"

Chuckling, he said, "I certainly hope so." Giving Clayton a light squeeze, Trey murmured, "Why don't you tell Miss Ressa bye? I think she's upset and thinks she hurt your feelings?"

Clayton rolled his head on his shoulders. "Bye, Miss Ressa."

The memory of Clayton's smile lingered, hours after he'd left.

It lingered even after they closed up and she was sitting at the computer, debating.

Debating hard, because she was about to do something she had no right to do.

Or she was *tempted*. She wasn't really about to do it, but she was closer to it than she was comfortable. Shit. How often did *she* get pissed when people tried to—or did—meddle in her background? She had plenty of things that she'd rather not have dragged out right in the open.

Actually, *pissed* didn't even touch on how *she* felt when people started meddling. There were some secrets she had that she'd just as soon take to her grave.

Besides, what was she going to do—general search for kids with the name *Clayton* . . . *five years old* . . . hey, she knew he had a birthday in September. That would *really* narrow the focus.

"What's up?"

Guiltily, she jerked her hands away.

One of her coworkers, Alex, stood on the other side of the desk, eying her.

"Nothing." Guiltily, she powered down the computer. "Is everybody pretty much done?"

"A few more wrapping up downstairs."

With a nod, Ressa picked up the little paperweight, carefully cradling it in her hand.

"Did somebody bring you a gift?"

"Yep." She displayed it, feeling as pleased as if she'd received chocolate and flowers.

"Who is it from?" Alex eyed it, his head cocked.

With a smile, she said, "Clayton . . . the little doll who shows up at reading hour."

"Ahhh . . . your shadow." He grinned knowingly. "That kid has a major crush on you, Ressa."

She grimaced. "Geez. That's great to hear."

"You're going to break his heart when you transfer out this summer." He tsked and shook his head. "You might want to break the news sooner, rather than later."

"Oh, shit."

"Not much you can do about it." Alex gave her a sympathetic look. "You need the transfer so you can be closer to school—these are the chores of being a parent . . . or a guardian as it were. Your cousin needs you."

Ressa nodded, her thoughts drifting to the child she'd been taking care of for so many years. "I know. Neeci is why I'm doing it."

Still, a heavy ache settled in her chest as she looked down at the molded heart she held. Funny . . . she was just now realizing how fragile it was.

Chapter Four

Week Thirty

Sheets twisted around him.

Dream and reality blurred together in that surreal way they did in that short time just before waking.

The twisted ropes of cotton weren't really cotton. They were long limbs, warm and golden brown. That mouth, always slicked with colors that made him think of sinful wines or lush fruits, moved against his. It was a seductive red today and as he fisted his hand in her hair, she sank her teeth into his lower lip.

"Trey . . ."

That was when he knew he was dreaming.

She'd never called him by name.

With a groan, he rolled them, putting her body under his, determined to enjoy it as much as he could, for as long as he could. She laughed against his lips, a husky sound that tripped down his spine. Who knew that a woman's laugh could be so erotic?

She might as well have reached between his legs and cupped his balls.

And then she *was* reaching down, one hand closing around his cock.

"Don't," he muttered, tearing his mouth away. "I . . . fuck, I can't."

"You can't what?" Ressa smiled up at him, dragged her hand up, then down.

"I can't . . . this. I just . . ." He shoved away from her, but she followed. Her hand milked him and he groaned, because the pleasure was there, leaving him hovering on an edge between pleasure and pain.

"I think you can." She sat up and he found himself staring up at her. Her breasts—or least the image his dreaming mind had conjured up—were full, her nipples a deep, deep brown. While she continued to pump her hand up and down his cock, she used her other hand to reach out, grab his wrist and bring it to her breast. "Touch me . . . you know you want to."

Want? "You think that covers it?"

"You never have done it." She lifted a brow. "Why is that?"

Any answer he might have given was lost, because she gave a slow, thorough twist of her wrist as she dragged it back up. Then she caught the fluid leaking out of his cock, smoothed it around the swollen crown.

He hissed out a breath.

She did the same and he didn't realize it was because he'd plucked at her nipple. "I'm sorry . . . fuck, I hurt you—"

"No." She shoved her breast into his hand. "Do it again."

Instead, he shoved upright and caught the tip in his mouth.

That warm, soft laugh echoed around him before fading into a moan. He settled between her hips and then the dream . . . shifted. Rolled.

IcantIcantIcant!

Her hands cupped his face and she rolled up against him. "Make love to me!"

He was buried inside her.

He went to pull out. Felt the smooth, sweet glide of her pussy against him and he shuddered.

"Sweet fucking hell," he breathed out. Then he drove deep inside her.

She cried out his name.

He might have sobbed out hers.

And moments later, he came awake just as he climaxed, one hand wrapped around his cock while the other twisted in the sheets.

Shuddering, Trey lay there, half-stunned.

"Son of a bitch."

He'd just orgasmed for the first time in more than six years.

"Son of a bitch."

"Are you just going to bite the bullet and ask her out?"

He glared at the phone on the bathroom counter. Razor in hand, he leaned forward. "Travis? I'll listen to your advice on my love life when you listen to mine."

"I don't have a love life."

"Exactly my point." He finished one pass down his jaw, rinsed the razor off, started another. "Look, it's just . . ."

He stopped, because there was only so much he was willing to tell. Even his twin. He sure as *hell* wasn't about to share certain humiliating details.

Unaware of the thoughts circling through Trey's mind, Travis pushed on. "Just *nothing*. It's been almost six years since Aliesha died. I *know* you're moving past that—or *have* moved past it. So it's not her."

"Don't." Even he heard the biting warning in his voice.

Travis's sigh came over the line. "I just worry about you, man."

"Same goes. And hey, I'm not the one who's working myself into an early grave, right?" He could still remember how Travis had looked in San Francisco when they all met up for their annual get-together. Mom insisted it wasn't necessary, but she still had that light of complete delight in her eyes when they all descended en masse, ringing the doorbell to the house their parents had lived in for years.

Travis had looked like somebody had dragged him, sopping wet and close to drowning, out of the Pacific.

"I'm not working myself into a grave," Travis said, his voice grim. "I refuse to die doing this shit work."

There was an edge to his twin's voice, one Trey hadn't heard before. "Everything okay with *you*?"

For a moment, there was just a taut, heavy silence. Then

Travis sighed. "Yeah. I'm just . . . tired. I need a vacation. I'll take care of that. Soon. But let's talk about this librarian. Who is she? What does she look like? Fess up."

"We're not in high school anymore, Trav."

"Too bad, because then I'd be able to figure this out on my own. Come on, I'll just work it out of Clay." There was a sly note in Travis's voice.

"Bastard." Trey finished up shaving and rinsed the foam from his face, using a towel to dry off. His hair hung in his face, too long, desperately in need of a trim. "How about I give you something else to hassle me over?"

"It won't be near as interesting," Travis said.

"Sure it will." He twisted the towel around his hands as he readied himself to say it. "I . . . uh . . . I committed to speaking at a writer thing next month. One of the writers at my agency had to cancel—some family emergency, and Reuben decided to take a chance at asking me. I said yes."

For a moment, there was just silence.

Then Travis said, "Repeat that."

"You heard me," Trey said wearily. "It's in Jersey. Not far, but . . ." Now was the hard part. "I tried to see if Al and Mona could watch him, but that's their anniversary and they are taking a cruise. So I called Mom and Dad. They . . ."

Shit. Hand shaking, he dragged it down his face, realized there was some stubble he'd missed. Maybe he should—

Quit stalling. Just spit it out. "They want to take him to Disney. Just the two of them."

"And you're letting them."

He gripped the counter. "Yeah. I'm letting them."

"Have you puked yet?"

That startled a laugh out of him. "Nah. But if I did, I wouldn't tell you."

"If you did, I wouldn't tell the others."

Now he smiled. "Yeah. I know." He checked the time. "Look . . . I gotta go. It's almost time to go to the library. I'm surprised Clay hasn't come up here and banged on the door already."

"Okay. Man, one second—listen. Make yourself a list or something. You do better with lists. And on that damn list, put down for you to just ask her out on a date."

"Shit." Trey rolled his eyes. "I can't be around her without my tongue sticking to the roof of my mouth, or worse . . . drooling." He grimaced. If he asked her out, then he'd have to worry about other things—what if he kissed her? What if *she* kissed him? What would happen when he started thinking about the void of his memory from that night? Drooling would be the *least* of his concerns. "Trust me, a date is no good."

"Fine. Put *no drooling* on the list. But stop sitting on your ass."

One hand closed into a fist as Trey stood there.

He hadn't just done that. He really hadn't made a stupid list.

He was going to kick Travis's ass over this . . . because, dumb-ass that he was, he had made a list. More than likely, nothing would come of it.

So, yeah. He'd made a list. Big deal.

Ressa Bliss was gorgeous.

She was outgoing.

She probably had a boyfriend. For all he knew, she might even be married. Not that rings really meant anything, but . . . blowing out a breath, he looked down at the one he had yet to take off.

Slowly, he reached up and traced the tip of his right index finger across the engraved surface of his wedding ring. It wasn't so much that he couldn't let go that kept the ring on his finger. He had accepted and acknowledged all of this a long time ago.

He grieved for Aliesha long and hard—probably longer and harder than he maybe should have, losing himself in a dark, ugly pit of despair. It had been easier to do that than focus on some of the other things that had gone wrong in his life. It hadn't been until the past year that he realized just how messed up he'd let himself get.

Oh, he'd hidden it.

He'd hidden it well from everybody except his twin . . . and probably Mom. Travis and Denise Barnes saw past the walls nobody else had even realized were there.

But only Travis had any idea of just how messed up Trey

probably was. There were missing hours that Trey still couldn't get back—followed by a morning where he had been forced to remember, all over again, that he'd lost his wife.

That void, those missing hours, they haunted him and all he wanted was to *forget*—the whole damn night, not just pieces of it.

Sometimes, he thought he almost remembered. A woman's laugh, the burn of whiskey.

Then a vicious pain.

He'd left the hospital with bruised ribs, bruised knuckles, and various other aches and pains. At some point, he'd gotten into a fight. The bartender said there had been a man in the parking lot, and he thought the woman Trey had been drinking with had left with him.

But beyond that?

He only had emptiness, questions—and a good, thirty-minute gap of nothingness that the bartender couldn't account for between the time he'd noticed the commotion on his security cameras and the time Trey had stumbled out of the bar.

The few dates he'd tried to go on since then, he could almost hear the echo of a woman's laugh in the back of his mind and it was like the fumes of whiskey clouded his head. Any interest he *might* have felt died under a rush of near memories.

So he'd just . . . stopped. Stopped trying to live again, lost himself deeper inside himself.

Until he'd seen Ressa. Staring at his ring, he closed his hand into a fist and slowly relaxed it. Then, without giving himself a chance to think about it, he tugged the ring off.

It wasn't a connection with his wife, really, that he was removing.

In more ways than one, it was his shield.

How he'd kept himself cut away from everybody and anybody save for his family and a few very select friends. If he took that off, then he had to admit to himself that maybe he was ready to move on.

He wanted his life back—or some semblance of it.

He wanted to feel a woman's skin against his own without memories of something he didn't even understand haunting him. Wanted to know he could touch a woman and actually feel that need—feel something other than the grief of Aliesha's death choking him.

How could one night change something so basic? How did something he didn't even *remember* change everything?

"Dad!" Clayton's voice rang through the house.

Wincing, Trey did exactly what he'd done for almost six years—compartmentalized everything. He'd think about all of this later. "Be down in a minute, buddy!" he shouted back, slowly putting the ring down on the counter. Whether or not he'd put it back on, he didn't know.

But he had taken it off. Even if it was just for a little while, that counted, right?

Picking up the little moleskin notebook he carried everywhere, he flipped to the middle and eyed the list he'd just made.

To-Do List

1. Clothes shopping

2. Get groceries—you're out of deodorant, moron

3. Ask her out

4. Try not to drool

The list was out of order.

And it was just as stupid as he'd thought it would be.

Abruptly, he went to tear it out of the notebook, but then he stopped.

If he didn't do this now, then when would he?

Abruptly, he grabbed his pen and scrawled something else down at the bottom.

5. Start living again

"Dad?" There was a pause, and then a more persistent yell with an edge of panic. *"Dad! I can't find my books!"*

Saved by the boy, he mused, stroking a finger down the list, lingering on the final item. *If nothing else, that one right there was something he had to do.*

He'd take it as a sign. So he'd think about it. Think about it and just see. See what happened.

Really, what could any of this hurt . . . nothing really, right? Not more than it hurt to dream about her at night, fantasize about that mouth. Or other attractive parts of her anatomy.

It was a seductive, taunting road, one paved with fantasies and frustration, but it was better than the desolate one he'd walked for far too long.

"In the basket on the bookshelf by the door," he called out as he shoved the notebook into his pocket. "Exactly where I told you to put them last night."

Single fatherhood was nothing if not a lesson in patience . . . and repetition.

Usually, seeing that head of buttery gold curls brought an instant smile to her face.

Today, though . . .

Ressa curled her hands into a fist, her nails biting into her palm as she saw CD walking with his little boy across the parking lot, long rangy strides shortened to accommodate his son's shorter legs. CD—her personal nickname for the man who haunted her dreams. *CD*—as in Clay's dad.

In time, Clayton would be just as tall as his father, she suspected. He seemed small for his age, but she could see the long limbs. It would just take time.

"Saying good-bye sucks, huh?"

Glancing back over her shoulder at Farrah, she lifted a brow. "Ya think?"

"Well, since ya never got around to getting Mr. Yummy Pants' name, I figured it wouldn't be *too* bad . . ."

"Saying good-bye to Clayton is going to break my heart," she said, painfully aware of the sulk in her voice, and unable to do anything about it. She didn't *want* to do anything about it. "I had to tell too many kids good-bye this week. I've only been here two years. How can it hurt like this?"

"Hey . . ." Farrah moved in and wrapped an arm around

Ressa's waist. "You know, you're *not* moving to Tokyo. You can come visit, drop in on your days off. Visit the kids then."

"I know, I know." Ressa shrugged away, out of sorts and still . . . aching inside. "This just sucks."

"You said he wasn't here last week."

She looked up and caught sight of the two males just as they cleared the top step and the ache in her chest expanded. "No."

A small, cowardly part of her kind of wished they wouldn't have come here today either. If they hadn't then she would have been spared this.

Didn't that just make *her* a coward?

Her heart twisted as the boy came rushing up to her a few minutes later. He was all smiles as he flung himself at her for a hug and she caught him, held him close.

"Aren't you looking handsome today, Mr. Clayton," she said, looking past him to see his father linger, just for a minute. Their gazes connected—he wore his trademark dark shades, but she could still feel that jolt.

His mouth parted and maybe it was ego—or just because she wanted so badly to believe it—to believe that he felt it, too.

She didn't look away.

Not that very second.

She should have. She knew that.

But she only had today left, right?

"Hey, um—"

"I was wondering if—"

They both started to speak at once, and then, they stopped, a nervous laugh breaking out between them. He gestured for her to speak and she linked her hands together, looking around. "I just . . . well, I want a few minutes with you . . . with Clayton after we're done. If that's okay?"

An hour later, Trey had less than five hundred words on the screen and his mind kept spinning back to the way she'd met his gaze earlier.

I want a few minutes with you.

He'd been about ready to just walk away, forget asking her out.

Terror and nerves had turned his gut to knots.

Unlike his brothers, he seemed to have missed out on that inborn charm—most of the family, on both his mother's side and his father's side, from his cousins, to his uncles and aunts, to his brothers—they all practically *breathed* charm and confidence.

Not Trey.

But then she'd said she wanted to talk to him and he'd felt something relax inside.

That hadn't lasted long, because immediately, his memory, always such a visual thing with him, had started to feed him back an instant replay of how she'd looked at him, her lips parted, the irises of her eyes spiking as she met his gaze.

No wonder he hadn't gotten shit done the past hour.

He heard the rise in voices that signified the end of the reading program and he saved his work, a dull pain throbbing in his wrist. After putting away the laptop, he grabbed a bottle of ibuprofen and tossed a few back dry.

Clayton was sitting at his desk studiously coloring away while the rest of the kids gathered around Ressa.

Both of them heard the words at the same time—

Good-bye . . .

We'll miss you—

Clayton's head jerked up.

Trey's hand clenched into a fist and he shifted the bag from one shoulder to drag across his chest as dread creeped through. Dread and . . . disappointment.

I want a few minutes with you . . .

Son of a bitch. With him . . . so she could tell Clayton bye.

"Why do you have to leave, Miss Ressa?" one of the older kids asked, his voice plaintive and loud, carrying through the entire library.

The crayon in Clayton's hand snapped and his gaze darted all around the room before landing on Trey with wild desperation.

Before Trey could reach the table, Clayton was up on his feet, practically running toward him.

"Let's go, Dad."

Clayton's small hand caught his, started to tug.

Yeah. He could get on board with that. But . . . "Wait a minute, Clayton."

"No!" He burrowed in against Trey, his voice already wobbling. "I want to go now. And I don't like this stupid lib'ary no more. I never want to come back. Can we get dinosaur egg oatmeal at the store? I want some for a snack. Let's go."

Eyes closed, Trey reached for some sort of fatherly wisdom to offer up. He came up short, as always.

"Clayton."

At the sound of her voice, Trey tensed.

Clayton tucked himself closer to Trey.

Slowly, Trey looked up.

Ressa knelt down next to the boy and in her hand, she held a book. "Clayton, I'm sorry . . . I didn't want you to hear that way. I . . ." She offered them both a smile. "I was actually going to see if you'd maybe let me buy you lunch or something and we could talk then. I . . ."

Clayton shoved his face against Trey's leg and sniffled. "I don't want no lunch. I'm not hungry. I'm not ever going to be hungry."

Well, shit.

"Come on, buddy."

His voice was low and soothing, while one hand rubbed up and down Clayton's narrow back.

Ressa tried not to focus on that part as CD spoke to his son. Clayton didn't want to look at her and she felt foolish . . . foolish and cruel and out of place.

"You've got a lady waiting to talk to you, Clayton. Come on, don't be rude. Just—"

"I don't care!" Clayton shouted. "She's leaving and she didn't tell me and I don't like her anymore."

Ressa managed to hide her flinch and she pasted a smile on her face. "Look, I'll just—"

"Wait." It was a command, plain and simple.

She narrowed her eyes at the stark order, but before she could say anything, he'd peeled his son away.

"Listen to me, Clayton," CD said, tugging off his glasses.

She managed, just barely, not to react when she saw his eyes.

His son had his eyes—a beautiful, surreal blue green. The kind of blue green you saw in pictures of the tropics—an impossible sort of color, but she had no doubt that amazing color was completely natural.

Swallowing, she forced herself to be still, to not move, to not *stare* as he continued to speak. "Now, I know you're upset, but you don't speak that way to people. You know that. You're angry and you're sad, but there's no reason to be unkind."

Clayton's lip poked out and he tried to curl in toward his father once more.

"You need to say something," his father said, shaking his head.

Clayton shot her a look. Then, as one fat tear rolled down his cheek, he whispered, "I'm sorry."

She opened her mouth to say, "It's okay."

She managed "It—"

And then Clayton hurled himself at her, wrapping thin arms around her neck. "I don't want you to leave," he said.

Break my heart, why don't you?

"Oh, sweetheart." She rubbed the back of his head. "I don't really want to either. It's just . . . well, sometimes we just have to do things we don't really like."

"But why are you leaving?"

Easing him back, she reached up and wiped away a tear. "You remember my cousin? The little girl I've told you about?" At his nod, she said, "You know how I've said I'm the one who takes care of her, right? Neeci starts school this year and things aren't going to work with me being at this library. So they are moving me to a different branch. It's closer to where we live and the school she's going to attend. I hate that I have to leave you kids, but I've got a little girl to take care of. And they've got good people here who will take over."

She waited for the next question—others had asked it when she put in for the transfer. *Why can't her mama take care of her? Why do you gotta go?*

But with her cousin, Kiara, that just wasn't an option.

All Clayton did was lean in and rest his head on her shoulder. "I'll miss you."

"Oh, honey. I'll miss you, too."

From the corner of her eye, she saw his father and her pulse sped up.

He reached out and hooked a hand over Clayton's shoulder. His fingers brushed her bare upper arm and she almost gasped as that light contact sent a jolt through her.

His eyes flew to hers and for a moment, they just stared at each other and her heart raced, so hard. So fast.

"Okay," Clayton whispered. "I'll . . . I'm gonna miss you." He dashed a hand under his nose and said, "I still like you, Miss Ressa."

"Oh, sweetheart." She stroked a hand down his hair. "I like you, too."

He nodded and then moved to his dad, leaning against his leg.

Then, as Clayton turned away from her, she awkwardly rose to her feet. It was better this way, and not just because she needed the change to work things out with Neeci and school. She'd miss the son, but it was probably a good thing that she was getting away from CD.

The man just wasn't good for her state of mind.

Taking a deep, steadying breath, she met his gaze, felt her heart trip up as those intense eyes met hers. "Did you still need to speak with me?"

One hand curled into a fist as she stared at him.

Trey knew, without a doubt, that he had been right.

She felt it, too.

But his son was leaning against him, still shaking, still crying, although he tried so hard not to. His fingers were kneading into Trey's legs in the way he always did when he was the most upset, like he just couldn't get enough physical contact.

The doctors had said it probably had something to do with a need for the stimuli. Clayton had spent weeks on a vent, and then the first eight months of his life in and out of the hospital. He'd made strides like whoa and damn as he caught up, but he'd missed out on so many things that a young baby was supposed to have. Instead of being hugged and held by his parents at any given time, getting that vital physical contact, he'd been under lights, hooked up to tubes and wires, while Trey stood at his side, holding his little hand and talking to him. Talking, instead of holding, stroking a hand instead of rocking.

And now his son needed him again.

"Not a good time, I guess," he said gruffly. Ducking his head, he scooped Clayton up and Clayton's arms came around his neck, clutching tight. "Man's had a rough day. I'll just . . . never mind. Good luck at your new library, Ms. Bliss."

He nodded at her, and as he walked away he focused on the soft, shaky breaths of his son.

"I don't want her to go," Clayton whispered.

"Yeah." Trey hugged him tighter. "I kinda don't want her to either."

Chapter Five

Try to relax . . . and if you can't relax, have a fucking drink—then relax.

The handwritten note left in his room made Trey smirk. Relax?

His agent knew him.

He ought to—he'd been working with him for coming up on five years now.

Which meant Reuben Mancusi ought to understand that one thing Trey wasn't going to be doing was *relaxing*. Not while he was here in Trenton, New Jersey—at a writer's conference, fuck him—and not while his son was in Orlando, oh, hey what was it? Over a thousand miles away. If he could get on a flight, in an emergency, he could be there in a few hours, but . . .

"You're going to make yourself sick thinking like that." He shook his head, then read the note over again, and then crumpled it up, shot it off to the side. It went straight into the trash can.

He barely noticed, too busy studying everything in the basket.

It was, without a doubt, customized just for him. Or the him he'd once been. Some of those interviews he'd done a lifetime ago had loved to ask questions like . . . *favorite drink, favorite book to read . . .*

Glenlivet had been the one hard and fast answer.

The book had almost always changed, because books changed with whatever mood he was in.

Hardly anybody knew that he'd stopped drinking. He had to admit, he was mildly surprised there wasn't any Valium in there, though. Or maybe he just hadn't looked hard enough.

Eying the bottle of Glenlivet, he pulled it out, turned it to the side and watched as the light glinted off green glass. Thoughtfully, he carried it with him as he hunted down a glass.

Curious, he cracked the foil, splashed some into a glass—

And the smell of it turned his stomach. The sense of smell was a powerful thing. For the first couple of years, even the smell of whiskey had been enough to send his thoughts flying back to the hospital, where he was flat on his back, while that pain clawed his brain matter out and then he slowly remembered, all over again, that he'd just lost his wife—that he'd almost lost his son. Those first few years, he'd almost lost himself.

He wasn't there anymore, but the smell of alcohol was still enough to turn his stomach.

He pushed the glass back and turned away.

So maybe he wouldn't have a drink, but he would try to relax, lie down for a little while. He was exhausted. He'd been up early and hadn't slept much the night before. Too busy thinking about Clayton's face after he'd put him on the plane with his father yesterday.

Dawn had only been a thought when he gave up trying to sleep and it was coming up on six now. At six thirty, he was supposed to be downstairs.

For tonight, at least, he had plans.

His old friend Max was waiting for him.

Max was the one who'd nudged his agent into calling Trey, and Max was the one who'd called him every few days, all but holding his hand as he got ready for this.

He was doing a speech for a group of librarians and he

was speaking on a couple of panels. Then there was a separate signing. All in all, it would take up maybe eight hours of his time.

He could do that, right?

The annual conference in Trenton was a low-key one, a mix of both readers and writers, but it wasn't anything that had people lining up for days.

He could do this.

Maybe.

Abruptly, he felt a keen longing for that whiskey and he wondered just how sick he'd get if he gave it a shot. But he wasn't about to tempt fate.

The absolute last thing he needed was to end up puking his guts up.

Instead, he closed his eyes and tried to just empty his head. That worked for all of fifteen seconds. He started going through the talk he had to do instead and was 99.8 percent certain he was going to sound like a doofus. Maybe he should rewrite—

His phone started to buzz.

It wasn't a call, though.

As much as he sometimes hated technology, this was one of those times when he loved it.

Within seconds, he found himself staring at Clayton Braxton Barnes. Clayton was the one bright spot in the time that signified a hell for Trey, but that bright spot was all he needed to push the shadows back.

That bright spot was marred, in a way. Lately Clayton was all caught up in one idea. *Can we maybe find Miss Ressa and ask her to my party?*

As much as he'd been tempted, Trey had pulled the distraction and hedging game that parents seemed to learn pretty much at the birth of the very first child. It wasn't wise, he'd already figured out.

He didn't know where she worked or where she lived, and it was better that Clayton just let her go.

Now, as Clayton grinned at him from the screen of his phone, Trey found himself amazed all over again at how much they looked alike. From the blue eyes to the shape of his nose and mouth and his ears. The only thing that wasn't his was that mop of messy blond curls. Those came from his mother.

"Hey there, man," he said as Clay grinned, displaying the two teeth he'd proudly lost within two weeks of each other.

"We went to Disney World!"

"Did you?" At the obvious happiness on his son's face, tension drained away—for real this time—and he rolled over onto his stomach. With the phone on the bed in front of him, he focused on Clayton.

For the few minutes he was in here, talking to his son, he could pretend they were both back in Norfolk and Clayton was only a few miles away, instead of that gut-twisting one thousand.

"I saw Darth Vader." Clayton's big blue eyes focused on the monitor, wide and avid, as he waited for his father's response.

"Did you kick his butt?"

Clay cackled and proceeded to tell Trey about his trip to Disney. In great detail. And Trey listened, hanging on to every word.

When the call ended, he flopped back onto his back.

Just a few more days and he'd be back in his house. Back with his son.

And he knew, down in some part of his soul that he was still hobbling along. Brooding, he thought about the notebook he carried with him, with the little list—and the item at the end. *Start living* . . .

A pair of wide, dark eyes swam through his memory and he blew out a breath.

Start living.

How the hell was he supposed to do that when the one woman he'd actually wanted to take a chance on was probably the woman he most needed to stay away from?

Ressa could maybe be good for him—she could definitely be good for Clayton. But on the flipside, all it would take is for things to *not* work out and Clay would be heartbroken.

You're a fucking coward, Trey.

The problem was, the one time he'd wanted to really reach out and maybe *try* to live again . . . well, life had just gotten in the way.

Or maybe that was just an excuse.

* * *

"My registration confirmation is right here."

Ressa Bliss put the hard copy down in front of the volunteer, tried to remind herself how many times she'd been the one sitting on the other side of the desk, and how unpleasant it was when people started snapping at her over issues that were out of her control.

Frankly, it sucked.

But this was ridiculous. She'd *paid* to attend this conference and she'd damn well attend.

"Ma'am. You're not registered," the volunteer said, not even pretending to be polite. "I've checked. You're not in the system."

"Then there is an error in the system, because I have my confirmation. I also have proof of payment." She pulled up the receipt in her e-mail and showed it to the woman—her name tag read Beth.

Beth didn't even give it a cursory glance. "I can only go by what the system says. Now, if you'll step aside, I have other people to get checked in."

"I'll step aside when you find me somebody who can help straighten this out. I'm moderating several panels and helping with two booths. I'm registered. People are expecting me to be here and I'm *going* to be here." She folded her arms across her chest and met Beth's glare with one of her own.

She was *so* not in the mood to be dismissed.

"Look, sister—"

"Sister? Ex*cuse* me?" Ressa demanded.

"Hi."

Before Ressa could explode, a new woman approached, a cool, but polite look on her face. She had a volunteer badge on—her name was Lynda and her plump face had that tired but friendly look to it—the kind that said she could do this all night if she had to.

As Lynda looked between them, Ressa sucked back her temper and forced herself to level out.

"Is there something I can help with, ma'am?" Lynda asked.

"Yes." Her professional, polite smile firmly in place, Ressa handed over her registration confirmation. "I signed up not

long after the event opened to registrations, but I'm not show-
ing up as registered. Can you help me out? I'm moderating two
panels, helping out with a couple and volunteering with several booths."

"Well. That is a problem." Lynda's smile twisted into a
grimace. "Give me a minute . . . I'll get you sorted out and get
you a name tag and everything."

"Lynda, she's not in the system—"

"I'll handle it, Beth." Lynda gave the other woman a polite
smile, but it somehow managed to speak volumes. Then she
looked over at Ressa. "I know your name. Actually, I was told
to keep an eye out for you—we're short two people on the lit
track and we need a sub. You were suggested by one of the
panelists . . . Max Hartfield?"

"Max?" She smiled, although inwardly, she wanted to curl
up into a ball and beg for mercy. She was going to throttle
him.

"Yes." Lynda gave her a quick and ready grin. "He told me
to tell you that he'd buy you a drink if you said yes and saved
him."

Ressa laughed. "Fine. Who do I need to talk to? I can't
make any promises, but I'll see what I can do—*if* it doesn't
conflict with anything else."

"Bobby Spears handles the lit track—trust me, he'll make
it all work out." Lynda gave her another grin. "Bobby is new
to the event this year, but so far, it looks like he can make just
about anything happen."

Well, so much for talking Max into wings and beer at some
dive. She'd kind of been looking forward to something easy
and fast.

"That sounds good."

"Come on." Lynda gestured to the side. "Let's move down
here and I'll start getting this straightened out."

Her phone started to ring as she worked her way in and out
of the throngs of people, trying to get to the end of the table.
Recognizing the ring tone, she answered, keeping her voice
low, "What in the hell is the matter with some people?"

"Ah . . . something in the water? Rabies? Solar radiation?"
Farrah sounded way too cheerful in Ressa's opinion, but Ressa
had been up since before four that morning. She was sleep de-

prived, caffeine deprived, and now, she was pissed off to boot, but if she really unloaded, she'd end up looking like an ass.

Farrah's prompt response made her laugh, though, and that helped undo some of the knots in her neck.

"What's wrong, sugar?" Farrah asked. "Was that drive that much of a pain in the ass?"

"Flying in would be just as awful." Getting to Trenton from any of the airports that were remotely close was a nightmare. "But no, it wasn't the drive. I'll explain later. When I'm in my room, with a big ol' glass of wine."

"Please don't tell me they lost your hotel reservation again."

"No." Ressa mentally said a prayer of thanks over that. "Not much better, though. There was a system glitch or something—my event registration disappeared. They're working on it."

"Well, that's fixable . . . I was worried you'd already met *him* and that he was a total dick."

"No." Ressa laughed softly, not bothering to ask which *him* Farrah was asking about. There could be only one, after all.

The *him* was the same *him* they'd tried to get into the library a hundred times. He lived in Norfolk, he was local, he was a *huge* name and from everything they'd been able to tell online, he was personable. At least, when anybody could get him to talk. Over the past few years, he'd gone into a cave so deep, nobody seemed to be able to pull him out.

Farrah probably knew more about him—she stalked the man, and if life was fair, she would have been here at the writers' conference, but it just went out six weeks ago that he was attending and Farrah needed her vacation time for her upcoming wedding.

So Ressa was here instead, and if she went by what Farrah said, she'd just look for the *hawt*-est guy around.

An image flashed through her mind. Overlong hair, falling into a lean, almost too lean, face. Blue green eyes. A mouth too perfect to be real.

The way he'd looked lingeringly at her that last time.

It had been two months since she'd seen him.

Two months, and she still dreamed about a man whose name she would never know.

And then there was Clayton, that little darling. She missed him in a way that didn't really make sense.

"Hey . . . you're drifting on me again," Farrah said, pulling her back down to planet earth.

"Sorry." Ressa focused back on the matter at hand. She'd promised her friend she'd pin down the elusive Trey Barnes for a few minutes.

He'd had a short visit with a local writers' group back in Norfolk just three weeks ago, so apparently he was rejoining the writing world.

Now she just needed to try and talk him into coming to the Norfolk library. Shouldn't be too hard.

In theory.

She'd give it a shot. He had to leave the house occasionally, and Ressa had been told more than once she could charm a snake when she set her mind to it.

A too-rigid lit writer should be a piece of cake compared to some of the people she'd dealt with.

"I told you I'd try," she told Farrah, watching as Lynda snagged a bag and then an envelope, pausing to speak with somebody sitting at the table piled with electronics.

"I wish you could have lucked out and gotten picked for his panel. I mean, you know Max and he suggests you all the time," Farrah said.

A little bell went *ding* in the back of her mind. *Max suggested you . . .*

"Ms. Bliss?"

"I need a minute, Farrah," she said, moving toward Lynda.

"I apologize for this mess, and for the inconvenience," Lynda said, smiling. "I've got you all set. I'll look into what happened with your registration, but I can't guarantee I'll find any answers. Sometimes the system just messes with us. I will report it, though."

"As long as you've gotten me taken care of, I don't care. I really appreciate your help." She accepted the bag, the envelope. "By any chance, do you know which panels they want me to help out with?"

"No." Lynda grimaced. "I'll be honest, I'm surprised I even remembered to pass the message on—they said they'd leave a message with the concierge so you'll probably have a voice-mail or something, too. I only remembered because of your name—*Bliss* . . . it's kind of pretty."

"Thanks." Rissa waggled the envelope again. "For everything. I've got Max's number so I'll just call him."

As she started to work her way through the crowd, she put the phone back to her ear. "I'm here."

"All fixed?"

"Save for the people problems," she muttered. "It's handled. They apparently want me to help moderate two more panels—don't know which ones—I'm going to be scrambling. But I'm a gofer for one of the panels he's on, so if nothing else, I'll sneak in a few minutes then." Up ahead, she spied the main elevator bank and she could have sworn her entire body breathed a sigh of thanksgiving.

"And that one is early tomorrow, right? Probably the best time to talk to him, before he gets pestered too much," Farrah said.

In the background, Ressa heard the deep voice of Farrah's fiancé, Antoine. "Baby, let her check into her room, at least," he said.

Ressa grinned as Farrah said, "Hush. I'm doing my job."

"Yes," Ressa said before Farrah could say anything else. She wedged herself—and her suitcase—in line. "I should have a chance tomorrow. Everybody, including the gofers, are supposed to meet up about fifteen minutes before the panel starts. I won't have much time to go over anything, but I'll put on the charm and ask him if I can buy him a drink."

"You'll flirt, you mean."

"Sure." Ressa was a natural born flirt and was perfectly fine with it. "If that's the card to play. Now can I get to my room? I'm exhausted and my feet are killing me. I want to lay down and crash for a little while."

"Oh, honey. I'm sorry," Farrah said, the switch from business to best friend flawless. "You do that. Let me know how things go tomorrow, though. And I expect *pictures*."

Ressa managed not to laugh.

She was well aware what kind of pictures Farrah wanted. Yes, the woman was engaged to one sexy beast, but it was no secret between the two friends that Farrah had something of a minor crush on one Trey Barnes.

"I'll get pictures," she promised soberly.

Then, as the elevator doors slid open, she disconnected.

Five minutes alone.

That was all she wanted.

Five minutes . . .

Chapter Six

Pizza delivery sounded better by the minute. Pizza, wings, an early night. An invitation from Max had changed his plans, but now he wished he would have just stayed with his initial plan of an early dinner, followed by bed. So far, Trey had done nothing but listen to the pompous ass who was Baron I. Capstone as he attempted to talk over and around everybody else at the table.

Trey was trying to figure out how to excuse himself—so he could get those damn wings—when she walked in.

He damn near choked on the tea he'd just swallowed.

Ressa . . .

Trey thought maybe his mind was playing tricks on him, but after he blinked and rubbed his eyes, she was still there. Although it could be a hallucination brought on by lack of oxygen.

That body ought to be illegal.

Get it together.

He swallowed, clenched his hands into fists—almost managed to suck in some much needed air.

But then she saw him.

She pursed her lips, frowned as though she was puzzling something through.

He saw the very *second* she recognized him and something that looked like dazed shock fell across her face. He could sympathize. He'd accepted the fact that they wouldn't see each other again, and that it was for the best.

That didn't mean he hadn't enjoyed every white-hot dream, and the rare, blistering climax that might follow.

Yes, he still thought about her.

Yes, he still dreamed about her.

And now . . .

She slowly resumed walking toward them and his heart started to hammer in his chest. Some wild hope started to jump and dance. *Maybe*—

"Hmmm. Boys, I've just found who *I'm* taking back to the hotel," Capstone murmured.

A rush of possessiveness, the kind he hadn't felt in years, slammed into him, catching him off guard.

He had no idea what he might have said if Max hadn't laughed. "Baron, son, you couldn't manage that if you lived a thousand years."

Then Max shifted his attention forward. "Ressa, sweetheart. It's been far too long."

All the puzzle pieces fell into place. Max . . . Max knew her. He'd mentioned he had a friend who could handle the moderating bit—*a librarian*, he'd said. *Has handled events like this before. You'll love her.*

Feeling a little dazed himself, Trey thought, *Yeah, Max. I think I could do just that. I could love her.*

Her gaze moved around the table and as it landed on him, need, longing attacked him with vicious, desperate claws.

"Hello, gentlemen," she said, her voice smooth and warm as melted chocolate. And her mouth—she'd painted it with some rich, vibrant red and he had to force himself to listen to what she was saying, instead of just watching her mouth as it formed those words. Her gaze landed on him and he inclined his head.

"Well . . ." She drew the word out, inclining her head. "This is . . . something of a surprise, Mr. . . . ?"

He grimaced. He'd heard that from her so many times. It

had become habit, dodging when people pushed, even for something as small as his name. His family had come in after Aliesha's death, surrounded him in the days that followed, and even though part of him had wanted them there, another part had dreaded it. Because if Zach was in town, and Sebastian, even though he'd just been a bit actor then, they were known names and the reporters had flocked around. Abby had been there too and any time she and Zach were together, that brought reporters out in droves.

It had been a small slice of hell, even as he took comfort in having his family around.

While he was grieving for Aliesha, and trying to deal with what was going on with his son, then—and the black hole of memories in the hours that followed after he'd left his family—he also had reporters dogging his every step. Normally, he wasn't one of the brothers who caught much attention when it came to reporters. Authors weren't that fascinating when it came to media attention, but nothing brings them out like tragedy.

Yeah, it had become second nature to avoid the media, to avoid having people recognize *him* period.

And it was time to get over it.

"Yeah, um . . . hi." He rose and glanced around. "Kind of a surprise to see you here, Ressa."

"Not as much as you," she said, arching her brow. "And again, you dodge the question."

"Ah . . ."

"Trey, it appears you know each other," Max said, leaning back in his chair, cocking a brow. "Ressa, you never mentioned you'd met this troublemaker."

"Well . . . we haven't *exactly* met. I've seen him more than a few times, but I've never managed to get *his name*." Ressa cocked her head.

She enunciated it this time and Trey winced.

"It's—"

He never really managed to finished because Max started to laugh, and Max had a laugh that boomed and echoed.

"This is a story I really do need to hear," Baron said, his voice low and packed with more innuendo than Trey would have thought possible.

Baron leaned forward then, elbows braced on the table as he studied Ressa. "You know, you look familiar to me. Have we met?"

"No," she said, her voice politely cool, the look in her eyes frosty. Then her gaze zoomed right back in on Trey.

Max chuckled. "Come on, Ressa. Sit down."

She huffed out a breath and started around the table, her gaze skewering into Trey.

He slumped lower into his seat, feeling both sheepish and disturbingly elated. He shifted uncomfortably to accommodate for his cock as it pulsed, reminding him of dirty dreams and fantasies he'd tried to forget.

Ressa slid into the seat next to him, bringing with her the scent that he'd *almost* managed to put out of his mind.

"So . . ." she drew out.

"So . . ." Max said, his voice underscored with laughter. "You've lived in Norfolk, oh . . . going on ten years now, I think. Been in that general area for most of your life. Am I right?"

Ressa just looked at him.

Max glanced past her to Trey and then asked, "All that time, and you're a librarian but that boy's famous face doesn't look at all familiar to you?"

Trey could feel the rush of blood racing up to flood his face. "Max. I can take you down, old man."

A laugh boomed out of him. "Yes, you can, Trey. Now shut up and let me have my fun . . . I'm an old man, remember?"

Chapter Seven

"Trey . . ."

She said slowly. Somebody had said it once earlier but it hadn't registered.

A number of eyes zeroed in on her, but she was only conscious of his—those amazing blue green eyes, that seemed so very familiar now.

And that face—lean, maybe leaner than it should be, now that she thought of it. He'd cut his hair, quite a bit, and the shorter length only served to emphasize how sinfully attractive he was.

That nagging sense of familiarity—

Trey—

Her heart kicked up because she could think of only *one* Trey who was appearing at the event this weekend.

A rush of other details slammed into her mind, almost too fast for her to process everything.

I'm gonna see Uncle Bastian this time . . . is Aunt Abby making cake?

Sometimes he even makes them up. He gets paid to do that, too.

Bastian. . . .

Trey Barnes's younger brother was Sebastian Barnes.

Abby . . . Abigale Applegate? She'd read about the marriage to one of the Barnes brothers. The sexy tattooed one.

Slowly, she said his name, one more time, hoping he'd correct her. "Trey," she said softly.

He seemed focused on the table now.

"I remember Clayton telling me that you told him stories . . . that you even made them up. You got paid to do it."

He gave her a lopsided smile. "It's a living."

"I imagine it is . . . Mr. Barnes."

He lifted his head now, faced her straight on. "Yeah, well . . . I could try to do something else, but apparently the one thing I'm really good at is making shit up."

"Somehow, that doesn't surprise me."

Still a little stunned, she looked over at Max, her gaze bouncing off the glass he had sitting in front of him. "I seem to recall that you owe me a drink." That said, she snatched his mostly untouched whiskey. If she knew Max—and she did, it would be good whiskey and that was just what she needed. "I'm collecting."

She tossed it back and closed her eyes as it burned its way down her throat.

"You know Trey, if you're forgetting the basics of civilized society—like how to introduce yourself to a beautiful woman, maybe you should trade me seats."

Ressa cracked open an eye at that low voice. Smooth, practiced and all but oozing with charm. And so pathetically obvious. His eyes roamed over her in a patently familiar way and she pointedly met his gaze, then looked away.

"Trey's just fine where he is," she said. "After all, this will be the perfect time to ask him for a favor . . . considering he'd been loitering in my library all that time."

She slid him a look as she said it, watched as his eyes widened.

"A favor."

"Don't worry." She gave him a cheeky smile. "It's almost completely painless."

"Baron, don't sulk. Ressa's not switching seats anyway." Max tipped an invisible hat toward him. "Ressa is my guest and

I'm going to be selfish—you'd talk her ear off and I haven't seen her in almost two years now. Far too long."

He patted her shoulder and she shot him a grin.

He wasn't being selfish. He knew her. He was keeping the peace. She knew far too much about Baron's type—the sexist, piggish man-whore had never appealed to her.

Shifting more comfortably in her seat, she took another sip of whiskey. Trey Barnes had knocked her off course.

Over the next few minutes, introductions were made and she mentally filed them away, nodding and smiling. All the while, her brain was mentally whirling.

Trey.

Her sexy *CD* was Trey Barnes.

How was that possible?

Although, really, if she'd looked, she might have seen it.

If Farrah had actually been able to spend five seconds in his presence, she probably *would* have seen it.

She settled into her seat and listened to the introductions, staying mostly quiet as the conversation flowed. It paused briefly as a server came around and took orders. Next to her, Trey shifted in his seat. She was painfully, acutely aware of the long, lean lines of muscle, tanned skin, elegant hands.

He glanced at her and she felt the rush of heat suffuse her. How she managed to just give him a casual smile, she just didn't know.

He quirked a brow at her and then glanced up at the server. While he placed his order, Ressa tried to get a grip. *So not prepared for this.* Not for seeing him here. Had she bumped into him and he was one of the bloggers, that would have been hard enough, but finding out he was *the* author she was supposed to hunt down?

Shit. He was probably on one of the extra panels Max wanted her to take over.

Which meant she'd be talking to him outside of this dinner, too.

Not prepared for that either!

Or for sitting next to him. He had a heady scent—cologne, very faint, though, mixed in with his soap, and under that, just *him*—it made her think of grass and the outdoors and sunshine. Sexy and male. She liked. So very much.

She definitely hadn't been prepared to have those intense, blue green eyes focused on her again. His eyes could be classified as a weapon of mass devastation. Sleepy, heavily lashed and the kind of blue green you'd expect to find down in the tropics. Trey had the kind of eyes that could put woman into a swoon if he put his mind to it.

Would Farrah absolutely *hate* her if she gave into this crazy heat that grew hotter and hotter every second she was around him?

She was debating that very thing, had even decided that Farrah would understand. It was just one of those fantasy crushes, and besides, her best friend was crazy in love, and engaged. Besides, this was just a . . . thing. Some sort of fluke and once it was done and he was out of her system, she could go back to thinking straight.

Decision made, she cocked her head and turned to look at Trey as he was reaching for the glass in front of him.

That was when she saw the glint of gold on his finger.

His ring finger.

On his left hand.

Hands that had always been covered by the gloves he wore—the gloves made sense now. Therapeutic gloves, she imagined. The kind worn by writers to help with their wrists.

And they'd hidden that ring.

An ice-cold bucket of water splashing in her face wouldn't have been more effective. Abruptly, she shoved back from the table. "Please excuse me for a moment."

Okay, Farrah had rambled on and on about how private the man was, even more so over the past few years. And Ressa knew—obviously—that there had been a woman in his life. But nobody ever came to the library. Clayton never talked about his mother.

It was like she just . . . didn't exist.

And how he'd given her that little paperweight for Mother's Day.

She'd assumed . . .

That's it, you assumed.

Feeling the weight of their combined gazes on her, she sought out the restroom. Once inside, she moved to the sink and braced her hands on it.

She'd almost made a move on a married man.

"You've done gone and lost it, honey."

All because a man had a beautiful pair of eyes and a slow, sexy smile.

Of course, she'd always been a sucker for a man with a beautiful pair of eyes and a slow, sexy smile.

Beautiful eyes, a slow sexy smile had damn near ruined her before and she'd fought long and hard to rebuild the mess that bastard had made of her life.

Her heart hammered and she sucked in a breath.

That man—she'd been right. She really *had* been better off getting away from him months ago.

He was dangerous.

"Just get through the weekend and you'll never have to see him again." The thought caused a hollow ache to settle inside her chest, though.

And instead of making her feel any better at all, it only made her feel worse.

Trey spent the next ninety minutes trying to puzzle out just what had happened.

One minute, she'd been easy and relaxed—oh, Baron—the prick—had gotten under her skin, but she'd handled him, and unless Trey had forgotten how to read people, she'd enjoyed knocking him down a peg, too.

She'd been warm, easy, relaxed.

And then, within the span of a heartbeat, something had changed.

He couldn't even put his finger on it, try as he might. And he wanted to know what it was. Part of him had kept thinking that maybe he should . . . should . . .

Should what?

Travis's voice seemed to nag him—a brotherly earworm—
Are you just going to bite the bullet and ask her out?

He'd almost done it. That last day, before Clayton had gotten so upset.

There was nothing in the way now.

Nothing except for that one thing. The one that made his brain shut down, panic crowding out everything. That, com-

bined with the humiliation that had happened the one time
he'd even tried . . .

So maybe it was better.

Maybe it was better that the air around them seemed to
drop by about thirty degrees and she'd gone from sliding him
those quick little glances, to barely looking at him at all.

None of that kept him sitting there next to her, thankful
that the table was a barrier that kept anybody from seeing the
evidence of just how much Ressa Bliss affected him.

Yeah. Maybe this was better . . .

But damned if he could really get himself to believe that.

"You really do need to think about taking that off,"
Max said as they headed down the hall to their rooms.

Since he didn't, at all, want to talk about it, Trey played
dumb. "Take what off?" Inside his pocket, he rubbed his thumb
across his wedding ring.

"Son, you know damn good and well what. That ring. The
one you use like a shield to keep women from getting too
close. The one you wear to pretend that maybe Aliesha isn't
really dead, isn't really gone." Max stopped outside his door
and looked back at him. "It's like as long as you wear that
ring, you don't have to let her go. You can keep that part of her.
But, Trey, she is gone. It's time you let go . . . and start living
again."

Jaw clenched, he looked away. Max couldn't be any more
off base if he tried, but Trey wasn't about to go into the real
reasons. But abruptly, he had a sickening realization.

Had Ressa seen his ring?

Son of a bitch—

The news of Aliesha's death had gone national—hell,
global—but not everybody followed some of the things the
media chose to sensationalize. Maybe she didn't know . . . ?

"Did I ever tell you that I was married before Maude and I
got together?"

Frowning, Trey shot Max a look.

But Max had a far-off expression on his face as he stared
down the hall. "Amelia. We met in high school. Married the
day after we graduated . . . man, I loved her so much." That

distant look cleared. "We were together for four years. Four of the best years I ever had . . . and then, one night while I was working, a man broke into our home, raped her, killed her. I thought I'd die, too. The man I had been, he did die. She'd been gone a year when I sat down to write my first book—the purest shit I'd ever seen. It took me three years to finish. The day I finished, I went into our room and sat. Then I started to cry. I hadn't cried. Not until that day." He closed his eyes and sucked in a breath, held it for a long moment. Then he looked up, met Trey's eyes once more. "That much time had to pass before I let myself cry enough to let her go. It wasn't until then that I realized I wasn't honoring her memory by keeping her so close. She wouldn't have wanted that." He clapped Trey on the shoulder and unlocked his room. "You should think about that ring, son. Think hard."

As he slid inside, Trey found himself standing in the hall, staring down at the gold band on his hand.

Maybe Max hadn't been as far off as Trey had assumed.

No, he wasn't still clinging to Aliesha's memory. He'd accepted her death. Let her go. But the ring was still a barrier. It was his shield, and sometimes a reminder.

And tonight, when he had actually thought about trying to reach out?

It had been the barrier he'd planned for it to be—only this time, he hadn't really wanted that.

Chapter Eight

Leaning against the door that opened out onto the balcony, Trey rubbed his thumb over the well-worn script of his notebook. Normally, the thing would be filled with notes by now and he might have even replaced it. And he actually *had* replaced it—in a way. But instead of just carrying one, he carried two. This one, with the *to-do* list he'd never finished and then another one that he used for more lists, more notes, the odd and random doodle. That one was on the table with his wallet, his change, his keycard, and phone.

This one, though . . . He stood there, staring at the list he'd written weeks ago.

Start living again.

Shifting his gaze to the ring he wore, he thought about the whispered conversation—if it could be called that—he'd had with Aliesha in the few minutes before they'd wheeled her off to surgery.

Aliesha had known.

His mom had called Aliesha an old soul. She'd been grounded and solid and so serene. Gentle, even. He'd fallen in love with that gentleness and her kindness and her humor.

And she'd lain on the table, gripping his hand and looked

at him with knowledge in her eyes. She'd *known*. She'd been born with a genetic heart defect and maybe that had given her a somewhat fatalistic outlook on life.

She'd been sick often as a child but she'd gotten stronger, healthier as she grew. Both her cardiologist and her OB/GYN hadn't seen any reason why she couldn't have a safe pregnancy, as long as she was careful.

Too bad the fucking drunk driver hadn't been *careful*.

As they were wheeling her into surgery, she'd looked at him with pain-bright, but clear eyes, her hand clinging to his.

Don't stop living.

Hadn't he, though?

That ring that he wore as a shield—he could psychoanalyze it to pieces. Those psychology courses he'd taken in college came up damn handy at times. If he flipped this all around and looked at it dispassionately, he knew it all made sense.

There were times he couldn't even stand to have a woman touch him. Not in any way that resembled intimacy. Aliesha's death, her funeral—the very *loss* of her, and then those dark, lost hours the night of the funeral, they were tangled up in a miasma of guilt he couldn't get free of.

He still didn't have those hours back. Whatever shit had been given him, it had been damn effective at turning his mind into a blank slate. He had the vaguest echoes of memory, but that was it.

The only bits and pieces he could call up from that night were the memory of whiskey—as evidenced by the fact that the smell of it still turned his stomach—and the echo of a woman laughing, and then shouts, followed by fury and pain. The fury and pain made sense, in a way. He'd ended up battered and bruised, so he'd sure as hell ended up in a fight with somebody.

And that was probably the last time he'd really let himself feel *anything* that didn't involve his son or his family. He'd shut himself down, locked himself up.

He'd done exactly what Aliesha had asked him not to do.

He'd stopped living.

Slowly, he tugged the ring off. It would come off for good this time, too. Something that might have been panic swam up, trying to grab him and pull him back down. He'd fought it before, fought the edges of panic even as he fought the depression that had eventually driven him into a shrink's office.

If it hadn't been for Clayton, he wouldn't have gone.

If he hadn't gone, he never would have realized just how utterly fucked up he was.

And because he knew how utterly fucked up he was, he made himself close his fist around that ring, made himself put it down.

The phone's harsh ringtone shattered the silence.

Trey jerked, sweat beading on the back of his neck, his upper lip, slicking the palms of his hands. His phone sat on the bureau, and the picture of his twin, his nose pressed to Clayton's, both of them mock snarling, lit up the screen.

He grabbed the phone like a drowning man. "Yeah."

There was a faint pause.

"You're a fucking mess, Trey," Travis said, his voice rough, heavy with sleep.

"Suck my dick," he said, all but collapsing on the edge of the bed.

Somehow Travis had picked up on the chaos Trey was feeling, and it had been enough to wake his twin up. Trey didn't bother feeling guilty. They'd been like this all their lives and more than once, he'd been the one to call his brother—or at least try—knowing something was up.

"Shit, man. If you're this worked up that I can't sleep, you might as well talk," Travis said, his voice a little clearer. "'Sup?"

"Nothing. Everything." He stared at his ring, because this was the one thing he couldn't, wouldn't share. "Look, my head, it's just . . ."

"I already told you that you're a mess. I got that part. Now tell me what's going on."

Abruptly, like everything had morphed into a boulder teetering on the edge of a cliff, Trey could feel himself on the verge of giving in. Letting it all out, like a poison.

"Shit. I *am* a mess. You remember that . . ." He stopped in mid-sentence, uncertain where to even go from here. *I saw her again. Ressa. I want her. Except I can't. And I mean I really, really can't—*

Travis's sigh carried across the line and then his twin said,

"Are you dreaming about Aliesha again? About the wreck? Trey, you know there was nothing you could have done."

Squeezing his eyes shut, he sat there for a moment. "No," he said, forcing the word out through gritted teeth. Then he opened his eyes, stood, and started to pace. "It wasn't the wreck. It wasn't her. It's . . ."

"Is it that night? Call the shrink." Travis paused, the words reluctant. He knew how much Trey hated to talk about this. "I know I'm not the—"

"I still wear my ring," Trey said, cutting in. He stared down at the bit of gold on his hand. "Not all the time, but when I'm out at a thing like this, or if I go to church with Aliesha's parents . . . if I head back to San Francisco. I wear it. Last night, I saw . . ."

Recognizing the ache that echoed inside him, Travis closed his eyes. Not all twins had that weird connection. Life might be easier if he and Trey didn't have it, but he wouldn't cut this out of him even if he had the choice. But he didn't want his brother feeling the rush of relief that punched through him.

"A woman."

Trey's laugh was dry, strained. "You could say that."

Something about that pricked at Travis—especially combined with a weird edge of panic. It was familiar, something he'd felt too often.

"It was Ressa. The librarian. Remember her?"

For a minute, Travis's mind went blank. And then, as a smile came over his face, he had to fight the urge to pump the air, or something else equally goofy.

Still, there was a reluctance, a heavy feeling of guilty.

Softly, Travis said, "Yeah. I remember her. Trey, this isn't a bad thing, right?"

"Fuck." A world of frustration came out in that harsh, decisive grunt. "The hell if I know. I just . . . I could . . ."

"You could what?"

A taut silence hung between and Travis held his breath, thinking maybe, *maybe*, whatever poison Trey was hiding would finally spill out of him.

But then Trey just said, "Nothing, man. I can't do this now."
Those words, softly spoken, made him close his eyes.

'Trey, look—"

"I can't. Look, I gotta go. There's a panel, and I . . . I think she thinks I'm still married. The ring."

"Then take it off, damn it." Travis paused then, as he felt something twist, almost savagely inside him. And it didn't come from him. "Trey?"

"It's not that easy." Then the phone went dead.

Trey disconnected and put the phone on vibrate before he tucked it into his pocket. He already knew what Travis was going to ask anyway and it wasn't anything he could answer just then.

Why isn't it that easy? What's stopping you?

It should be that easy. Nothing *stopped* him.

Yet something vital *did*.

He hadn't had sex in so long, he might well have forgotten what it was. There had been exactly *three* chances in the past six years—*three* dates, each with a different woman and each time had resulted in spectacular failures.

The first one had just been a series of stops and starts and when Cassie had looked at him expectantly at the end, obviously waiting for a kiss, he'd just nodded at her so *she* had tried to kiss him and he'd backed away so fast, he'd ended up tripping over the planter she had on her porch.

Lizette, the cute single mom from Clayton's play group, had ended up finding another group after their disastrous date and he couldn't blame her. He'd gone to kiss her and she'd closed the distance and he'd just . . . locked down. Completely.

Then there was the debacle with his neighbor Nadine. Their pathetic date still made him cringe.

It wasn't just guilt—the psychologist had told him it was normal to feel guilty—*normal* although there was nothing to be guilty about. But it was more than guilt. Trey didn't even want women *touching* him now.

Even theoretically, it wasn't appealing.

Or it hadn't been, until he'd met Ressa.

He sat on the edge of the bed, staring at the ring he'd all but ripped off his hand. It gleamed at him from the table. Sweat built at the base of his neck.

Swearing, he shoved up and paced the three steps across the floor and grabbed it, hurling it across the room. The platinum and gold band hit the wall and then fell.

It lay there, on the far side of the room, glinting at him, the gold and platinum shining in the dim light of the room. Mocking him.

That didn't change anything.

It took twenty minutes and a lot of sheer determination to get to the room set up for his panel. He kept his head down, his sunglasses on, and his hands jammed into his pockets so he wouldn't see his naked left hand.

He kept his mind focused on a plot kink in one of his side projects. The heroine was difficult, fighting him. Too much in her past was just not coming together and he couldn't figure out why.

That was enough to keep him distracted until he found the right room, trying not to notice the long line that had already formed. A few people saw him and when he heard the speculative whispers, and more than a few whispers of his name, he hunched his shoulders and just moved faster, letting the door all but kick him in the ass as he ducked inside.

Once there, he just stood, took a deep breath. The scent of coffee—

"Mr. Barnes."

Blood drained, slowly, from his head all the down to pool in his groin at the sound of her low voice—smooth as honey, potent as whiskey. He hadn't craved that in years, but now, he had a need to taste it. On her.

He had another need, too. The one that seemed to flood him whenever he was near her. Muscles tensed and tightened and it was, yet again, just sheer will that allowed him to blank his face as he looked over at her. He could stand this close to her and still feel it, that need to touch, to taste, to take . . .

Yeah, *theoretically*, he wanted her.

And fuck the theory—he just plain wanted. Wanted her with a need that bordered on obsession, and it all but blinded him as she stood there, giving him a polite, professional smile.

He cleared his throat and managed to return her smile.

"Ms. Bliss. Ah . . . how are you?"

"Fine, thank you."

Trey found himself trying not to stare at the way the high-waisted skirt she wore clung to curves so lush, they were all but imprinted on his brain already.

Remember item number four on your list . . . try not to drool.

He could all but feel his smile wobbling on his face now and he looked around, half-desperate. Spying the coffee urns lined up on a table at the far wall, he nodded at her. "Ah . . . I need coffee."

Coffee. Coffee would work—if it didn't focus his brain, he could dump it on himself and use it as an excuse to run back upstairs and change. Getting through the panel with a hard-on was not going to—

"Morning there, Barnes. You look nervous. Guess those movie star genes from your brothers weren't passed onto you, huh?"

The sound of Baron's voice scraped against his already ragged temper and raw nerves. But it served to cool the flare of heat that had been burning through him. Heat faded, replaced by irritation. And the irritation wasn't just because Baron stood between him and caffeine.

Teeth bared in a mockery of a smile, he met Baron's gaze. "What makes you think I'm nervous?"

"A little red in the face, looking kind of desperate." Baron shrugged. "It's not a big deal. Not like you do public appearances. These sessions are being recorded, you know. Streamed live, and then shared later for those who couldn't attend. Has to be nerve-wracking—"

Trey started to laugh. As he edged around Baron, he said, "Thanks to one of those movie star brothers—and actually, Zach didn't do movies, he did TV—but thanks to Zach, I was used to growing up around cameras and having people ask me crazy questions. I probably had more screen time by the time I was fifteen than you've had in your entire career."

There was a soft laugh from the back of the room. He ground his teeth together and focused on the coffee setup over at the side of the room.

The forty-five minute panel passed in a blur.

There were laughs from the audience, there were questions and grins from the panelists—Ressa remembered that. She did her best not to think about the cameras—there wouldn't be a day when the thought of *those* wouldn't turn her stomach, but she kept her body angled to the side and went with the flow.

When another assistant signaled it was time and she had to tell everybody they had to wrap up, there was a groan that echoed through the crowd.

She took that to mean she'd made it through another one.

Half the time she felt like she was faking it and more often than not, she didn't even remember *exactly* what had happened until she listened to the podcasts or watched the videos that streamed out in the days that followed these sort of events.

As much as she hated the videos, she always watched.

But she didn't have to look at a video or listen to a podcast to know how this one had gone.

One look at Max's face and she knew.

He caught her hand as she stepped back from the podium. "You knocked it out of the park, sweetheart. Good job."

Rolling her eyes, she blew out a theatrical breath, although she really did need the oxygen. "Thank you."

As readers started to approach, she moved away. She'd done her job, now she was going to stand by and watch as the people at the table continued on with theirs.

"How long has it been since you did this?"

Trey studied his numb hand closely. Yep. Still shaking. That had been . . . kind of a rush, he decided. Nerve-wracking in a crazy way, thus the shakes. But fun. Tucking his numb, shaking hands into his pockets, he flashed Max a grin as they moved out into the hall. "About six and a half years. I had that three week tour when *Odd Girl* came out."

Neither of them mentioned the conference he'd been at

when Aliesha was in the wreck—he'd barely even had time to meet a few people, talk to some of his fellow panelists, before he received the call.

Eyes squinted in thought, Max stared at nothing in particular for a long moment. "That was your first one, wasn't it? First tour?"

"Yeah." He sighed as the adrenaline started to drain away, as if those words had just pulled some unseen cork right out of him. "First and last."

"It's only been your last because you have too much going on in your life," Max said softly. "Hard to handle that sort of thing when you got your son to take care of. Can't really spend two or three weeks flying around the country when you got a young son, now can you?"

"Some people think I can." He jerked a shoulder in a restless shrug, thinking of the publicist he'd fired only six months after Aliesha's death. The son of a bitch had insisted it was time that Trey start focusing on his career again—*enough time had passed, right*?

Max clapped a hand on his shoulder. "You put your son first. You still do. Not a thing wrong with that, Trey. You're all he's got and he needs you."

I need him, Trey thought. Out loud he just said, "I know." They'd been so busy in the room that the next session of panels was about to start so they managed to slip through most of the crowd.

He wanted to go up to his room for a little while, sit down. Call Clayton—

"Hi!"

A punch of heat that was becoming almost brutally familiar slammed into him, catching him in the throat, the gut—lower.

Ressa cut in front of them, so close now that he could smell whatever she'd smoothed on her skin. She was glowing, the grin on her face was a cross between ecstatic and nervous—sort of how he felt.

"That turned out pretty good, didn't it?" The words tumbled out of her, a hard 180 from the easy calm she'd shown both last night and during the panel.

Arching a brow, he opened his mouth, but she was already talking.

"Don't you think? Max, I know you said it went well, but you always say that. What did you—" She stopped, snapping her mouth shut and then blowing out a sigh while the smile on her face turned sheepish. "Sorry. Nerves. They never really hit until I'm done."

"I get that." Trey smiled as that blast of heat melted away into something . . . softer. Easier. She wasn't just sexy as hell, he realized.

Just then, she was . . .

"You know what? I think I'm going to go up to my room for a little bit," Max said.

Both of them whipped their heads around to look at him.

Trey almost shot out a hand to catch him by the arm.

"But—" Ressa opened her mouth, closed it.

"I'm getting too old to pound the floor all day," Max said, grinning at her. "I'll see you both around later. It was a great panel, Ressa. You know better than to think I'd lie."

As Max disappeared, Trey ran his tongue along the inside of his teeth. He should do the same thing. Go up to his room. He needed to call Clayton. Relax, maybe change into some shorts and go running or something. Swinging his head around to look at Ressa, he opened his mouth.

The words that came spilling out shocked the hell out of him.

"Would you have a cup of coffee with me?"

Her mouth fell open. "Ah . . . excuse me?"

What the hell . . . The words couldn't be pulled back, but he realized, now that they were out, he didn't want to take them back.

Elation, and nerves, pounded inside him, but he managed to hide all of that behind a grin as he took a step closer.

It was like riding a bike, he told himself. He hadn't thought it through, and he hadn't ended up flat on his face.

In a matter of seconds—a blink, really, her lovely, wide eyes cooled.

"I'm afraid not. I try to avoid having coffee with married men."

Then after a scathing look that left him feeling like she'd just sliced the top layer of his skin off, she turned on one ice-pick heel and strode off.

He was distracted enough by the sway of her hips—and the delightful, round curve of her ass—that it took him another fifteen seconds to make himself move.

Yeah, maybe he should have explained that part first.

"Hey, wait a minute."

As he ducked into the elevator with her, Ressa folded her arms over her chest. "Afraid I can't, Mr. Barnes."

Her icy tone drew the eye of more than a few passengers in the elevator. She started to tap her foot, watching the numbers speed by.

The floor stopped at eleven, fourteen, fifteen—

"Ressa, wait."

She pushed through the bodies as the elevator slowed at seventeen. "I've got a busy afternoon, Mr. Barnes, so if you'll—"

She hissed as she turned to see him coming off the elevator after her.

Not a single damn soul said a word, although more than a few watched with rapt gazes until the elevator doors slid closed in their faces.

"I guess I didn't make myself clear," she said. "Let me take care of that now."

"I think I should go first." He shoved his hands into his pockets, inclining his head.

"Oh?" With a cool smile, she waved a hand. "Please do."

Despite herself—and the disappointment—and heaven help her, that knee-jerk reaction she'd had to say yes to whatever he wanted to do—she wondered what excuse he'd pull out of his ass.

He lowered his head, reaching up to rub at the back of his neck. With his left hand, one that was noticeably bare today.

He was nothing but another player. It pissed her off, too. She'd *liked* him. He'd seemed so . . . nice. He was an amazing father, and he adored his son and he was . . . well, he'd seemed almost *perfect*. Taken, yeah. But still . . . perfect.

He went to drop his hand, head still bowed. But as he was lowering his hand, he stopped, pausing, staring at the pale strip where his ring would have been.

He looked at his hand like he'd never seen it.

"We only had a few years together," he said, his voice soft, almost distant. "We met in college and . . . that was it for us. We just knew. We waited until we graduated to get married."

Something about his tone had her stomach twisting. *Stop it. You've heard these lines before.*

"My wife . . . she . . ."

"Look, if you all are separated or whatever, fine. But I don't date married guys. So—"

"She died almost six years ago." He looked up then, his gaze flat. So flat, almost cold. He looked back at his hand, staring at the place where his ring would have been. "I was at a conference. She was pregnant with Clay and there was an accident—a drunk driver crossed the lines while my wife was on her way to her OB appointment. She . . ." He stopped and looked away, but not in time to keep her from seeing the diamond bright glint in his eyes.

"She went into early labor—died during the C-section." He cut another look her way. "The ring . . . well. I know she's gone. It's not like I'm clinging to her memory or anything. It's just . . . things were . . ." He stopped and shook his head. "Never mind. I'm sorry I bothered you."

With her heart tangled up somewhere in her throat, Ressa stared after him as he walked away.

Chapter Nine

"I rode the roller coaster!"

Back braced against the headboard, Trey smiled as Clayton peered up at him from the screen of his iPhone. His grin was a mile wide and he had a smudge of chocolate or something on his nose, and the sight of the boy soothed the ragged ache in Trey's heart.

"Did you throw up?"

"Gross! No. Have you ever thrown up on a roller coaster?" Clayton asked.

"Nope. One time, though, when we were kids, your uncles and I ate like three hot dogs—"

Two seconds later, his mother was on the phone. "Don't you dare, Trey Malcolm Barnes. You hear me?"

"Ah, hi, Mom. How are you?" He summoned up his best smile, knowing it wasn't going to do any good. It hadn't, even when they were kids.

Denise just narrowed her eyes at him.

That made him laugh. "So that panel earlier was . . . kind of intense."

"Don't you go putting any ideas in that boy's head," she said, ignoring his attempts to distract her.

"Mom. He's my kid," Trey pointed out. "He was probably born with those ideas imprinted on his DNA."

"Exactly. I'm hoping they'll stay there—inactive—and here you are, telling him about . . . *that*."

He laughed, felt more of the shadows fall away. He could practically see his mother shuddering as she remembered *that one time*. A hot dog binge, three kids on a coaster—Zane had proven to be smart enough to not do it—although *he* had dared them. Sebastian had been too short, and of course, he'd cried the entire time. Right up until they all started getting sick and then he'd laughed. And laughed. And laughed.

"Okay. I won't give him ideas while he's at Disney with you." That was the most he could promise. "Now, can I talk to Clayton? Please?"

Her aggravated sigh only made him smile wider. "You boys, it's a miracle I still have any hair left."

"So did you throw up after?" Clayton asked.

"Tell you what, Clay. We'll talk about it—all about it— once we're home. Grandma doesn't wanna hear about puke and stuff. We don't want to make her unhappy."

"Oh. Okay." Clayton was quiet for a second and then veered onto the next topic. "When are you going to be done? I miss you."

"Soon, buddy." At the knock, he rolled off his bed and moved to the door. A quick look through the security hole had him frowning. No. He didn't think he wanted to open the door. Turning away, he moved out of the bedroom to the narrow little strip that served as a balcony. There was another knock just as he shut the door.

He had no idea what Ressa wanted, but he'd already decided it was better to just let it go.

"I want a Darth Vadar backpack for school."

At that, Trey pulled his attention back to what mattered— focusing on the excited boy on the other end of the line.

He'd surprised himself, though.

He'd taken the ring off.

He'd asked her out.

Start living again.

Yeah, he'd do that. Later. He could still feel something inside, he'd proven that. But he'd try again . . . later. With somebody who didn't have the power to rip a hole in him with just a look.

He wouldn't lock himself back up again.

He'd made himself that promise when he came back inside his room and saw the ring on the floor. It wasn't meant to be a shield and it shouldn't have been worn as a reminder of . . . whatever had happened that night.

It had been a sign of a promise, one that both he and Aliesha had honored, until death had come between them.

Now he just had to accept it—and let go of those things he couldn't remember.

Feeling a little sick, Ressa stared at the coffee she held—a peace offering—and then back up at the door.

He was in there. She knew it for a fact, because she'd heard him, the low rumble of his voice. She had no idea who he was talking to and she hadn't heard anybody else, but he was in there—ignoring her.

Sighing, she lifted her hand to knock a third time, but in the end, she turned away. Eying the narrow table behind her, she shrugged and figured it wasn't going to hurt.

She left the coffee sitting there, with a note scrawled across the side in scrawling black.

T.

   I'm sorry.

R.

"It's the hottest one yet, I'm telling you." Ellie Barrister leaned across a table roughly the size of a dinner plate and tapped the postcard she'd slapped on the table earlier. They'd made it through the first days of the book fair—tomorrow was the final day. Tonight was for chatter, a few drinks . . . and brooding.

"I hear you. L. Forrester, whoever she is, puts some of the best I've ever read to shame. I just wish she'd do interviews."

Tori Caldwell clicked her beer to Lynnette's cosmo. "Signings, a book tour . . . something. She's practically a hermit."

Ressa snorted and shook her head. Sitting at a table surrounded by her friends, they were talking books and men and life in general. "Sounds a lot like somebody else I know." Although, to be fair, there *was* information out there on Trey. She just hadn't *looked*.

At the curious gazes directed her way, she shrugged. "Actually, there are a few authors I can think of who fit that bill. Some of them are weird. You ought to know that by now."

"True. And if *weird* translates to *amazing* . . . then fine. Be weird. But she could at least *talk* to me. I mean, listen to this . . ." Lynette flipped through the book and stopped close to halfway through.

Ressa winced. "If you spoil that book for me, I'll smack you over the head with it."

"I've already finished mine." Ellie grinned at them. "If you're nice, Ressa, I might let you borrow it, as long as you return it. I need to read it another three, four . . . ten times to decide if it's my favorite or not."

"Nothing is going to top *You, I Desire*," Ressa said, absolutely certain.

"Guys? Hush." Lynnette reached for her cosmo, took a sip and then started to read.

"She shouldn't be here." Lynnette looked up, winked. "This is our heroine, by the way. Nina. She's seducing a billionaire."

"She's telling us to hush," Tori muttered, shaking her head.

"Another billionaire?" Ressa rolled her eyes. "You know I hate billionaire books."

"Me, too." Tori slumped in her chair, her gaze roaming the room. "I want another drink. Should I go to the bar or hope we can flag our server?"

"The bar. It's packed," Lynnette said. "Ya know, I'm not big on billionaire books, but sometimes they work for me. I was kind of surprised Forrester did one. But this one was fun, and Ressa, you especially are going to love it. The guy is a geek. *And* borderline awkward. He made eggs explode when he tried to hard-boil them because he got distracted reading Patricia Briggs. He goes to SF/F cons and the first time he saw her, he had this crazy thought that he might believe in love at first sight."

Ressa started to laugh. "Shows that a woman is writing it. Men don't believe in love at first sight. Sex, yeah . . . but love?" She shrugged. "I don't know if *I* believe in love at first sight."

"I do." A wide, satisfied smile settled over Ellie's face. She had just celebrated her tenth anniversary—and she married a guy she'd known under a month.

"I think I could believe in it . . . if I met the right guy. Now let me read." Lynnette cleared her throat, and then she started to read, getting into it, too by the way her voice changed oh, so slightly.

She shouldn't be here. She liked this guy—she wasn't supposed to like him. It was a job—he was a job. She was supposed to get to know more about him, understand what kind of guy he was now and how he'd gone from Geek Central to Mr. GQ and then . . . then . . .

" 'Nina? Hey, what are you doing here? I thought you—' "

Fuck the job. With need and want a vicious tangle inside her, she launched herself at him. His mouth opened under hers and it was a vivid, almost vicious delight when his tongue rubbed against hers. His arms came around her and her head started to spin—

"Oh. Oh, wow. Who in the hell is that?" Tori whispered, interrupting Lynnette. She jabbed Ressa in the side, staring at somebody in the doorway. "Damn. Isn't he pretty?"

Ressa looked over her shoulder and damn near choked. "Sweetheart, you don't want that."

"Yes, oh, yes I do." She hummed a little under her breath as she leaned forward.

"You all are killing me." Lynnette put the book down with a snap. Ressa took advantage of that and snagged it, flipping through and looking for the spot where Lynnette had been reading.

"Hey!"

Grinning, Ressa continued to turn the page even as she glanced up at Tori. "Girl, that man is a prick—with a capital *P*. He loves the sound of his own voice. Shit, he probably loves his voice so much, he jacks off to the sound of it."

Lynnette and Ellie laughed while Tori shot her a dark look. "You could let me have my fantasies, you know."

"Okay. Fantasize away."

"Ah . . . he's coming over here, ladies." Lynnette lifted her cosmo. "I don't know about any of you, but I have absolutely no time for—"

"Ressa. How lovely to run into you again."

She didn't bother smiling as she looked up at Baron. "Baron." Then she looked back at the group. "So, has anybody speculated much about—"

"Ladies, I was wondering, if maybe—"

Teeth grinding together, Ressa turned her head. Jack ass

With a sweet smile, she met his gaze. "Yes, Mr. Capstone? Did you need something?"

He studied her, a smile flirting with his lips.

Just as he was going to respond, though, Lynnette whispered, "It's him." Then her hand shot out. "Please, Ressa. You have to introduce me. Please. I'm dying. I . . ."

Baron turned his head at the same time as Ressa.

Her belly sank.

She thought maybe she'd just like to disappear as Baron lifted an arm. "Max. Trey. Why don't you come over here? Trey has some . . . fans."

He gave Ressa a charming smile. "Why don't you join me for a drink while they chat? I swear, you really do look familiar to me."

The look in his eyes made her skin crawl and she wanted, very badly, to put a lot of distance between them. "I already have a drink, Mr. Capstone," she said, lifting hers and smiling.

He opened his mouth, but before he could say anything, she pushed back from her chair, watching Trey and Max. A funny little twist of heat went through her at the sight of Trey.

Heat . . . and awkwardness.

"Max." She looked at him first, managed to smile. Then she slid her gaze to Trey. His blue eyes were blank. Almost carefully so. "Mr. Barnes. If you two have a moment, I've got some friends who wanted to meet you. And . . . I . . . ah . . ."

Just get it out. Before he disappears and you can't. If she didn't say it, the words would burn inside her, like an open sore—festering and raw.

"I needed to apologize, for earlier. I'm sorry."

Trey's lids flickered.

You should have said yes, a small voice inside her murmured. Regret was a living, breathing thing inside her.

"So!" With a bright smile that she didn't at all feel, Ressa turned around. "May I introduce Lynnette, Tori, and Ellie? We've been friends online for forever and once or twice a year, we try to hook up at one of these events. Guys, this is Max . . ." She moved to stand at his side, pressing a quick kiss to his cheek. "And this is Trey Barnes. Sorry, Max, but it's him they really want to talk to."

Max chuckled. "That's okay. I'm used to being tossed aside for the younger, better looking guys these days."

She breathed out a nearly silent sigh of relief as Trey moved forward to talk to her friends.

". . . join us?"

She blinked, caught off guard a few minutes later.

Max tightened the hand he'd laid on hers. "Ressa, are you feeling well?"

"I'm fine. My mind was just wandering. What were you saying?"

"We're all getting sort of hungry and thought we'd order something." Max cocked a thick brow. "Are you going to join us? We'll need a few more chairs."

"Oh. Well . . ." She shot a look around the table. "Um, no . . . no, I don't think so." She eased her hand away from Max and edged around Trey to grab her bag. She caught Lynnette's eye and held her friend's gaze, hard, for a long moment, before she turned around, her gaze skating past Trey to meet Max's once more. "I'm actually heading to bed. I'm still dragging from that drive in. Raincheck?"

"Breakfast, right?" She glanced at her friends, saw the speculative glance in Lynnette's eyes, saw Ellie opening her mouth—then wincing. Probably because Tori had just kicked her under the table.

"Breakfast!" Tori smiled. "You're buying, remember. You owe us."

Ressa bit back a groan and then nodded at the group in general, before turning on her heel.

She had a bottle of wine in her room. Ellie had brought it when she drove in from Albuquerque—her friend *hated* to fly and drove everywhere.

Ressa was going to crack that baby open and drink the whole—

"That was smooth."

She practically came right out of her skin. Whirling around, she glared at Trey. He stood less than two feet away.

"You . . ." Heaving out a breath, she pressed a hand to her racing heart and then looked past him into the hotel restaurant. Max had settled into her seat and Baron was shouldering his way deeper into the crush.

Nobody looked their way. At all.

"Mr. Barnes—"

"It's Trey," he said, his voice mild.

Narrowing her eyes, she continued to speak. "Unless you needed something, I'd like to go on up to my room. My panel is at eight thirty in the morning. I don't know who thought that was a good idea, but I need some sleep if I'm going to be functional."

"Okay." He shrugged. "I just wanted to tell you thanks for the coffee."

As he cut around her, she reached up and pressed her fingers to her temples. "You are a very frustrating man, you know that?"

She watched as he turned around, still walking, backward. "So I've been told. You didn't need to apologize. You didn't know. We'll just chalk it all up to an . . . awkward experience."

Then he headed off down the hall.

She should have just let it go.

Just let it go at that. Really.

"Oh, it's been an experience. Not really the kind I was shooting for, but yeah. It's been an experience."

This time, when he turned around, he didn't keep walking backward. Instead, he moved toward her, his steps slow, his eyes thoughtful. "Yeah? Exactly what sort of experience were you shooting for?"

Ressa thought about the ring he'd worn, the one he'd taken off and how he'd stumbled and fumbled through trying to explain it.

She thought of the storm of emotion that had been in his voice, in his eyes. It wasn't just grief—there was a storm of emotion that she couldn't even begin to understand.

Then she thought about the faint smile that tugged at his lips, that heat she'd seen in his gaze.

Don't. Just don't—her common sense screamed.

"I've got wine in my room. I was going to drink the whole bottle. Want to save me from myself?"

"I don't drink much these days," he said softly. Then he blew out a breath. The words were laden with things unsaid. Then he shrugged. "But I can maybe keep you company."

Chapter Ten

It took almost twenty minutes to get to her room, thanks to the crush at the elevators. During that twenty minutes, Trey waited for the voice of reason to ruin things.

Waited for that awkwardness that had accompanied the last three dates.

Waited for his gut to start to churn at the thought of sitting down over a drink—it did, every time. He dealt with it, smiled through it and handled the headache after.

Waited for a rush of guilt, for the elevator to get stuck, an earthquake, a meteor strike . . . anything that would signify this was just a bad, awful idea.

But with each minute that passed, he just wanted to be in her room—at this point, *any* room would do, so long as he had some privacy—because he was dying to touch her.

He didn't know exactly what she was offering.

Part of him thought he did, and he was almost certain he was right, but Trey was a realist. He was also more likely to believe in the negative with some things, because it was easier that way. Disappointment sucked.

He was also fully aware that more than likely, even if she *was*

interested in . . . anything, this was the most likely scenario—
if she touched him, his brain was going to screw everything up
and then he'd look like a basket case in front of a woman he
wanted more than he wanted his next breath of air.

His hands were shaking.

To hide it, he shoved them into his back pockets as they
waited for their turn to shuffle onto the elevator. Finally, they
managed to wedge themselves in and then more people
wedged themselves in after that. Trey found himself so close,
he could have turned his head and he'd be able to bury his face
in her hair. Soft, wild twists of curls . . . what would she do—

"Oh! Sorry!" There was a giggle, a squeal . . . and then like
a bunch of dominos, people half fell, half crashed into others
as the woman in the front continued to giggle. "Oopsie! Too
marny—ah, too many marnis—too many martinis!"

A couple of snorts, a couple of snickers and more than a
few curses. Trey barely heard any of them. Ressa had ended up
crushed against his chest and he was pinned to the wall. Her
hip was pressed snug to his crotch and even as he tried to ease
her away, her gaze shifted, lifted . . .

His cock started to pulse, throb.

Her gaze dropped to his mouth.

Her hand fisted in the material of his shirt as she licked the
full, ripe curve of her lower lip. If he didn't at least taste that
mouth—

The elevator dinged and bodies spilled out. As the person
next to them escaped the press, Ressa eased back. Dusky color
rode along her cheekbones as she slid her eyes up to meet his.

Tearing his gaze away, he looked at the lights flickering
above the elevator door.

It hit her floor and as she turned away, she slid her hand
down, caught his.

Sweat beaded at the nape of his neck and he had one brief
moment of lucidity.

Trey Barnes was a man who liked order. He liked to be in
control.

But he had absolutely no idea what in the hell he was doing.

And he was absolutely fine with that.

* * *

Her heart was still racing.

Despite the fact that they'd been packed into that elevator like sardines in a can, for one brief moment, it had just been the two of them. Voices had faded away. The press of too many bodies and a woman's drunken laugh. Everything faded.

The only press she'd felt was his . . . the press of his body to hers, his arm under her breasts as he steadied her, his cock against her hip, pulsing in a way that had her core tightening in response.

The only voice she'd heard had been an internal one that whispered, *I need to touch him. So bad. I need . . .*

Now, as she swiped her key through the card reader, her hands were sweating, almost shaking.

And the damn key card wouldn't work.

"Figures," she whispered, her voice hitching.

A warm hand came around, took the key. "Let me see," he murmured, his voice way too close to her ear.

Eyes closed, she stood there, struck dumb from the want ravaging inside her. The door clicked and she opened her eyes as he came around her to turn the handle, push it open. Then he turned his head, stared at her.

Waiting. On her, she knew.

Do or die, she thought, a little desperately.

Kind of extreme, maybe. But it felt apt. Because in that moment, she knew if she didn't take him inside . . . and then just take him—let them take each other—some little piece inside of her would feel like it had died.

She slid past him, brushing up against his body as she did so. She felt his ragged intake of air and that hot, hungry need inside trembled, swelled.

She didn't turn on the light.

As the door clicked shut behind her, she kicked off the spike heels and then turned to look at him.

Abruptly, a line from the book Lynnette had been reading danced through her mind.

With need and want a vicious tangle . . .

Yes, this was a tangle, one that was entirely too twisted, considering how short a time she'd known him. Hours, really. Just a handful of hours when you added it all up.

None of that mattered.

She moved toward him.

He met her halfway and as his arms came around her, everything inside her breathed out a sigh of delight . . . even as the need inside her demanded for *more*.

The curls he tangled around his hand were every bit as wild, as soft, as crazy as he'd thought they'd be.

And her mouth was pure, silken sin.

Spinning her around, he pressed her to the wall and caught her hips in his hands, boosted her up. Her dress caught, stopped him from spreading her open and he snarled, shoved it up—only to stop, sanity trying to intrude.

You should pull back. Pull back now before this just goes to hell—

Pull back?

Ressa hooked one leg around his and rolled her hips.

Rolled her hips against him and his cock throbbed, pulsated behind the barrier of his jeans. Desperate, he shoved the skirt of her dress the rest of the way up and cupped the lush curve of her hips, fingers digging into the silken flesh. With a groan, she wrapped her legs around his hips and started to rock, rubbing herself up and down.

His eyes all but rolled into the back of his head.

She was already wet—he could feel her, through something silky and thin.

Tearing his mouth from hers, he braced one hand on the wall, eased back.

Ressa continued to roll her hips against his and he could hear the shuddery, shaking breaths as they escaped, felt his own echo within his chest as he looked down. He was still completely dressed. So was she—but her dress had been pushed up to her waist and a pair of panties painted a murder-red swath across her hips.

And still she moved against him, like that contact was vital.

To him, it was.

But . . .

But . . . that voice of reason demanded to be heard now. *You can't do this. You know better. You have to be in control, more in control. You have to be careful.*

"Ressa." Her name was a ragged, broken whisper.

She reached up. "I've got something in my bag," she said softly. "I'm healthy. Haven't been with anybody in two years. You'll use a rubber, though."

Easy, practical . . .

The voice of reason went silent, soothed.

She stroked her hand down his chest and his body leaped, all but ready to lunge and pounce and take. He kept waiting for something else—for his body to freeze up on him like it had the last time he'd tried to so much as kiss a woman.

"Trey . . ." She leaned in, pressed her mouth to his neck.

Fuck this. Trey pushed away from the wall and turned, half stumbling toward the bed.

If it all fell apart, well, he might as well enjoy it as much as he could before then.

He bumped into something on the way to her bed, swore. Did it again and then swore again, tearing his mouth away from hers only to have her catch his head and try to draw him back. Three boxes, a suitcase and a desk the size of a postage stamp turned the room into an obstacle course. Shifting his grip on her, he edged around the desk, a box—her teeth caught his ear. "You're taking too long."

He grunted as he reached the bed, slowly lowering her to her feet. "Sorry." Holding her eyes, he reached down, catching the material bunched around her waist, dragging it up. "Can we do away with this?"

"Let's." She turned, presenting her back and sweeping her hair out of the way.

Catching the tab of the zipper, he dragged it down, watched as the material spread open. Lust slammed into him as flesh was revealed. The band of her bra, the same bright murder red she'd slicked across her lips, interrupted the smooth skin of her back. But that wasn't the only color.

Flames.

Twining around elegant, scrolled print. It started at her nape and ran down the line of her spine.

Desperate to see more of her, he shoved the material down

over her arms. It caught at her waist, bunched there and he
shoved it lower until it hung over her hips. She went to wiggle
out of it but he caught her waist, eyes locked on the tattoo. And
despite how his cock was throbbing, despite the need that had
his hands all but shaking, he found himself smiling, almost
charmed.

"'You are who you choose to be,'" he murmured, running
his finger down the script, the flames that danced all around it.

"Now if you don't recognize that quote, I think we're gonna
have to call this whole thing off, baby."

He went to his knees, intrigued by the bit of color he could
just barely make out under the material that tangled at her
hips. "Please." He leaned in and pressed his lips to her spine.
"Give me some credit."

Her breath caught as he smoothed the dress down, leaving
her clad in scraps of lace and silk. It was a picture that would
leave him with fantasy material for a good, long time, he
mused. Then he smiled even wider, leaning in to press a kiss
to the little figure tattoo at the very base of her spine. Whoever
had done it had been good—the robot was no more than a few
inches, but it had some of the finest detail he'd ever seen, and
while he wasn't as big into ink as some, he figured he knew
talent when he saw it.

"The Iron Giant." He rose, sliding his hands around, pulling her back against him. "Favorite movie?"

She laughed easily. "Oh, I like it well enough. But that line
stuck with me. Decided maybe I'd keep it with me as a
reminder."

"Hmmm . . ." He slid one hand up, up, up until he could
trace his finger over the triquetra inked onto her chest, dipping
low between her breasts. He wanted to turn her around, press
his mouth just there—where the softly rounded point disappeared between those lush curves. His cock pulsed and she
reached back, cupping his hips in her hands, tugging him
closer.

No. He better not do just anything yet—

Control. Find some control first.

Voice raw, he reached around and trailed his fingers over
the tattoo where it ran between the valley of her breasts. "This
one?"

"My first one." Something of humor touched her voice and he slid her a look. She angled her head back, met his eyes. "I was feeling all wise and philosophical. Read that it had something to do with beginnings and endings and how they were all connected. Part of me wanted to get something that signified a slamming door—as in *kiss my ass*—but then I got to thinking about how I needed to remember how something ended, so I wouldn't go back there. It's all connected."

That humor faded, and fast. Because he didn't want whatever had moved through her mind to come between them, he leaned in and nuzzled her neck. "I've got to tell you—whatever it means, why ever you did it . . . , it's sexy as hell."

His voice stroked all over her skin, almost like he'd run his hands along her body instead of that light brush across the tattoo. She *wanted* him running his hands along her body.

And she wanted him naked.

Wiggling around until she faced him, she reached up and toyed with the top button of his shirt. "What about you?" She lifted a brow. Her mind went hot and hazy as she remembered the day she'd seen him running—and she knew it had been him, but she wasn't about to point out how she'd all but drooled over the quick look she'd gotten as he pounded the pavement outside her library. "You got any ink?"

"I guess you'll have to find out." He dipped his head and pressed a kiss to her upper chest, right at her collarbone.

"Going to make me work, huh?" Ressa gasped as he flicked the skin with his tongue, felt her pulse kick up when he nibbled his way up her neck. "I'm good with that."

He straightened, staring down at her, his gaze hot, raw, and so intense, it threatened to steal her breath. She leaned in and pressed her mouth to his, taking her time as she moved down and took care of the second, then the third button. Unable to resist any longer, she smoothed one hand past the cotton of his skirt and laid it flat against his chest. Skin, warm and firm, met her hand, and when she scraped her nails over his flesh, a rough noise escaped him.

She caught his lower lip between her teeth and tugged.

His hand twisted in her hair when she would have pulled

back. "Come back here," he said, and his voice was rougher now, lower.

Her nipples drew into tight, hard points just at the sound. When he stroked his tongue across her lower lip, then dipped inside her mouth, she felt her toes curling.

Enough with taking her time. She finished the rest of the buttons in a rush, but instead of shoving the shirt off his shoulders, she curled her arms around him and pressed herself tight against him.

He responded to that by falling backward on the bed, taking her with him. Delight whispered through her and she automatically shifted, placing one knee on either side of his hips and undulating against him. The length of him, the heat, the way she could feel him pulsing inside his jeans—something liquid and fiery spread through her veins, coalescing between her thighs.

Dying to have him inside her, she sat up and shoved at his shirt. Strong, hard lines, toned muscle. He was lean, skin stretching over firm muscles, his belly flat with a ribbon of hair running down to disappear behind his jeans, but his chest appeared to be bare of any tattoos. "Hmmm. No ink here," she murmured.

"Maybe you're just not looking." He came up onto his elbows, a grin crooking his lips, and then he cocked his head as her fingers danced along the line of his abdomen.

Arching a brow, she shifted her attention down. Black ink, something rounded, peeked above the waistband of his jeans, situated just above his hipbone. "Well, now. I need to take a look."

"By all means." His voice was steady, but as she unbuttoned his jeans, she heard his breath skip.

She was watching him, his face, the way his blue green eyes went dark, then started to blaze hotter as she dragged the zipper down and tugged at the waistband.

The hunger was eating her alive and she didn't give a damn about the ink, didn't care, she just wanted to get him out of those damn jeans—absently she flicked a glance over at his hip.

Ressa stopped. Cocked her head as she studied it.

"Is that like . . . a warning or are you bragging?" She

slid him a sly look as she stroked her finger over the number inked onto him and to her delight, a faint blush crept over his face.

He snorted and then, as a laugh spilled out of her, he reversed their positions. "You can't mean to tell me you aren't familiar with *that* number," he said, pressing his mouth to her neck and then moving lower.

"Well. Maybe. Although I was kinda hoping you were . . . advertising." She groaned as his tongue slid along the scalloped lace edge of her bra. His fingers danced along her side, moving lower and lower until she was arching up against him. *More . . .* "Are you telling me that you tattooed 9¾ on yourself because you're a Harry Potter fan?"

"Well, you tattooed a robot on your ass." He flicked at the catch between her breasts and she caught her breath as he sat up, straddling her thighs. "I figure you don't have much to say about my Harry Potter tattoo."

"I . . ." She had a comeback for that. Really. But in the next moment, her brain went blank and her lashes drifted down. Long-fingered, skilled hands cupped her breasts and she instinctively arched into his touch. Her hands came up to cover his, a whimper falling from her lips. "Trey . . ."

The bed shifted under her and she opened her eyes just in time to see him bending down. She didn't quite manage to muffle her cry as he caught one nipple in his mouth.

Her hands cupped his face and she held him like the thought of him stopping would just absolutely end her. Trey could have told her there was nothing to worry about there— the need inside him was a vicious scream. *Take take take . . .*

No. He wasn't going to rush this. He focused on the scent of her skin, the way her hands tangled in his short hair, the way she arched close, like she couldn't stand any sort of distance between them.

Stretching his body out against hers, he slid one hand down and cupped her, pressing the heel of his palm against her. She was wet—he could feel it through the silk of her panties. His cock gave a hard, demanding jerk.

"Please . . . just . . . will . . . *Trey!*" Broken words, none of them connecting or making sense, fell from her lips, but the hunger behind them, *that* he understood.

Trey pushed himself to his knees, ripping his shirt off and throwing it away. Then he caught the bra that was still tangled around her shoulders, tugging it away before he hooked his hands in the panties that rode low over the sweet swell of her hips. "Condoms. Where?"

She blinked, her gaze unfocused, hot. Then she pushed to her elbows, her tongue sweeping out to wet her lips as she looked around. "My bag. I don't . . ."

He shoved off the bed and spotted the deep purple leather lying a few feet from the door. He snagged it and was back on the bed in seconds. She caught it in her hands and upended it with an urgency that might have made him smile if he hadn't been tempted to start pawing through everything that came tumbling out.

She caught a strip of foil in her hand and he tore it from her. Then, with a quick sweep of his arm, he swept as much of the stuff from the bed as he could. "I'll apologize for that . . . later," he promised.

"Like I care. Just hurry." Her eyes roamed over his body and he could feel it almost as if she'd been touching him with her hands.

Then she was and that made *his* hands shake. He fumbled with the strip of condoms, managed to tear one off and then tossed the rest near the head of the bed. She scraped her thumbnails over his nipples and he swore, feeling that touch echo all the way down to his balls. As her hands moved higher, he shoved the condom packet in his mouth and shoved his jeans and boxers down, hands unsteady.

"What's this . . ." A low, husky murmur escaped her as she slid one palm over the black head of the raven that curved along the top of his shoulder.

He ripped open the rubber, tossed the foil down. "We can talk tattoos later, darlin'." He didn't think he'd fumbled with a condom that much since his first time, but he finally managed, and then he tumbled her back down onto her back, cupping her face in his hands.

Hurry, hurry, hurry . . .

His hands shook and that feeling of losing control, of panic, seemed to edge closer. As he slanted his mouth over hers, he settled between her thighs. She brought her knees up, rocked against him. "This is crazy," she said, her mouth moving against his.

"I'm fine with crazy." Then he reached down, caught her knee.

She slid one hand between them, wrapped her hand around his cock. The feel of her hand on him shoved some of the panic back—he wrapped his hand around hers, squeezed until she tightened her grip and then he thrust into her hand, practically mindless.

"If you make me wait much longer, I'm going to hurt you," she said, her voice cutting through the fog.

The laugh that ripped out of him was half-need, half-desperation.

Tucking the head of his cock to the heart of her, he held his breath. Then, a shudder rolled through him. He could feel her, and it was the sweetest thing. He could feel her heat, and how wet she was, how hot—slowly, as his nerves bled away, he sank inside.

She closed around him, a snug, hot fist. When he pulled back, then surged back in, she gripped him tighter and tighter, milking him in a taunting, tormenting way.

"Aw, hell . . ." He caught a fistful of the duvet in his hand, clenched it while his balls drew tighter and tighter against his body.

She surged against him and he felt the tight buds of her nipples dragging across his chest. Half-blind, he shifted until he could catch one of her breasts in his free hand, then he pushed it up. She filled his hand to overflowing, her nipple plump, and when he caught it in his mouth and bit down, she shrieked and bucked against him, pressing him tighter and tighter.

Control splintered, shattered.

Ressa couldn't breathe.

He shifted back up and caught her mouth with his, demanding and hungry, damn near ruthless and she couldn't get enough and she couldn't breathe—

Tearing her mouth away, she turned her face to the side, panting.

"I can't . . ." He tugged her face back to his, his teeth scraping along her lip. "I can't breathe . . ."

"Do you have to? Kiss me, Ressa." His voice was a rumble against her lips and she opened for him with a sigh.

Who needed oxygen?

Even the small bit she'd managed to pull inside her evaporated as he stroked inside her, so deep, so hard—he filled her to the hilt, and then even after he'd buried himself within her, he flexed his hips, like it wasn't enough. It had him rubbing against her clit. Desperate for more, she worked herself closer and shuddered around him as hot little shivers started to race through her.

Blood pulsed, hot and thick, through her veins, and every beat of her heart drew her tighter, pulled her even deeper into the need. He pulled out, slow, lingering—it was as though he couldn't stand the thought of not being inside her, and then, as he surged forward, she felt the pulse of his cock. It had her heart stuttering and her skin started to feel too small to hold everything she had inside her. Again, as he buried himself completely inside, he flexed his hips, held there—that light friction against her clit was too much.

When he started to pull out, she caught his hips, her nails digging into his ass as she worked herself against him. "Don't . . . just . . . ahhh . . ." Blind to everything but the orgasm rising inside her, she held him within her and then, as it started to explode through her, he snarled.

When he started to move this time, she couldn't stop him.

There was nothing slow and lingering about his movements now. Hard, brutal, fast—and even as she started to drift down from the vicious pleasure of her first orgasm, another slammed into her.

Without even having the breath to scream, she clung to him as he stiffened over her.

Trey . . .

His name echoed through her. Even when she didn't have the breath to speak it, even when she didn't have the ability to think past the pleasure, that simple thought remained.

Trey . . .

* * *

Ranged out over her trembling, damp body, Trey barely had the energy to keep some of his weight braced on his elbows. It was enough that he wasn't crushing her into the mattress, but that was all he had in that moment.

He couldn't move.

His mind was just . . . not there.

He could almost imagine it had completely shut off. Ressa curled her arms around him and stroked a hand up his back.

He shivered a little as her fingers traced the raven.

"I saw you."

He tensed at the words.

"What?"

"Running." She slid a hand up his spine. "I've got a confession to make, Trey. I've been half in lust with you from the first time you walked into the library and I'd just watch for you . . ." She pressed the flat of her hand to his spine.

He focused on the touch, his skin prickling under her hands. His mind tried to spin away on him and he lashed it down, focused. The guilt—the guilt he'd half expected earlier—tried to rise up and bite him on the ass and he set his jaw.

"Trey?"

Her voice was sleepy, but even he could hear the concern in it.

He reached behind him and caught her hand, twining their fingers. Pressing the back of her palm to his thigh, he forced his mind to work, focused on her words and not on the mess inside him.

"You saw me out running," he murmured. He found himself smiling, to his utter shock, over the insanity of it. "I was there because I wanted to see you."

He felt her reaction in the way her hand tightened on his. Slowly, he levered his weight away from her and sat up. With his back to her, he smiled over his shoulder at her.

Ressa followed suit, settling behind him with her naked breasts to his back. "Is that a fact?"

He dragged in a breath and caught a headful of her scent—it was on him now, all over him and just that simple thought was enough to have his cock twitching.

"Yeah." She eased back and ran a hand down the tattoo. "I was almost positive it was you. I saw this tattoo and that just drove me a little more crazy than I already was."

She pressed her mouth to his shoulder.

He closed his eyes, felt her tugging her hand free of his. But when she went to scrape her nails over his lower belly, he stood up. "I'll be back in a minute," he said gruffly.

A minute later, locked alone in the bathroom, he discarded the condom in the trash and washed his hands. Then, hands braced on the counter, he stared at his reflection in the mirror.

His face was pale, eyes darker than normal.

Son of a bitch.

Closing his eyes, he blew out a breath and braced himself, waiting for the rush of guilt to return. But it didn't.

Instead, there was . . . relief. And that crazy, desperate need he'd felt almost from the first moment he'd laid eyes on Ms. Ressa Bliss.

Chapter Eleven

"It's a raven."

Trey lay sprawled facedown on her bed.

There was a box with a few bits of crusts and one half-eaten slice of pizza. They'd destroyed the better part of a bottle of wine. Okay, *she* had destroyed the better part of a bottle wine. He'd taken half of a glass, and she couldn't say for sure if he'd even taken a sip of it.

And out of the five rubbers she'd had with her, there was only one left.

It was one in the morning and both of them were exhausted but she couldn't sleep. The burning edge of hunger had eased, yet she couldn't sleep.

Didn't want to sleep.

Bent over his back, she took her time studying the amazing beauty of the raven on his back. The eye was red, glinting with a wicked light that spoke of omens and warnings. Save for the eye and the beak, just about everything else was black and the raven took up just about all of Trey's back, its head tucked against his shoulder, curved, as though he was looking up at the man, wings outspread.

"Ding, ding, ding," he said.

She slapped his butt. Then, because his butt was yet another work of art, she squeezed. "Why a raven? Another literary thing?"

"Quoth the raven." He popped one eye open and smiled. "One of my brothers does tattoos."

"Hmmm. I know. Zach." She leaned forward and grinned down at him, but he seemed too busy looking at her breasts. When he finally looked up and met her eyes, he looked abashed, but she just winked at him. "I know who he is. I have that TV series on Blu-ray. Love it."

Trey groaned and buried his face in the pillow. "If you tell me you're one of his zealots, I'm leaving."

"No." She laughed, all too familiar with what he was talking about. Over the past few years, Zach had developed a huge following on Facebook. They called themselves Zach's Zealots and they followed him with a zeal that would have driven Trey nuts. Zach ignored them—completely. He had cut himself out of Hollywood like that part of his life had never existed.

"Did he really tell a TV show producer that he kept the bodies of ex-girlfriends in a freezer?"

"Probably," Trey said, his voice still muffled. "I don't ask because it just feeds into his crazy. He doesn't need that, trust me."

Ressa chuckled, amused by the idea. "So . . . did he do this?"

"Yeah." He turned his head back toward her, popping one eye open. "Zach nagged all of us, kept telling us he needed the experience and shit, but honestly, I think he just liked making us bleed then charging us money for it. I figured if I was going to do it, I'd make sure it would be something that was important. Poe and Potter—those are the kind of stories that turned me into a storyteller."

She studied his face. "When did you know you wanted to be a writer?"

"Always." His lids drooped lower again, a soft sigh escaping. "I'd been jotting stories down in notebooks for pretty much forever. Didn't do much with it until . . . college."

The pause was long enough that she knew there was something else he'd been planning to say, but he'd stopped himself. Stretching herself out at his side, still absently tracing the raven with her fingers, she watched him. "It had something to do with your wife, didn't it?"

His back rose and fell and then he levered up on his elbows, a faint smile twisting his lips. "Yeah. Something." Then he shrugged. "Pretty much everything."

He rolled around and sat up, presenting her with his back. It was a nice view and maybe under other circumstances, she would have enjoyed the view of the tattoo, but she wanted to kick herself. She pushed herself to her knees and crawled to him, settling down with her front pressed to his back. Sliding her arms around him, she pressed her lips to his shoulder "I'm sorry. I didn't mean to make you sad. I should have left it alone."

"It's okay." He covered her hands with his. "You didn't make me sad. I just . . . I don't want to think about this tonight." His body tensed. "I should probably go."

Common sense told her it was a good idea. But she shoved common sense into a tiny closet in the back of her mind.

He turned his head to look at her.

It was so easy to just lean in, kiss him. It was a soft kiss, soft . . . gentle. Tender enough to make her heart ache. She brought one hand up and murmured against his mouth, "Stay."

Dawn came in like a golden ribbon through the curtains when he woke. It didn't matter that he'd been up way too late. By his internal clock, Trey had overslept and even though he knew Clayton wasn't going to come in looking for breakfast, his body was already awake.

A warm, female body was pressed against his and he closed his eyes, let himself enjoy it for another moment before he let himself start to think.

He could do one of two things. She was still sleeping, so he could leave.

Or . . .

There wasn't much thought required to make his decision.

One night and she was already an addiction.

As she continued to sleep, he slid under the covers, his

mouth tracing over the curves he'd committed to memory last night. There was strength here. Strength and beauty and softness, so much it made him ache for more, and more.

He caught one nipple—already tight—in his mouth. She curled an arm around his neck, mumbling, not entirely awake but getting there. But when she would have tugged him closer, he moved lower, his lips skimming along the slight curve of her belly, her hipbone, the crease of her thigh.

"This is one hell of a wake-up call."

Catching the covers in one hand, he slid his gaze up over her body, staring at her in the dim light. Her eyes were still closed. He smoothed his palm along the outer curve of her thigh, watched as her chest hitched—and the way it caused her breasts to move. Warm, smooth brown skin, her nipples just a few shades darker. His mouth watered as he rubbed his lips against her pubis.

Her hands tangled in his hair.

"You keep teasing me like that, boy, and we're gonna . . ."

He laughed softly, although the feel of her, the scent of her already had his cock throbbing. "It's not teasing so much as . . . wanting."

She arched against him. "Please."

He opened his eyes, saw her staring at him.

There was naked need in her eyes. Naked need, naked trust.

With a groan, he lowered his mouth to the mound of her sex. He opened her with one long, slow lick and the taste of her had him growling, jerking her closer, one hand going under her to lift her tight against him.

"Trey—"

It was a harsh, choked cry, her hands clutching at him. He barely even heard her over the rush and roar of blood in his ears. Not enough. Nowhere near—

He drove his tongue into her, blind to everything but the taste of her and the feel of her straining against him.

And then even that wasn't enough.

Lowering her to the bed, he moved up and hooked her knees over his elbows. Mindless, he thrust deep, spearing her on his cock. She erupted around him, her pussy milking him like a fist as she started to come.

He caught her cry in his mouth, the hot, wet grip of her driving him mad.

"Son of a—"

He stiffened and shoved up onto his hands, unintentionally driving himself even deeper.

She whimpered, rolling her hips against him and that sent chills shuddering down his spine. "Ress . . ." he choked out, squeezing his eyes closed as the feel of naked, female flesh, wrapped around his cock, threatened to push him over the edge. "Stop . . . just . . ."

Her hands clutched at his torso. "What?"

"I . . ." He bit the inside of his cheek, hoping that slight pain would bring him some measure of control, but the ground under him was crumbling too fast. "I forgot the fucking rubber."

It took seconds for the words to penetrate and then, as her body went tense, he started to pull back.

She wrapped her legs around him.

The sensation of her, slick and wet, hot and wild, sent his brain on meltdown.

"I'm on the pill," she said against his lips. "Do we need . . ."

Shuddering, he rolled his hips against hers, felt himself falling.

Flying.

Bracing one arm around her hips, he locked her tight against him, heard her startled cry as he drove himself home—hard and deep.

Her nails sank into his shoulders and she rocked up to meet him, another female cry falling from her lips when he surged back into her.

Slick, soft, so hot—

"Trey . . ."

Blindly, he sought her mouth, caught the next moan and swallowed it down.

The control he'd been scrabbling for wasn't even a memory now.

Ressa barely even had time to catch her breath.

It was like she'd thrown herself into a storm—willingly—and was now lost to it.

Trey's body moved, hard and fast, driving her across the bed until she had to slam her hand against the headboard to brace herself. One arm hooked under her knee, opening her and she whimpered as it took him deeper, as each deep stroke had the head of his cock rubbing against her G-spot in a way that was almost too much. She sucked in a breath, a moan rising in her throat, but he caught her lips in a deep, drugging kiss.

Her head started to swim and she couldn't breathe.

Shoving her free hand between them, she tore her mouth away and gasped for air.

"Trey, I—"

He twisted his hips and the orgasm slammed into her, hitting her with nuclear force. She felt herself flying into a thousand pieces, sensation wracking her, and still he thrust, rising up onto his knees, gripping her hips now as he shafted her, slower now, but just as deep.

He stiffened, just as she was starting to come down, and she whimpered when his cock jerked and he started to come. The sensation of it, his length pulsing and throbbing inside her, set her to shuddering all over again and it was so intense, her vision started to gray out on her.

Dangerous, she thought dazed as he slumped down, his head resting between her breasts.

This man really was dangerous.

Chapter Twelve

Getting by on less than two hours of sleep wasn't as much fun as it was cracked up to be.

Trey had thought he'd be ready to get the hell out of dodge, but as the panel droned on and on, all he could think about was trying to track down Ressa and . . .

And *what*?

That was the kicker.

And what*?*

His body still burned with the memory of the past night, his shoulders and back tender from her nails. He was both more sated than he could remember feeling in years and at the same time, he was already burning, already hungry for more.

And still, the endless panel dragged on endlessly.

Baron T. Capstone droned on, loving the sound of his own voice, the sound of it like an ice pick in Trey's ear. The pompous prick talked over everybody, including the moderator and interrupted people non-stop. Finally, Trey just started ignoring him and finished up with his comments, raising his voice to be heard when necessary, doing what he could to answer the questions directed at him.

Once, when he'd finished, Baron had given him a quelling look and asked sourly, "Are you done yet?"

"For a minute."

The room had laughed for the first time since the panel had started and Trey stopped waiting for the moderator to handle Baron and did it himself. After that, the questions flowed a little easier and the other authors managed to get a few words in, too. And with every passing minute, Baron seemed to grit his teeth more and more.

When it ended, a publicist from his publisher cornered him.

"I need an hour of your time," she said.

Trey thought longingly of his plan to pin down Ressa. But Sylvia gave him a beaming, hopeful smile and instead of turning tail and running, he pushed his hands into his pockets. "Why? You going to yell at me over the panel?"

"Hell, no. I'm tempted to buy you a drink." Sylvia rolled her eyes. "Of course, I didn't say that."

She grinned at him and, after a minute, he smiled back. "Okay, then. What do you need?"

"Come on. You'll see." She hooked an arm through his and led him away.

As they were walking through the halls, a familiar laugh caught his ears and he looked up.

There she was. Ressa, on her way into a panel—

"Ah, can this wait a couple of minutes?"

Sylvia smiled. "Of course."

He barely managed to catch Ressa before the door closed and the soft rush of dusky pink staining the warm gold of her cheeks had him wanting to find out how low the blush went. Then he just wanted her naked.

"Ah, hey. I was . . ." He blew out a breath, the nerves that hadn't been present for most of the night now rushing up to steal his voice.

"I need to get in there," she said, her voice soft.

"Yeah, I know. Look, I was just wondering . . . we, ah . . . well. We never got around to getting coffee," he said.

Ressa laughed. "I think we kind of did an end run around coffee."

"So." He shoved his hands into his pockets. "Can I call you sometime?"

"Call . . ."

Oh, no.

Ressa swallowed back the emotions that immediately leaped to choke her. Excitement and fear—equal amounts of both. *Call me?* Trey wanted to call her?

"Ressa!"

Hearing her name, she glanced behind her, even as the fear started to edge out the excitement.

She swung a look back to Trey again. "Ah . . ."

In the end, though, it was the fear that won out. Fear, maybe because she couldn't quite forget the way somebody had watched her all weekend. *You look familiar . . .*

No, Baron didn't know her, but what if he had?

Trey wasn't a mid-list writer—or even a mega writer who lived in some shack in the middle of nowhere, eschewing the media.

While he didn't exactly chase the media spotlight, he had people in his family who were media darlings. The cameras, the press . . .

Her stomach lurched on her and, abruptly, she backed up. "I don't know if that's such a good idea," she said, pasting a casual smile on her face. "We . . ."

She shrugged. "Look, we had a nice night, but that's probably all it's ever going to be."

His brows dropped low over his eyes and as something passed through that surreal blue—*hurt?*—she turned away. "Take care of yourself, Trey."

It was the right thing to do, she told herself. Not just for *them*, but for the people close to them.

But still . . . she felt like she'd just punched herself, right in the chest.

We had a nice night.

Trey couldn't shut the voice up.

It had taken nearly thirty minutes for him and Sylvia to make their way to the room where she had hoarded boxes of books. And he had replayed in his head endlessly those two minutes—hell, it might have been less than sixty seconds— with Ressa.

"This is going to take more than an hour," he muttered. One bed held boxes of the hardback he had coming out in a month. The cover bore his name in red, standing out on the black background, the almost ghostly image of a woman looking away, eye-catching in its simplicity.

The other bed was loaded down with boxes of another book. He moved closer, pulled one out. Like the other book, this one featured a woman on the cover. But she was nude—or that was the appearance. The lower curve of her breast, the indentation of her waist, the flair of her hip. She wore a tie, although all the viewer could see of it was the way she held it out from her body, to the side. The tie, oddly enough, had a cartoon character motif.

He ran his finger along the hot pink foil lettering of the title. *Exposing the Geek Billionaire.*

Aliesha had dared him to write it. For a couple of years, she'd nagged at him—all because he'd complained that he was getting tired of writing stuff that sometimes depressed even him. But he was *good* at it—it sold well, so he did it.

Then try something else, she'd told him.

L. Forrester had come to life all because of that dare, but this book, in particular, was because of her.

Write me a funny story, baby. Something funny and sexy.

He'd laughed and tried to tease her into bed. *Let me just do something sexy instead.* She'd smacked him with a copy of the book she'd been reading. The third one he'd published. She'd read it through while he wrote it and while she'd sniffled and brushed at tears as she read it, he'd had more than a few rough spots as he wrote it.

I'm serious. You've got a wonderful way with telling a love story, but you always kill one of them. You should write something fun . . . a billionaire, but not some suave guy . . . make him geeky or something. Then give him some classy, controlled girl, and he's all fumbling around her . . .

He'd fumbled her out of her clothes and into bed, instead.

For two years after Aliesha's death, he couldn't write a damn thing—the stories he'd written before no longer worked.

Then one day, he'd lain in bed, that memory circling through his head, over and over again, like it had been on a loop.

He'd sat down at his computer and started to write, almost in a daze. Travis had been there and it was a good thing, because for the next two weeks, he'd barely existed outside that book. It had been *this* book, although he'd had to rewrite it five times before it felt right.

Two other books had come from L. Forrester before he felt confident enough to try this one, even though it had, technically, been the first.

"You realize everybody thinks you're a woman, right?"

Trey smiled as he pulled one of the trade paperbacks out. Shrugging, he said, "Yeah. I don't care."

He started to sign, ignored the cramping that started up in his hand after the first ten minutes.

Near the end, Sylvia gave him another one and said, "If you can, personalize this one—Max asked you to."

Trey looked up at her. "Since when does Max read romance?"

"Since never." She rolled her eyes. "Although I'm still trying. No, he saw them when he was in here signing his and asked if I'd get a copy for a friend of his. She's a huge fan."

"Sure." Trey tightened his hand on the pen. "What's the name?"

A few seconds later, as he scrawled Ressa's name inside the cover, he tried yet again to silence the sound of her voice.

We had a nice night . . .

"Heading out soon?"

Distracted, Ressa gave Max a quick glance as she checked to make sure she had everything. Clothes were packed, makeup . . . everything. Why did it feel like she was missing something?

Her heart tugged a little, but she ignored it.

"Yeah. I'm dropping Tori at the airport and then hitting the road. What about you?"

"I don't fly out until the morning. Taking the night to

relax." He glanced around and then caught her elbow. "I need a minute."

He caught Tori's eye. "Would you mind? It won't take but a second."

Ressa really didn't feel like chatting just then. Chatting, talking . . . being around people, even a friend. What she *wanted* to do was go track down Trey, tell him she was sorry.

And maybe, if that worked, ask him if coffee was still an option.

But she knew that was stupid.

Monumentally stupid.

"What do you need, Max? I'm kind of scattered right now so I hope it doesn't take brain power."

"No." He laughed and turned over a messenger bag, stuffed with books. "Here, just a special thank you. Ah . . . you might want to keep it closed for now."

Then he winked.

Curious now, she peeked inside and then almost dropped it as she saw the books inside. "Where did you . . ."

"Trade secret."

Flipping through them, she felt a maniacal grin curling her lips and then, it froze. A cover caught her eye—sucking in a breath, she pulled it out and Max sighed. "Now I told you to wait, young lady."

She ignored him, practically cradling the book for a few precious seconds before she went to flip through it. Then she stopped.

Her name was scrawled inside.

Ressa,

I heard you were a reader. I hope you enjoy.

L. Forrester

Her name jumped out at her, even as she took in the broad scrawl of the handwriting, the quick, almost careless loops and strokes.

"She's *here*?" she demanded. Wow. If she could talk to her—

Max laughed and reached out to take the book, slipping it back into the bag. "Oh, don't go getting any ideas. You're not going to track the author down—you could hunt night and day and it won't happen. I asked the publisher to get me a copy. I heard you were a fan."

She processed that, and then, after tucking the book back into the messenger back, she stared at Max.

"You know her."

Her accusing tone only elicited a grin from Max. "When you've been around as long as I have, you tend to know a great many people, Ressa." He leaned in then, kissed her cheek. "You better go. Your friend is looking this way."

She glanced back, saw Tori tap her watch.

Swearing, she hitched her bag up. "We're not done talking about this, Max. I wanna know how you know her."

"Same way I know you, Ressa. We bumped into each other somewhere along the way." He nodded at her. "A pleasure, as always."

A pleasure. She scowled and then rushed back over to Tori.

Tori was glaring at her. "We need to go."

"I know!"

As they hit the doors, Tori asked, "What did Max want?"

Ressa thought about the book, practically burning a hole through her bag as it rested against her hip. "Just had something he wanted to give me," she said vaguely. Then, because she didn't want Tori to ask, she outright lied. "He was also checking up about a con he's doing in New York, asked if maybe I'd be up there again."

"That suspense thing? You doing that again?"

"Hell if I know." Another lie.

"Maybe you oughta look and see if Mr. Hottie will be there."

They had to jump back out of the way as somebody came speeding in front of them. Tori shouted after the driver, flipping him off for good measure. The interruption gave Ressa time to compose herself and by the time they crossed the street to the parking garage, the heat had faded from her face and she had a curious expression as she eyed Tori. "Mr. Hottie?"

"Yeah. You play all nice and innocent," Tori said, laughing as she shifted on her seat. "But I saw how you were looking at him. *And* I saw how he was looking at you. I'm not blind. So, tell me . . . what, did you two jump each other's bones?"

Ressa felt the blood rush up to stain her face and busied herself with digging her keys free. The rollaway bag she had, had felt so light earlier, and now it seemed to weight a ton.

Tori grabbed her arm, pulling her to a stop when Ressa stayed silent. "You *did*," Tori said, her eyes rounding. "Oh, man, you *did* . . . please tell me that he's as beautiful in bed as he is outside of it."

Once more, heat flooded her face, while an ache settled in her chest.

"I don't know what you're talking about," she said, managing a somewhat lofty tone.

Tori wasn't fooled. "Son of a bitch. You *totally* jumped him in the elevator."

"I most certainly did not," she snapped, turning her head to glare at her friend. "I in no way jumped him in the elevator."

"Okay." Tori waited a beat. "Did you wait until you got to your room or did he take you to his?"

To that, Ressa really had no response. Oh, she could have lied, but there was no way she'd be able to pull it off, not when the need for him was rippling through her, a need that was growing stronger and stronger—damn it, she was supposed to have gotten him out of her system.

Instead, that need was worse.

"I don't believe this. The man spends most of his career tucked up in his cave and the *one* time he ventures out, you end up doing him." Tori shook her head. "I don't know if I'm jealous or just in awe."

"Oh, shut up." Ressa unlocked her trunk and shoved her bag inside. One hand braced on the trunk's lid, she looked at Tori. "Do you want to make it to the airport or not?"

"So did you get his number?"

Can I call you?

Now that ache in her chest spread. Eyes closed, she braced her forehead on her bicep. "Tori, can we just let this go, please?"

"Hey . . ."

When Tori brushed a hand down her arm, the knot in her throat grew larger and, to her horror, she thought she just might cry. She managed to fight it back, shoving all that misery down the way she always did.

"What's wrong? Did he just up and leave right after? Shit, he's not lousy in bed, is he?"

Ressa snorted. "If he was, trust me, I wouldn't be sitting here miserable. It was . . ." Now she found herself smiling, and she realized this was the first time in her life she truly understood the term *bittersweet*. "Ever had one perfect night?"

"Maybe." Tori shoved long brown hair back over her narrow shoulders, then she grinned. "But if I have, I was too drunk to remember it the next day."

Sighing, Ressa looked up and smiled. "It was probably the closest to perfect I'll ever know. But that's all it was. One perfect night."

Chapter Thirteen

Hands slid smooth and agile down his chest. Followed by a warm, seeking mouth. Crazy, wild curls trailed over his skin and he let his instincts guide him. He fisted a hand in her hair as she continued to move lower, lower . . .

When she closed her mouth around the head of his cock, Trey groaned, arching up.

The snarl that ripped out of him was choked and harsh, so ragged, he barely recognized the sound of his own voice.

Don't stop . . .

He tried to say the words.

Maybe he did and just couldn't hear it over the roar and rush of blood.

Don't . . .

Her laugh teased his ears as she lifted up and trailed a hand up his thigh. *I won't. I'm having too much fun.*

Music crashed, cutting through the dream. Trey jolted and then sat upright in bed. The dream fell to pieces around him as he looked around the room.

It had been a month since New Jersey—over a month since he'd seen . . . tasted . . . touched . . . Ressa.

He still dreamed about her.

The theme song from *Buffy the Vampire Slayer* was blaring from his phone. The display had one simple word on it, and while maybe it wasn't exactly the apocalypse, he felt like he needed to gear up for battle.

Grabbing the phone, he studied the display for a second longer and then silenced the alarm.

School.

Clayton started school today.

It was six in the morning, still too early to get Clayton up. He had wanted it that way. He needed to get his head clear, brace himself. Psych himself up or something.

The phone rang as he finished up in the bathroom and he answered with a sigh. "You realize that I can handle this myself, Mommy."

"Fuck you," Travis said easily. "How's my boy doing?"

Trey smiled despite the stress that tried to chew him up inside. "Excited. If I could work up even a tenth of Clay's excitement—hell, a hundredth of it, I'd be doing just fine with this."

"Today will be the worst. I . . . uh. Well, I had plans to be there, maybe drag you out to breakfast or something, but work wouldn't let me off. Bunch of dickheads."

"It's cool, Travis. I got this." He moved to the window, staring out at the eastern horizon. He loved this spot—had spent many mornings just here, watching as the colors bled from deep purple to pink then gold as the sun rose higher. With one arm braced on the cool glass of the window, he stared outside. "Much as I appreciate it, you can't always be there to hold my hand."

Silence caught, hung there. Then Travis blew out a heavy breath. "Fuck, Trey. You've spent the past few years shutting down more and more. Don't act like you haven't. I feel it. I just . . . you're scaring me. And don't try to lie to me about this. I—"

"Travis. I'm okay." He cut his twin off. Turning away from the window, he moved to his dresser and stared at the gold ring that had rested there for the past few weeks. He'd put it on for the trip home, but since then, it had rested in that very spot.

The need to put it back on any time he ventured outside, whether it was to the library, to the grocery, or even those monthly trips to church with Aliesha's folks, was going away.

He could handle life without that shield.

He'd even handled a few mild flirtations—not on his side— without feeling like he needed to bolt.

And maybe it was just because he needed it, but it seemed the ghosts that hung around him were a little lighter.

Of course, there was a ghost haunting him. *We had a good night but . . .*

"Trey—"

"I'm *okay*." He touched the ring. "I took my ring off. I was out running and this cute blonde started asking me about my tattoo. I didn't turn into an Olympic sprinter in my desperation to get away. I ran into a woman in the produce aisle and she asked me for my name and I didn't bolt."

"Did you give her your name?"

Trey winced. "My name, yeah. But when she asked for my number . . . well. I wasn't interested."

Travis scraped his nails across the growth of stubble on his face. If he hadn't been laid up in a hospital bed, he'd be on the other side of the Atlantic—and that had him pissed. He was more pissed off about the fact that he was laid up dealing with blood loss than the fact that he'd been shot two days ago.

Damn, but he wanted out.

He didn't want to be here. He wanted to be back in the States.

He'd wanted to be there for his twin. Had been prepared to talk Trey through this. But oddly enough, he wasn't feeling all that conflict he'd expected to feel. He eased up on the choke chain he'd lived with and realized something was . . . different, very different with his twin.

Normally Trey felt like a barren landscape.

"You are okay," he murmured.

"No." Trey's voice was honest.

"Fuck, man." Rubbing at the back of his neck, he tried to put his finger on just what it was he felt. There was something.

He could feel it. "Did you . . . hey, you finally went out with your librarian, didn't you?"

"No." Trey laughed and the sound was bitter, humorless. "No. That didn't work out."

"Okay." He frowned, tried to figure it out. "What is it then? Something's different with you. You feel . . . hell, you . . . aren't as empty."

"I'm not," Trey said, his voice blunt. "I can't say I'm back to normal, but I'm getting there. I've got a promise to keep. You, though . . . man . . ."

Trey went quiet.

Travis braced himself, the lie already there.

But Trey just sighed. "Something's up with you, I think. Let me know when you're ready to stop holding back on me. Listen, I gotta go. I need coffee if I'm going to get through the morning."

Brooding, Trey took that coffee out to the pergola, watching as the early morning sunlight glinted off the pool. It was early yet, but despite the coolness of the morning, he didn't bother going inside for a shirt as he sat there and continued his brood.

A faint ache still lingered in his side, although it didn't come from him.

More than once, he'd dealt with this from his twin, although it had been less and less over the years.

He wouldn't pry. Hadn't then, wouldn't now. But damn if he didn't want his twin to stop holding back from him. Especially when shit like *this* happened.

The door creaked open behind him. *Slowly.* Although the coffee was still fairly hot, he took a healthy swig and swallowed gamely before leaning forward. Still acting all nice and casual, he put it down, taking care to nudge it far out of reach before he leaned back and laced his hands behind his head.

With a lusty sigh, he waited.

His internal clock told him he still had a good fifteen minutes before he'd planned to wake up Clayton.

That didn't matter.

The floorboards shifted as the boy crept closer.

He managed not to grin.

Lowering his lashes, he waited.

Then—*oomph*—

"First day of school! First day of school!"

He caught Clayton before the kid could drive that knee any farther up into sensitive parts of his anatomy. Flipping Clayton onto his back, he stared down into eyes as blue as his own. "What?" he asked, although his ears were still ringing from Clayton's screech.

"First day of school!"

"I think you've watched *Finding Nemo* too many times." Hauling Clayton up for a hug, Trey sighed, taking a minute to just . . . enjoy. Clayton was still all warm from his bed and he smelled like the soap he'd scrubbed with last night. "I think your calendar is off. School starts *next* week, I bet. Besides, you can't be going to school already. You're not old enough."

"I'm almost *six* years old, Dad. I should have started *last* year." Clayton wiggled free and moved around until skinny, *sharp* knees were driving into Trey's thighs.

"Nah. Besides, you didn't turn five until it was too late to sign you up. I remember, they told me. Still I'm not sure you're old enough. Maybe I should call and check . . ." He fixed his face into his best *thinking* expression. "And I'm sure it's not this week."

"And it is too this week. You reminded me last night and made me go to bed *early*. Did you forget?"

Trey scrunched his face, thought harder.

Then he sighed. "I guess maybe I did. Since you seem pretty certain it's today, I reckon we ought to deal with breakfast and stuff, right?"

"Right." A sly look crept across Clayton's face. "Since it's school and all, that's like a special day. I bet it's even special enough for chocolate chip pancakes."

"Nice try." Amused, he stood up, hooking his arm around the boy and then swinging him around until Clayton was on his back. "We can talk chocolate chips on the weekend. How about some plain waffles instead? I can whip those up in half the time."

* * *

Six a.m.

Ressa studied her phone after she'd turned off the alarm. With a sigh, she went to her notifications and eyed her schedule for the day.

She had to get Neeci up and off to her first day at school and Ressa had a late day at the library. Her mother was helping out on the late nights—they'd worked it out a while ago and it was going to have to suffice, but days like today would suck because she might not see her bed until eleven or later. She still had work to get done on the blog, once she had Neeci settled.

Already she was tired, which sucked because she had to be at work at her regular time tomorrow.

I can do this, she told herself, and she knew she could. The words had been her mantra ever since she'd taken over guardianship of her niece back when Neeci was a baby. Neeci had needed a stable life and Ressa was the only person who could offer it. She loved the little girl like she was her own, but there were too many days when she found herself questioning things—like whether or not she was equipped for the job that had been thrust upon her.

Child, nobody is ever equipped for the things they find themselves doing . . . you just do the best you can. Words Mama Ang had told her, years ago, rose to steady her as she sat up. Yeah, the best she could do. She could do this.

With that in mind, she dismissed the notifications and went to the calendar on her phone. She couldn't function without her agenda.

A series of notifications, an alert from her voicemail, and a list of the calls she'd missed came up.

She grimaced when she saw that her cousin Kiara had called.

Kiara, Neeci's mom.

Once, Ressa had thought Kiara was like her guardian angel. She ended up being more like an albatross. Ressa loved her dearly and she knew Kiara loved her, but it was a poisoned, toxic sort of love.

It was the same kind of love Ressa had had for her father.

The same kind of love Ressa was determined to keep away from Neeci.

She had to wonder what Kiara wanted. She never called

over anything good. Kiara either wanted money or a favor or to see Neeci, and that always ended up with the girl crying and despondent for days on end.

Doubt gnawed at her, but she deleted the voicemail without listening. She'd seen Kiara a few weeks ago. She had plans to see her again in a few weeks on her birthday, and Neeci would see her, too. If it was important, Kiara could call again, or write. Morse code . . . something.

She tossed the phone down and climbed out of bed, determined to face the day without dread.

Or with as little dread as possible.

After all, it wasn't every day her little cousin started school.

"I wish Mama was here."

Flicking a look up, Ressa met Neeci's gaze in the reflection. "I know, baby."

"Granny Ang is picking me up, right? She won't forget?"

"No." Ressa managed not to chuckle. Like Angeline would *ever* forgot Neeci. She'd *never* forget her baby. "She won't forget you."

"Why can't you pick me up?" Neeci demanded.

"Because I'm working, sugar. You know that."

"That's stupid. They can just let you come home. For today." Neeci dropped her head—or tried to—onto the bathroom counter. *"Ouch!"*

"Be still." Ressa figured she'd told her cousin that five times in the past five minutes. In fifteen minutes or so, they'd be done—the good news was that they wouldn't have to do this every day. The bad news, well, it didn't matter to a five-year-old that you only had to deal with your hair like this every week—or less—the five-year-old still wasn't going to go for being still.

"I *hate* getting my hair done." Neeci stood there, her lip poking out and her bright eyes miserable.

Ressa's heart broke a little and she put the brush down. Sitting down on the toilet, she smoothed Neeci's bangs to the side. "We're almost done," she promised. "Come on now. Aren't you excited for your first day of school?"

Neeci's gaze darted away and she shrugged, one small shoulder jerking up and down. Then she brought her hand up to her mouth, automatically going to poke her thumb inside.

"We're not doing that anymore."

"I bet Mama wouldn't care," Neeci said, mumbling around the thumb even as Ressa went to pull her hand down.

Finally succeeding, Ressa cocked a brow. "Maybe she wouldn't, but she's not here and she's not in charge. I am. Besides," she said, shifting into a no-nonsense tone. "Think about all the stuff you'll be touching at school. Desks and doors and chairs . . . everything you touch, somebody else touched. So if you touch whatever *they* touched and then stick your thumb in your mouth like that, baby, you've got those nasty germs in your mouth."

"What kinda germs?" Neeci wrinkled her nose.

"Gross kinds. What if somebody picked up used gum from the ground? Or went to the bathroom and didn't wash their hands? That's just nasty."

Neeci's eyes rounded and she looked down at her hands. As those hands crept back behind her back, Ressa hit back a smile. Neeci had never much liked germs.

With a sigh, Neeci leaned in and rested her head on Ressa's shoulder. "What if nobody likes me? What if I don't make friends? I had a couple of friends at preschool, but none of them go here. What if I never make another friend my whole life?"

"Oh, honey." Now her heart was twisting and turning all over. Pulling her cousin into her lap, she hugged her. There was nothing the girl could have said that would have hit home harder. "Neeci, there is absolutely no reason you shouldn't make friends. You're funny and you're nice and you like people. All you have to do is be nice and you'll find people who like you."

Neeci was quiet for a minute. "But you're funny, and you're nice. You like people. But you had all kinds of problems getting people to like you. I heard you talk about how you didn't have many friends in college and you didn't have a lot in school either, and the friends you did have was trouble. What if I'm like that?"

"*Were* trouble," she corrected automatically, even as she thought about little ears. Just what had she been talking about and what had Neeci overheard?

There wasn't an easy answer to this, was there?

"I didn't make friends all that well, you're right," she said slowly. "We've talked about this, Neeci, you and making friends. We've talked about it a lot. Yeah, I did some bad things growing up and I hung out with bad kids. I did stupid things that could have gotten me in trouble."

"And your daddy was an asshole."

"Neeci!" Ressa glared at her in the mirror.

"I heard Granny Ang say it," Neeci said defensively.

"What Granny Ang says and what you can say are two different things." Ressa blew out a breath and shrugged aside the knee-jerk instinct to defend her father. Not only was he past the point of needing defending, he also *had* been an asshole. A terrible father, even if he had loved her in his own twisted way. Bad people can still love. That doesn't make it healthy— for anybody. "My father wasn't a good man, no. He did stupid things and made bad choices, but that doesn't have anything to do with what I'm telling you. I made my own choices, too. And once I started making better choices, sweetie, I made better friends. I found people who liked me."

"Did they like you even though you did stupid stuff?"

Snapping a band around the last plait, she turned Neeci around and bent over so they could see eye to eye. "When it comes to stupid stuff and your friends, that's how you know who your real friends are, baby. Your real friends are the ones who are going to love you . . . even after they know all about the stupid stuff and the bad mistakes. They know . . . and they love you anyway."

Neeci scuffed the toe of her new pink sneaker on the floor. Not looking at Ressa, she said softly, "I was talking to Mama about school and she said since I was so pretty, people were gonna like me. But what if people don't think I'm pretty? What if other girls are prettier?"

Typical. Ressa didn't even bother giving in to the urge to be frustrated. "There's a lot more to being a friend than being pretty." She rubbed her hand over Neeci's neck, turning it over in her head. Then, easing back, she waited until Neeci looked up. "Hey, you know old Tom? He lives in the place across from Granny?"

"Yeah!" Neeci's face lit up. "He gives me suckers when Granny isn't looking and he tells cool stories and he lets me read his comics."

"I know, right?" Ressa grinned at her. "He's got a classic set of Marvel Comics that he let me read . . . *if* I didn't take them out of his sight. Anyway, so he's nice. Fun to be around, yeah?"

"Yeah. He's really nice."

Twining one of Neeci's plaits around her finger, Ressa lifted a brow. "But what about those burns on him? They twist his face all up, and when he smiles or talks . . . Doesn't that make him scary?"

"No!" Neeci looked outraged, her eyes flashing and her small face folding into mutinous lines. "How can you . . . Oh."

She pulled away and wagged a finger at her cousin. "Ress, that wasn't nice. Mr. Tom is awesome."

Ressa rolled her eyes. "Mr. Tom is *beyond* awesome. But those burns did mess up his face—and he'll be the first to tell you he'll never win any beauty pageants. Not having a pretty face doesn't make him less of a friend, does it?"

"No." Moving back to the sink, Neeci stood there and waited. "I'll make friends . . . right?" Her face was hopeful, her eyes so sad.

Moving back up behind her, Ressa took the brush. "I think you will. And don't go telling me that you don't have any friends around here. You've got a bunch of friends. The Logston girls love playing with you and so does Jacob down the street. Should be a piece of cake to make more."

Neeci smiled, but with her solemn eyes, that smile did more to tug at Ressa's heart than anything else.

Sometimes, she thought, she could just shake Kiara.

Ressa had been Neeci's guardian for years and *still* Kiara managed to sink all these hooks of doubt into her daughter.

Ardmore Elementary was in a pretty, borderline exclusive neighborhood. At times, she felt as out of place there as she had when Mama Ang had practically dragged her, kicking and screaming, into the household she shared with Bruce MacAllister.

She'd been fifteen and had lived on her own for nearly four months, using up her precious cash and paying the bills, working under the table for more cash and doing just fine.

But then Mama Ang tracked her down.

Mama Ang had been doing a search for her brother, Darnell—she did them once a month, and this time, she'd found his obituary. She'd spent weeks trying to track Ressa down, first in the foster care system—where Ressa *should* have been, and then she'd just started checking out all the places her brother would have lived.

Sometimes Ressa wondered, if they'd left her alone, maybe Kiara would have turned out okay. Who knows what Ressa would have been doing, but maybe . . .

Maybe . . .

Maybe . . . maybe if she'd talked to a certain someone a few weeks back, she could—

Maybe. The most useless word in the English language.

Stop. I'm done with this. There was never any maybe there. It was just a fantasy. A fling. Nothing would ever happen— could ever happen there.

You know how he'd react if he knew the truth about you?

She squared her shoulders. Yeah, he'd react pretty much the same way just about every other guy in her life had. Screw the maybes.

"Ressa, you're squeezing my hand really hard."

Grimacing, Ressa let go and looked down to see Neeci wiggling her fingers. They'd parked in the lot the e-mail had directed them to—most days, parents weren't allowed in, but they made a few allowances for the first day of school and kindergarteners. Which was good, because Ressa had two heavy totes loaded down with supplies—crayons, folders, tissues, wet wipes, paper towels.

She sure as hell didn't remember having to lug all this stuff to school when *she* had been Neeci's age. Nodding to the doors she'd been looking for, she said, "That's where we go in."

Neeci shoved her hand back into Ressa's. "I'm scared."

"Aw, now. Don't be scared. It's going to be fun. Just give it a chance." Ressa hoped she wasn't lying.

The scents of crayons and books and children hit her as she walked in. It was something unique to a school, Ressa decided, and it tugged on memories long forgotten—a few of them were even pleasant. When she *had* gone to school, she'd enjoyed it, and for the most, she'd attended fairly regularly. She'd only graduated a year behind, thanks to the determination of Mama Ang.

Well, that, and the love for books Ressa had discovered.

Hopefully Neeci would find herself as addicted to learning as Ressa had been, even if Ressa had discovered her love for it a little later in the game.

Moving with the flow, she pointed toward some of the signs on the walls, watching as Neeci giggled at a handmade shark that towered over one door—*Fourth graders are friends—not food.*

"That's silly," Neeci said, a smile slowly replacing the nerves.

"Yeah. But funny. I hope sharks can read."

Neeci rolled her eyes, an expression that was so patently like her mother that Ressa could only shake her head.

"Here we go— Oof!"

She almost toppled as a boy-shaped tornado tried to run her down. His face was pale, his eyes huge . . . and filled with tears. Instinctively, she went down to one knee.

"Oh, hey now . . ." She reached up and brushed a hand across his hair. Golden blond curls tumbled right back into his face and brilliant, blue green eyes stared up at hers.

Her heart wrenched.

"Clayton?"

Half-wild, he shook his head, his eyes wheeling all around.

"Clayton!"

A shiver raced down her spine.

She squeezed her eyes closed.

Oh, no . . .

"Ressa, what's wrong?" Neeci asked in a tiny whisper.

Oh, just about everything . . .

Chapter Fourteen

The rush of emotion that slammed into him was too intense to define.

Especially in that moment.

Ressa Bliss was kneeling in the doorway, one arm draped around his son, and the sight of the two of them was like a punch straight to the solar plexus.

As he stood there, Clayton blinked and seemed to focus on Ressa. "Miss Ressa?"

"Yeah. What's wrong, sugar?" she asked.

He just shook his head, and threw his arms around her neck, clinging to her.

"Clayton."

Clayton wordlessly shook his head.

The image of his son, clinging to Ressa, imprinted itself on his memory, an afterimage that lingered even when he paused and closed his eyes for a span of a few seconds to make sure he was actually *seeing* what he thought he was seeing.

When he opened his eyes, she was still there and she'd shifted her attention from Clayton to him. She lowered her lashes and then looked back at him, and when she did, the surprise was replaced by the sort of pleasant blankness he'd expect from a stranger.

Okay, not liking that, he decided.

But he'd deal with it later.

People were trying to squeeze in around them as they huddled in the doorway.

Ressa noticed as well, and she stood, boosting Clayton up. Then she held out a hand to the child with her and eased back out into the hall.

The little girl watched it all with wide, pale gold eyes that took in everything around her.

He tried to puzzle that one out—was the girl her daughter? Some vague memory of Ressa mentioning a little girl worked free and the puzzle was solved a minute later as the girl leaned her head against Ressa's hip—he envied her for a minute there. She asked, "Ress, what's wrong with him?" She went to poke her thumb in her mouth.

Deftly, Ressa caught her wrist. "Remember that talk about germs, Neeci," she said, her voice absent.

She met Trey's gaze steadily, but she wasn't as steady as she pretended to be.

"Here," he said, his voice gruff.

She passed Clayton over, although the boy clung tight to her neck. Once he had Clayton in his arms, the boy did the same thing to Trey that he'd been doing to Ressa, clutching tight in a child's version of a stranglehold, his face in Trey's neck.

Trey blew out a sigh, bringing his hand up to cup the back of the boy's head. Turning away, he asked quietly, "What's up there, man?"

Off to the side, he could hear Ressa talking in a low voice, while the girl started on an endless tirade of questions.

Tuning them out, he rubbed his cheek against Clayton's head, still waiting. "Come on, Clay. Talk to me."

"They have their moms. Everybody." His voice was watery now and when he spoke again, he was louder, his response perilously close to a sob. "They all have their mommy with them, but I don't!"

Trey felt his heart crack, right down the middle.

But before he could find any way to answer, a soft voice said, "I don't."

Clayton stopped in mid-sniff. Head now tucked against Trey's chest, he shifted around until he could see the girl. From the corner of his eye, he watched Ressa rise, resting a protective hand on the girl's shoulder.

"You don't have your mommy here?" Clayton asked, his voice just above a whisper.

The girl had old eyes, Trey thought. And when she spoke, her voice held the edge of an anger that didn't suit that delicate face or her youth. The girl slid Ressa a look, caught between defiance and a child's hurt. He found himself wanting to hug her close, stroke away some of the hurt he sensed behind the anger.

"No. She's . . ." She stopped, her words trailing off.

"Gone." The hand Ressa had placed on the girl's shoulder tightened gently. Ressa looked at Trey for a quiet moment before shifting her attention to the boy. "Neeci doesn't have her mama here either, sweetheart. She knows how hard it can be. Maybe the two of you can hang out. It's easier, I bet, with a friend."

Clayton eased back from Trey's chest, stared at the girl curiously. "You're a girl."

Neeci blinked. "And *you* are a boy." Then she folded her arms over her chest. "I run fast."

"I bet I run faster." Tears momentarily forgotten, Clayton wiggled until Trey put him down. Standing in front of Neeci, he rocked back and forth on his heels. "I don't like dolls and stuff."

"Neither do I." Neeci rolled her eyes, a look that was far too grown up considering how young she had to be. Then she smiled. "I'm Neeci."

A few moments later, the two of them were inside the classroom and Trey breathed out a sigh of relief as the band around his chest loosened. None of the kids had seemed to notice.

Painfully aware of the woman who was taking great pains to avoid him, he spoke with Clayton's kindergarten teacher— Mr. Boyd Franklin. Round cheeked and a little thick around the middle, he looked to be in his late twenties, and he'd already introduced himself to most of the parents and most of the kids, taking care to chat, even if it was only for a moment.

He noticed things, something Trey could appreciate.

He'd definitely noticed Clayton's momentary panic.

"How long ago did his mother die?"

Trey folded his arms over his chest, watching as Clayton and Neeci giggled over one of the books he'd found on a bookshelf. "It's . . . complicated," he finally said. "But Clayton never had the chance to know her. Being around the other kids, their moms . . . it's going to be hard for him, I think."

"That's rough." Boyd didn't offer any empty sympathy, just stood there in silence and then, after a moment, he smiled. "It looks like he's made a friend already."

It did, indeed.

Trey gave it a few more moments and then broke away, cutting through the sea of backpacks, desks and small bodies to crouch by his son. Better to leave now while there was still chaos, he figured. Clayton would be so busy he would barely notice anything else.

"I'm going to head on home, big guy," he murmured when there was a break in the conversation. One that involved bugs . . . and bug guts, he noted with some revolted amusement.

Clayton whirled around. "But . . ." His mouth opened, closed. Then, small shoulders drooping, he reached out and touched his father's cheek. "What are you going to do all day? Aren't you going to be lonely without me?"

"Very." He caught Clayton's nose and pinched it lightly. "But I'll be okay. You have to do this kindergarten thing so you can go to college next week and be an astronaut by Christmas."

Clayton grinned. "It takes longer than that, Dad."

"Oh. Well, you still have to get started." Leaning in, he pressed a quick kiss to Clayton's brow. His heart squeezed and memories from six years raced through his mind.

Slowly, he pushed to his feet and forced himself to smile. "Do me a favor," he said. He sounded steady—how about that? As Clayton flashed him a curious smile, he ruffled the boy's hair. "Now I know you want to know everything under the sun, but don't come home and be smarter than me already. Wait until tomorrow before you do that."

Clayton laughed and turned back to Neeci. "It will take a lot longer than that, Dad. I don't know if I'll ever be *that* smart."

He managed to make it out the door.

And that was when he saw that Ressa was loitering there . . . as if she'd been waiting for him.

Half-blind, he kept on walking. He needed to breathe. For just a minute.

Trey left the school like a man possessed and he didn't even seem aware that she'd followed him, not until he heard the sound of her heels clicking on the pavement.

Slowly, he turned and looked at her.

"Rough day?" she asked softly.

He jerked his head away, one shoulder rising and falling in a shrug. "Always heard the first day is harder on the parent than the kid."

"If that's the truth, I kinda feel like giving both of you a cookie and a teddy bear."

Frowning, he swung his gaze back to her.

Because he seemed to need the company, she moved in closer and leaned against the truck next to him. Not close enough to feel his heat, but close enough to wish she could.

"You know, you are the last person I thought I'd see here," she said quietly.

He slid her a look from the corner of his eye, and she didn't think it was her imagination that the shadows seemed to lessen from his gaze. A faint smile kicked up the corner of his mouth and then he tipped his head back to the sky. "I have to say the same."

Common sense told Trey to get his ass in the truck and leave.

She didn't want anything from him. That had been made almost painfully clear.

We had a nice night, but that's probably all it's ever going to be.

A nice night? Yeah. He equated a *nice* night to one that didn't involve a temper tantrum or him forgetting that he had something in the oven or that he'd left a load of clothes in the washer for two days. If he got through a day without some sort of minor disaster and could relax at the end and maybe not have a headache? *That* was a nice night.

What they'd had, for him at least, had shot up past *nice* into the realm of *blow the top of my head off.* Or maybe his cock. He couldn't go more than a few nights without dreaming about her, although after years of what had felt like an almost sexless existence, he wasn't entirely bothered by the dreams.

He was just bothered by the fact that a night that had all but shaken his world had just been . . . *nice.*

He was still craving a whole lot of everything from her and she wanted nothing from him.

Just his luck.

Ressa bit her lip as she pushed off the truck, moving to stand in front of him. She had to fight the urge to smooth that misery from his brow, hold him until it all eased away.

"So why do you want to give me a cookie and a teddy bear?" he asked, his gruff voice cutting through the fog of thoughts tangling in her head.

"Hmm." Unable to keep her hands to herself, she let herself lift one up, intending to brush his hair back. But he caught her wrist, held her hand there, trapped in mid-air.

Their gazes locked.

She forced a smile.

"I'm past the age where a teddy bear will help, Ressa." His thumb stroked over her wrist and then slowly, he let go of her hand.

She let it fall to her side, stung by that blunt rejection, although she supposed she shouldn't be. She was the one who'd pushed him away. "I can't help it. You look like you need it," she said, smiling to cover the emptiness she felt.

"We'll save it for Clayton." He glanced toward the school. "He needs it more than I do."

"Yeah. I guess he does." Sighing, she followed his gaze, her heart aching for the boy they'd left inside. "Guess maybe the teddy bear idea is a little much for you."

She looked back at him, watched as a faint smile crooked his lips. "Yeah. Well, I never say no to cookies. But I don't need somebody to hold my hand over the fact that my son is starting school. I just need to . . . deal."

Starting school? "This isn't just about him starting school, is it?"

Through his lashes, he studied her. "Why are you asking?"

"I . . ." Frowning, she looked away.

"That weekend we had is over, Ressa. You made it clear that was all you wanted, so what does it matter if I need a cookie or whatever?"

It stung. And if she wouldn't have hated herself for taking the easy way out, she would have just told him to forget it.

But as she stood there struggling for some sort of answer, he took a step toward her. His mouth grazed her ear, sending a shiver through her. "I still wake up smelling you on my skin. A cookie, a teddy bear, a friendly chat isn't what I want from you. Since you already decided you didn't want anything more than beyond what we had in that hotel room, I'd just as soon not try to do . . . whatever it is you're doing."

He went to cut around her.

Insanity struck.

There was no other explanation, but *logic* had nothing to do with what she did next. She caught his arm in her hand. "Almost every night, I find myself dreaming about you. It's not a matter of not *wanting* more."

Under her hand, the muscles in his arm went tense.

He was watching her. She didn't want to meet his eyes, but she couldn't avoid it forever. Mouth dry, she slowly lifted her gaze to his and found that blue green gaze cutting into her, stripping her bare, and all she wanted to do was erase the past five weeks. No. Not the past five weeks—there was another period of her life she'd love to undo, but that just wasn't possible.

"It's just that this is too complicated," she said.

"Complicated." He shifted around.

Ressa found herself caged between him and the truck. His arms bracketed her shoulders and his mouth was only a whisper away now.

"Sometimes we make things out to be more complicated than they really are," Trey said, and his voice was imminently reasonable. So reasonable and logical, it caught her off guard when he slid his knee between her thighs. She wore a full-cut skirt, but the material was thin, very little barrier, and she gasped at the feel of him rubbing against her inner thighs. "Let's simplify. I want you. I want to know more about you and I want to spend time with you. Either you want the same or you don't."

As he brushed his mouth against her cheek, he murmured, "Which is it?"

"I want that, but . . ."

He kissed her.

Ressa moaned, grabbing his waist to steady herself, but he ended the kiss too quickly and moved away, watching her with hooded hungry eyes.

"Then we either try this out or don't." He stood four feet away now, hands hanging loose at his sides. His gaze focused on her mouth and Ressa shuddered at the hunger she saw there. *We don't.*

Logic whispered inside her head. She knew better. "I'm something of a mess, Trey," she said, managing to keep her voice level. "I'm raising a child who isn't mine. There are complications involved with that. There are other things in my life that are just as complicated, if not worse. I don't think I'm the ideal woman for a man like you to get involved with."

"I'm a single father." He took a step toward her.

"And you're doing a damn fine job with him. That's not the sort of complications I have going on." There was a war going on inside her. Logic and desire, for once, completely at odds.

Trey reached up and fisted his hand in her hair. She'd left it down, and the weight of it was heavy on her neck.

He tugged on the curls, forcing her head back as he moved in closer. "I've got four brothers—one of them is a movie star, the other is a former child star and we can't get together without the damn paparazzi stalking us."

He brushed a soft kiss across her cheek and she felt that light caress all through her body.

"My son has nightmares, convinced that I'll die just like his mother did, and sometimes I wake up, convinced he died in the wreck that killed his mother. The night my wife was buried, I went out, got completely wasted and managed to get in a fight and I don't remember any of it—the whole night is a black hole, but whatever the hell happened was enough to turn me off alcohol—even the smell of whiskey is enough to make me sick. I know plenty about complications, Ressa."

She reached up, fisting her hands in his shirt.

"It's simple . . . either you want to spend time with me . . . or you don't."

He made it sound so easy.

"I'm going to ask you again and you just tell me the first thing that comes to mind—after this, I won't bother anymore."

Ressa stilled.

He smoothed a hand down her back and then pulled away. Only a few feet separated them.

It felt like a mile.

"I'm going to go grab a cup of coffee. Would you like to join me?"

Before she could answer, a voice interrupted them.

"Trey!"

At the sound of that voice, Trey closed his eyes. Staring down at the ground, he muttered, "Son of a bitch."

"Trey? Hello!"

Her answer lodged in her throat, Ressa turned. Next to her, Trey took a deep breath and she had the oddest feeling he was bracing himself.

She slid him one final look and then met the gaze of the woman in front of them.

It was . . . well . . . June Cleaver.

That was all Ressa could think.

She looked like a modern-day version of June Cleaver. Her ebony hair was cut in a short, sleek bob that accentuated a long, elegant neck. Not that her neck needed the extra accent, but there was a strand of pearls that glowed against oh, so, perfect skin. Her cardigan was mossy green and matched her wide eyes. The cardigan that picked up the green in her full-cut skirt . . . a skirt that looked like a watercolor garden. Roses and lilies against a misty background.

Those mossy green eyes looked at Trey and she all but had her heart written in them. If the woman had handed him a letter declaring her love, it wouldn't have been any less clear.

"Um . . . hello," she said, her voice soft, breathy before it steadied. "I thought I'd come see you and Clayton. Since it's his first day and all. Has . . . school already started?"

"Ah, yeah, well, that's nice of you, Nadine, but yeah, it's already started. Clay's in class, ready to go." Trey gave her a casual smile.

Casual, maybe, but to Ressa, it looked frayed around the edges.

Nadine shot her another look from the corner of her eye. Some part of her wanted to apologize, just for standing there, and she thought maybe she should just excuse herself—

Trey reached out a hand, rested it on her waist, almost as if he'd read her mind.

"I wanted to be with the two of you." Nadine's voice was softer now. Almost a whisper. "He's been so excited, and you've been so worried . . ."

If Ressa hadn't been standing next to her, she wouldn't have noticed, the way he tensed, so subtly. But nothing showed in his voice, on his face, as he shrugged. "The first day of school is supposed to be a roller coaster ride, but we handled it."

She nodded again, looking away. "I can see that, I . . . well. I just want to help, to be there for you. As much as I can." Another one of those glances at Ressa, and this one lingered.

Unable to stay quiet anymore, Ressa gave her a wide, brilliant smile. "Hi."

Trey's thumb stroked her back.

Nadine's throat worked as she swallowed, her gaze darting off to the side.

"You . . . well, you've got the whole morning ahead of you now. It's going to be awfully quiet at home. Why don't we go have some coffee?"

Ressa felt, as much as heard, Trey's sigh.

"I'm sorry," Ressa said, the words popping out. Her tongue was moving and her brain had *no* idea what was going on. "Trey and I were just getting ready to head out. We already had plans."

Trey's hand fisted in the material of her blouse.

"What . . ." Now Nadine's gaze flew to her. "But . . ."

"Nadine, this is Ressa Bliss." Trey let go of her blouse, but not of her. He curled his arm around her waist and he moved closer, pressed his mouth to her temple. "A friend of mine."

Nadine looked back and forth between them. "But . . . I . . ." She blinked and looked away. "We didn't have any time to talk today."

"With Clay starting school, the morning routine has to change." Trey smiled. "It was nice of you to come by, Nadine."

She nodded and slid another look back at Ressa.

Ressa felt something cold slide through her—those mossy green eyes had gone chilly.

There was something under that June Cleaver mask.

"That woman is working you," Ressa murmured as she watched the woman climb in her car a few yards away.

"Nah. Nadine's just . . . lonely. Her husband died a couple of years ago and she's shy, doesn't know how to talk to people very well."

Shy, my ass. "She's working you." Ressa slid away, turning to study him. "And *you* clearly were falling for it. She's good . . . I think I almost fell for it, too. What's the deal about your morning routine?"

Scowling, he rubbed at his jaw. "We started having coffee together in the mornings a while back. We just sit on the porch while Clayton eats his breakfast there. It's not a big deal or anything. It's not like we're dating."

"Maybe not to you. She thinks she's got a claim on you."

Trey rolled his eyes and then moved in, cupping her chin. "And is that why you decided you'd have coffee? Or was *that* just to distract her?"

"No." She swallowed and hoped like hell she wasn't making a mistake. "I want to . . . have coffee."

His thumb swept over her lip. "Just coffee?"

"For now." Then she eased back. "But I'm not joking. That woman thinks you two have something going, Trey. Why else would she show up here? That's a mom thing—or a serious girlfriend thing."

He opened his mouth, then shut it. "She probably just didn't think about it."

"She did." Rolling her eyes, Ressa muttered, "Men. Sometimes you're so blind."

"And what do you want me to do about it?" he said, crossing his arms over his chest.

She ran her tongue across her teeth. "Well, for one . . . if we're going to have coffee . . . or anything else . . . you need to make sure she knows you're not interested."

"Nadine knows that."

Ressa cocked a brow, and as Trey's face went red, curiosity flooded her.

"We . . . ah . . . look, we tried a date. Once. It didn't work out. At all."

Cocking her head, Ressa asked, "Was this before or after the coffee deal started?"

"Before. Months before." He frowned. "Why?"

"Because I suspect she thinks you two have had a lot of dates *since* then that have worked out—every morning you have coffee together. You need to make her back off. Have her give you some space . . . What?"

He sighed. "She makes you feel like you've kicked a puppy. I . . . Fuck. Sometimes when Clayton and I head out for breakfast, just the two of us, she gives me this look and it's like I kicked a puppy right in front of her."

"I told you—she's working you. How do you feel when you keep doing whatever it is she wants? Like just now, when you saw her here? What did you feel?"

How in the hell had the discussion gone from him trying to talk Ressa into coffee to his somewhat annoying and needy neighbor?

Trey did not know.

Ressa eyed him coolly, an arch look on her face, as she waited for an answer.

Trapped. He winced and looked away. Nadine was a sweet woman. She helped out with everything. She didn't have any kids, but she helped out with a local Boy Scout troop. She volunteered with Big Brothers/Big Sisters. She headed up clothing drives and made sandwiches to pass out down at a park where some homeless people tended to gather on weekends.

She was a *sweet* lady.

They'd tried one date and he'd only said yes because the few times she'd stammered out her obviously nervous invitation to the movies or dinner, she'd left him feeling like he'd broken her heart when he said no.

They'd gone out to dinner and a movie and when they came back, she'd been the one to make a move.

She'd kissed him.

Everything inside him had gone cold.

There had been absolutely no interest—in fact, he couldn't wait for her to *stop* kissing him.

Turning away, he rested his hands on his hips and looked up at the clear blue bowl of the sky stretching overhead. "Trapped," he bit off. Every time he was with Nadine, he had that same sensation. He didn't know why, but that was how he felt. And it *wasn't* because of anything Nadine did.

"I'd feel trapped, too, if somebody kept trying to manipulate me into shit I didn't want."

He stilled and shot a look over his shoulder, meeting Ressa's gaze. "What?"

"I'd feel trapped, too." She shrugged and moved toward him.

She was so close . . .

Reaching out, he caught her waist and pulled her against him.

She didn't resist.

Leaning back against the truck, he took the soft weight of her body on his and his cock stirred, blood draining down and pooling in his groin.

Her lashes lowered.

A soft sigh shuddered out of her.

"No more coffee," he said softly.

Then he trailed his fingers up the inside of her ribs.

She was right, he suspected, and it made him feel stupid that he hadn't seen it before now.

"She'll make you feel like you kicked a dozen puppies." Ressa slid her hands up his chest.

"Too bad. If I'm having coffee, I'd just as soon have it by myself . . . or better yet, with you."

"We are still talking about coffee here, right?"

"Sure." Then he bent down and nipped her lower lip. "Unless we're not. But don't worry, I'll tell her."

Mentally, he braced himself for it. He could already see the look in her eyes, too.

"You're like an open book sometimes."

He met her eyes.

"You're thinking about how much you're going to hurt her feelings, aren't you?"

There was a zipper under her arm and he lifted a brow. "Well, this very second, I'm thinking about how easily I could pull this down . . . but . . . yeah."

"You're going to do it anyway. No matter what you say or how you do it."

"I can be nice, you know." He scowled at her.

For a moment, she stared at him.

Then she laughed.

"You are blind. Trey . . . she's in love with you. And the sooner you make it clear it's not going to happen, the sooner she can move on."

There was only one way to describe how he felt in that moment. He summed it up in two words. "Oh, shit."

Chapter Fifteen

The coffee shop was just down the corner from work. The new branch where she worked wasn't as big, or as high tech, as the branch near the waterfront had been, but the children's area was nice and they had a great program.

That was always a plus.

By an unspoken mutual agreement, they kept their discussion casual—the sort of talk they would have had if this had been their first date.

Well, technically, it was, even if they were doing things out of order.

Usually the date came before the crazy hot sex.

It didn't negate that first, mild awkwardness that came with any first date, though, and Ressa was even more nervous because on the drive over, she'd had too much time to think through what a stupid decision this was.

Ressa pointed out, nice and casual like, how much the Norfolk library loved it when local authors came to visit. She hadn't gotten around to that before, and now, at least, she could say she'd sown the seeds.

Now, as they sat on a low-lying brick container wall, the riot of summer flowers blooming behind them, she sipped at an iced coffee while Trey actually managed to drink regular coffee. In this heat. She didn't know how people did that.

He stared toward the library, sunglasses shielding his gaze from the vivid rays of the sun. "How long you worked there?"

"For this branch? You forgot already?" She wrinkled her nose at him when those dark lenses angled toward her. She wanted to snag them off. If he never again hid behind a pair of sunglasses, it would be too soon. "Oh, guess you meant the library in general. I've been with them since college, at one location or another."

"Always wanted to be a librarian?"

"Yeah." She suspected he wouldn't be one of the ones who didn't get it, so she told him the truth. "You know how books are a casual escape for some? Books weren't just an escape for me—they rescued me."

His brow lifted, his expression somehow conveying . . . *go on* . . . all without him saying a word.

She blew out a breath. She could do this—get this part out. If he learned this much of her and didn't handle it well? Then that would be answer enough and she'd know before she got in over her head.

"I wasn't . . . a good kid," she said finally, just laying it out on the table. "My mom died when I was little. I can relate to Clay there. But my dad . . . well."

She shrugged. "He got in trouble a lot. In and out of jail. I'd live with his sister when he was locked up. He did a stretch of three years, got out when I was seven and seemed to straighten up—or so people thought. He just got smarter. We moved around a lot. He was dealing drugs . . ." She paused and then blew out a breath before she added, "And he used to have me helping him."

Now she looked up.

Trey didn't look shocked or appalled or disgusted.

He just sat there. Listening.

She swiped a finger through the condensation on her cup while her gut twisted into ten thousand knots. "There were a few times when he'd get arrested off and on, but he never got charged, never got held. He was killed when I was fifteen. I ended up going to live with his sister." She smiled now, unable to stop it. "Mama Ang. She pretty much changed my life. And not just because she introduced me to books. I wasn't easy for her to live with—at all—didn't think I needed anybody, kept trying to run away—school was awful . . . but she kept at it, kept at *me*. Six months after I'd gone to live with her, I got in a fight at school. Somebody was on me again, about my dad, and I lost it. Got suspended. Mama Ang locked me in my room. No TV. I could come out for meals but that was it. The only thing in the room was the schoolwork I had to do and books. Eventually, I got bored enough to pick one up. I didn't even hear her come in the room—she'd been calling me for dinner and I never heard."

She flicked a look at him. "It was Tolkien. She asked me if I was enjoying it and I lied—told her it was the most boring piece of shit I'd ever read. Mama Ang just laughed. The next day, she brought me more books and told me a whole world lay inside them."

Ressa paused, thought of the hours, the days, the weeks that followed. "It took a while. It wasn't some *Reading Rainbow* after school special where I changed overnight, but . . . I found myself spending more time inside a book, getting in trouble less . . . doing better in school. Not on purpose, but it happened. And I liked *me* more. I'd read about these people who were . . . decent. Like Mama Ang. I didn't understand why they could be like that and I couldn't. So I told myself I'd just pretend . . . and maybe I'd figure it out on the way."

"I guess you did."

Ressa stared at her watered down coffee for a long, long moment. "It took a long, long time."

"Sometimes that's how it works."

Silence fell between them as they drank their coffee under the shade of the tree, the day growing hotter and brighter around them. It was probably a good five minutes before he spoke again. "You know, I never go to this branch."

Thankful for the change in subject, she smiled at him over her cup. "You're more than welcome to come. And . . . for the record, you've been invited—an open invite to any of the branches. More than once."

"Uhhhh. . . ."

Ressa laughed, the embarrassed look on his face delighting

her. "Hey, don't freak out on me. My boss would love to have
you come visit—naturally, she'd *prefer* if you came to the
main branch, but any of them would make her day. Her month.
Her life." She winked at him. Then she looked down. "I . . .
uh. Well, I was supposed to try to talk you into it if I had the
chance in New Jersey, but it didn't ever work out. Seems like
you're not big on public stuff anyway."

He'd put a shadow in her eyes.

He wanted to take it back, but at the same time, he realized
if they were going to try for . . . coffee or anything else, shadows came with it.

Now she was smiling at him again and he wanted to see her
smile, then laugh.

And he wanted to kiss her.

The longer he sat there, the more he wanted to kiss her. The
more she *breathed*, the more he wanted to close the distance
between them and cup her face in his hands, take that wide,
lush mouth with his and just . . . have.

Just have.

Take.

Give.

Because he knew he'd give in to temptation if he kept staring at her, he dragged his attention away and focused on the
pigeons gathering near one of the windows.

"It's not the public thing that bothers me, really." He rubbed
the back of his neck. "I'm not too crazy about doing anything
where I live, just . . . well, it feels weird. But up until recently
it was more of a matter that I just . . . can't. Couldn't."

"Clayton."

Her understanding, so softly spoken, was just another tug
toward her, another strand in a tangled web he could feel spinning around them both. Reaching up to tug his sunglasses off,
he dropped them on the concrete and rubbed at his eyes.
"Yeah. Clayton. We don't have family here. My family would
come if I called—man, my mother would be *overjoyed*. She'd
probably do backflips. And Travis—my twin—he comes out
as often as his job lets him. The others would help if they

could . . ." Then, abruptly, he laughed. "Maybe not Seb. He's a good kid, but he's not quite ready to handle the responsibility of taking care of *himself*, much less my son."

"I have to say this, just once." Ressa puffed out her cheeks and then heaved out a heavy breath. "I can't believe I'm sitting here next to a guy who refers to *Sebastian Barnes* as *a good kid*. Man, Mama Ang practically drools when she sees his name anymore. But he's a *good kid*."

Trey slid her a sly look from the corner of his eye. "Well, as long as it's her drooling, and not you. Gotta say, I'm not too fond of the idea of you drooling over my baby brother."

"Well." She winked at him. "He's prettier, but I think you're way sexier."

"Seb is pretty," Trey agreed. "And he knows it. Any woman who takes him on is going to have to be prepared to fight him for counter space and her fair share of time in front of the mirror."

The low laugh that escaped her settled down low in his belly, adding fuel to the fire that was already licking through him. Sliding a little closer, he reached up, toyed with one of the fat, round curls spilling down her neck and shoulders. "Vain. A man that pretty is going to be vain. I'm not surprised."

"Oh, he's a peacock," Trey said, nodding. "But Zach's just as pretty as Sebastian is. He's not a peacock."

"Zach . . . he's got some pretty ink."

"Ressa . . ."

You're getting ready to complicate things. It was a resounding echo in the back of his head, one that echoed and echoed and echoed as he lifted a hand to cup her cheek.

"Yeah?"

Dipping his head, he pressed his lips to the corner of her mouth. "Quit talking about my brothers. Matter of fact, don't think about them . . . forget what they look like."

"And why would I want to do that?" She murmured the words against his mouth.

"Because I'd rather you just think about me." He kissed her then.

She opened for him on a moan, her mouth parting as his lips covered hers and he had to do that, too, take advantage and slide his tongue inside, tasting vanilla, coffee . . . and under that, *her* . . . the taste that had haunted him for the past five weeks.

How did one night turn into such an addiction?

He didn't know, but it had.

Before he could forget where he was, he pulled back, lingering long enough to press his brow to hers. "You're getting under my skin, Ressa Bliss. How are you doing this?"

Then he settled back as she blinked at him, her eyes wide, dazed.

He lifted a hand, stroked one finger over her lower lip. Then a slow smile curved her lips, and that smile had his blood pumping hot in his veins. And the look in her eyes— damn— that look, all lazy and lambent. He wanted to bite her, strip her naked, taste her everywhere he hadn't—

"You're under my skin, too, honey." Then she sighed and looked away. "And that wasn't something I was at all prepared for."

He shifted on the brick wall, his erection becoming a painful—and noticeable—problem.

"So. Tell me about the other two."

Half-formed thoughts faded into nothingness as he slid her a look. "Huh—oh. Well, there's Zane. He's the oldest." He studied his coffee for a long moment. "He does photography . . . I think there's going to be a wedding soon."

"A wedding?"

He crooked a grin at her. "Yeah. Keelie . . . she works with Zach, the one with the pretty ink . . ." He gave her a playful snarl and she swatted him. "Zane's been waiting—he does that. He watches. He waits. She finally figured it out. I hear they are like tripping over themselves happy in love."

"That's . . . sweet," Ressa said after a moment. "Are you happy for them?"

"Yes." He said it without hesitation, without reservation. "Zane's always been that way. He'll stand there, watch things, wait for things . . . he never really chased them and sometimes I wondered why, but I guess he had his own timetable. I don't know Keelie as well as some of the others—I can't travel to Tucson as often as some of them can, so I haven't really gotten to know her that well, but if she makes Zane happy, that's all I need to know."

"And then there's the other one . . . your twin, right?"

"You've been reading up on us." He chuckled and shrugged. "You probably noticed you didn't find much about him. He's the odd one. Went into accounting."

"You say that like he decided to stitch together cat skins for clothing and yodel naked on the streets while eating nothing but haggis and drinking only rotgut." The glint in her eyes said she was clearly amused.

Trey laughed, shaking his head. "Well, accounting confuses me." Then he shrugged. "I guess it shouldn't seem so out of place. Mom was going to be a lawyer. Dad dealt with stocks before he retired. The rest of us . . . actors, photographer, writer . . . and there he is, crunching numbers."

"He's probably got the more stable occupation." She wrinkled her nose. "And the most boring one. If it makes him happy . . . ?"

Happy. He shrugged. "Yeah. That's the bottom line." Which was the problem, really. Travis *wasn't* happy, but it wasn't like Trey could pull him out of it or anything, could he?

"You're closest to him, aren't you?"

He just nodded.

"I always wondered what it would be like, having a sister." She slid him a look. "I've got cousins—none of them are close except Kiara. That's Neeci's mama and we don't have an easy relationship. What's it like, having a big family like that? Were you ever lonely?"

"There are always times when somebody can *feel* alone," he said softly. "But when you've got a family like mine—and it's not the size of the family, really, but being close—all you have to do is pick up the phone. Knock on a door. I didn't always knock when I should have, didn't pick up the phone."

She linked her hand with his and for a long moment, both of them were quiet.

It was an easy quiet—he liked it. He could see the two of them sitting just like that. And his mind started to spin up scenarios of maybe her sitting in the living room with him, just like this . . .

"I'm going to have to head out soon."

Ressa's low voice cut into the hazy fantasy winding into

place in his head and he cleared his throat. He was messed up. He was here with a beautiful woman—one he'd already slept with, tasted, touched, a woman he wanted like mad—a woman who'd then brushed him off.

Complicated.

Yeah.

That pretty much summed it up.

Still, it would be worth it. Whatever her complications were, whatever hurdles they might have, he thought it would be worth it.

"I . . ."

"Look . . ."

They both spoke at once, and he grimaced, looked away.

"I want to see you again," he said when she stayed silent. "Often. A lot. I'm going to be blunt and say it flat out—I want to see you in my bed. I want to take you out on a date, I want to press you up against the nearest hard surface and kiss you until we're both senseless. I want to take you and Clay . . ." Then he paused, grinned. "Your cousin. Neeci? Her, too. We can go to the beach and they can run each other wild while we take it easy. I want all of that."

She opened her mouth, her eyes going hazy.

Trey pressed his thumb to her mouth. "But I've already told you I wanted more with you. So . . . we've had coffee. Now you decide if we try for anything more or if you'd just rather everything stay in the past." He paused and then added, "But if that's what we're doing, then you need to know . . . I'm not trying to be an ass, but I don't want to pretend like we're friends from here on out, either. I can't be near you without wanting you and I'm not going to pretend otherwise."

She caught his wrist, tugged it down.

"And if those complications I told you about turn out to be more complicated than you thought?" she asked softly, nerves dancing across her face.

Something inside him unknotted. Relaxed. He felt like he could breathe deeper, see clearer. "Unless you've got the Russian mafia out after you, then I'll deal."

"No . . ." She leaned in and dropped her head against his shoulder. She smoothed a hand down the shoulder of his polo, like there was some imaginary wrinkle. If there was, he was going to put in a dozen more to just have her touching him again. "No mob bosses running me down, Trey."

"Then maybe you can go ahead and give me your phone number." The way her mouth curved up ever so slightly was going to drive him nuts. "Maybe we can . . . I don't know . . . grab coffee again. Or dinner."

"I love both."

"What's up with you?" Farrah eyed her suspiciously as she came into the employee area.

"What? Nothing. Hey . . . why are you here?"

Immediately, she knew she'd been a little too jumpy with her answer, but she tried to skate by anyway, feigning a look of wide-eyed innocence, one that fooled nobody. Farrah made that clear by the way she crossed her arms over her chest and started to tap a tiny foot.

"Oh!" Ressa focused on the glittery, strappy silver sandal. "Where did you get those? They are so *cute*!"

"Zappos. Now let's get back to the subject. You . . ." Farrah walked closer, circling around Ressa with narrowed eyes. Lips pursed, she raked a gaze over Ressa and then stopped in front of her, planting all five foot one inch of herself in the middle of Ressa's path. "What is up with you?"

"Not a thing." Ressa smoothed a hand back over her hair and then glanced down at her clothes. She'd spent the past thirty minutes or so wandering around, trying to clear her head because being with Trey muddled it. Muddled it enough that she'd lost track of time and had almost been late.

She'd ducked into the bathroom before she'd hurried in here, worried the wind or the heat or . . . something . . . would show on her face, but with a smile that seemed to be perpetually locked in place, she thought she looked fine.

Apparently she'd missed something. "I swung by the coffee shop and had a panini and iced coffee before I came in. I don't have spinach between my teeth or anything, do I? What brings you out this way?"

It wasn't *completely* a lie. She'd eaten the panini on her way in, and now she was worried she *might* have something trapped between her teeth.

"No." Farrah raked her with a rueful look. "You look gorgeous as always. You look like you've been . . . son of a bitch. Did you hook up with somebody last night?"

"What? No." Ressa edged around Farrah and shoved her purse into the locker she'd been assigned. "You do remember that I have a five-year-old child living with me, right?"

"Okay. This morning. Did you hook up with some beautiful piece of man flesh this morning after you dropped her off? Oh! Hey, how was my baby's first day?"

Beautiful piece of man flesh—Ressa made the lightning adjustment as Farrah's mind jumped from one track to the other. "I think she'll do fine." *That's good. Focus on Neeci.* "The first day, she's worried . . . wishes Kiara was here."

Farrah rolled her eyes. "Sooner or later, she'll realize how lucky she is that her mama *isn't* here." Then, with a lift of one slim brow and a sly grin, Farrah's mind shifted track once more.

Back to the beautiful piece of man flesh, and yeah, that described Trey rather well, although he was so much more.

And they didn't *hook up*. They'd done that already.

"No. I didn't have a hook up this morning," she said tartly, looking back at Farrah over her shoulder. "I dealt with Neeci, went and had coffee, some food. Came here. Fascinating morning."

Farrah didn't look like she entirely believed her. But she shrugged. "Okay, girl. If you say so. Anyway . . . I took half a day off. I have to go get fitted—"

"*Shit!*" Ressa squeezed her eyes shut. "That's today."

"Yep." For a moment, Farrah's face all but glowed. "Just a few more of these things and then . . ."

Farrah sighed happily. Ressa would have rolled her eyes at the almost rapturous look of bliss on her friend's face, but in truth, she was more than a little jealous. "I want pictures," she said.

"I know, I know. I just wanted to remind you that *your* fitting is in tomorrow. And I've been told to tell you—*eat.*"

"Yes, *ma'am.*" Ressa didn't need the pointed look to drive

the comment home again. She'd lost a few pounds between the original fitting and when she'd gotten to try the dress on again after the hem had been brought up.

The cause for the change in her weight? A total lack of appetite. Brought on by lack of sleep, a terminal case of lust, and loneliness, all of which started in New Jersey. And now she was worried it might start all over again.

"Don't worry," Ressa said with a game smile. "I'll fit in the da—the dress."

Farrah studied her, and it was too hard to hold her friend's eyes so Ressa busied herself putting on the lanyard that held her ID card and checking her hair.

After a few more seconds, Farrah just sighed. "Okay, honey. I'll see you tomorrow night, right?"

"You bet." She listened to Farrah's heels clicking on the floor. Farrah paused by the door.

"I'll call tonight, okay? Send you pics and we can giggle over the dress," Farrah said. The door squeaked as she went to open it.

Ressa squeezed her eyes shut. "Sounds like a plan."

"Perfect . . . so . . . what's his name?"

"Tr . . ." She clamped her mouth shut. Then, slowly closing the locker, she looked back at Farrah, standing with her back against the door. "You're a sneaky bitch, you know that?"

The other woman looked unfazed. "A girl only gets *that* look in her eye when she's met somebody. Now, let's get to the good part. What's his name?"

Swiping a hand down her skirt, Ressa nibbled her lower lip for a second. Then she just plunged ahead.

"Trey Barnes."

For a second Farrah gaped at her.

Then she started to laugh. "Oh, okay. That's funny. That's . . ."

She stopped laughing when she caught sight of the look on Ressa's face. "Wait a second . . . you're *serious*?"

"Yeah." Ressa braced herself.

"*The* Trey Barnes. As in the sexy motherfucker I'd die to get my hands on?"

"You're getting married," Ressa pointed out, trying to ignore the curl of possessiveness that tugged at her.

"I mean if I *wasn't*." Farrah waved a hand through the air like that was just a given. She glanced around the lounge and then moved closer, eyes narrowed by retro-chic glasses. "I thought you had trouble getting him to talk to you."

"Ah . . . it wasn't that. Exactly." Ressa blew out a breath. "I need to get out there. The manager here isn't quite as laid back as my old boss." She used the most charming smile she had in her arsenal.

And it didn't do jackshit.

"Oh, no, you don't," Farrah said, catching Ressa by the elbow. It would have been funny—Farrah barely topped five feet and soaking wet, she might weigh one hundred pounds. Ressa, on the other hand, was five eight and although she wasn't constantly on the diet lingo, she hadn't been below one seventy since high school and she generally had to fight to keep it at one eighty.

While Ressa might outweigh and outreach her, there was nobody who could out stubborn the other woman.

"What?" Exasperated, Ressa tugged her arm free and propped her hands on her hips. "What more do you want to know? Look, I told him you'd like to get him in here, although I don't know if it will happen. He's not big on doing anything where he lives. That's a huge part of it. He's pretty private. I wouldn't call him shy, but . . ."

"I don't care about that!" Farrah's eyes rounded and she advanced on Ressa, poking a finger at her. "You're *seeing* him and you didn't tell me."

"I'm not . . ." She stopped, blew out a breath. "We're not. Not exactly."

"What's *that* mean?" Farrah gaped. "Son of a *bitch*—are you *sleeping* with him? Please, please, please tell me you did—tell me you fucked him and that he can fuck a woman the way I think he can."

"Would you drag your mind out of the gutter?" Huffing out a breath, she turned away so Farrah wouldn't see the answer in the rush of color in her cheeks. "It means we're not seeing each other *yet*."

It wasn't a lie. And she hadn't answered Farrah's other question, either.

It worked. She hoped. Moving over to the watercooler, she

got herself a cup of water she really didn't need and took a sip before looking back at her best friend. "We . . . well, we talked a lot in New Jersey." It wasn't a lie. Not really. They'd just talked a lot in between bouts of amazing sex. "But I . . . I didn't want to try to pursue it. He . . . did you know he was married?"

Farrah's eyes softened. "Honey, his wife *died*. A while ago. Didn't you know that?"

"It's not like I'm one of the Trey stalkers on that Pinterest page. I don't follow his every move the way you do." Although she had to admit she had a certain interest in some of his moves now. Very specific moves. Mouth suddenly dry, Ressa took another sip, focused on the wall in front of her. "And yes, I know that. *Now.* He was still wearing his wedding ring."

"Oh." Farrah glanced toward the door as voices drew near. "Oh, sweetie."

"Look, it's not . . . I don't think he's still hung up on her. It was rough when she died. She was pregnant—he almost lost his boy, too." Then she shook her head. "This isn't a good time to be talking."

"No, it's not. Look, I know it was bad. You were . . . well, that was back when things got bad with Kiara—you had your hands more than full. It was a big splash in the news around here for a while. Anyway. So, forget me calling. I'm coming by after my fitting. We'll talk." Farrah nodded. "I'll grab Chinese. You grab a bottle of wine."

Ressa winced. "I don't know . . ."

"Are you going out with him tonight?" Farrah cocked a brow.

"No, but . . ."

"Then I'm coming over. Because we are not *done.*"

Trey had made the shift from being a night owl to learning how to focus in the morning once it was clear that afternoons were a bust, because that was when Clayton *really* seemed to want to make the most chaos and noise imaginable. His son might have started school, but he suspected nights and afternoon were going to be just as manic as before.

Half lost in a world that involves silken skin and soft sheets and shaky sighs—a book, not a dream about Ressa—he didn't hear the first time the doorbell rang, or the second.

But by the third, when he was trying to convince the hero and the heroine they couldn't have sex . . . *yet* . . . the jangling noise managed to cut through his concentration.

Scowling, he eyed the clock, looked back at the open project on his computer.

His hands were numb at this point.

He'd managed to get a couple thousand words written on the next Forrester book. But he didn't want to go answer the damn door.

The bell rang again.

With a sigh, he shoved back, a little off-kilter as he realized how late it was. He'd set the alarm on his phone—not that he expected he'd ever lose track of time that much, but he wanted to make sure he was on the road well before school let out.

It was after one. He had to leave in another fifty minutes.

That much time had passed. The silence in his house was almost eerie.

He wasn't used to that much quiet in the middle of the day. By now, there should have been at least a hundred demands to go swimming, to go to the beach, to go to the Nauticus—or even just riding his bike—something.

But all day long, it had been quiet.

Muscles in Trey's neck were stiff, letting him know how much time it had been since he'd moved, and he rolled his head from one side, to the other.

The doorbell had fallen silent and he breathed out a sigh of relief. Nadine. Had to be. The only other people who'd hang that long were his brothers and they'd call. Besides most of them had keys. Except Seb, and he'd had one; it had just gotten lost.

He peered through the Judas hole and then groaned silently, resting his head against the polished wood.

It *was* Nadine.

And she was still out there, busily writing on a little notebook.

He opened the door, because in the back of his mind, he could hear Ressa's voice. The longer he waited . . .

She jumped as the door swung inward but he forced himself not to apologize, not to invite her in. He just smiled. "Hi, Nadine."

"Oh . . ." Her hand fluttered up to her throat, toying with the necklace there. "Trey, you . . . you startled me. I didn't think you were home. You took so long to answer."

"I was working," he said, shrugging. "I get caught up and don't hear the door."

A nervous laugh escaped her. "Of course." She stood there, her hands clasped at her waist, an expectant look on her face.

Guilt gnawed at him. That vague sensation of something closing around him rose inside him. Refusing to give in to the guilt, he pushed his hands into his pockets. "Can I help you with something?"

"What? . . . Oh." Her shoulders slumped, so very slightly, and then she brushed her hair back. "I wanted to know if you needed anything. I thought I could pick up Clayton and take care of dinner for you." She gave him a slow smile. "You could get more work done . . . maybe tell me what you've been working on lately. We don't talk much anymore, do we?"

She's in love with you—

The sound of Ressa's words danced in the back of his mind and Trey fought the urge to shut the door and just disappear. Instead, he squared his shoulders. "Afraid that won't work out, Nadine," he said, shaking his head.

"Silly me." With a tentative smile, she eased closer. "I forgot you said you had plans. Maybe tomorrow?"

She reached out to touch his arm.

He caught her hand in his, squeezed gently. "No." Carefully, he nudged her hand back down. Then, forcing himself to hold her eyes, he shook his head. "Nadine, I don't know what you think you see here, and it's not that I don't appreciate the intent, but . . . Clayton and I aren't ever going to be anything more than neighbors to you."

Her dark green eyes widened and judging by the flash of hurt there, he realized Ressa had been right. "Trey . . ." She reached out again.

This time, he stepped back. "Nadine, you've helped out a lot the past few years . . ."

"You just need more time," Nadine said, her voice tremulous and soft. She took a step closer, then another.

He held firm where he was now. She was five feet nothing and if he gave her a chance, she'd back him right inside the house and it would take forever to get her to leave.

"No. I don't need more time to understand what's going on here." Once more, he felt like he was kicking a puppy dog, but he flattened, hardened his tone because if he kept using that soft, gentle one, she'd hear what she wanted, not what he had to say. "Nadine, you're a nice lady. You're my neighbor and you've been helpful in the past . . . but that's . . . that's it. There's nothing else between us. There's not going to be."

"But . . . but . . . we kissed!" She half shouted it as she stood there, and suddenly, that sweet expression fell away. Her hands balled into fists. "We kissed and we've seen each other every day and you made me think it could be more. You can't tell me there's nothing there."

"Yes, I can." It was easier even, to look at her, now that she wasn't twisting her hands and looking all around like some shy, nervous girl hiding along the wall at a dance. "My head was a mess for a long while after Aliesha died. I was lonely. We went out one time, and yeah, we did kiss. Once. Yes, we see each other . . . We live next door to each other. But . . ."

He stopped, staring at her for a long moment. Then softly, he said, "You're a friend, Nadine. But that's all you're ever going to be."

"Why?" Nadine asked and her voice broke a little. Her eyes were wild and she still had her little hands closed into fists, banging the right one on her thigh. "If . . . I mean . . . haven't I been good to Clayton? Don't I try to take care of you? I can do better."

This sucks, Trey thought miserably.

She moved closer and rested a hand on his chest. "I can be *whatever* you want."

Her hand slid lower.

He caught it, blood rushing up the back of his neck.

"The only thing I want you to be is a friend, Nadine. I'm sorry."

"No . . . no . . . no . . . you don't mean that. You don't. You . . ." She jerked her hand away and pressed it to her lips, tears welling in her eyes.

Aw, hell . . .

He felt himself lifting a hand, helpless against that misery. Even though that sensation of being trapped started to settle in—

But before he was even close to touching her, she spun around and stumbled away, half tottering on the heels she always seemed to wear. He swore as she bumped into the railing of the porch and he went to catch her arm.

"Don't touch me!"

She jerked away with a venom that chilled him.

Slowly, he let her go, his fingers uncurling.

"Go ahead," she said, her voice warbling. "Throw me away. But nobody else will ever love you like I do. I would have done anything for you."

She gave him one last, accusing look and then headed over to the house next door.

Trey closed his eyes and when he heard the door slam, he dropped down to sit on the top step, resting his head on his fisted hands.

Chapter Sixteen

Trey was ready for two things. A burger and some quiet.

He would have thought he had all the silence he could handle during the day. Kindergarten wasn't anything like the two-day preschool deal Clayton had done at a local church for the past two years. That had been for two hours and that was it.

But today, Clayton had been gone from morning until midway through the afternoon and those hours in between had been abnormally quiet. Oh, he'd gotten plenty of writing done, but he just wasn't used to that sort of . . . quiet.

Now there was anything *but* quiet.

Clayton hadn't stopped chattering since he'd buckled himself into his booster seat in Trey's truck.

Now, as he listened to Clayton talk about how he and Neeci *both* hated eggs, how they *both* hated lima beans and how they *both* loved peanuts but couldn't stand those little skin things, he thought that maybe burgers were just the ticket. Burgers. On the grill. Where Clayton could swim while Trey grilled and at least got some remnant of quiet.

"Dad! Isn't it funny how we both hate eggs *and* lima beans?"

"Nah." He forced a smile. "It just means you're smart people. I mean, *I* hate eggs and lima beans."

Clayton laughed and went to launch into yet another discussion about how Neeci lived with her cousin and how she never got to see her mama, and how she sometimes spent the night with her grandma and how funny it was that her cousin was Miss Ressa.

The words were tripping out of him so fast, Clayton barely had time to catch his breath before yet another five-minute ramble.

"Okay, man. How about you go put up your backpack?" he asked, interrupting Clayton during those few seconds he paused to breathe.

"But . . ." Clayton looked down and stared at it.

He'd been unpacking it for about the past twenty minutes.

Trey might be new at the school thing, but he was positive it shouldn't take that long.

"But?"

"I wanted to show you my schoolwork."

Realizing this was going to take as long as Clayton could let it take, he tapped his watch. "Five minutes, then the backpack goes up."

Clayton gave him a wide grin and then shoved his hands back into the backpack, coming out with more stuff than Trey thought he could have accumulated in one day at school. "Some of this is yours," Clayton announced, displaying a stack of paper with pride. "You gotta sign it and stuff."

Figures. You think the schoolwork is done when you leave school. He moved to the kitchen table and took the packet, absently pulling a pair of glasses from his pocket. Once he had them on, he skimmed through it. *Classroom rules, room parent . . .*

Man.

"Look!"

A piece of paper with Clayton's characteristic scrawl was shoved in front of him. "I write my name already. Some of the kids can't."

"It's not a competition, Clay," he said, but he smiled at the lopsided name and address written on the ruled paper. Below it was what Trey assumed was their house, with flowers in front of it. There were two stick figures, one taller than the other.

"That's us." Clayton hugged Trey's waist and pointed at the stick family. "Me and you." Then he sighed. "A bunch of other people had a mom and dad and brothers and sisters. Some had dogs or cats. But it's just us."

Trey smoothed a hand down Clayton's sunny hair. "It's not just us, kid." Putting the drawing down, he boosted Clayton up. "You've got a huge family, one that loves you just as much as I do. You got Grandma and Grandpa, all your uncles. Uncle Travis is here so much, he might as well move in."

"Yeah." He sighed softly and tucked his head against Trey's shoulder. "But it's not really the same. I want a mom."

Trey closed his eyes.

"Neeci has a mom. But she never sees her."

Rubbing his knuckles up and down Clayton's back, Trey started to rock him, like he had years back. "Sometimes it happens that way, kid."

"Why? If I had a mom, I'd see her all the time."

"I know." He pressed a kiss to Clayton's temple. Then he lifted his head, waited until Clayton's eyes swung up to meet his. "I have to tell you something, though. Now I don't know what's going on with Neeci, and I'm going to ask—man to man—that you respect her privacy. You know how important privacy is, we talk about it a lot. If she wants to tell you, that's fine. Respect it, though, and don't go telling friends at school." He thought of the grim, sad look he'd seen in Ressa's eyes the few times she'd mentioned her cousin. There was a story there, all right, and it wasn't a happy one. He lifted a hand and stroked it across Clayton's head. "Some people don't make good parents. I don't know if that's what's going on with Neeci. You don't say that to her, or anybody else, you hear me?"

Eyes solemn, Clayton nodded. "Aunt Abby had a bad mom."

Instinctively, Trey locked his jaw. Forcing himself to relax, he studied his son's face. "Where did you hear about that?"

"I heard her talking to Grandma once. She was upset. Her mom had called—yelled at her because she was marrying Uncle Zach and not that sumbitch who'd dumped her."

Trey closed his eyes. *Sumbitch*.

Well, that described Abby's former fiancé well enough. "Two things, Clay. That word you just used, don't use it again—"

"What word? Sumbitch?"

"Yeah." He nodded. "That one. It's a bad word and we don't use it. Abby only used it because . . . well. You're mostly right. Her mom wasn't a very good mom and the guy who dumped her wasn't a good guy, either. You're too young to know about this, but you're not wrong. We are *not* going to talk about this, you hear? I just . . ."

With too-old eyes, Clayton said, "If Neeci might have a bad mom, you want me to know why she might talk about her, and maybe that's why she has this sad-mad look in her eyes."

"Exactly. If she wants to talk, then be a friend." He leaned in and pressed a kiss to Clayton's brow. "I told you not to come home smarter than me."

"I get sad-mad, too, Daddy," Clayton whispered. "Because I don't have my mom."

"I know. I get the same way sometimes, Clay." As much as he hated it, Trey wasn't surprised Clayton had noticed that look in the girl's eyes. He had, too, and his son had always been sensitive to that sort of thing.

"Now . . . you gave me your schoolwork—and mine—so go put up your backpack, and then take a look and see if you can figure out what you're going to wear tomorrow."

With a quick pat on the kid's rump, he sent Clayton off. At the arched doorway, Clayton paused and looked back. "Dad . . . do you think Miss Ressa's pretty?"

Trey ran his tongue across the inside of his lip. "Why are you asking? You think you're going to ask her on a date?"

"No." Clayton giggled. "She smelled really good though. I thought she was really pretty, too. And you smiled at her. A lot. It wasn't like that look you get with Miss Nadine."

Then Clayton took off. Trey didn't wait another second. He snagged some sweet tea out of the fridge.

With the echo of Clayton's voice ringing in his ears, he took a slow drink and tipped his head back, staring up at the ceiling.

After another minute, he took one more drink, then another.

Leaning back against the counter, he decided it had been one hell of a day already.

He thought of Ressa's number, saved into his phone—and the not particularly great picture he'd found on Facebook of the panel they'd done. He hadn't been snooping. Somebody had posted pictures of the panel to his Facebook page and she'd just happened to be in one of them—it wasn't a great picture, her face averted, hair half obscuring her face, but it was the only one he had.

He had that picture in his phone, with her phone number.

He was going to wait until tonight.

Then he'd call her.

He didn't know just what was going to come of it . . . but he'd call her.

For now, though, he studied the stack of papers waiting for him on the table and scowled. Brooded. Debated.

Then he flipped them facedown.

He'd go over all that mess later . . . after he took a few more minutes of the relative quiet.

"Spill."

Legs crossed, skirt hiked up to her thighs, Farrah chowed down on chow mein and waited.

"You're so subtle," Ressa said, shaking her head. "I just love how you work up to these things."

"Screw subtle. Spill." This was spoken around a mouth full of noodles and punctuated with a pair of chopsticks jabbed her way.

Ressa picked up her wine and took a long swallow, bracing herself. As she lowered it, she said, "Don't go getting all excited about this. I don't know just what is going on right now . . . it might not be anything."

She picked up a piece of crab Rangoon but instead of eating it, she just plucked it apart. "So . . ."

Just how did she say this?

"Son of a bitch."

She looked up.

"You slept with him."

Ressa winced.

"You *did*. You went and slept with him," Farrah said. She put down the box of carryout and leaned forward, speculation on her face. "Didn't you?"

Ressa caught her lower lip between her teeth for a second, then she shrugged. "There wasn't really a whole lot of sleeping."

"Don't tell me that." Farrah drained her glass of wine and grabbed the bottle, giving herself a refill. "Considering your answer, I'm going to assume he *does* fuck as beautifully as I'd have hoped."

"Ah . . ." Ressa felt her mouth going dry as she remembered the way his mouth had felt moving over her, his hands—his body. *All* of him. "Yeah. You can assume that."

"Details." Farrah sat back down on the couch and leaned forward, eyes wide, laughing.

"No!" Ressa glared at her. In self-defense, she popped a piece of the mutilated crab Rangoon in her mouth and chewed. As she was chewing, her belly let out a yowl, reminding her just how long it had been since that panini.

With her appetite kicking in, she reached for her dinner of General Tso's chicken and a set of chopsticks. "You'll have to do your sexual gossiping with somebody else. But yeah, we slept together in Jersey—the last night. I figured . . ."

She trailed off and popped a bite of chicken into her mouth. Acutely aware of Farrah's watchful eyes, she shrugged. "I figured that was it. It was great, but . . ." She let the words trail off, unwilling to go into details about everything else.

Farrah was one of the few people who knew most of Ressa's secrets. And because Farrah loved her, she didn't care. But she wouldn't understand.

"But what?" Farrah asked softly.

"Well . . ." Keeping her head tucked, she shrugged. "A lot of things. The . . . his ring."

Yeah. That was a good cover-up.

"Ohhhh . . ." Farrah nodded. She nipped a bite of noodles from her chopsticks. "If he's still wearing his ring, honey . . . well, that's a mess waiting to happen. You might want to check things now. That can't lead to anything but trouble."

"He already took it off." She frowned and poked at her rice.

"What does that matter?" Farrah's expression was troubled. "I know that look in your eyes . . . you're already falling. You don't need to be falling for a guy who's still carrying a torch for his dead wife."

"I don't think he's still pining for her." How did she explain this? Yeah, the ring was an issue, but there was something powerful between her and Trey. "I get a feeling that ring was just as much of a security blanket for him as anything else."

She stopped and shook her head. "No, not even that. It was a shield. I think he uses it to keep people at a distance—women, at a distance."

"I guess that could make sense." Farrah's voice was neutral. Ressa looked up.

"Honey . . ."

"Stop worrying." Ressa didn't know what Farrah was dancing around, but whatever it was, she just wanted her to get it over with. "You don't have to baby me, okay?"

"I can't help it." Farrah wrinkled her nose. She took her time over another bite of noodles and then put the box down. "Listen, she was young. So was he. I think I read once that they'd been together since their first year in college—they just hit it off. And if she died right after the baby was born—"

"During," Ressa said, her voice soft. "She had to have a C-section and she died during the surgery. Clayton . . ."

She stopped as Farrah's eyes widened.

Oh, she hadn't gotten around to explaining that part, had she?

"Clayton . . . *what*?"

Wincing, Ressa said, "I didn't tell you about that, huh?"

"No, you did *not*!"

"Ah. Yeah." She put her food down and got up, taking only her wine as she started to pace. "Well. It turns out that he's actually been coming to your library for a while. Isn't that funny?"

Seconds ticked away. Finally, Farrah said, "Are you telling me that Mr. Tall and Tattooed, the daddy of that adorable little boy who just about broke your heart is *Trey Barnes*?"

"Well." Ressa shrugged. "We thought he looked familiar, right?"

Farrah all but wilted back against the couch. "I can't take this. Please. Just . . . I think I'm going to faint."

"Let me just go get my smelling salts." Ressa understood, though. She had to fight the urge to toss back the plum wine like it was two-dollar whiskey. "Now stop being so dramatic."

She huffed out a breath. "Clayton . . . he almost died. I read about what happened to his wife—there was a drunk driving accident. Apparently it almost killed his son, too. After all of that, I think it just made him all but shut down."

Farrah got up to pace. "The baby was born early," she said after a minute. She gave Ressa a sheepish smile. "You know how obsessed I get with these things. Anyway . . . I know he all but lived at the hospital for a while. I think his son was sick a lot."

"Makes sense," Farrah said, shaking her head. "His wife dies, he almost loses his son. The baby didn't even leave the hospital for the first couple of months, I don't think. He went from being this super social guy to a recluse. That poor guy. Ressa, he had the media hounding him non-stop. It got to the point where his twin was even running interference half the time, pretending to be him just so he could get in and out of the hospital without people harassing him. And when the media figured out what they were doing, they gave him even *more* grief . . . they came up with these bullshit stories about how he couldn't really be grieving if he and his twin were playing games with the media."

"Assholes," Ressa muttered. She couldn't imagine how hard that must have been for him. And yeah, it made sense why he'd gone into the hermit mode.

Then Farrah came back to her, held out her hands.

Ressa accepted them, a knot swelling in her chest.

"I get it." Farrah's eyes were dark and kind and gentle, so full of understanding, it made Ressa's throat get tight. "I do— and sweetheart, if I were you, I'd be all over him. A crazy weekend with a beautiful man like that?"

"But . . ." Ressa waited.

"But . . ." Farrah squeezed her hands. "You're already twisted up about him. You were months ago, and you're just as crazy about Clayton as you are about him. What if he is still in love with her? And . . ." She bit her lip and then hurriedly asked, "And are you sure he's ready to handle everything else that comes with you?"

Ressa tugged her hands away and started to pace. She thought about the way he looked at her. The way he touched her and how everything inside her lit up, and how everything inside seemed to just *slow*—and wait. It was like she'd been waiting. Just for him.

She thought about the way his eyes lingered on her, how he stared at her as if nobody else existed.

When he looked at her, it wasn't the memory of his dead wife he saw. And he wasn't caught up in the memory of anything else either. He saw her and only her.

"I'm complicating this," she said, swearing. Then she glared at Farrah. "*We* are complicating this. We like each other. I like how I feel when I'm with him and I know he likes being with me." Then she paused in front of the mirror and added, "If nothing else, when he's with me, I know he's not seeing me as some sort of replacement. I saw pictures of her— she was like some Nordic princess. She was this tall, elegant thing, all legs and boobs and yards of ice blonde hair."

Farrah grinned and her gaze dropped to Ressa's chest. "Well, you're not short . . . and you're definitely not lacking in the curve department, Ress."

"Ha-ha." Ressa continued to study her reflection. A black woman stared back at her, her hair done in soft curls around her face, her mouth a deep wine red. The tank top she'd paired with her pajama pants had ridden up, revealing the outline of the newest tattoo design she was working on. It was a tower of books, one that threatened to topple over. It started on her hip and climbed up to just under her right breast. And when she looked in her own eyes, she saw the shadows and the insecurities she'd fought to hide for so long. "I've got tits, yeah. But he won't look at me and see Nordic anything."

After a moment, Farrah came up to stand next to her, leaning in so that her head rested against Ressa's arm. "So what do you think he sees when he looks at you?"

"I don't know."

If she knew the answer to that, this would be a lot easier.

"Are you two going out?"

"I think so."

There was a world of caution in Farrah's eyes.

"Okay . . . then answer this. If he sees *all* of you, is he going to be okay with it?"

She heard the warning. She heard the love that came with it. If she was smart, she'd pay attention to it.

The phone rang and in the time it took Ressa to grab her phone from the coffee table and see his name on the display, she decided the time to be *smart* had come and gone.

Heart hammering, she hit *talk* and lifted the phone.

"Hello?"

Chapter Seventeen

It had been so long since he'd been out on a date, Trey wasn't entirely certain he remembered how they worked.

Okay, in theory, yeah.

He could remember in *theory*.

Unlike Zane, Travis, and Sebastian, Trey hadn't ever had the revolving door thing with females. He hadn't pined for one woman for most of his life like Zach—Zach had only ever loved one woman and all the relationships he'd been in had been casual. Trey had had two serious girlfriends in high school—and then on a trip to Canada with Travis the summer after graduation, there had been this ballet dancer . . . Giselle had pretty much destroyed his mind. He couldn't recall much about their time outside the bedroom, because he doubted they'd spent much time together outside of it.

But his experience with the opposite sex started and stopped there—those three not-really-serious relationships, and then Aliesha. In all, four first dates.

He wasn't sure the first date with Giselle really counted as a date since they'd bumped into each other at a club—literally—and she'd wrapped her arms around him and pulled him onto a dance floor. From there, they'd ended up in her flat, a place that wasn't much bigger than the bathroom he had now. In that flat, he'd learned more about the female body than he had ever dreamed it was possible to learn.

Because they had totally sucked, Trey decided not to count the first disastrous dates he'd had since Aliesha's death.

It wasn't a lot of experience. Trey realized that. Maybe that was why he was almost as nervous now as he had been the day he'd shown up to take Marisol Hammonds to the junior prom—she'd been girlfriend number one and they'd been together from sophomore up until right before their senior year. That was when she realized she was more into jocks and she'd broken up with him by way of leaving a message on the answering machine. His brothers had ragged him something awful about that.

Actually, he thought he was *more* nervous now. Back then, he hadn't stood and stared stupidly at his clothes for ten minutes before finally deciding that absolutely, it was just fine to wear a button-down shirt and a nice pair of trousers.

When he realized he was second-guessing the choices again, he scowled at his reflection. *Enough already, man. Keep this up and you'll never make it out the door.*

Clayton had poked his head into the bedroom, eying him with wide, puzzled eyes. "Why are you wearing your dress-up stuff? We can't go to church. It's Friday. Did somebody die? Nobody died, did they?"

"Nobody died." The rush of questions had Trey smiling. "And no, we're not going to church, although Grandma Mona wants us to come with her to church soon. She's been asking— I just keep forgetting."

"Okay." Clayton slid inside the room and took a running leap to land on Trey's bed. "Why you wearing nice clothes?"

"Remember what I told you earlier?"

Clayton's forehead wrinkled. "The date thing. Oh, yeah. You and Miss Ressa are going out on a date." For a minute, just a minute, he forgot his concern over the dress clothes. "I knew you thought she was pretty."

"You never miss a thing, do you, pal?"

"Why you gotta wear nice clothes if you're just going to take a girl to a restaurant? Is she going to be your girlfriend? Like Keelie is Uncle Zane's girlfriend? Are you going to—"

"Let's try one question at a time," Trey suggested. Tucking his shirt in, he moved back to the closet and studied his belts. Before he could start the deliberation thing, he just grabbed one at random. It was black. His shirt was some kind of grayish blue, pants were black. The belt would work. No deliberation needed.

Turning away before he could think about it another second, he eyed Clayton. "I'm wearing nice clothes because I bet Miss Ressa will wear them and I want to do the same thing."

"Why?" Clayton crossed his legs and focused his attention on Trey. These questions—and the answers—were serious stuff, in Clayton's mind. Of course, *all* questions were serious in Clayton's mind. Even the very silly, and very strange ones.

"If she goes to the trouble of looking nice, I should do the same."

Clayton shrugged. "You should just tell her to wear jeans, then you could, too."

"Well. . . ." Trey pretended to think that over. "I guess I could, but I think Ressa would rather wear what she wants to wear."

"But then you have to wear stupid dress clothes."

"I bet Ressa won't think they are stupid." He moved to the bed and caught Clayton's nose, tugged it. "Your aunt Abby loves seeing Zach dressed up. And think about how all those magazines and TV shows go on and on about Uncle Sebastian when *he* gets all dressed up."

"Those are goofy." Clayton rolled his eyes. Then he looked down, plucked at a loose thread on his shirt. "A boy at school called me a dumb liar. I saw a poster with Uncle Sebastian on it and I said who he was and the boy said I was lying."

Trey sighed and crouched down in front of him. "You might hear that some. You know you're not lying."

"Everybody was going on and on about how awesome he was. I really know him. He's my uncle. And they laughed at me." Clayton's lip poked out.

"I'm sorry." He hugged Clayton closer, brooding. "You need to remember, though. Sebastian is your uncle—he's not a prize to brag about or anything."

"I wasn't bragging." Clayton's thin shoulders rose and fell.

"There was one girl who said her sister likes to kiss his poster—that's weird. Isn't that weird?"

"Very." Easing back, Trey ruffled his hair. "You should have seen some of the girls I went to school with and how they acted about Uncle Zach. I bet they were just as weird."

"*Girls* are weird." Clayton sniffled. Then he said, "Neeci isn't, though. Neeci is just Neeci. She believes me. She said she's never seen any of his movies, but she believes me." At that, Clayton slid Trey a sly look. "I told her I hadn't seen too many of them, either. It's not fair. He's my uncle. I should be able to see more."

"Nice try." Trey grinned. "When you're older. Besides, there's that one coming out on Blu-ray soon—you were too little to see it in the theater last summer, but we can watch it together now."

"But—"

Clayton's would-be argument was interrupted by the sound of a chime—the alarm system Travis had nagged him into installing years ago—its computerized little voice announcing. *Front door—*

"Anybody here?"

Clayton's eyes rounded and he bounced up off the bed and ran down the hall. "Uncle Travis!"

"Sounds like," Trey said. As Clayton pounded down the stairs, Trey grabbed his shoes, a pair of black leather ones—again, not giving himself any chance to deliberate.

He was halfway down the steps when he caught sight of his brother, and the worry punched a hole in him. Too thin. Too pale. Travis was even skinner than Trey was.

And if he asked what was wrong, Travis would lie through his teeth.

As though he'd heard his thoughts, Travis turned his head, met his gaze.

"Well. Look at you," Travis mused.

"Look at you." Trey told himself to ignore it. That was what he *should* do. Travis knew how to take care of himself. He'd been doing it for a long time, and Trey knew that. But right now, he looked like death warmed over. "Travis, hope you don't mind me saying, but you look like . . ."

Travis lifted a brow and glanced at Clayton who was tearing into a bag.

"Yeah." Travis shrugged. "Rough few days at work."

What in the hell are they doing? Feeding you to the lions when you don't crunch numbers fast enough?

A taut silence passed between them, as things Travis wouldn't tell, and Trey wouldn't ask, hummed in the air.

That silence was shattered by a shriek from Clayton.

"Cool!" Clayton yanked something out of the bag—it looked like a new video game. He flashed it at Trey and then tossed it down and ripped into the bag again.

Still staring at his brother, Trey moved the rest of the way down the stairs. If he let himself focus, he could catch the faintest edge, no matter how hard Travis tried to keep him out. Yeah, there it was . . . exhaustion, irritation . . . and a lingering pain. With a caustic smile, Trey asked, "So what are they making you do at work these days? Lay down on the road and let your clients drive trucks over you or what? That's about the only thing I can think of that might make you look that run-down."

"I'm fine." Travis's voice was short, almost brusque.

The hell you are. He glared at his twin and watched as Travis narrowed his eyes, glaring back. Then, because they didn't have time for it now, he shrugged. "We can talk about it later, though. You in town long?"

"Yeah. I . . ." Travis cocked his head like he was searching for the words. "I'm on leave right now—I'm between jobs at the moment. Looks like I might be moving into a consulting capacity once I go back, or at least sometime in the very near future. But for now, I'm on leave. I've been . . . sick, had to take time off."

Sick—instinctively, he went to step between Travis and Clayton even though a body wouldn't stop germs.

Travis rolled his eyes. "Relax. I'm not contagious. Not like I'd come here if I was. I'm here more for the downtime anyway."

"You didn't get fired, did you?" Trey had to admit, considering how rough Travis had looked the past few months—hell, the past few *years*—it wouldn't bother him at all if Travis ended up needing to look for another job. And *bullshit* that Travis had been sick—that wasn't what had him looking like hell.

"No. I've got a job. I'm just taking some time off—we'll re-evaluate in a few months." Travis shrugged.

Was it him or did it seem that his twin's mouth went tight at the movement? Like it hurt? Trey wasn't sure.

"You're staying here, then." Trey didn't ask.

Travis just grunted. "I was kinda looking forward to pizza and movies, but looks like you have plans."

"Daddy has a date," Clayton announced as he finished ripping the paper off a Nerf gun.

For the next breath, the only sound was the boy's desperate, determined efforts to tear the packaging open. And then, Travis lifted his head, a wide, wicked grin on his face, one that chased away the exhaustion and the irritation. "A date . . . do tell, Daddy."

"A date. In my case—and yours, it would involve social interaction with a female," Trey said. "You're familiar with the general idea, I think."

"More familiar than you are, I'd say." Travis bit his lower lip, held it there a moment as he crossed his arms over his chest. "Now why haven't I heard anything about this? Last I heard, the only woman you were interested in, things didn't exactly work out."

Feeling the creep of red as it spread up his neck, Trey shrugged. "Not much to say, just yet. I asked her out a couple days ago, she said yes. We haven't even gone out yet."

"So this is a first date."

Before Trey could respond, there was a knock at the door. Travis moved aside as Trey headed to the door. "It's the babysitter."

Travis grinned at his nephew. "A babysitter, kid? Is she pretty?"

Clayton went red. "She's a girl!"

"Well, yeah. The best ones usually are. Is she pretty?"

Clayton darted a look at the door.

Trey hesitated a minute. "She's saving for college."

"Hey, *I'm* not babysitting. I'm on vacation, man." Travis

ruffled Clayton's hair. "I want pizza, though. I'll buy. Then I'm probably going to crash early."

"But . . ." Clayton poked out his lip. "Movie? I thought you said a movie."

"We'll do that tomorrow when Dad can join us." Travis bent down and whispered something to him.

Trey heard the word *date* and *girl* involved. It made Clayton giggle.

Shaking his head, Trey opened the door to let Annabeth Hawkins in.

One thing about having his brother crash like this . . . it had taken his mind off the panic. For a few minutes at least.

Ressa whipped off the dress and tossed it on the bed with its three predecessors. The black wiggle dress was a little *too* sexy. The red polka dot one was *cute*. That was the problem. It was too *cute*. The pink square neck one was just fine . . . if he was taking her home to meet his mother.

Snarling under her breath, she stood in front of her closet, a closet *full* of clothes, too, thanks to her somewhat problematic love for shopping. She wore a black bra shot through with a red lace ribbon and a retro piece that was both girdle, garter, and panties. It was moderately comfortable, sexy as hell and it managed to smooth things down so that *if* she had gone with the black wiggle, she would have filled it out just fine.

But it was a first date and the message she was going for wasn't *Fuck me now*.

Even if that was the message she had on her mind.

Even if that was the message she'd had on her mind pretty much from the first minute she'd seen him again—well, it wasn't the *only* thought on her mind.

She had other thoughts, too. Like how much she loved his smile. And how much she missed seeing him and Clayton. And of course, the occasional worry wiggled its way in— mostly about Neeci. She was spending the night with Ressa's aunt, Neeci's "Granny Ang" and although Neeci loved Granny Ang, sometimes things didn't always go well when she didn't sleep at home.

Which meant she needed to warn Trey about a potential problem. She suspected Trey, more than most, would understand, but just the thought of it made her gut clench, and yet again she thought that maybe she should just cancel the date.

Cut and run, because she could see herself falling for Mr. Trey Barnes, in the worst sort of way.

Fall for him, then end up walking away, or crawling away, when things ended badly or she ended up battered and bruised, brokenhearted.

Coward.

But really, did it hurt to have a real date with him?

Maybe once they had that one real date, she'd realize they didn't really have that much to talk about. Sure they were combustible, but she'd had heat before.

Doubt started to niggle inside her and she went to sit down, but her gaze landed on the clock. Twenty minutes. She only had—

The phone rang. Panic grabbed her belly. He wasn't calling to cancel, was he?

If he does, I'll hurt him.

And then that bubble of panic popped as she recognized the number. With a jaded eye, she studied it, then without a blink, ignored the call.

Talking to Kiara always put her in a bad place. *Always.* She had to coach herself into going to visit her, into calling her. Sending her quick little notes wasn't possible, although she did write—there was just nothing quick about it. It took three or four days to get the right words down, the words that said . . . *I love you, but I don't want to talk about the past anymore.*

"You ought to be the one in here!" The sound of Kiara's voice, even now, still echoed in her ears. That wound was mostly scarred and it helped that Kiara had mostly come to accept the truth, but still, the rawness was still there.

The phone went silent as she moved to stand in front of the mirror.

Catching sight of the little clock she kept near her bed, she swore. Down to eighteen minutes. Her hair was done, her makeup was done, but she really should have something on when he knocked on the door.

Swearing, she grabbed a red dress off the hanger. She'd just ordered it and other than trying it on, she hadn't worn it yet. Pulling it on, she smoothed it down over her hips and went to the mirror. The embellished design of the bodice accentuated her curves there and also left her tattoos bared. She fingered it absently, half thought about wearing something with a higher neckline, even as she gave the rest of her reflection a critical look.

The nipped-in waist definitely met with her approval and the skirt flared out in a way that flattered her full hips. She looked curvy rather than frumpy—that was good. She'd been hoping that would be the effect with the dress. She'd gotten pretty good at picking out the right styles, but shopping online could still be hit or miss. The fabric worked, too.

Frowning, she turned a little, eying the embroidery on the shoulders—each shoulder featured a cheekily grinning pin-up girl.

The cut of the dress was almost conservative.

A few months ago, if somebody had told her she'd be going out to dinner with Trey Barnes, *conservative* was exactly what she would have suspected would suit him. Of course, she'd have laughed her ass off, and then gone out of her way to find something completely *not* conservative.

But with the way the dress *fit* her, the dip of the bodice over her breasts, the sassy little pin-up girls and how it exposed her tattoos . . .

"Well, it's sure as hell me," she mused.

She turned away from the mirror.

Nothing in the closet was going to work any better.

Except maybe that wiggle dress, but if she put that on, she might as well issue an invitation for him to come on in and stay awhile. She'd bought it in a mood, not too long after that weekend she'd never been able to forget. She'd been thinking about him when she'd bought it.

Thinking. Missing. Wanting.

If she put it on, she'd do nothing but think about him peeling it off.

The phone started to ring again while she was pulling on a pair of heels, but she lunged for it this time. Farrah—it was the ringtone she used for Farrah and she needed her nerves soothed. Balancing on one foot as she fought one-handedly with the strap, she answered. "Make me feel better," she ordered.

"Why?"

"Because my cousin just called and I didn't talk to her and now I feel guilty and he's going to be here soon," she said in a rush.

There was a faint pause, and then Farrah said, "Fuck her. Half the time I don't know why you even bother."

"Because it's my fault."

"No," Farrah said, her voice cold and hard. "No, it's not."

Ressa sighed. "Logically? I get that. Emotionally? Different story. Look, she's my cousin. I love her. Now, tell me something to make me stop thinking about her," she said, moving to deal with the other shoe.

"Are you ready?"

"No. I'm still buck-nekkid, with my hair in rollers and I'm shoving my face full of ice cream," she said tartly. Her belly gave a demanding grumble. Maybe ice cream wouldn't be a bad idea. Take the edge off. Ice cream made everything better, right? If she ate something now . . .

"Yeah, right. What are you wearing?"

"That red baby-doll dress I showed you a few weeks ago."

"That?" Farrah's disappointed tone did not go unmissed. "Why not that sexy black number?"

"Because that sexy black number says one thing—*Do me*. We're going out for dinner."

"Any reason you can't have both . . . him *and* dinner?" Farrah sounded sly now.

"Whatever happened to the girl who was teaching me caution a few days ago?" Ressa asked wryly.

"Well, I want you to be cautious. Don't get your heart broken. But if you can manage to have fun with him while it lasts and *not* get your heart broken? Go for it."

Fun . . . while it lasts. Odd that even thinking that way made her feel kind of funny inside. Like she was already setting herself up for a heartbreak.

"I plan on having fun. Without jumping back into bed with him the very first time we actually have a date." Rolling her eyes, she stretched out her feet, studied the shoes. They worked.

Then she glanced toward the hall, thought about that pint of ice cream she kept on hand for emergencies.

This wasn't really an emergency, though.

Sighing, she turned her back on the thought of ice cream and made herself focus.

"Talk yourself out of a bite or two of ice cream?" Farrah asked.

"Yes. Damn it." Ressa pressed a hand to her belly.

"Good. The dress fits perfectly now. Don't go getting the nervous eats, okay? We don't want to do another fitting. Now . . . how do you feel?"

"I'm nervous. I can't remember the last time I was this nervous about a date." Ressa grimaced.

"I don't think I've ever seen you this nervous about a guy."

"Oh, I've been this nervous," she said quietly.

There had been a guy. Ressa had cared about him. Enough to come clean with him about her past. He'd said he loved her. But when he learned about her past, he'd walked.

"He never really loved you. He just loved what he thought he knew," Farrah said quietly. "You ready to go that route again with Trey? What if he's the same way?"

The question had Ressa tensing. She had to focus, had to concentrate to make her muscles relax. Leaning forward, she scowled at the faint smudge in her eyeliner. She used one of the sponges to fix it before she answered. "It's not the same thing; *he's* not the same."

"If that's the case, then you see all the problems ahead of you, too, right? I mean, assuming this thing turns out to be anything . . . you know what kind of mess you could be asking for?"

"What problems?" She forced a light note into her voice. "Let me think . . . well, other than the fact that he's this hugely successful author who is still dealing with some baggage—" That was a safe way to explain it, she figured. "He's a widower with an adorable kid. Or maybe you're talking about my mess."

"There's that," Farrah said, her voice flat. "And other things. He's white, you're black."

"Really." Ressa eased away from the mirror, studying her reflection once more. "I never noticed."

"That could be a problem . . . if it got serious. That, and a couple of things. Have you thought about that?"

"Yes." Sighing, she turned away from the mirror. She didn't want to think about serious. Not yet. Not right now. "You and I both know I'd just be hiding from the truth if I said otherwise. If . . . look, if we think we've got something, his skin color isn't going to matter to me. I won't care. I don't think *he* will, either."

"It affects more than just the two of you, though. It's Neeci, it's his little boy," Farrah said quietly. Her sister had married a white guy. Her parents supported her . . . but the guy's family? They'd cut him off. It had caused some rough spots.

Rubbing her thumb along the lines of the tattoo on her chest, Ressa said, "Mama Ang won't care who I fall for, Farrah. All she ever wanted was for us to be happy."

"Yeah . . . it looks like your cousin really got *that* memo." Farrah's voice was thick with sarcasm.

"Please." Ressa closed her eyes. "Don't. Okay? Just . . ."

"I won't, honey. Although Kiara makes me crazy. Mama Ang, she tried so hard—Bruce, God bless him, *he* tried. You tried. Anyways . . . it's not just about you all, you know that. Kids change everything."

"We're talking about things that might not even be an issue. For all I know, we'll go out and we'll bore each other senseless." Plus . . . her gut started to twist, and as much as she didn't want to think about Kiara, her cousin started to creep back into her mind.

Kiara.

The things that Ressa had done her best to overcome, to move past.

But they were still a part of her.

Shit.

The doorbell rang. "I've got to go. I think he's here."

"Honey, you already know you're not going to bore each other senseless. That's why you need to be careful . . . and maybe why you should put on that black dress and get him out of your system, now. While you can still can."

Chapter Eighteen.

Trey knew what it was like to have the breath knocked out of him. Normally, he didn't associate the sensation with good things. He'd felt that way when he'd fallen out of a swing when he was a kid—when he'd gotten knocked on his ass time and again in middle school during his very, very brief interlude with school sports. Maybe he'd enjoyed basketball when it was one on one, or when he was playing with his brothers, but team sports had never been for him.

That hadn't kept Travis from nagging him into trying out for football one year. Trey had given it a shot—for that one year. During that time, he'd spent so much time getting tackled, knocked down, thrown around, that he'd ended up feeling like the ball himself.

He'd given it up—he was more for individual sports. Swimming was his thing and even then, he'd known what it was like to feel breathless—or worse, like he was drowning. Like when he'd gotten a charley horse while swimming a few times.

Then there had been the day he'd gotten the call about his wife . . . when they wheeled her in the surgery. Those unending moments when the doctor came out and told him the news.

His first look at his son, hooked up to a vent as he struggled to live.

Trey knew all about how it felt to have the air knocked out of him, but he generally associated it with pretty shitty things.

He didn't think it had once felt like this.

Ressa opened the door, standing there in the doorway with light spilling out around her while she wore a dress of red that cupped her breasts and skimmed in over a waist that dipped in and all but begged for him to curve his hands around it, before flaring out over those lush, round hips.

She'd twisted her hair up and back in a way that made him think of a time gone by—drive-ins and diners and girls in poodle skirts and muscle cars. Her mouth was once more painted red and made him think of sin and sex while his mind went blurry and hot. Her eyes were smoky, smudged, and as he tried not to gape at her, she lifted one brow, an almost-amused expression on her face.

"Hello."

He opened his mouth.

Closed it.

Then he tried again and had to clear his throat before he managed anything more than ". . . Uh . . ."

Now a smile curved her lips and she leaned against the doorway. "What's the matter, Trey? Cat got your tongue?"

It was the smile that did it.

He should have a little more class than that, more subtlety, better moves or something.

Considering what was going on with him, he should've had a little more *fear*. But as she continued to stand there, grinning at him like that, his mind just clicked off and instinct clicked on and he moved, caught her around the back of the neck.

A startled noise escaped Ressa—she might have been trying to say something but by the time his mouth slanted across hers, it became a moan and her hands curled into the lapels of his shirt as she rose up onto her toes to meet him.

It was like the past few weeks had fallen away. Nothing else mattered in that moment as he fell into a spell of lust, heat, and need. He licked at the seam of her lips and then pushed inside, craving more.

She opened for him and he banded an arm around her waist,

hauling her close. The taste of her—sweet, sweet woman and coffee—flooded him and he thought he just might go crazy if he ever had to wait so long to kiss her again.

It was the sound of a car blasting by that had him jolting to his senses. Common sense told him to put some distance between them.

His cock pulsed against the warmth of her belly and her open door beckoned them. He could have her inside there in just a few seconds . . . naked in just a few seconds more, although really, naked wasn't necessary, just tug up her skirt and . . .

Stop. Now. Before you turn into a drooling maniac.

Instead, he eased back and rubbed his lips across hers. "I've only thought about doing that a thousand times in the past six weeks."

Her lashes fluttered up. "I've only thought about you doing that a thousand times," she said, her hands still curled into the front of his shirt.

Pressing his brow to hers, he forced himself to let go. It took more willpower than he thought he had, but he was able to manage it, uncurling his arm from her waist, releasing the grip he'd had on her neck.

She was slower to let go of his shirt, smoothing the wrinkles away. Finally, he put a few feet between them and looked around. "So. This is where you live. Nice place." Then, he added wryly, "Not a bad neighborhood."

"Well, seeing as how I live about a half-mile away from you, I'd hope you like the general area." A bubble of laughter escaped her. "I kind of like it myself. You want to come inside, see the place?"

His eyes came to hers and the heat inside them almost turned her bones to mush. Ressa thought her legs would dissolve, she truly did.

Sucking in a slow breath, she casually braced her weight against the wall at her back.

If he said yes . . .

If he said yes, then she'd damn well take him inside and screw the date.

"I want to." Then Trey's lashes swept down over his eyes and he stepped back another step. "Which means I'm going to stay right here while you lock up. We're having a date. Dinner. Conversation . . ."

"Any reason why we can't do that if you come inside?"

"If I come inside, we aren't going to leave for a while." His gaze traveled down to her mouth. "We both know that." Then, her heart clenched inside her chest as he reached up and cupped her face. "I want to spend time with you . . . get to know you. That means I can't go inside."

She'd been prepared for a lot of things.

Ressa had gone on more than her share of dates. First dates weren't anything new to her. She'd had more than a few where she'd called a friend from the bathroom to help her bail out gracefully because she didn't want to hurt anybody's feelings, a couple where she just hadn't *cared* because the guy was such a roach—and a couple of times she'd had to call a friend when one of those roaches had up and decided *You think you can brush me off like that, bitch?*

And then there were the dates that had been on the verge of flipping a coin—*Should I let him pay or am I going Dutch . . .*

She had everything from hot dogs and canned sodas to gourmet meals and candlelight, but she hadn't known what to expect from Trey Barnes.

It hadn't been *this*.

Now she'd *heard* about this place, but she had absolutely no thoughts about getting inside—it wasn't even open . . . yet.

Eying the unlit sign as he held open her door, she held out her hand. "I don't know if now is a good time to point out that I am kind of hungry."

"Well, since I did tell you I wanted to take you out to dinner, I was kind of hoping you *would* be hungry." He grinned at her and shut the door as she shifted her attention back to the not-yet-opened business in front of her.

It was set in one of the older buildings and although she knew they had been working to renovate it, if she hadn't been aware of it, she'd think she was looking at the place as it had been built maybe two hundred years ago. Towering, imposing . . . and maybe slightly spooky.

Perfect for the themed restaurant that would open in the next couple of weeks.

As of now, though, the place *wasn't* open.

"So. . . ." She drew out. "If this place isn't open, how are we supposed to eat?"

Trey's grin widened a little farther. "That's easy." He slid a hand into his pocket and pulled out a key ring. "I've got an open invitation . . . and they are still doing the finishing touches on the final menu. I called earlier and asked if maybe I could come by . . . bring a date."

Ressa's mouth dropped open as she stared at the keys.

Then she swung her head around and stared up at *Chillers*.

Local media had been talking about this place for months now and with the opening getting closer, the place was being talked about more and more. She definitely had plans to come—once the madness stopped, but she'd expected that would take a while. It wasn't every day that a couple of bestselling writers got together and decided to open up a joint like this. *Chillers* wasn't being billed as a typical restaurant. It was an entertainment venue, complete with private areas for large parties; they were going to have live music, and she thought she'd seen a mention that they were already booked, as far as musical acts went, for the next six months straight.

Chillers had a bookstore as well—one that would carry mostly genre books, with a heavy focus on thrillers, suspense, and horror—but they weren't skimping on any of the others, either, and they were also going to be doing author events. The last she'd seen, they already had seven lined up over the next few months, including a local writer who was fairly popular, a big-name romance writer, and a couple of fairly well-known urban fantasy and science fiction writers.

Every time she thought about this place, the book lover in her got a little giddy.

"We get to eat here," she said slowly. Absently, she reached up to rub her fingers across her lower lip, forgetting about her lipstick. "Tonight."

"Yep. You were specifically requested to tell them exactly what you thought about the place—from how it looks, to the menu, and anything else you thought might be useful."

She slanted a look at him. "I take it that you know the owners."

"Yeah." He shrugged, jerking one shoulder up as he studied the place. Then he canted his head in her direction, a somewhat embarrassed grin on his face. "I . . . ah. Well, this is between us, but Mitch and Guff—when they were putting the plans together before they went to the bank, they talked to some friends about it. Asked some if they'd be interested in maybe offering some money for the start-up. I was—thought it would be a hell of a place to have in the area. So I've got a vested interest in seeing it take off."

This had been a good choice.

Trey had been torn between trying this or a nice little Italian place he knew about or even something more casual—a chain place somewhere close to the mall. It would be easy to keep things nice and casual if they'd gone for the Italian place or a chain restaurant.

Casual was crucial right now because if he had too much time alone with her, it was going to shatter his ability to think. Maybe even destroy his ability to talk. It had taken a lot more focus than he'd thought possible just to drive here, because it had required taking his eyes off her and he just hadn't wanted to do that.

But here, he'd have some semblance of privacy—not a lot of it because he knew Mitch Watkins and Les MacGuff weren't going to give him *that* much privacy. Not when he was bringing a date. They got together often enough—BBQs a couple of times in the summer, and both Trey and Guff had boys the same age who got along well. Neither of the men had been able to resist digging for information when Trey had called to ask about maybe coming by. With a friend.

So he'd have to put up with their nosy asses.

But that was fine, because Ressa had just turned to look at him, a smile on her face that was nothing short of delighted.

He didn't even have time to brace before she launched herself into his arms. "This has got to be the coolest thing ever," she said, her mouth moving against his neck.

It sent shivers down his spine and he closed his eyes.

Behave. It was a stringent command to his body.

But at the same time, part of him wondered *why* it was so necessary that he behave. Well, yeah, clearly it wasn't a good idea for him to push her up against the closest available surface. Or even the broad, large railing that led up to the veranda.

But really, did they have to be here?

Yes, his mind insisted.

A date.

They were having a damned date.

That didn't stop the blood from draining out of his head, from churning hot and ready, from pulsing all in one direction—straight toward his cock. To try and get his thoughts on something other than how soft she was, how good she smelled, he said, "Well, don't say that now. Guff and Mitch are raving about the kitchen crew, but for all I know, we'll go in there and everything will taste like kibble."

"I don't *care*," she said, pulling back and planting a loud, smacking kiss on his mouth. "You can fix that. Or they can. Fire the crew, hire better kitchen help. But . . . wow. I'm eating here before anybody else."

He licked his lips, tasting her on them. He was a split second from pulling her back against him, just so he could have another, longer, deeper taste.

But then she turned around and her lids drifted down low, a tiny smile bowing up the corners of her mouth. "I can already tell you, baby, that's not kibble cooking in there. I smell steak . . . and bread . . . whoa. Let's go eat."

She caught his hand and he let her tug him along behind her. He'd go pretty much anywhere she wanted at that point.

The restaurant had three floors.

She loved every single one, but thought maybe, the third floor with its dimmer lighting, the slow, smoky blues playing in through the speakers, and the semi-private booths was her favorite.

"So the first floor was more for the classics. Stoker. Poe.

Doyle." She smoothed a hand down the glossy hardwood, eying everything around her. "Second floor was geared for all the modern writers—I saw books from the big horror writers like King, as well as the major suspense and thriller writers—I loved seeing references to J.D. Robb mixed in with Lehane and Coben." There had been what looked like a body bag affixed to the wall—she wondered what some poor diner might think of that, and the toe tag used to identify the body—as well as what looked like memorabilia from the futuristic romantic suspense series, side by side with similar items that played up books from the other authors.

When she'd asked how they'd picked what authors and what books they'd gone with for the décor, they'd shrugged, then one of them had answered, *We went with who we like to read . . . who we like personally. Once word got out what we were doing, we had plenty of people offering to help out, but we went with who appealed to us.*

She liked that, knowing that they had their hands all over this place.

But she still couldn't quite figure out what was up here on three. Well aware that she had three men watching her, she stopped in the middle of the floor and tried to place the connecting theme.

The low light coming out from smoky shades.

The sultry music.

There were framed pieces of cover art and she caught sight of a few shadowboxes that had actual books in them, but they all looked old. "You already did the classics. I'm not quite sure what you were focusing on here."

"Crime noir." Guff shoved his glasses up his nose, smiled. He had a round face that was just this side of homely—but that smile made him almost beautiful. It was warm, welcoming and so genuine, she couldn't help but smile back. "That was the only thing we could figure out to make this floor work."

"Oh?" Puzzled, she gave the surroundings another look. Was she missing something?

"It was the answer, Guff, my friend. Not the only thing—the *answer.*" Mitch was louder, more flamboyant than both Trey and Guff and he flirted with anything breathing. Her, Trey, and Guff. Trey ignored him. Guff just rolled his eyes. She was hovering somewhere around amusement and irritation, but he was so good-natured with it, it was hard not to laugh, although a couple of times, she'd seen Trey give him a dark look.

"The answer to . . . ?"

"We wanted something sexy." Mitch's grin was wide and slightly wicked. "See how it's quieter up here? Even with the music blasting downstairs, you hear only an echo. Plus, the entire air of the place, it's just . . ." He paused, and then, voice lowering, he murmured, "Intimate. We thought we'd offer this for those wanting a quiet night. It's already booked solid for the next eight weeks."

"You're kidding."

He winked at her. "No. But for tonight, it's all yours, honey." Then he shot that grin at Trey. "Well, yours and Trey's. Maybe I'll send up a bottle of Glenlivet and then just lock the two of you in here."

"Very funny," Trey said, but there was an edge to his voice. "How about you go hassle your staff or align the edges of the napkins, Mitch?"

"My therapist has told me I'm not allowed to align things anymore." Mitch gave a theatrical sigh.

Guff snorted. "You probably put your therapist in therapy. Come on, Mitch. We'll send one of the servers up with menus, the whole deal. We need to see how everything is running. We have a test run next week, but you can be our very first guinea pigs as far as orders and all that goes."

It took less than sixty seconds for them to be alone.

Now, with that soulful sax wrapping around her and the dim light casting Trey's face into shadows, Ressa felt her breath catch in her chest, just looking at him.

The low lights played with the planes and hollows of his face, making his eyes look darker. A man as beautiful as he was really didn't need the extra help to look so beguiling. He took a step toward her and she spun away, moving around the decidedly smaller dining area, her heels muffled by the padded carpet. "They really have gone all out here, haven't they?"

"Yeah."

She shot him a look as he leaned his hips against one of the tables.

"Mitch . . ."

She stopped and turned to him, laughing a little. "Don't worry about him. I got his number."

"Yeah?" Trey smiled halfheartedly. "Is it tuned to the *I'm a sex-fiend* dial?"

"Nah." She decided she wanted the little booth tucked against the windows. Sliding onto the bench, she turned her gaze toward him and lifted an expectant brow, waiting.

Once he joined her, she slid her hand over the table, linked their fingers. "He strikes me as somebody who does it just to get a rise out of people."

"He does." Trey shrugged. "He's mostly harmless."

"I already figured that." With a happy sigh, she leaned back and looked around once more. "This place is something else. I can't—oh!"

"What's wrong?"

"The bookstore! I wanted to see inside!"

Now it was his turn to laugh. "Both Mitch and Guff have keys and they've all but been living here lately. Guff's wife, Zelda, too. We can get them to show us the store. I wouldn't mind seeing it myself." He paused, frowned. "They keep asking me to set up a signing there."

He was rubbing his thumb over the back of her hand, a thoughtful, almost absent caress. It sent shivery little thrills racing through her each time.

"Will you?" Her voice came out a little less than steady.

His eyes slid slowly up to meet hers, pausing to linger on her lips.

Oh . . . don't do that . . .

Chapter Nineteen

"Is Loki really dead?" Travis asked, faking interest in a movie he'd seen a hundred times. Well, maybe not that many. Although he already knew the answer, if he managed to get Clayton going, it just might distract him from the nausea twisting through him. It felt like somebody was playing Twister inside him—with spiked gloves and boots.

Amy narrowed her eyes at him and then whispered, "Don't tell him. You don't want to ruin the movie."

Clayton stared at Travis with suspicious eyes. "I think he's already seen *Thor*. Dad told me that Uncle Travis collected all these comics and he knows more about these movies than probably anybody else."

Travis kept his face blank. "Hey, that was when I was a kid." He watched the scene play out, then he shook his head. "I don't know. I think he might be. He got all white and stuff."

Clayton focused on the screen for all of two minutes.

His next question almost had Travis choking on his beer—and the wound in his side all but screamed as he tried not to laugh.

"Do people kiss each other on dates?"

Torn between agony and amusement, he eyed Clayton. "Aren't you a little young to think about dates and kissing?"

Clayton rolled his eyes. "*No*. I see Uncle Zach kissing Aunt Abby. And Uncle Zach posted a picture on Facebook of Uncle Z kissing Miss Keelie." He scrunched up his face. "I bet Uncle Z will ask Miss Keelie to marry him."

"How do you feel about that?" He poked Clayton in the foot, glad the kid was distracted from his father and potential kissage.

"I like Miss Keelie." He displayed his bicep. "She drew Captain America's shield on me at the wedding. It washed off, though. I'll get a real one when I'm big. And I'll have her do it."

"Uncle Zach might have something to say about that."

"He can do the Hulk. A giant Hulk. On my back." Clayton gave him a gap-toothed grin.

"You got it all planned out, huh?" Travis thought maybe he could breathe now without feeling like the fires of hell were eating him.

"Yep! You think my dad will kiss—?"

Travis reached over and covered Clayton's mouth. "Enough. I'm the uncle. I don't talk about kissing. You got questions about kissing, ask your dad."

Amy laughed and then leaned in, whispered something in Clayton's ear.

Travis couldn't hear it, but whatever it was, it sufficiently distracted the kid. There was no more talk of kissing.

Personally, though, he sure as hell *hoped* his brother did some kissing. The man needed to start living again.

"I can't."

Trey laughed and scooped up the last bit of Irish Delight. It was a debilitating mix of Guinness fudge cake, caramel made with Jameson Irish Whiskey and creamy icing that tasted of Baileys Irish Cream liqueur. Normally, it was way too rich for him—he'd be happy with a few chocolate chip cookies.

But now he wanted to know how to make it—maybe Abby could do it and send him a few to stick in the freezer, so he could see that look on Ressa's face. Often. Not that he'd tell Abby that's why he wanted the cakes.

"One more bite." He held the spoon in front of her mouth.

Ressa rolled her eyes at him and then leaned in, closed her lips around the spoon. As she drew back, humming in pleasure, he had images of her doing something similar . . . only not with a damn spoon.

Her lashes lifted.

She finished the bite and then lifted a brow. "What's that look for?"

"It's not a particularly polite thought."

"Who said I was looking for polite?" She pushed the plate away and then leaned forward, elbows on the edge of the table. That position did devastating things for her breasts, plumping them up and sending a whole new slew of images rushing through his mind.

"It involved your mouth, and you doing just what you just did . . . but not with a spoon."

Confusion clouded her eyes, but only for a few seconds. Then she reached for the wineglass at her elbow. "You shouldn't put thoughts like that in my head, honey. I just might forget we're in a public place," she said a moment later, and he didn't think he was imagining the lower, huskier rasp to her voice.

She'd sounded like that just after he'd made her come.

He'd heard that voice in his dreams. Too many times. Now he wanted to hear her sound like that again, in reality.

"Then I guess I won't mention how sexy your voice sounds right now," he said, leaning back from the table before he did something stupid. "That you sound pretty much exactly the same way you'd sounded when I made you climax."

Her eyes widened, pupils spiking before her lashes drooped. "No. Let's not mention that."

A soft, shaky sigh escaped her and then she slid out of the booth, moving to pace around the room. Trey stayed where he was, blood pulsing too hot inside his veins. The dim light practically caressed her skin and his hands started to itch, just thinking about feeling her again. Under him, against him, above him . . .

It was a thought that made his hands start to sweat.

But all he could think about was touching her. Hearing that voice break as she whispered his name. Hearing her moan.

She swung her head around, staring at him over her shoulder. The power of her gaze held him mesmerized as she turned and slowly started toward him.

"You keep looking at me like you're seeing me naked, we're going to have problems, Trey."

His heart practically stopped as she went to her knees in front of him, her palms resting on his thighs. Through the material of his trousers, he could feel the imprint of her hands, each finger, the heat of her.

He wanted to shove his hands into her hair, haul her against him—up, into his lap, so he could push her skirt up, free his cock and drive into her.

It was a hot, brain-numbing fantasy.

But as she slid her hands up, he caught her wrists.

"You've got no idea," he murmured, lifting one wrist and pressing his lips to the inside.

The feel of that beautiful mouth on her skin was a tease, a caress . . . a promise. It sent a shiver racing through her entire body and Ressa was tempted to plaster herself against him and do everything she could to make him forget who he was, where they were . . . everything that didn't include getting naked.

If she didn't have so much conflict inside her, she could just do what Farrah had told her . . . enjoy the ride.

But she didn't want to enjoy the ride while it lasted.

There was too much going on to make her think she could have this for a little while and then just let go.

It was there in his smile. In the way her heart tugged when he looked at her.

The way he laughed when she told him about some of the things she'd seen at the library—a couple of teenagers she'd caught making out at the stacks, or the sympathy and irritation that had lingered on his face as she talked about how a group of *concerned citizens* had descended on the library to discuss the moral repercussions on the community when the library

actually purchased *sexual-type books*. That had been the
phrase they'd used when they'd lined up in front of her one
Saturday afternoon. *Sexual-type books.*

Enjoy it while it lasted?

I think I could enjoy him forever.

As he lowered her hand, his gaze moved to hers and he
reached up, cradled her face in his hand. "You look a thousand
miles away all of a sudden."

And you see too much.

Forcing a smile, she shrugged. "You know, a friend of
mine thinks I should just . . . enjoy the ride."

Heat flooded his gaze, even as he arched a brow.

"Enjoy what ride?"

She reached up and cupped his cheek. "You. This."

"I can't say I'm opposed to you enjoying me," he said, his
voice dropping lower. He covered her hand with his, his thumb
stroking back and forth over her skin. "But I think there's
more to it than that."

"I think we both know there's a lot more going on here than
just a couple of casual dates . . . a casual weekend, and then
we say, *See you around.*"

He moved and she caught her breath as he pulled her into
his lap. He did it with ridiculous ease and when she settled
there, astride his thighs, it was with her skirt riding high on her
legs. The table pressed into her side but she ignored it, looking
at him, his mouth just a wish away.

"Is that what you want?" Trey studied her.

Ressa felt something in her chest tighten. Sitting there, with
his eyes boring into hers, she felt stripped bare. Vulnerable.
She could lie. Let this go. Just see what happened. Right?

"That's a loaded question, honey." She leaned in and
pressed her brow to his. "I already told you . . . my life is complicated, and I seriously mean complicated. I don't know if
you getting involved with me is the best thing for you."

He went to speak and she pressed her finger to his lips.
"Don't. I'm not just blowing smoke. But at the same time, I
hate the idea of *not* seeing you. The past six weeks? They've
pretty much sucked, Trey."

"Tell me about it." His lips pressed to hers. His hand curved
over her neck as he looked into her eyes. "Maybe you should

let me decide about whether or not I want to get involved with you, Ressa. These complications . . . are they really that bad?"

Her gut twisted.

He pressed his thumb to her chin. "Whatever it is, Ressa . . . I want to be with you."

A million words, a million questions, a million hopes and doubts and wishes crowded up her throat to spill out of her. But before she could even voice one, there was a noise coming from the hall—almost deliberately loud, and the voice was too cheerful.

And *obnoxious*. "You all are far too quiet . . . is that a good thing or bad?" Mitch called out. "Should I come back? Speak now or forever hold your peace!"

Trey sighed and let go of her waist.

"And what if I was about to tell him to come back?" She wiggled free and smoothed her dress down.

"Not a good idea," Trey advised. "We'd never hear the end of it, and knowing him, he'd sneak up anyway or try to, thinking he'd get a look at something he shouldn't."

"A bit of a pervert, huh?" She grabbed the rest of the wine and tossed it back, her throat dry, her heart racing. *What am I doing?*

Enjoy the ride, while it lasted—that was the best thing, the smart thing. Ressa wasn't going to be smart, she realized. She wasn't going to be smart at all. There was no point. Her heart was already involved.

"No."

As Mitch came in the door, Trey shot him a look. "He's not a bit. He's a full-fledged perv. A card-carrying member of the local degenerates club."

"Who?" Mitch grinned. "Me?"

Then he rolled his eyes. "You two don't even looked mussed. What is wrong with you?"

I was just asking myself that very question, Ressa thought.

Chapter Twenty

The bookstore was as perfect as the rest of the place.

Small, quaint and cozy, it was tucked off the back of the building. If somebody had asked her to design the perfect bookstore, this just might be it. Lots of dark wood, soaring shelves that held the extra stock, and little book nooks tucked into every available space. There was plenty of light, and during the day even more would pour in through all the windows.

She found herself eying the little seat built into the space under a staircase and felt a thread of envy moving through her. "I want this," she said. "I want just this. That's it. I'm remodeling, just so I can have this."

Behind her, Trey chuckled.

When he slid his arms around her, it felt perfectly natural to lean back against him. "They'll have people coming in here just to read," she said.

"Read, and hopefully buy." He pressed his lips to her neck.

"You going to sign here?" Turning in his arms, she tipped her head back so she could see him, and when he winced, she grinned.

"I . . ." His face slowly went red and he blew out a rough breath. "I honestly haven't decided."

"Why not? You did fine at the book fair."

"I know." He let go of her with one last, lingering stroke of her sides and then he stepped away to pace edgily. "That just felt . . . different. I don't know. It's easier to flick the author part of me on when I'm not here."

Running her tongue across her teeth, she skimmed her eyes across the bookstore. Mitch had let them inside and then left, saying he'd be back in a bit. The man seemed determined to leave them alone as much as possible, she'd noted. "I'm going to assume that you mean *here* as in Norfolk . . . not this bookstore."

"Yeah. *Here* . . . home. It just feels weird. I like not worrying about screwing up and saying something stupid if I bump into somebody. If I start being author me, that kind of goes away." He shrugged and shot her a grimace. "That probably sounds stupid."

"No." She shook her head. "It sounds like you just want to have a part of your life that stays separate . . . yours. But Trey, people here already know who you are. If you say or do something stupid, it won't matter if you are in your home space or not."

He rolled his eyes.

"Do you know there are a few pages on Pinterest? Trey sightings?"

"What?" He blinked at her.

"Yep. Some locals who grab pictures of you when you're out around town—the post office, grocery store. That sort of thing. You aren't anonymous here, even if you want to be." She watched the expressions on his face flit from surprise to frustration to resignation. She decided she wasn't going to mention that a few people she knew kept up with those *Trey sightings*. Finally, he just sighed and shook his head and she reached out, touched his cheek. "I guess that's not making it any easier for you to think about doing anything here, huh?"

"I'm not thinking about it." He shoved his hands through his hair. The thick, gold-streaked strands of brown immediately fell back into place, but he barely noticed. "I'm not thinking about it tonight at all."

"Okay." She shoved off the wall and moved toward him. "Seems fair. I want to . . ."

She stopped and studied the book dump tucked at the end of the aisle. The section was labeled *Romance* and the book, with its spring green cover and the mostly nude female torso, was very familiar.

"Looks like they don't care if romance writers play in their pool," she murmured, reaching out for one of the L. Forrester books. She started to flip through it and then stared at the signature on the title page. Just below the block font was the bold, vivid scrawl—the exact same scrawl she had in her book, although hers was personalized. "She *signed* these."

Trey stopped at her elbow. "There are quite a few signed books in here," he said. He gestured to another display. "Those are signed, too."

"But she doesn't *do* this. She doesn't do interviews, blog tours, nothing." Frowning, she put the book down and picked up another, scowling at the signature.

Trey picked up a book and flipped through before putting it down. "You a reader?"

"Of *her*? Hell, yes. I love them. She makes me laugh and . . ." She paused, pursing her lips. "Well, if I'm ever reading one and you're around, I'd want privacy."

The back of Trey's neck went red even as his eyes flashed hot.

"That a fact?" He picked a book back up. "Maybe they'll sell me one early then."

"I have one." She laughed a little and then went back to studying the signature, then the book dump. "I wonder how they got her to come in here and sign."

"That's not necessary." Trey gestured at another display. "He doesn't live here either. If the publisher makes arrangements and the author is okay with it, they can get signed books from the author. It just has to be coordinated."

"Well, so much for that idea. I was hoping Mitch or Guff knew her. I was going to press for clues." She sighed and put the book down. "The information on her website can't even be called *sketchy*. It's more like she thought about being sketchy and then took an eraser and cleaned up most of the sketch before she let anything go up."

"Some people are kind of big on their privacy." Trey shrugged.

"But . . ." Then she stopped and put *Exposing the Geek Billionaire* down. "Never mind."

He slid her a look. "But what?"

"She's good. Damn good. I guess I just don't understand why somebody that talented wouldn't want to do interviews and that kind of thing."

"Maybe for the same reason I don't much like doing book signings." He cocked a brow and put his copy of the book down, too. "Some authors just aren't all that good at being social, or they feel weird talking about their work—so weird they can't get past it. Others have different reasons."

"Yeah. Fine." She rolled her eyes and shook her head. "Whatever."

Then she cut around him. "What books do they have of yours? I should probably read a couple of them."

There was a faint pause. And then he said, "Read a couple?"

She shot him a wide grin over her shoulder. "Oh, relax. I've read two of your books. I just figure I'll read a couple more. I normally go for something a little less . . . depressing, though."

"Gee, thanks." He gave her a sidelong look and then jerked his head to the side. Something about the look he'd given her told her he'd had this conversation before. Then he confirmed it by saying, "You do realize that dating me doesn't make my books required reading."

Dating me . . .

"Dating you." She glanced over her shoulder at him. "So . . . does that mean we're doing this again, Mr. Barnes?"

He caged her in, up against the end of one of the book-shelves. She felt the wood against her back, the heat of him against her front and her heart started to race.

"I think you're the deciding vote on that, Ms. Bliss. You already know what I want."

She smelled so good.

It was a scent he wanted to lose himself in.

Trey wanted to lose himself in her altogether really. Then

she turned in his arms, a smile on her lips and he felt that strike him square in the heart.

Feeling a little dazed, he wrapped his arms around her. "So what's the decision?" he asked, the words sounding a lot rougher, a lot more demanding than he'd intended.

Say yes—

"I'm definitely considering it."

"Okay." He caught her lower lip between his teeth. Then he let go. "Just so you know, I make excellent arguments. If you need me to convince you . . ."

A bubble of laughter escaped her. His lips twitched at the sound and he pressed his face against her neck as she laughed. Her arms curled around him, one hand sliding into his hair. "Well, now. You know . . . maybe that won't be necessary."

He lifted his head.

She met his eyes and lifted a hand. She touched a finger to his lips and traced, following the line of his mouth. With a far-off look in her eyes, she murmured, "I think it's time for me to stop considering and just enjoy the ride." Now her gaze cleared and she focused on him. "I'd like to see you again. It's not always easy to work out—I don't usually let Neeci go to a sitter. It's me or Mama Ang, my aunt."

"I'm a parent, too." Stroking his hand up her side, Trey leaned in and rubbed his lips over hers. "You know, Clayton talks about Neeci non-stop. I think the two of them bonded pretty much from the get-go."

"Didn't they?" She leaned back and he loosened his hold enough so that she could rest against the shelf behind her. The smile on her face widened and her eyes glinted with humor. "I swear, there are times that I hear nothing else. It's *Clay this* and *Clay that* and by the way . . ."

Ressa grimaced and looked away, although she shot him a look from the corner of her eye. "She . . . ah . . ." She licked her lips. "Neeci wants an autograph. I figured I should tell you soon before she sees you at pickup or something."

"She wants my autograph?" Confused, he studied her face. Neeci was seriously *not* his audience. Not for a good ten years or so.

"Nooooo . . ." Ressa drew the word out. "She wants your

little brother's autograph. She kind of heard that Sebastian Barnes was your brother, and. . . . well, um . . ."

"Ah." Now he started to laugh. "I can manage that. I'll make Clay ask him. Seb will probably get a kick out of it—he'll bend over backward for Clay."

He reached up and pressed his finger to her lower lip. "Hey, if you're not busy tomorrow, why don't you bring her over?"

Ressa blinked. "What?"

"To the house. You and Neeci come over. They can play together . . . and one of my brothers dropped into town. You can meet him."

"Please tell me it's Zach. I've seen some of the tattoos he's done on his website." She looked delighted now.

"No." He rolled his eyes and tipped his head back. "People always want to meet Seb or Zach—I have four brothers, you know. Those knuckleheads are only two of them."

She laughed. "You jealous there, gorgeous?"

"You coming over?" he countered, leaning in and nipping her lower lip. "And no. I'm not jealous. I got used to people asking about them—well, Zach, before I was even five. Are you coming over?"

It had taken more determination than Trey had thought he had not to push for more than a quick, *almost* chaste kiss when he'd dropped Ressa off at her place.

If he'd lingered more than a minute, he would have gone back to kiss her again—and he'd told her that—as he pulled away. The look she'd given him made him all too aware she wouldn't mind if he'd done that. Over and over. But he needed to get home.

He was already pushing it, time-wise, and it didn't matter that Travis was there to help out. He needed to get Amy home, get to bed—or maybe climb into a cold shower.

He almost relished the fact that he *needed* the cold shower, although the ten minute drive was nowhere near enough to cool his blood. Of course, the fact that he kept replaying that *almost*-chaste kiss . . . or picturing Ressa in her dress, peeling it off of her, none of that helped level him out.

Pulling his truck into the driveway, he noted that Clayton's light was off. He was in bed, sound asleep. Just as he should be, which meant Amy had been in charge, not Travis.

The door opened before he'd cleared the steps and he saw Travis there, his face looking even more haggard than before. Trey shoved the alarm down. Sooner or later, that son of a bitch was going to tell him what was going on and, if he didn't, Trey would take drastic measures. He'd fight dirty and just tell Mom.

Travis might be able to bullshit his way through anything, but if Denise Barnes realized that Travis was bullshitting *her*, the man was going to suffer the torments of the damned.

But for now . . . Trey stopped at the top of the steps and rocked back on his heels. "You survived."

"Piece of cake." Travis shrugged and glanced behind him. "Amy, he's here if you're ready to go."

Amy appeared less than a minute later, her eyes heavy, a smile on her face. She barely glanced at Travis, smiled at Trey. "Everything go okay?" he asked.

She nodded and hefted her bag higher up on her shoulder when it started to slide down. "I don't know how much I was needed, but thanks anyway. The money comes in handy."

"You were needed. If I let Travis be in charge, then Clayton would still be awake, he wouldn't have had a bath and dinner might have included something like pizza and chocolate, followed by chocolate brownies and chocolate ice cream. With chocolate cookies for a bedtime snack."

"And what's wrong with that?" Travis asked, his voice mild.

"You're not a five-year-old boy who'll wake up sick to his stomach." Trey just shook his head and stepped aside so Amy could head to the car. "Let's get you home."

As he climbed in, he noticed that Travis had made himself comfortable on one of the Adirondack chairs on the far side of the porch. He didn't look like he was in any hurry to move, either.

Trey was tired. Crazy tired. But if Travis was in a mood to have a chat, that suited him just fine. He had more than a few things he wanted to say, too.

* * *

Trey was irritated with him.

He'd have to be an idiot not to notice that. While Travis might be many things, he wasn't an idiot. It hadn't taken even fifteen minutes to run Amy home and make the return trip. Travis stayed where he was, legs sprawled out, eyes closed.

Once he had felt eyes on him and he had slowly lifted his lashes. From his angle, he could see the side of the house a few yards down—and how the curtains swayed in one window, only to fall back down.

He'd caught sight of the woman there once or twice. Whoever she was, she was nosy. He thought maybe it was Nadine. Nadine Armstrong. Yeah, that was right. She drove Trey a little nuts. Apparently she had a thing for spying, too.

As Trey pulled his truck back into the driveway, the light in the window next door went black and Travis rolled his head on the back of the chair, listening to the solid sound of Trey's shoes striking the sidewalk.

It had him blowing out a breath. This wasn't going to be one of their peaceful chats. "I think I might grab a beer. You want one?"

"I'll get it." Trey paused and then added, "You still look like you're going to fall flat on your face anyway."

As the door shut behind him, Travis dragged a hand down his face. No, he wasn't going to fall flat on his face. He wasn't even close to falling flat on his face. But he sure as hell felt like shit. Barely a couple of minutes passed before the door opened again and Trey came striding back out.

"You know, judging by the look in your eye, I'd almost say you must have had one lousy-ass date. What did you do, spill food in her lap?" Travis asked.

"Funny." He passed over a bottle of brew and dropped down into the other chair, stretching out his legs in a mirror of Travis's sprawl. "The date went fine."

Now Trey was smiling. A faint smile, but the smile was there and his eyes had that same goofy look that Zach's tended to get when he was thinking about Abby. "Another one bites the dust," Travis muttered under his breath.

"What?"

"Nothing. So, what's her name?"

"Ressa." Trey slid him a look.

"Ressa . . ." Travis studied. "Well. I'll be damned. How are things going with your sexy librarian? Hey, wait a second—I thought you never got around to getting her number?"

"You could say fate intervened," Trey said, lifting a shoulder.

"Fate." Travis studied him. "Do tell."

"We bumped into each other at that conference."

Something in Trey's voice had Travis biting back a smile. He mentally blocked everything else—some things a man just didn't need to know about his twin, no matter how close they were. And there were vibes coming from Trey that fell into that *didn't need to know* category.

"I'm not going to ask you to define *bumped* there, brother." Travis snorted.

"Yeah. Don't." Trey threw a beer cap at him.

Travis had to fight to instinct to grab it out of the air and lob it back. It sailed past his shoulder to hit the window as he smiled. "So. Then what?"

Trey just shrugged. "We hit it off. But it was just the weekend. When I asked for her number, she seemed to think it was better to just let it ride. That should have been it." He rose, still holding the beer he had yet to drink. "Then I take Clayton to school and there she was."

Travis just waited.

"She's got a cousin. She was dropping her off. I . . . I kinda get the idea that the mom isn't in the picture much—if at all. Ressa takes care of the little girl. Anyway, she's coming over tomorrow. Her and her cousin."

It was tossed out, so casual like, and Trey stood there, taking a drink while Travis all but had to pick his jaw up off the floor. Practically six years of being by himself—just him and Clayton, and now . . . "Just how many times have you two gone out?"

"Technically speaking?" Trey shrugged as he put the bottle down. "Once."

"Not including tonight?"

"No. Tonight was the first date. Jersey, well . . . we didn't really do anything we could call dating."

It might have been Travis's imagination, but he was almost positive that Trey was blushing. Yeah. He was pretty sure he wasn't imagining it.

"Let me get this straight," Travis said slowly, feeling uneasy. It was probably all in his head, but he couldn't help it. After the hell his twin had been through the past few years, Travis automatically defaulted to protective.

Getting to his feet *hurt,* and he hoped like hell he didn't give any sign as to how much. Once he was upright, he took another drink. He just might end up puking it out on Trey's feet, but if he tried to talk then, Trey would hear the pain in his voice so he needed the minute. Now, then. About as steady as he was going to get. He crossed over to study his twin's face, just a few inches away. "You see this woman you've been moon-eyed over for . . . what, six months? You run into each other at a conference. You're not spelling it out, so I'll just take a stab at it—it sounds like you two spent half the time fucking, am I right?"

Trey's eyes narrowed, but Travis steamrolled right over him. "Then, you two up and part ways. Now you find out your son and her cousin share a class. Doesn't that sound kinda . . . coincidental to you?"

"Anybody ever tell you that you're a paranoid son of a bitch?" Trey said, his voice almost pleasant.

Travis just crossed his arms over his chest. "This doesn't sound kind of . . . weird to you? This woman you've been drooling over shows up in not one, but two places for you to trip over her? First the conference, and now, out of the entire city, she ends up having a kid in the same class as Clayton and you don't think any of it sounds a little too pat for you? Come on, Trey."

"You think she up and somehow managed to get her cousin into Clayton's class, that she manipulated Max into asking her to handle the panels?" Trey snorted. "Let me guess, I bet you think she moved here, just so she could set all of that up. You know what, Trav? Fuck you."

He edged around him and headed for the front door.

"Aw, man. Come on, I didn't mean . . ."

"You didn't mean what?" Trey spun around and glared at him. "You think I'm not capable of making a decision about the woman I'm dating? Fuck off, man."

"Trey, look . . . I just . . ." Uncertain how to proceed or what to say, Travis stumbled for the words. "I'm just worried. You've spent the past few years alone and now . . ."

"I've spent the past few years alone." Trey snorted. "*Alone*. You think that touches it? Yeah, I've been *alone*. I've been *empty*—and I *wanted* it that way. It was easier—safer. Up until I saw her, I didn't realize just how empty and hollow I was."

He turned away then, staring out into the night. "People talk to me and they try to help and they say all these nice things that don't mean *shit* and I'm still empty. I still feel like . . ."

He stopped, shaking his head.

"For six years, I've just felt *alone*. The few times I've even tried to talk to another woman, I barely even *saw* them as women—I can't remember the last time I wanted to kiss a woman—spend any amount of time with somebody who wasn't family, and sometimes even that's hell."

Trey looked away.

Travis closed his eyes.

"You got any idea how fucking *lonely* it gets?" Trey asked, his voice barely more than a whisper. Now he turned, their gazes locking.

Feeling like blinders had been ripped off, Travis stared at his twin, suddenly aware of the fact that he wasn't the only one capable of holding back. There was a giant void inside Trey, one he'd never even been aware of.

Swallowing the bile that suddenly rose inside him, Travis closed a hand into a fist and focused on a point somewhere in the middle of Trey's chest. How had it become so hard to look at his brother's face?

"You all try," Trey said gently. "I know you do. It was hard enough to get through those first few months, that first year . . . grieving for Aliesha, worrying about Clayton, thinking I might lose him. But I didn't even know who I was—I didn't feel like anybody, not the man I thought I knew. By the time I realized how messed up I was, I was so far down in a pit, I couldn't see the top. Daylight wasn't even a memory for me. I've been pulling myself up and things started to get better. Maybe I feel alive again. But I still . . ."

Trey's voice faded away.

Travis finally dragged his eyes up but saw that Trey was more focused on the bottle he held than anything else.

"I quit drinking after that night. Tried once—cracked open a bottle of bourbon you'd given me one year. It was about a year after Aliesha died. The smell of it made me sick and it was like I was reliving that night all over again, like I'd lost her, all over again. Even now, the smell of alcohol turns my stomach." He closed his eyes and took a slow sip of the beer he held. He sat there in silence, waited for what seemed like forever before he sighed. "It's all in my head. I shut myself down . . . and I know it. I'm going to finish the fucking beer. I'm going to see Ressa tomorrow and I'm going to stop hiding."

He slanted a look at Travis. "I know what I feel when I look at her. I know what I see when she looks at me. I don't know what it is about her, but she cut right through me and I'll be damned if I let you breathe your paranoia down my neck and make me question that."

"Trey, look." Travis didn't know if the word guilt touched on what he suddenly felt. He didn't know if confusion did. Panic crowded around him and he could hardly breathe. There were few in this world who mattered to him and the one who mattered the most stood right in front of him. And he'd managed to hurt him. "I didn't mean anything by it. I just . . . look, I'm worried about you."

"Some advice," Trey offered. "Worry about yourself, because for once, I'm doing fine. You, on the other hand, look like you'll keel over, and don't think I didn't notice that you felt like you were going to puke up your guts a minute ago. Now leave me the hell alone."

He turned and headed for the door. But before he went inside, he paused, waited. "And Travis, you better listen to me . . . she's coming over tomorrow and if you do one thing to make her uncomfortable, I promise you, I will beat you senseless. You hear me?"

Trey didn't wait for a response. He went inside, closing the door with a quiet snick.

Travis stood there, staring at the door, something a little sick moving through him. "Well," he muttered into the silence of the night. "I went and fucked that up good and proper, didn't I?"

Chapter Twenty-one

"Day-yum," Ressa murmured under her breath

"What?"

"Nothing, baby," she said, putting the Mustang into park as she took one more moment to admire the sprawling Colonial in front of her.

She'd thought Bruce's place—*no, it's my place now . . . mine*—but she'd thought that place was nice.

This was . . . beyond.

She couldn't quite call it a mansion, but the house on the double lot was amazing. The lawn was lush and green, flowers flooded in a brilliant rainbow of color, and the brick and glass somehow managed to reflect both old-world charm and modern comfort.

She hadn't been sitting there thirty seconds when one of the house's double doors opened and a blond tornado came spilling out.

Neeci was already tearing at her seat belt. "Hey, hey, hey! Slow down, baby."

Neeci rolled her eyes.

"Now, listen. You need to remember—"

The door opened and Neeci was gone, tearing up the sidewalk to meet Clayton. With a weak laugh, Ressa finished. "Remember your manners and no running in the house."

Movement caught her eye and she looked past the kids to see Trey. Her heart made a weird little lurch inside her chest and gripped the steering wheel convulsively. "And you need to remember *your* manners. No drooling on the host. No grabbing him in the hallway. Behave."

She wondered if she'd be able to do that.

A few minutes later, she met him on the sidewalk and had the delightful pleasure of him leaning in and closing his mouth over hers. It was a soft, sweet kiss, even more chaste than the one he'd given her last night, but it still made her muscles feel hot and loose, while her heart skittered and jumped like crazy.

"Ewww!"

Against her lips, she felt him smile and then he pulled back. "I don't think it was ewww," he mused, glancing over at Clayton and Neeci. Then he slid her a sly look. "But maybe I should try it once more, just to make sure."

She slapped a hand against his chest when he would have leaned in. Lifting a brow, she said, "Nice try."

"Can't blame a man for trying," he said, covering her hand with his. "Why don't we take them inside? I'll show you around and . . ."

He stiffened beside her. It was subtle, almost imperceptible, but she was becoming adept at picking up those minute changes in him. From the corner of her eye, she saw where his gaze had shifted and she followed it, saw the man who somehow managed to slide quietly onto the porch. For a second, she could only stare.

It was like seeing double.

But then her brain kicked into action and she saw the differences. They were slight, but they were there. Trey was observant, something she'd already noticed.

His twin left him in the dust.

In the seconds it took her to sum up the man on the porch, he'd already taken her measure and was probably already at work forming an opinion. She wondered what it would be. Those eyes—they were the same lovely blue as Trey's, but so different. They held a hardness.

"My brother," Trey said. "Travis."

"Thanks for telling me. I wouldn't have figured it out on my own," she said dryly as he led her up to the porch.

"Yeah, well. He's the ugly one," Travis said, moving forward with slow, easy grace, those eyes still resting on her face. It was like he wore a mask, though. He watched her with good humor and curiosity and maybe that wasn't a lie, but it wasn't altogether real, either. There was somebody else below that expression—that mask.

"Trey tells me you're a librarian," Travis said as he shook her head.

"Yes." She smiled. She could almost bet what he did. The look in his eyes was a dead giveaway. She'd never seen anything about him mentioned—he was the only Barnes sibling who had absolutely no public persona at all.

Trey had a good-humored sneer on his face. "If we didn't look so much alike, I'd swear he was a changeling or something. He went and ended up in the most boring job imaginable."

Yeah, she mused, remembering now. Trey had already told her that. But . . . *an accountant*?

Ressa looked back at Travis, listened as he exchanged what sounded like well-used jibes and insults. That shrewd look he'd given her suddenly made her feel more than a little nervous, though.

She had to fight the urge not to look over at Necci, not to place herself protectively between her and her cousin.

It was practice that let her smile at him, practice that let her keep herself from tensing up under that all-too-keen gaze.

An accountant? Like hell. The only place she'd ever seen anybody with eyes that watchful was when she'd been forced to talk to cops.

If he was an accountant, then she was Marilyn Monroe.

"I like her."

Trey hefted a bucket filled with ice from the counter and headed for the door. He didn't look back at his brother. "You just met her."

"Talked to her for a while already. That's enough," Travis said. His voice was carefully neutral, but the message was there. An apology underscored every word. "I like her. And I was an ass. You going to stay mad at me all day?"

Trey shrugged. "Who says I'm mad?"

"Well, since we've kinda known each other for . . . I dunno, our whole lives, I've gotten pretty good at reading the signs." Travis closed his hand around the door handle, but instead of opening it, he stood there, keeping Trey from moving outside.

Now Trey had to look at him.

Once their eyes locked, Travis said, "Look, I'm sorry, okay? I can't help but worry . . ."

"That's a fucking joke, coming from you," Trey snapped. "You have more secrets than the CIA, don't think I can't tell. But *you* worry? Give me a break. Look, I'm not mad. I'm just . . ."

He stopped, eyed Travis. "What?"

There was a faint echo of surprise in the back of Trey's mind, there for a blink, then gone. Travis hadn't expected Trey to pick up on so much.

Trey almost snarled.

"Look . . . it's . . ." Travis was staring off into empty air. "I . . . son of a bitch. Look, yeah. I hold stuff back. I guess I never realized how easy it would be for you to pick up on it. But you don't have to worry, and I'm sorry about last night."

His twin meant it. Trey could tell that much. He was sorry, and . . . yeah. He didn't think Trey should worry. There was a sincerity there that Trey could feel. But what did any of that mean? Trey had no idea.

Blowing out a breath, Trey said, "Open the door, would ya?"

"Should I go?" Travis continued to stand there, watching him. "I can crash at a hotel."

"Like hell. Just stop being such a dick, okay?"

The door opened and he cut past his brother. Some of the tension that seemed to wrap around them both dissolved, like sticky threads of cotton candy caught in a rainstorm. But it wasn't gone. Sooner or later, they'd have to have this out. He was tired of Travis hiding away like he was.

But all that could wait.

* * *

Both of them swam like fish.

Ressa smiled to herself as Clayton and Neeci chased each other around in the shallower end of the big pool. So far, Ressa had managed to stay out of the water, and even mostly dry, although every few minutes, a giant splash would come her way. She didn't know how long she would be able to evade them. But she had every intention of doing so for as long as she could.

"I like your suit." Trey's voice was soft and low and he laid a hand on her hip, the warmth of it almost shocking even in the heat of the day. Because he was there, because it was too tempting not to, she let herself lean back against him, and the solid wall of his chest against her back was a delight that she'd remember for a long, long time.

Even if—

If—

Broodingly, she made herself silence that *if.* For some reason, that *if* had been whispering through her brain a *lot* today. Ever since she'd met the too intense gaze of Trey's twin.

Maybe those thoughts weren't fair—hell, she knew they weren't. Not to her, not to Trey. Maybe not even to Travis, even if he did have cop's eyes.

As his thumb stroked over the ruby red retro suit she'd pulled on, she forced herself to focus on Trey and not the worries that had chased her over the past hour. "The suit? This old thing?"

This old thing—she'd spent about thirty minutes debating on the right swimsuit and had ended up going with the red because it highlighted her breasts, her hips and her butt and she liked how it showed off her ink, too.

"Yeah." Trey stroked a finger down one of the tattoos on her arm, smiling. "This old thing. Although you could be wearing sackcloth and I'd still be intrigued. I think I'd like nothing best, but . . . not a good idea right now."

"No." She turned her head up and met his eyes. "Probably not." She glanced across the pool where Travis lounged on a chair, gaze shielded by a pair of dark sunglasses, his face supposedly relaxed. But he was watching every damn thing. She could feel it. And there was a weird tension between the brothers. "Seems like there's something going on between you and your twin. Everything okay?"

"It's fine." He kissed the tip of her nose. "You got family, right? You know how it is. We just bumped heads last night. The jerk has a hard one."

"Oh, I got family. I doubt we're as close as y'all are, though." She covered his hand with hers and looked back at the pool. "The way those two play, you'd think they were born joined at the hip."

Trey chuckled. "When I told him you two were coming over, he all but bolted out the door looking for you. Then I had to tell him it wasn't until this afternoon. You'd have thought I told him the world's candy supply had disappeared overnight."

"Likes his candy, huh?" She slid him a look.

"Like you wouldn't believe." His lips brushed against her shoulder.

That light touch sent a shiver through her. "Trey . . ."

"Sorry." His hands tightened around her waist and then he stepped back. "Damn if you don't go to my head, Ressa."

Slanting a look at him, she said, "Now it wasn't like I told you to *stop*." She already missed the feel of him standing there so near she could feel his body heat.

"Standing that close makes it hard for me to think." He shook his head and instead of moving back to where he'd been, he moved around and cut behind her, settling onto a tall stool sitting at the nearby bar. His gaze settled on the pool where Neeci and Clayton had decided to play an enthusiastic, but slow, game of water tag. "Do you realize I don't even know all that much about you?"

She stiffened, then forced herself to relax. "What do you want to know, honey?" Then, mentally, she wanted to kick herself. She had secrets, so many that she didn't ever want to share. Some of them weren't even hers, and some of the ones that were still made her look back at the years behind her and wonder what she'd been thinking.

He must have read something on her face and she gave him a wide, easy smile. "I'm an open book," she said, the lie falling too easily from her lips.

A smile lit his face. "An open book. No woman is. That's why you drive men crazy . . . and why we love you."

She pursed her lips as she considered that. "I think I like that." Then she shrugged. "There's no reason for you to know that much about me. Or for me to know that much about you. We just met not that long ago."

"True." His voice was soft. "And yet I find myself thinking about you all too often. In the morning. Halfway through the day. At night. And that was before we met back up because of those two. I never was able to stop thinking about you, even when I told myself there wasn't going to be anything more for us."

"Did you want more?"

She looked away from the pool to meet his gaze.

He was staring at her and the intensity of his gaze sent her heart into overdrive.

"I wanted more pretty much from the first moment I laid eyes on you." Then he shrugged and looked back at the kids. "But life kept getting in the way."

"It's got a way of doing that."

Trey didn't know if he'd ever noticed a woman's eye-lashes until he'd met Ressa Bliss.

He'd certainly never had quite this fascination with a woman's mouth. She had this way of sucking her lower lip in, biting it ever so lightly and then letting it go . . . it made him think about biting her lip, her neck, her . . . lots of things.

But then her words connected, and he lowered his head, staring down at the polished wood of the bar top. He rubbed his thumb against the surface and wondered if he was ready for all the emotion already surging inside him.

What do you want to know . . . I'm an open book.

No, she wasn't. Trey was pretty good at picking up on stories and he'd seen the story in her eyes before she gave him that wide, easy smile.

"You know, we've all got shadows, Ressa," he said softly. "We all have secrets behind us."

A squeal, cut short, had them both looking at the pool and then Trey swore, moving off the stool with a muttered apology.

"Clayton, watch the roughhousing in the pool," he said as he strode past her. "Neeci isn't me or one of your uncles."

"But she—" Clayton started, a scowl forming on his face as Neeci surfaced, her hair dripping, a look promising retribution on her little face.

"Did you hear me?"

Clayton's face folded into mutinous lines, but he nodded and then turned to the steps. "I don't want to play no more."

"Anymore," Trey corrected.

"That either!" Clay shouted. That was the last thing he got out before Neeci took him under.

"Neeci!" Ressa snapped.

"He did it to me first, Ressie!"

"Oh, boy." Ressa shoved past Trey. "That line doesn't fly for me. You know that. Out of the pool."

Neeci's eyes widened. "What . . . you—" She gulped. "You're not making us leave, are you?"

Clayton came rushing to her defense. "I did it to her first. I don't want her to go. It's my fault."

"I think both of you need to get out for a while," Trey said, moving to Ressa's side. "Maybe it's time for them to eat. You think?"

"Yeah." A smile quivered at the corner of her mouth, but she kept her face straight as they all but slumped in relief—not exactly the best thing to do in the pool. "Both of you can settle down a little while. Besides, I'm getting hungry. Come on out, guys."

"I'll help them dry off and get them moving inside."

At Travis's voice, Trey looked up. His brother had left the far side of the pool and approached without him even noticing. He looked a little less haggard and he'd torn through more than half the food Trey had made that morning. He still looked like he needed to put on a good ten or fifteen pounds, but maybe in another week or two, he wouldn't look like he was getting ready to put in for a casting call for *The Walking Dead*.

Trey glanced at Ressa. She shrugged in response. "We'll be in in a few minutes."

After the door had closed, she looked over at him, that familiar, teasing smile curving her lips up. "I don't think she's ever been so worried about consequences before."

Trey backed her up against the low-lying brick wall, his hands coming up on either side of her hips to cage her in. "Sometimes the consequences are a bitch." Then he leaned in and nuzzled her neck. "And then sometimes, the ride's worth it."

"Trey . . ." She curled her hands around his waist, her fingers stroking the feathers of the raven that just barely reached his side. "I get the feeling you're talking about something entirely different."

"Am I?" he asked, moving to rub his mouth against hers. He could taste her and it went straight to his head.

Before he had a chance to deepen the kiss, though, she pulled away. "Even on the drive back, I already missed you. It's crazy. I watched you, wanted you for months before I even knew your name," she said, staring up at him. "Then we had a weekend. One night, really . . . crazy, amazing sex and a few hours together where it was just us. Not much in the scheme of things, but it felt like I was missing some vital part of me when it ended."

His heart did the weirdest little spin inside his chest—it couldn't be healthy for a body organ to do that, Trey was almost certain of it. But it felt so right, staring into her eyes. Cupping her face in his hands, he bent his head, pressed his brow to hers. "It didn't end, though. Just a time-out. Now we just gotta figure out where this is going. Yeah?"

"Yeah." She closed her hands around his wrists and smiled. "Yeah."

They talked her into the pool.

She did it only after they promised not to splash her, and that held for all of ten minutes and then Clayton and Neeci gleefully pounced on her and she gamely let them take her under.

Since she was already soaked, she took off after both of them as they swam away and she caught Neeci, tossing her into the air and watching as she landed with a giant splash. Neeci came back out of the water, laughing and squealing for her to do it again. Clayton took a wide-eyed look at her and then swam for his dad.

"Don't expect me to save you," Trey said, laughing and moving out the way. "She told you not to splash her. I think you're in for it."

From the side of the pool, his legs in the water from the knees down, Travis watched all of it, an amused look on his face.

Realizing he wasn't going to find any help from his dad, Clayton took off for the next best bet. He climbed out of the pool and ran around the brick surface to hide behind Travis. "Don't let her get me," he begged.

Travis snorted. "You trying to put me in the middle of this?" He sighed and shook his head. "Clay, kid."

"You're stronger than she is! Besides, you don't want to kiss her and Dad does."

Travis shot Trey an amused look. "I'm pretty sure your dad and kissing has nothing to do with any of this. But . . . here. I'll make it easy, cuz your dad doesn't want to kiss me." He hooked his arm around Clayton's waist and flipped him in.

Clayton hit the water with a giant splash and surfaced with a dark glare for Travis. "That's not fair!" There was a grin on his face as he started to swim for his dad. "I'll make Dad dunk you. You're too big for me."

"I'll dunk him later, Clay. Your uncle looks like a puppy could kick his butt right now." Trey slid him a look across the pool. "Makes it too easy. He's not dressed for the pool anyway."

For some reason, the idea of a puppy beating up his uncle Travis struck Clayton as hilarious and he went into a fit of giggles—which made him oblivious to the fact that Ressa had slid under the water and swam up behind him. She caught him around the waist and came up out of the water, twisting and plunging them both under. Clayton's screech of delight was cut short and he came up sputtering.

"That was sneaky," he said, swiping the water out of his eyes.

"Next time a woman tells you she doesn't want to get wet," she advised. "Listen."

Then she winked at him and swam over to the far side, hoisting herself out and sitting on the edge to watch.

Losing one of his playmates had Clayton swimming back to Travis.

Looking down into a pair of blue eyes that were almost a

mirror of his own, Travis lifted a brow. The kid was up to something, he knew it.

"You gotta come in now." Clayton propped his arms on the brick and gazed at him soulfully.

Yeah, that's not going to happen. Travis gave him a game smile, but shook his head. "Your dad's right, kid. I'm dragging so bad a puppy *could* kick my tail. I've been sick. Don't think I'm up to a swim."

From the corner of his eye, he saw his twin's gaze narrow on him, and he felt the intensity of Trey's gaze as well. *Oooohhh*, yeah. He was going to get it. If it wasn't for the stitches, he would have just gone in.

But he couldn't get them wet and he wasn't going to explain them either. No way to hide the injury if he took off his shirt, and that was a talk that just couldn't happen right now— or ever, if he had his way.

"Oh, come on." Clayton pouted.

"Leave him alone, Clay," Trey advised. "Look, you two can tag up on me. We'll do sharks and minnows."

Clayton stared at Travis for another few seconds and then turned away, his shoulders drooping. "You gotta be the shark. The whole time. It's only fair cuz you're so big, Dad."

It only took thirty minutes of that to wipe them out.

Ressa had to give them credit.

She helped Neeci change out of her suit in the cute little outbuilding Trey had offered them, and then, after dodging behind the door her cousin had left wide open, she rolled her eyes and changed into her clothes, a pair of denim capris and a shirt with cutout sleeves that left most of her arms bare and dipped down low on her back.

Her hair had moved into disaster territory and there wasn't much hope for it right now. She'd have to wash it tonight. For now, she tidied up the braid she'd twisted it into—she'd figured she'd end up getting wet anyway—and then she gathered up the clothes.

Heading out the door, she promptly crashed into Trey, hitting him with an *oomph*.

His hands came up to steady her.

"Sorry," she said, grinning. "I think I left my grace at home today."

His arm banded around her waist, pressing their lower bodies together. "Sorry . . . for what?"

"Pervert." She wrinkled her nose at him and glanced around for the kids, but they weren't outside.

"They went inside, hounding Travis to get them a snack since he didn't have to change. Might as well make himself useful since he's going to be a layabout for a while." He glanced down at the bag of wet swimsuits and towels she held. "They might even be distracted for five minutes."

"Not long enough," she said loftily. Twisting out of his reach, she started up the brick walkway. "So . . . is he on vacation or something?"

"Or something." Trey sounded resigned and took up pace next to her. "He's got a weird job. Travels a lot. Lately, it's wearing him out."

Stay out of it. That was what her common sense said. Well, *mostly.* But in her gut, she knew that man wasn't an accountant. Running her tongue across her teeth, she gave him what she hoped was a casual look. "So he's an accountant, huh?"

"A forensic accountant." Something that might have been pride crept into his voice. "We all razz him about it, but he does important work. It's mostly white-collar stuff—he doesn't talk about it, but I've researched that kind of thing. He always had a megabrain. He went and put it to use—has something to do with white-collar crime and that kind of thing."

White-collar, huh? She thought of the grim look she'd caught on the other twin's face a time or two, the knowledge. She didn't think he'd caught that from doing a lot of white-collar shit. He looked like a man who'd carried some weight.

But she wasn't going to point any of that out.

"I have to tell you this, I don't really see you as wasting your brain." She caught his hand, laced their fingers. "The books you write, what you do . . . it makes a difference. Books made a big impact on my life. You have to know that you do something important."

"Well, I'm not saying it's nothing. I went into it because

books made a difference to me, too." A faint grin curved his lips as he lifted her fingers to his lips. "Seems like the two of us have a lot in common there."

"Don't we just?"

Travis had a bad feeling.

He tried to ignore it, told himself it was because he was still on edge because of the fight with Trey last night.

But it wasn't and he knew it.

It was the way Ressa watched him.

When he managed to pin her alone in the library, her hands behind her back as she studied the books lining Trey's shelves, that feeling only intensified. He hadn't made any noise but within seconds, she grew aware of him and her body went tense. Slowly, she turned her head and although she had a smile set firmly in place, her eyes were guarded.

"Hello."

He inclined his head, kept his expression easy. "You should have seen this place before Mom got her hands on it in the spring. It was kind of scary."

She just arched a brow.

"Trey's a pack rat," he offered helpfully.

"Is he now?"

"Yeah." He came inside and paused in front of a shelf that held Trey's favorites. He'd been sitting in the window seat with a beer when Mom came in here, armed with boxes and bags and a feather duster. Trey had been grim and accepting, until she'd turned on that shelf. It was the one time he'd ever seen his brother refuse Mom anything.

She wasn't allowed to touch that shelf, and no, it did *not* matter that half the copies on that shelf were held together with tape.

But she'd cleared out a box that held duplicate copies—Trey hadn't realized he'd bought that many doubles. She'd also found probably a thousand dollars in receipts he'd forgotten to turn over to his accountant, three checks he hadn't cashed, and Travis had forgotten the rest of it.

She'd also convinced Trey to turn one of his empty rooms

upstairs into a storage area for business stuff. Instead of author copies lining the floor in here, and bookmarks spilling out of boxes, they were neatly organized in that spare room.

"It used to look like a disaster zone."

"I can imagine it did." She shrugged and went back to studying the shelves. "He's got interesting taste."

As she pulled down a romantic suspense, a grin lit her face.

"Well, he overheard Mom talking to her friends about all the *s-e-x* in those. We were in high school . . . naturally, we weren't *allowed* to read them. There wasn't more you had to say to get him curious." Travis shrugged.

"I see." She glanced at him. "Did you read it?"

"Only the good parts." He studied his nails. "I was too cool for the mushy shit, you know."

"I bet." Amusement lurked in her voice as she put the book back on the shelf. "So . . . you're an accountant."

He heard it in her voice.

Looking up at her, he saw it in her eyes, too.

"Forensic accountant," he corrected. "It's not exactly the same thing. So don't go asking me to help on your taxes."

"I figure I can handle them on my own." She picked up another book. Poetry, this time. "Seems like you're the black sheep in your family."

"Seems that way."

She didn't say anything else as she flipped through a book. Keats, Travis noticed. He'd never been one for poetry.

She looked up at him for a long moment and then back down at the book.

Travis had the weirdest urge to just tell her. Which was insane, because he was used to keeping quiet. But . . .

"I know all about being the black sheep," she said, cutting through his thoughts, her gaze still on the pages. "Had some . . . trouble, I guess you could say, when I was a kid. It would have been worse if it wasn't for my aunt. And then of course I had to go and end up on my ass again, figure things out the hard way. Both my cousin and I, we probably broke my aunt's heart. I straightened up. My cousin? Not so much. Some of us, I guess we can only learn things the hard way."

She watched him now with a message in her eyes.

And she was all but challenging him.

Lifting a brow, he shrugged and tucked his hands into his pockets. "Sometimes the hard way is the only way to learn."

"Maybe. Sucks, but I guess we all learn in our own way." She put the book of Keats back and started for the door. Sliding past him, she went to go down the hall and then paused. Over her shoulder, she said, "I like Trey. A lot. Whatever you find, I hope you keep that in mind."

Travis closed his eyes.

Son of a bitch.

Oh, yeah. She knew something.

She'd pegged him for a cop, he'd bet that in a heartbeat. He wasn't. But she'd come a hell of a lot closer than anybody else ever had.

Her gut churned as she settled on the couch next to Trey.

She needed to round up Neeci and head home, but for some reason, she needed this.

No.

Not some reason.

Every reason.

All the reasons.

She'd seen it.

She was right. That man wasn't an accountant any more than she was. Or maybe he *had* been one . . . or something. Undercover, maybe? She didn't know. She was curious why he had his family thinking that was what he did. Not that it was any of her business.

The one thing that was her business was what would happen when Travis found out.

And he was going to look.

That was what his kind did. They nosed around, dug around, looked for answers.

Would he leave her alone?

Or would he tell Trey?

Maybe she should just tell him . . .

Wasn't that one hell of a thing to drop into a conversation. *So, baby . . . let me tell you this trouble I got into. My cousin and me, actually. You know, Neeci's mama? You're just going to love this.* Shame and misery twisted in her and she had to fight not to squirm.

A series of giggles had her looking toward the TV and she smiled at the screen as she caught sight of one seriously beautiful man—being cornered by a couple of devious kids.

It was Sebastian Barnes, playing the role of a hardened military man who came home to find his brother's kids orphaned and himself left with the job of raising them.

"He looks comfortable in that role," she murmured.

"Yeah. He took it after he spent a couple weeks here with me and Clayton. Said he had more fun with kids than he'd thought he could. Of course, one of those kids almost made him go and get himself snipped," Trey said, grinning. He toyed with her fingers as he spoke and the sight of that sent a pang through her heart.

"Yeah? A terror?"

"Beyond. According to Seb, the kid missed his cues, stepped on his lines all the time, and when they were doing those wrestling scenes you saw earlier? He actually kicked Seb in the . . ." He stopped and ran his tongue across his teeth. "Well. His shots were on target the first few times. Then Seb wisened up and started wearing a cup—the kid got mad when he hurt his foot and complained to his mother, who *then* complained to the director."

She almost asked if he was joking, but judging by the smirk on his face, she knew he wasn't. "And what did the director say?"

"He suggested the kid remember he wasn't actually supposed to kick him. She wasn't pleased, I'm told."

"Wow." Eying the screen now, she tried to figure out which one it was. He'd mentioned the wrestling, but it had been two kids on the lone adult. The ruddy cheeked, angelic looking boy who looked to be six or seven didn't seem like a good fit. The only other option was the teenager. "Was it that older kid? Seems like he'd know better."

"He did." Trey lifted a brow as he turned to look at her. "It was the little kid. Apparently under all those golden curls, he's got a set of horns. And his mom is one of the worst stage moms ever."

"Stage mom?" She eyed him curiously.

Trey laughed. "Sorry. You've got normal moms—those who are just that . . . normal. Like our mom was. Even though Zach practically lived on set, and then later, Seb, and all of us were around it because of them, she made sure we had a normal life, or as normal as possible. Then you've got stage moms—the only thing that matters is the next part. Their child is the most important person on the set—even if it's just a bit part and you've got Sean Connery acting next to them, that kid is *everything* and if makeup doesn't kiss his ass, the world ends. We saw some crazy shit. Seb said he overheard this mom going after wardrobe because the kid ripped his jeans and they didn't strip him onset to replace them."

"That's awful. I kinda feel bad for your brother," she murmured, eying the angelic looking boy with new eyes.

"I don't," Trey said with relish.

"Why not?" she demanded, turning to look at him.

"Because Sebastian deserves it."

"Does he ever," Travis said as he came into the room.

She didn't let herself stiffen as she glanced at him.

He settled in an armchair on the other side of the room. "Mom had to pop that kid's bubble on a regular basis. Some people grow into their arrogance. Sebastian was born with it. And he was probably ten times worse than that kid and Mom was constantly reeling him in."

"Yep." Trey chuckled and the sound was more than a little diabolical. "Now he's getting a taste of his own medicine. I bet it tastes really bad."

"You are awful." Shaking her head, she settled a little more comfortably against him and tried not to think about the fact that the other, quieter twin was sitting just a few feet away. He wasn't looking at her directly, but she was all too aware of his gaze.

The side of the car was still warm from the heat of the day, although it was rapidly cooling down.

Not that she was cold.

Caught between the car and Trey's body, she could barely think.

One hand tangled in the back of her shirt, the other spread

on her neck while he used teeth and tongue to slowly destroy her sanity.

Moaning into his kiss, she clutched at his shoulders as the strength drained out of her. A dark, rough growl came out of him as she sagged back against the car and he followed, his weight pressing more firmly against her as he started to move, oh so slowly.

It was . . . devastating.

Her sex clenched and she could feel herself growing hotter, wetter in readiness. His cock was a heavy, thick brand and she rubbed herself against him. Half mad with the need, she found herself reaching for him, ready to tug his jeans open and shove her hand inside.

"You're going to kill me," he muttered, catching her wrist and drawing her hand back.

Belatedly, she remembered. Where they were. What she was doing.

Neeci was in the car, asleep.

In the house a few yards away, Clayton was in the same condition.

And Travis—

That was a bucket of cold water in her face. Curling her fingers into her hand, she tugged free and turned her head.

Staring out at the street, she breathed slowly. After a minute passed, she said, "You make me lose my mind, Barnes."

"Same goes." He cupped her cheek, guided her face back until they were looking at each other yet again. "What's wrong? Where did you go?"

"I didn't go anywhere." She hooked her fingers through his belt loops and tugged him close, giving him a wicked smile as she arched against him. "Why would I want to do that anyway?"

He rubbed his finger across her lower lip. "You've been disappearing half the day."

"No, I . . ." Ressa stopped, heaved out a sigh. "It's nothing, Trey. It's just . . . that complication stuff."

Observant eyes studied her. "You sure that's it? Nothing I said? Did?"

"No." She rose up on her toes and wrapped her arms around

his neck. In case that wasn't enough, she pressed her lips to his, said it again. "No."

She eased away, but he didn't let her go far. "Then what is it?"

She laid her cheek against his. "It's just . . ." She blew out a breath. "Trey, I just have stuff in my head. It's not you, I promise. It's just . . . all that complication stuff we keep talking about. We should probably have that talk soon."

Tension held him tight as he turned his face into her hair. A moment or two passed before he spoke again. "Yeah, maybe so. Because this sure as hell isn't going to get any less intense on my end."

Something that might have been fear, might have been delight, twined through her.

"So. We talk soon." He pressed a kiss to the corner of her mouth. "I wish you didn't have to leave."

"But I do. I need to get her to bed. We're meeting Mama in the morning for breakfast. Besides, I don't think you and I need to talk about spending the night with each other yet. At least not when there are kids around, anyway."

She kept telling herself that as she drove away a few minutes later.

It was even the truth.

It didn't do jack to untangle the knot inside.

And nothing could help with the bigger, uglier knot of fear that wedged itself deep into her gut.

"Stop worrying," she told herself.

It wouldn't do any good anyway. Wasn't like she could change the outcome of anything.

Chapter Twenty-two

Whatever you find, I hope you keep that in mind.

Those words had managed to do two things—stir his curiosity and make him check her out. Travis hadn't really planned to do much of *anything*, to be honest. He didn't make a habit of digging around in the backgrounds of the people his brothers were dating.

Well, not right off the bat.

If somebody struck him as off? Well, then, that changed things.

Ressa, if it hadn't been for the interlude in the library, he wouldn't have gone nosing around, at least not right away. Even though she had managed to set his instincts off.

He liked her. She was blunt and funny and Clayton clearly adored her. She treated the kids—both the little girl and Clayton—well, and to him that mattered a hell of a lot.

So, she clearly didn't trust law enforcement types. She wasn't the only one, and plenty had a reason not to.

And if she hadn't said anything in the library, he would have just made himself let it go. Now, though . . .

It had been four days since she'd been over with that doll of a little girl. Each day, he'd had to force himself not to go digging anything up. He didn't have a reason to. She wasn't doing anything, right? Just dating his brother.

His rich brother.

His single brother.

His widowed brother who really didn't have that much experience with women.

That was the nagging little voice of evil, that red devil that rode his shoulder.

The other voice, well, he couldn't call him an angel, but maybe it was the voice of common sense, he spoke up and reminded him, *You like her. Trey's not an idiot. He's got decent instincts, even if maybe he has been out of the game awhile—or never even in the game to begin with. Just let it go.*

Yet Ressa had all but told him there was something in her past that he wouldn't like. That meant Trey wouldn't like it. And she hadn't told Trey, either.

Why was she keeping secrets?

It didn't take much time at all to figure out just what she'd been warning him about.

By the time he was done checking everything out, his head was pounding and he didn't know if he wanted to warn Trey . . . or just find Ressa and tell her to get it over with.

"About damn time you talk to me. What did it take, Mama fussing at you?"

Ressa closed her eyes at Kiara's words, trying to ignore the stab of guilt. She didn't need to feel guilty. Yes, it had taken Mama Ang nudging her, but she'd called, right?

"I'm calling, right, Kiara?" she asked softly. "How are you doing?"

There was a faint pause, and then finally, she said, "I wanna see Nceci."

A headache settled at the base of Ressa's head. "K, we've talked about this. You saw her not that long ago. You can see her at Thanksgiving. But—"

"Damn it, Ress! She's my baby. I want to see her!" Kiara's voice skipped, hitched. That heavy, harsh, needling whine underscored those words.

Ressa closed her eyes to the pain and focused on what

mattered—Neeci. She used to allow it, whenever Neeci wanted it, whenever Kiara wanted it. And Neeci had nightmares. Used to wet the bed all the time, cry all the time. The counselor had suggested maybe they try something different.

It had broken her heart, but in the end, Ressa knew it was the right thing.

Neeci was a child and she needed more stability than Kiara could—or would—ever be able to provide. She needed to be safe and secure, and she needed something that Kiara just couldn't offer.

"We've talked about this. If you want to write her a letter, you're more than welcome to. You're welcome to do a phone call, if you remember the rules. But you're not going to put her through this."

"I'm not putting her through *anything*," Kiara half shouted. "She's my little girl and you are *not* her mother."

"No." Ressa steadied herself. "I'm her guardian. You signed away parental rights and there's nothing you can do or say to change that, Kiara."

There was a faint pause and then finally, Kiara said, "Yeah. You're her fucking guardian and I'm the one who's in here. And whose fucking fault is that? But it may not stay that way. Not forever."

Guilt twisted inside. "Kiara . . ."

"Don't!" Kiara shouted.

In the background, voices raised.

"What does that mean?" Blood started to roar in her ears.

A harsh, bitter laugh drifted through the phone. "We'll talk next time you're out here, cuz. I'm not telling you on the phone. But you and Mama Ang need to come out here, and soon. Since you don't have anybody to leave my baby with, you'll have to bring her."

"I don't think so." Ressa gripped the phone tighter.

"Well, you don't have much choice," Kiara said, her voice sly. "There are things I have to tell you and I need to tell you both. So what else are you going to do?"

"I'll make arrangements." Ressa set her jaw, her mind automatically flashing to Trey. "I already have somebody in mind. Kiara, what's going on?"

"You'll do anything to keep my girl away from me," Kiara

said. Sullen temper underscored her words. "When you going
to be here?"

Sighing, Ressa skimmed a hand back over her damp hair.
She still needed to deal with her hair, needed to call Mama
Ang now, needed a drink. "Look, I'll talk to Mama Ang. See
what I can work out. I'll let you know."

"Yeah. Fine. Whatever."

"Kiara . . . I love you."

Kiara said nothing, for the longest time. And then she murmured, "I know."

The line went dead a moment later.

For the first time in . . . ages, really, a story had
sucked him under.

It helped, he supposed, that Travis was there. He volunteered to pick up Clayton and Trey just grunted, only vaguely
aware. He surfaced again when his alarm went off, signaling
that it was time for him to leave, but since Travis was already
gone, he only paused long enough to fuel himself with coffee
and a hastily slapped together sandwich, and then he lost himself back in the story.

It had been nearly eight before he found himself winding
down and then he was famished, eyes bleary, and guilt had
him seeking out his son.

Clayton was snuggled up against Travis while they watched
Captain America. Trey paused briefly to shake his head—
the two of them had already watched every single movie in the
Avengers franchise—and some of them twice—and Travis
hadn't been there that long.

But that didn't keep him from attacking the fridge—he
rolled his eyes at the leftover pizza. Then he ate a slice cold
and reheated what was left before joining them in the living
room.

While the captain was grieving over Bucky, Trey looked
over at his twin. Trying to keep his voice casual, he asked, "Did
anybody call or anything while I was off in another world?"

"Nope." Travis lifted a bottle of beer to his lips, drank deep,
then shot him a look. "Were you expecting a call?"

Yes. He shrugged. "Just wondering."

He pulled his phone from his back pocket, eyed the lack of messages and then blew out a breath.

"You're watching the movie with us, right, Dad?" Clayton asked, his voice soft, gaze still locked on the screen.

"Yeah, Clay. I'm watching." He did send her a text, though. *Hey . . . how you doing?*

There was no answer, though. Even when he was tucking Clayton into bed, even when he returned to his office and tried to catch up on some of the non-writing work he'd ignored all day.

He'd only been at it twenty minutes when Travis joined him, his feet silent. Travis had always been quiet, but Trey had always known when he was there, too.

"You and Ressa going out this weekend?"

Trey looked up at his brother, studying him. He'd been in town a little over a week now and he was looking less gaunt by the day.

Less gaunt, less tired . . . but his eyes were still grim. He looked older, too.

Older, and harder.

Trey couldn't think of a better way to put it. Travis had been born three minutes before Trey, but there were times when it looked like a decade separated them.

"I don't know." He shrugged, and wished he *did* know. They'd had coffee twice this week. He'd had sex with her—about a hundred times—but it was all in his head, or in dreams, and if he didn't remedy that soon, he thought his balls might bust.

Of course, sometimes, he had second thoughts, and third, and fourth. Occasionally those thoughts were followed by a panic attack because he worried about just what he'd do—what Ressa would think—if things got all hot and sweaty between them and then he had another freak-out session in the middle of a make-out session.

More than once, he'd had to mentally kick his own ass, because he'd decided he was moving past this. Moving on with his life—because he actually wanted to *have* a life.

They were still dancing around that *talk* . . . despite the fact that they talked on the phone every night. Sometimes it was just for a few minutes. But then there had been a couple of nights when they walked for a good two hours after they put their respective kids down.

He didn't know if he'd see her that weekend and the thought that he might not made his mood take a turn for the lousy.

"Haven't made any plans?" Travis settled in the beat-up chair next to him, elbows braced on his knees.

"What is this, twenty questions?" Eying his inbox with acute dislike, he said a silent prayer that his assistant Meg would be back to work next week—she'd been on vacation while he was at the convention plus the following week and right before she was supposed to come back, her mother had passed away.

He knew she needed the time away. Shit, if his mother had died, he had a feeling he'd crumple like a baby and want to hide for about a year. He got it, really.

But at the same time, he was lost without Meg being here.

Deciding the search-and-destroy method would be best, Trey did a search for the stuff he knew he wouldn't mess with—all the promotional stuff that was sent his way—he tagged and filed all of that into a folder for Meg to deal with when she was back and up to it. Then he did another search for the people he knew he had to answer sooner rather than later, although those people tended to call. There was a mess of stuff from his agent and his editor, including a new cover.

"You never did answer me."

"What?" Trey only barely registered Travis's voice as he studied the cover. He didn't know what to think about it. It was another L. Forrester book, about one of the secondary characters he'd had in the last one. The heroine had a friend on the quiet, shy, almost gawkish side . . . and somebody who'd worked with the hero in the book had fallen for her.

This one was called *Seducing the Scholar* and instead of a sexy girl with a tie, it had a guy. Trey didn't care what it said about him. He much preferred the pretty girl over the bare-chested pretty boy they'd slapped on this one. He'd told them he wanted something in the same vein . . . and this was definitely that. But he much preferred the beautiful woman.

"Hell, Trey, are you even on . . . what is this . . ."

He went to slap his laptop shut but Travis stopped him, moving entirely too fast as he jerked the laptop out of his reach and all but sprinted around the desk until he had it between them.

"Give me that damn laptop," Trey growled, rising and bracing his hands on the surface of the desk.

"*'Seducing the Scholar'* . . ." Travis drew it out, eyes narrowed. He looked up and the screen was reflected in miniature in his gaze. "So. Who is L. Forrester?"

"You jackass, give me the computer."

"Answer the question." Travis just backed up, an unholy light gleaming in his eyes. "You devious little bastard. It's *you,* isn't it?"

If he could have managed not to blush, he would have bluffed. He knew how to bluff, even his twin. At least he *thought* he could have bluffed.

But it was a waste of time to even try because that telltale hot flush he could feel spreading up his neck, then his cheeks, was a dead giveaway. "Give me my damn computer, you moron."

"Has Mom read these?" Travis sidestepped another grab for the computer, moving easier than he had since he'd arrived. He backed up farther out of reached as he grinned at his brother. "Does she know you went and picked up a pen name?"

"No, you fuckwit."

"Fuckwit." Travis chuckled as he cocked his head, studying the cover from one side, then the other. "So is this one of the billionaire books? You giving up the *cry me a river* books?"

"No." He gauged the distance, the desk, and then hurtled over it. One hand slipped on a piece of paper but he made it. Travis was already dodging out of reach. "You piece of shit—"

"You kiss that pretty lady of yours with that mouth?" Travis snapped the laptop shut and turned it over. "So what is this? What's the L. Forrester stuff?"

Steaming, tapping the laptop against his leg, Trey debated beating his brother senseless or just leaving the room. "You are just as annoying now as you were when we were kids," he finally said.

"Probably." Travis looked cheerful. "You going to answer the question? I can always call Mom. I bet she's heard of this L. Forrester person. I'll see what she . . ."

"It's romance. Okay? Aliesha wanted me to try something different."

Travis's face, still lit with teasing laughter, slowly sobered.

Sighing, Trey turned away. "Don't look like that. Okay? I started working on it a couple of years after she died. It was . . . therapy. The first idea was something I bullshitted over with her, and she told me I should try it. I decided to and my editor liked it, but the imprint doesn't do romance, so we went with another imprint at my publishing house. It did well. I had fun with it, so we did another. And . . ."

He stopped, shrugged. "I like those *cry me a river* books," he said, sliding his brother a dour look. "It's what I'm good at. But every once in a while, I want to do something different. This is. And apparently I don't suck at it."

"Are you still doing it for Aliesha?" Travis studied him.

Trey glared at him.

Holding up his hands, Travis said, "Hey, don't look at me like that. I'm trying to understand, trying to help. I loved her, too. I . . . I just . . ." He stopped and looked away. "But I see how you looked at Ressa. If you're doing this for Aliesha . . . ?"

"It's not for Aliesha. She's part of my past, but Ressa . . ." Trey didn't even have to think about it. His heart ached just thinking about Ressa. It ached, even as a smile seemed to fill every empty part of him. "I look at her and I hurt. I look at her and I want things I thought I'd never want again. I didn't think I'd ever feel that way again."

He turned away, putting the laptop on his desk as he moved to the window. Shoving the window open, he unlatched the screen and leaned out.

He needed air.

A good twenty yards away was the dark, looming presence of Nadine's house, and as he stood there, he thought he saw one of her curtains flicker, then fall back into place. He scowled and then pointedly looked away.

Quietly, he said, "Aliesha's gone, but I didn't do this for *her*. It was for me. I needed to find a way to close the door, say good-bye . . . something. That's what the first book was. The first chapter was the first step in letting go . . . it just took me a while to figure that out."

Travis was quiet.

He was quiet for so long, Trey started to wonder if he'd slipped out.

But when he turned, he saw his brother standing exactly where he had been. "Can I suggest you do something else for you, then?"

Trey narrowed his eyes.

Travis shrugged. "The kid's asleep. He'll stay that way until you wake him up. Chances are Ressa's little girl is sleeping, too. Why don't you go spend some time with your woman, Trey?"

He opened his mouth, but Travis cut him off. "Both of you have kids you have to keep in mind. I can stay here with him. The two of you need to grab some time for yourself and stop dancing around each other like cats."

Brooding, Trey went to shake his head. *Not a good idea.* Of course, his entire body was already hard at the thought, blood thrumming in his veins.

"Go on," Travis said. "You should have seen your face when I told you nobody called, and don't act like you weren't expecting her to call. Go see her. Take some time for you."

For a long moment, Trey stared at his brother and then, without saying another word, he headed for the door.

"By the way . . ."

Trey paused in the doorway and looked back.

"I already knew your little secret," Travis said, grinning at him. "You have all those other books—the hot girl with the tie—up in the spare room. If you didn't want me knowing, you should have locked the room or told me to stay out."

Trey just flipped him off.

Hey . . . how are you doing?

She'd picked up the phone, stared at the text about a dozen times.

And about a dozen times, she'd almost called him, because she needed to hear his voice. She wanted to see him. But if they talked, he'd hear something in her voice, she knew it.

And this wasn't something she could go into over the phone.

They needed to have *that* talk before she launched into a full-on sulk about the things from her past, and how her temperamental, and troubled, cousin still tangled up everything. So Ressa remained in her bed, curled up on her side and trying to pretend she could sleep, that the past few days hadn't happened.

She stroked the screen of her phone like a talisman, keeping her thoughts on Trey. If she thought about him, she wouldn't have to think about the fact that this weekend, she and Mama Ang would be going to see her cousin, and she'd find out just what that sly note in Kiara's voice meant.

She needed to talk to him, though. See if he'd mind keeping Neeci with him. There were a few others she could leave her cousin with, but nobody she was as comfortable with and nobody that Neeci would like being with.

Whose fucking fault is that? Kiara's words rang in her ears. Groaning, she rolled onto her belly and buried her face in her pillow.

"Think about something else," she told herself.

She shoved the phone call out of her mind, tried to think about Trey, but instead, her mind spun back.

Years back. Back to the time when everything had gone wrong.

"Wow." Kiara stared around her for a long moment before looking at her cousin. "How are you affording this?"

She shrugged. "You ready to go?" On her way out the door, she grabbed her jacket but Kiara stopped her yet again, her eyes going wide at the buttery-soft leather jacket she'd pulled on.

"Oh . . . Ress. That is nice!"

"Thanks. Come on. We're going to be late for the movie. We hardly ever go out anymore."

"That's because you're always busy," Kiara said, laughing as she gave the leather jacket one more envious stroke. "If I didn't know better, I'd think you were out there following in your dad's footsteps or something, the way you got this place fixed up, your clothes . . ."

"Very funny." Ice skated up her spine, but she pushed it

away. *"I don't mess with that stuff. I told you that. And you better not either."*

It had taken her forever to get her life somewhat normal. She wouldn't mess it up now.

"So are you working or what?"

"Would you let it go?" She glared at Kiara and herded her out the door, locking it behind her. They'd almost made it to Kiara's car when a quick shout had them looking back.

"That your roommate?" Kiara asked as Hannah came jogging down the stairs, holding the cordless in her hand.

"Yeah."

"Ress, if you cancel on me again, I'm never talking to you again," Kiara said, a sulk threading its way in her voice.

"I'm not cancelling." She wanted to go see a damn movie with her cousin.

Hannah was closer now and caught the last half of the conversation, her eyebrows going up. She paused, looking back and forth. *"It's . . . your boss,"* she said after a pause. *"They had a no-show and need you to come in. They'll pay double tonight."*

"No." She glared at Hannah and gestured to Kiara. *"Let's go. We're going to be late."*

"But . . ."

"No." She gave Hannah a hard look and hurried around the car. Kiara gave her an odd look as she slammed the door.

"You really got to tell me what kind of job this is—a place that pays double if you come in? I need that kind of job."

It was almost two in the morning before she made it home.

The memory of her movie date with her cousin wasn't much more than a memory—that had been over a month ago and everything since then had been a blur of classes, dinners, parties—and very little sleep.

Maybe the dinners and parties would sound fun to some.

But when she had to do a cocktail party at three and then a dinner party that lasted until midnight, followed by a brunch that started at nine, on top of keeping up with her class load . . .

Sometimes she wished she'd never told Hannah she'd talk to her friend, Sharon.

". . . that easy."

That voice made her pause.

Sharon.

Speak of the devil.

She paused in the hallway, head cocked as she listened in.

The next voice had her shoving a door open and she gaped at the young woman sitting across from Sharon Hightower— the woman responsible for the money she now had in her bank account.

She didn't know who was more surprised—herself, or her cousin.

Kiara recovered first, smiling widely at her. "Hey, Ress!"

"Kiara." She set her jaw. "What are you doing here?"

Kiara stood up, nervously smoothing down a red dress that looked suspiciously familiar. It looked almost dead like the one she owned. "I came by to see if you wanted to grab dinner, but you weren't here and . . ." She shrugged, tried for a smile. "I started talking to Hannah."

She turned her attention to Hannah and the pretty blonde smiled. "She's pretty, Ress. She asked some questions and I answered, then she wanted to know more so I asked Sharon over."

"Yeah. And she's smart and she doesn't need to do this." Fury pulsed inside her. Fury—and fear.

"Oh, come on . . ." Sharon spoke to Ressa for the first time, a pleasant smile on her face. "It's harmless. Look at what it's done for you."

If she was as smart as she liked to think, Ressa would have punched Sharon Hightower in her pretty, perfect nose.

But she hadn't.

Sighing, she snuggled deeper into her pillow, still clutching her phone like a talisman. Now . . .

The knock on the door caught her off guard.

Swallowing, she looked down at the workout gear she had on, her heart slamming hard against her ribs. Her head spun, bile churning its way up her throat, compliments of the memory of that night. She'd thought if she pounded away her grievances on the treadmill, she'd feel better, but no luck.

There was another knock, harder this time and she swore, rising from her bed and moving toward the stairs. Whoever that was, he was going to wake Neeci up—

He.

Her heart lurched up into her throat.

Even though her gut told her who it was, wariness had her approaching the door slowly, and she clutched her phone tighter as she paused a few feet away.

It was past ten now. Fears from childhood, old but not forgotten, rose up. A girl didn't grow up the way she had without learning more than a little caution.

From several feet away, she called out, "Who is it?"

And at the same time, she moved to the antique table near the door and grabbed one of the ugly metal sculptures that Bruce had loved to collect. She always made fun of them, teased her stepfather about them, but after he died, getting rid of them had seemed impossible. Now, the solid weight of it felt good in her hand.

The sound of Trey's voice made her heart race all that much harder. "It's me."

"Trey . . ." Her mouth went dry. Bracing one hand on the door, she leaned in, staring through the Judas hole centered on her door. He had his head bowed and it looked like he mirrored her pose, one hand braced on the door while he waited. Waited for what?

Dread twisted, shifted.

Aw, now . . . what is this shit? Don't I have enough going on?

Hard times, girl, they will make you or they will break you . . . the echo of Mama Ang's voice came up from the recesses of her mind, and she squared her shoulders before she reached out to unlock the door.

Face expressionless, she opened it, pondering the bottle of wine she had in the fridge. She couldn't think of too many things that would have him on her doorstep this late.

Looked like the twin brother had gone and ratted her out.

The son of a bitch.

* * *

Trey had planned to say something. Anything, really.

But as the door slowly opened to reveal her standing there in clothes that skimmed her thighs and hips, a tank that drooped over one shoulder, leaving luscious skin and all those fucking sexy tattoos bared, every thought he had drained away.

Should they talk?

Yeah.

She seemed concerned about whatever secrets her past held. He had some shadows of his own—shadows that had haunted and strained his life for nearly six years. Should he explain those?

Oh, hell, yeah.

But all he could think about was the sad, somber look in her eyes.

What's hurt you?

He wanted to ask—no, demand. Then he wanted to kiss the misery away and make it all better.

One hand clenched into a fist as he let his gaze roam lower, over the gray tank, the tattoos he'd kissed his way across, the curve of her breasts.

His gaze caught and lingered over the heavy-looking metal sculpture she held in one hand.

"You always answer the door with pieces of art in your hand?" he asked.

She glanced down, a frown drawing her mouth tight.

"Ah . . . no." She shook her head and turned away, putting it down on a table a few feet away. "Come on in."

He came inside, easing the door shut, studying the tension that held every line of her body tight.

She still stood with her back to him and he was a breath away from going to her when she spoke. The tight sound of her voice froze him in his tracks.

"Is everything okay? You're out kind of late."

"No." *You tell me,* he thought. But then he decided to let it go. For now. Reaching up, he trailed a finger down her nape, watched as she shivered. "Everything's not okay. It's been four days since I saw you. Four days since I kissed you. And way too long since I made love to you."

He heard the soft catch of her breath and that was all he needed to lean forward and press his lips to her neck, brushing aside the thick tail of her hair where it rested against her skin.

She practically melted against him, some of that tension draining out of her body. Sliding his arms around her, he pulled her back against him. Lust bit into him as her butt pressed up against his cock, but he gritted his teeth, forced himself to think past the need.

"Ressa," he murmured, resting his chin on her shoulder. "What's wrong?"

Her voice was unsteady as she answered. "Nothing. Nothing is wrong."

She was lying. He knew it.

As she turned in his arms, he studied her face, saw the darkness in her gaze, the misery. "Talk to me," he said, rubbing his lips against hers. "You look like your world is coming apart."

"No." She curled her arms around his neck, leaning against him. "I just . . ."

She leaned in, licked his lips.

Groaning, he gripped her hips, tried to ease back. "Ressa, wait . . ."

"No. You're right. It's been too long. I need you."

He clung to sanity by his fingernails. "Where's Neeci?"

"In her bed. Asleep. Nothing wakes that child once she's down," Ressa said, pressing her mouth to his neck. He felt the hot brush of her lips against his skin. She spoke again, and this time, her words were a plea. "Make love to me. I need this."

He couldn't have denied her anything in that moment.

"Your room . . . Where is your room?"

She waved toward the stairs and the two of them half staggered, half ran toward them. Halfway up, he took her down and pressed her to the steps, feasting on her mouth and shuddering at the taste, the feel of her. Thoughts of regret, fear, hesitation faded away. Thoughts of *control* faded away.

He cupped her hips in his hands, her skin burning hot through the thin material. Against his chest, her breasts went flat and that was good, but not enough. He caught the tank top she wore and started to drag it up.

She caught his wrist.

"Upstairs." She bit his lower lip and then said it again, the demand heavy in her voice. "Upstairs . . . *now*."

He caught her around the waist, and rose, one hand around the bannister. He felt half drunk—drunk on her. Pinning her against the railing, he said, "Upstairs."

Then he returned the favor and bit her lip, reveling in the feel of her reaction, a full body shudder.

It seemed forever before they finally reached the top of the stairs, even longer before they stumbled into the room Ressa pointed out. *Finally*—

Trey spun, trapping her against the door. A startled gasp erupted from her as he caught the band of her sport bra in his hands. He would have torn it away from her if he could and he was cursing by the time he was able to toss it to the floor.

Her full breasts swung free and he caught them in his hands, hunger a spike in his brain. He teased dark brown nipples, already drawn tight.

"Kiss me," she demanded, locking her fingers around his neck.

He didn't even have a chance to follow that hungry order because she tugged his mouth to hers, kissing him with a greedy need all but put him on his knees. Tongue and teeth clashed. Her breasts pressed flat against him and it was a sweet, sweet torture . . . but *still* not enough. He broke the kiss to tear his own shirt away and then grunted in pleasure at the feel of their upper bodies pressed bare to each other.

She rubbed herself against him and he shuddered, feeling the drag of her nipples over his skin. Ressa moaned out his name and it sent a tremor racing through him. His fingers tightened on her and he had to force himself to be gentle, but even as he tried to do that, she sank her teeth into his lip, hard enough to bring pain. He did the same and she moaned into his mouth and arched her hips to his.

Desperate for more, for all, he shoved his hands inside the waistband of her tight workout pants, working himself against the heat between her thighs, but still—*not enough*.

She whimpered as he went to his knees, jerking her pants down. When they tangled at her calves, he stopped and leaned in, pressing his face to her cleft. Soft curls hid her from him, but that didn't deter him. He flicked his tongue against her clit and when she bucked against him, satisfaction ripped at him.

The scent of her rushed up to flood the air and he thought he just might go mad for the want of her. He stripped the pants away and used his hands to tug at her ankles until she widened her legs.

"I need to taste you," he muttered. Taste. Have. Love . . .

Love . . .

The thought should frighten him.

Everything in this moment should frighten him—or at least worry him, because he felt too out of control, scrabbling for any remnant of it. But all that mattered was having her. Branding himself on her . . . and having *her* brand herself on *him*.

Leaning in, he licked her, using his tongue to open her before going deeper, hungry strokes that had her rocking against his face.

She panted out his name, her hands clutching the back of his head. "Please . . . I want . . . I need . . ."

When she tried to pull at his shoulders, he caught one wrist, guided it away.

"Stop," he muttered. "I need this. I need to taste you . . . your pussy, fuck . . ."

A broken sound left her throat and he looked up, saw her eyes flare wide and then she tugged him back. "Do it then. Put your mouth on me."

She was slick and hot, and getting hotter, slicker with every minute as he licked at her. He shifted to close his mouth around her clit, sucking at it gently, then harder as her nails bit into his shoulders and her broken moans turned to breathy, desperate cries.

Sliding his hand between her legs, he tucked two fingers against her entrance, felt her tense. Then, slowly, he screwed them in.

She tightened around him and he felt her muscles grip and clutch and grab—

He paused, taking a moment to lick at her clit before he

looked up. "When you start to come, I'm going to stop. I'm going to be inside you."

"Damn right," she whispered, her voice shaky.

His cock pulsed, throbbed, demanding he be inside her *now*.

But . . . no. Not yet.

Another taste. Another slow stroke of his fingers inside her. She moaned, her sheath tightening—

Again.

Again—

She bucked and he felt it coming on. Shoving to his feet, he pulled out one of the condoms he'd brought with him. She moaned, her hips rolling in a circle like she already had him inside her. His fingers trembled as he tore the foil open and they trembled even more when he fumbled with his jeans.

"Hurry," she whispered.

He looked up at her, saw how her eyes had all but gone blind.

I'm not taking my time.

Condom on, he leaned in, pressed two fingers against her and rubbed. "Are you still there?"

She bucked against his hand. "Are you trying to drive me crazy?"

He did one slow circle around her clit as he answered. "Yes. I want you as crazy as you've made me, as hungry, as mindless."

For a moment, she just stared at him and then a Mona Lisa smile curved her lips. "Well, then fuck me already, because I'm going out of my mind."

He caught her legs behind the knees, lifted her, her back braced against the door. Without another word, without even another breath, he pushed inside, shuddering as she wrapped around him, drawing him deeper, deeper . . .

Ressa gasped as he stroked deep inside. Filling her . . . her body, her heart, her soul.

Even as her heart and soul felt like they'd shatter.

No man ever had consumed her as totally as he had. It scared her, too, because she knew what that meant. He owned so much of her, without even asking, and that meant he could break her—without even trying.

That terror had her shoving her hands into his hair, drawing his mouth to hers. Desperation had her rocking to meet every thrust, kissing him like she feared this might be the last time, the very last.

I don't want to lose you . . .

The thought of it terrified her.

His teeth nipped her lower lip right before he tore his mouth away and buried his face in her hair. His hips surged against hers, swiveled. Deep inside, she felt his cock swell, the head of it rubbing against her in a way that left her feeling like she'd somehow explode, even as her skin started to feel too tight, too hot. There wasn't enough room inside her to contain this—

She slammed her head against the door, barely noticing the pain as sensation swamped her. "I . . . damn it, it's too . . ." Her lids drifted down and she tried to gather up the pieces of herself that tried to scatter.

Trey reached up, cradling the back of her head. "Stay with me," he ordered, his voice harsh, rough. "Look at me."

She stared into eyes so blue, it hurt to look at them. He rubbed his mouth against hers, whispered, "I need you."

Too much. A sob welled inside her as he slowed his thrusts, that driving hunger falling away into devastating gentleness. No, no, no . . . the hunger was better, easier to lose herself to . . .

Trey flicked his tongue along her lips and she opened for him. He shifted position on her body, gathering her in closer, lifting her higher, and she shuddered as he started to drag his body back and forth against her clitoris with every stroke.

A scream built inside her and she swallowed it down, digging her nails into his skin instead, clutching at his hips with her knees. The swollen head of his cock pulsed as he twisted and pushed into her again, harder, deeper, but so devastatingly slow—

She shattered with the next stroke and he went mad, as though he'd been waiting for just that before he let go. As she gasped and shuddered under the force of her orgasm, he snarled, his body going tight, muscles rippling as he thrust deep, once, twice—then again, again . . . harder each time until he shoved her, unbelievably, into another, more powerful orgasm.

He growled her name just before his mouth caught hers in a deep, drugging kiss.

He would move.

At some point.

Back braced against the door, Ressa lying half sprawled, half draped over him, Trey knew he couldn't stay on that miserable, hard floor for too long, but for that moment, he was just fine. More relaxed than he could remember feeling in too long, and if he had his way, he'd talk her into letting him stay for a while, and he might end up even more relaxed.

Ressa was limp in his arms. Turning his head, he pressed a kiss to her neck.

She sighed, curling one arm around him, hugging him tighter. He worked up the energy to look at her, but she had her eyes closed.

"I'll move. In a minute. Ten tops."

"I was thinking in an hour," she said, her voice rough.

"That sounds good, too." He kept studying her, hoping she'd look at him. He wanted to see her eyes.

She just traced her fingers along the tattoo on his lower abdomen, a slightly ticklish sensation. It made his skin prickle and even that light touch had his body stirring. He could see himself flipping her onto her back, sliding between her thighs, burying his dick inside her, but for now . . .

All he wanted was this.

This very moment.

"You didn't call tonight."

The minute she said it, she wanted to jerk it back. She was still half-sprawled against him and her body ached in the sweetest way, and instead of inviting him to her bed, instead of pressing her mouth to his neck, then moving down, instead of doing any number of wonderful things, she had to go and say that.

The last thing she wanted to do was sound like a needy, desperate woman. Except she felt terribly needy and desperate right now.

Trey *had* texted her. She could have called him back, except she'd been too busy letting her cousin mess her head up. Again.

But the words were already out, hanging there between them and there was nothing she could say or do to unsay the words.

All Trey did was skim a hand down her side. "I . . . uh . . . well, you probably need to be prepared for this kind of thing if you're going to get involved with a writer. We don't always live on planet Earth. I kind of got lost in another world and didn't surface until after seven. Travis was there to take care of Clayton and . . ." He shrugged. "It was the first time I've been able to lose myself like that in a while. I was going to call but they were watching a movie and Clayton . . ."

Now she felt like a pathetic loser. She'd been feeling sorry for herself and brooding, while he was simply spending some time with his brother and his son. "Hush. I just . . . I missed you. I should have called you. Nothing was stopping me."

Except the fact that I'm a mess.

"I'm sorry. I wanted to talk to you. I sent you that text, but you didn't answer and I thought, hey, I could always call tomorrow. But then I . . . well. I wanted to see you." He rubbed his cheek against hers. That simple caress made her heart melt. "I miss you. Seeing you a couple of times a week doesn't feel like enough."

It made her heart melt a little.

At the same time, it made her heart break a little.

Because she remembered why she hadn't texted.

And the fear that had rushed through her when she'd seen him at the door. She'd thought he was here because Travis had dug into her family's past, that Trey knew.

She'd kept this from him. She couldn't anymore. Once she dropped this on him, would he feel comfortable watching Neeci? Oh, he'd probably do it, because he was just that kind of guy. But she wouldn't ask him.

She could already imagine what would happen—she'd seen

it play out several times once it had happened with a guy she'd really cared about.

Nobody had ever mattered as much as Trey.

But she couldn't put it off anymore.

I have to tell him.

Tucking her head against his shoulder, she barely managed to keep from clutching at him, holding tight.

"Can I stay?" Trey murmured, unaware of the nerves already tangling inside her. "At least for a while."

She swallowed. It didn't keep her voice from being husky when she answered, "Yeah. Yeah, I'd like that."

Then, before she could chicken out, she finished in a rush, "I think there's something I need to tell you anyway."

Trey felt like he'd just gotten off one of the coasters at Busch Gardens—he'd gone up, then down, then up . . . and he was about to crash down again, he knew it. The adrenaline high he'd been riding on was about to give out, too.

They were downstairs now, in her kitchen, because she'd wanted a glass of wine. She'd offered him one, but his mind was already spinning and he knew better than to try alcohol now. So maybe he'd been able to have a beer with his brother—even if he'd done it to challenge himself.

He wasn't going to push his luck, considering the look in Ressa's eyes.

She stood on the far side of the room, a glass of the red wine in one hand, her gaze on the floor. She opened her mouth, closed it. Then abruptly, she said, "Let's go back to my room."

Once there, he gathered up his clothes, tugging on his jeans. He had a feeling this wasn't going to go well and if he was right, he wanted to be able to just get dressed and leave.

He didn't know what she was going to say, but it wasn't going to be fun.

He'd seen that look too many times—it was the look that said, *I've got bad news and you're not going to like it.*

Besides, bad news and being naked just didn't mix well together. There was something about being dressed that just made hard news a little more tolerable, he decided.

Taking any kind of bad news naked was just a double punch to the gut.

Apparently, she agreed. She pulled a black robe over the sexy blue sleep shirt she wore, but she left the robe untied and the black framed her goddess-like body as she started to pace.

"I . . ." She pursed her lips and blew out a breath. "Look, this isn't the easiest thing to tell you. It's not something I generally talk about much. There's not really a graceful way to work this into a conversation. If all we'd had was Jersey, then it wouldn't matter. But now . . ."

He just waited as she looked down, her shoulders slumped, the coils she'd twisted into her hair falling to shield her face.

Slowly, she looked up and took another breath, deeper this time, like she was gathering herself.

Her eyes were solemn.

She looked like she was braced for a blow.

What is this? he wondered.

A taut, heavy silence stretched out, and then finally she threw the words out, almost like a challenge.

"My cousin is in prison . . . and it's my fault she's in there."

Chapter Twenty-three

Trey just stared at her.

She crossed her arms over her chest and started to tap her foot. "Did you hear me?"

"Yeah." He hooked his hand over his neck, rubbed the muscles there for a minute, and then he stood up, moving to stand in front of her. "Is this Neeci's mom?"

"Yes." She lifted her chin, almost in challenge.

"Okay." Then he scowled. "Well, I guess it's not okay—it's got to be hell on you all, but . . . I don't see what this has to do with us."

She just stared at him for a long moment and then she tossed half the glass of wine back, like it was pure moonshine. "Are you serious? Didn't you *hear* me?" she asked when she was done. She thumped the glass down with so much force, he was surprised it didn't break. "My cousin is in jail—we were like sisters and *I* am the reason she's in there and you don't see what it has to do with us?"

"Well. No." Tucking his thumbs in his pockets, he rocked back on his heels, eying her narrowly. He couldn't quite tell how to take this mood of hers. Not at all. But he wasn't tracking this line of thought she had, either. "It's not like I'm dating her."

"You should probably rethink if you want to date *me*."

"Why the hell would I do that?" he snapped. Now he was getting pissed.

She stormed over to him and poked him in the chest with a finger. "You think about what the headline on some of the gossip rags will read like if this goes anywhere, hotshot? *I* have. *Learn the scandalous secrets behind the girlfriend of Trey Barnes, publishing's golden boy*."

"I'm *not* anybody's golden boy." Capturing her wrist, he held it in his grasp when she would have tugged away. He hauled her up against him, using his free arm to wrap around her waist. She glared up at him, but it did something to the ache and the anger forming inside him when she didn't pull away. Trying to hold that anger in check, he half growled, "And for the record, I don't give a damn what any gossip rag says about me. We lived through all of that shit growing up. You think I *care*?"

"But most of that was probably *just* gossip," she said, her voice rising. "They'd have a field day digging up things about *my* past . . . and then there's Kiara. This isn't gossip, Trey! It's reality."

She jerked her hand away and the venom, the remnants of horror in her voice caught him so off guard that he let her go. Her eyes shot hot, brutal sparks at him and then she spun away, her strides erratic and jerky.

She fumbled as she tied her robe, then, as though the admission had chilled her to the bone, she rubbed her hands up and down her arms.

The roaring in his ears faded as the seconds ticked by. His hands felt empty.

"Ress."

"Don't," she said, her voice low. "Just . . . don't. I need a minute."

Slowly, she lowered herself to sit on the edge of the bed, arms crossed protectively across her chest as she huddled in on herself. It hit him then, how she waited, the way she'd looked at him. Like she was braced for some violent blow.

And that was what she'd expected.

She really thought he'd push her away over this.

She needed a minute? No, he thought. That wasn't what she needed at all. Slowly, he crossed the floor and knelt in front of her. She flinched and tried to pull away.

He reached out and caught her behind the knees, holding her in place.

"Whatever it is," he said slowly, waiting until she lifted her chin and met his eyes. "*Whatever* it is . . . she did it. How can it be your fault?"

An erratic breath escaped her and then she shoved past him. He ended up on his butt while she moved to grab her wine. Sighing, he levered himself onto the bed and watched as she tossed back half the glass.

"Yeah," she said, her voice thick and scathing. "*She* did it. But she never would have gotten involved if it hadn't been for me . . . and I'm the one who turned her in."

She turned back to face Trey now and her eyes glittered with tears—both rage and misery shone there. In that moment, he couldn't think.

"She got herself in a mess of trouble and there's no denying that. But that's not going to make a difference when push comes to shove and Neecl asks why her mama is in jail—and I have to tell her the truth."

"Ressa— "

"Shut up!" She hurled the glass. It shattered, the glass splintering on impact. She barely noticed. "You don't *know*, okay? You don't . . . you can't . . ."

Droplets of wine clung to her lower legs. Bits of glass sparkled around them as he rose. He crossed to her, sidestepping the glass. He caught her, ignoring as she tried to jerk away. "Be still," he growled.

"What do you know!" she half shouted, half struggling as he dumped her on the bed. "You got this perfect family . . . movie star brothers, perfect parents. Since when in your perfect life has anything *ever* gone wrong?"

The second the words left her mouth, she stilled.

Trey stared at her.

Slowly, he backed away. Glass crunched under his feet and pain shot up his foot. Turning away, he looked at all the glass while her words echoed through his head.

My perfect life.

"Trey, I . . ."

"Where do you keep your dust pan and broom?" he asked, the words sounding oddly wooden, flat.

"Trey, listen . . ."

"Where?"

"Shit, I . . ."

He turned his head.

"There's one in my bathroom closet," she said, turning her head and staring toward the window.

He barely remembered the next few seconds, barely remembered the sweeping up the glass, dumping it in the small trash can inside her blue and silver bathroom. The bloody red streaks on the floor had him stilling and he frowned, staring at it until he realized it was coming from his foot.

He sat on the toilet and stared at the sole of his foot, the small, jagged bit of glass barely visible.

"Let me help."

He ignored her as he tried to catch it between his thumb and forefinger.

My perfect life.

She nudged his hands aside and he averted his gaze as she used a pair of tweezers to pull the bit of glass out. The small pain barely fazed him and he took the pad of gauze from her when she would have pressed it to the cut.

"I'm sorry."

He just shook his head.

"Trey, look, my head is all messed up. I . . ."

"Don't worry about it," he said brusquely. He caught sight of the neat little first-aid kit she'd put on the counter. He flipped it open and found a bandage.

"Trey. Look . . ."

"It was a bad idea," he said shortly as he dragged on the rest of his clothes. "Coming over here like this. I'll go. We'll . . . talk. Sometime."

He was down the stairs and halfway to the door when she shouted at his back. "It *was* my fault!"

The misery in her voice froze him. He wanted to be gone, wanted to leave and just . . . hell, he didn't want to go home. He thought maybe, just maybe, he actually wanted a drink. No. No, he wanted to get drunk, even craved that oblivion.

But he knew better.

He just stood there and waited.

"She . . . I . . . she was like my little sister. Her mama— Mama Ang—she's the one who got me off the streets. She saved me," she said softly. "Kiara was . . . she was like my sister, you know. We lived here, in this beautiful, nice house . . ."

"This was . . . it was Bruce's house. I bought it from Mama Ang a few years ago. Bruce was Kiara's stepfather, but they never got along well. When he died, he left the house to Mama Ang. He gave me the Mustang and some money, left his other car to Kiara and some money—a lot of it, really. But it was held in trust. She couldn't get it unless it was used for college. Once she turned twenty-five, she would get twenty thousand a year for the next five years, but . . ." Ressa sighed, the sound shaky and soft. Tired. "She hated it. Didn't know why I got the car and money, but she had to wait. She was three years younger than me, still in school. I'd already started college . . ."

Her voice trailed away.

"Fuck. If he knew . . ."

Turning, he found her standing in the middle of the room, arms once more wrapped around herself. "If he knew what I was doing, he wouldn't have given me shit." Ressa said, her voice harsh.

Now she looked up at him. "Seven years ago, I was arrested on suspicion of prostitution."

He just stared at her.

Those blue green eyes had gone blank and she couldn't read anything from him.

When he just stood there, silent, she lifted a brow. "What . . . Don't you have anything to say?" She moved into the living room, unable to keep watching him. For a moment, she just stood there, her chest aching as she took in the world that she now lived in. A world that she didn't really deserve. Hearing the creak of a floorboard, she moved farther into the room and settled down on a wide, fat chair. Bruce had bought it for Mama Ang, placed it right here in this spot by the fireplace so she could read. He'd ended up using it more than she did.

Mama Ang hadn't been able to sit in it since the day she'd found him in it—lifeless. That big heart of his had just stopped.

Aware of Trey's watchful gaze, she crossed her legs, taking her time to smooth down the robe. Then she met his eyes.

"Are you just going to leave it at that or are you going to explain?" he asked, his voice oddly calm.

"What's there to explain?" She shrugged lazily. "My senior year of college, I was arrested for prostitution."

"How about you tell me whether or not you were guilty— and if so . . . *why*?"

The question—both of them—caught her off guard.

She'd expected him to just walk.

That was why she'd done it. It would be easier. That was why she'd tried to keep him at a distance ever since that morning in New Jersey. She'd felt herself on this slippery hill that very morning. Or maybe she'd been slipping even before then.

She wanted to protect herself—that was even why she'd told Travis. If *he* went and told his brother and Trey pushed her away, then she could blame him. If he walked without her explaining, then she could still blame him.

But now . . .

Lowering her head, she caught the end of her belt and started to twirl it around her finger. "No," she said softly. "I was willing to do plenty of things for money, but I wasn't a whore."

Even though she didn't hear him, she knew he'd crossed over to her and she caught her breath, not daring to move. When his hand brushed her cheek, she continued to stare at her fingers, worrying the black silk.

"Why don't you just tell me, Ressa?"

Because when you walk away, it's going to be because you know the truth . . . and it won't be anybody's fault but mine. She swallowed around the knot in her throat. The ache in her chest threatened to choke her.

"I had the money from Bruce," she said softly. "But it was just barely enough. I was working at a fast-food place, up until midnight, cramming for all these classes . . . trying so hard to

keep up. It seemed like everybody else around me was having
a good time and there I was, struggling just to hold my head
above water. December rolled around and Mama Ang called,
wanted to take me and Kiara to Florida for a vacation over the
break, but I couldn't go." She shrugged. "I tried to act like it
wasn't a big deal, but my job . . . they wouldn't let me have the
time off. I'd just started and all. I was in my room, sulking,
and my roommate came in. She was always out—dressed like
Cinderella, and I thought she must have had one hell of a
Prince Charming, because she'd come back with gifts and she
was never hurting for money. Her parents weren't loaded or
anything—they had a dairy farm up in Indiana and she was
there on scholarship, just like I was."

Resting her head on the back of the couch, she thought of
the last time she'd seen Hannah. She'd looked just as scared,
just as miserable as Ressa had felt. "Hannah asked me if I'd
like to maybe stop working so hard. She knew how I could get
enough money to cover my books and everything that my
scholarship wouldn't cover—plus still have money left over. I
told her to get the hell out. Figured she was talking about drugs
and I'd finally gotten clear of that. Took a long time to get away
from everything my dad had done—the mistakes I'd almost
made. But she laughed. It wasn't drugs. Wasn't anything illegal. Was usually even fun. She told me I could do a trial run,
even."

Sighing, she looked back at him. "Hannah was an escort—
there was a teacher's aide who'd set it up. About fifteen girls
from that school and a community college a few miles away.
It was easy money. I'd get anywhere from two hundred to five
hundred dollars just to spend an evening or a day with some
guy who didn't want to go to a party by himself. A few times,
I'd fly to some event—there was one in New York, one in
Miami. I'd make more on those. It seemed like a dream come
true."

Unable to sit there any longer, she got up and moved to the
fireplace. The hearth was empty and cold. The mantle held
pictures—a few of Mama Ang and Bruce, a couple of Kiara
from high school but most of them were of Neeci.

There wasn't a single one of Ressa.

She still felt like an imposter here.

"Dreams never last though, do they?" She picked up a picture of Neeci and Kiara. She'd taken it when Neeci was a year old, when she'd taken the little girl to see her mother.

"What happened?"

"My cousin found out how I was making money. If it had just been that . . ." She shrugged. "But she wasn't happy. There she was, with a nice chunk of change coming to her but it had to get doled out in bits and pieces until she was twenty-five. She'd gotten used to having everything she wanted. Bruce had spoiled her, trying to get her to open up to him . . . it didn't work, but she sure as hell came to like having somebody who'd give her every little thing her heart desired."

Bitterness choked her and she had to stop for a minute. Forcing herself to breathe, she put the picture down. How many times had she wished she'd had a father like Bruce? Too many. Oh, she'd loved her dad, even when she hated him.

He'd taught her how to con people, used her to distract people while he robbed them blind.

Remember how we do it, baby . . . that woman right there, the little lost girl act. That's what we're doing.

Later, he'd used her to carry the drugs he'd started to sell because cops wouldn't search a child.

He'd ended up in jail anyway and later he'd ended up dead and she'd been the one they'd come to, looking for the money he owed.

"Hannah told her about it, one day when I was out. Sharon—she was the woman who set it all up—she'd always pay a bonus to whoever brought a new girl in and Hannah loved the bonuses. I think she liked the bonuses more than the actual jobs. She told Kiara . . . and Kiara was determined. She got involved in it—lied about her age, even. She was only seventeen when she started going out with these guys, but she'd always looked older. Acted older. They loved her. Some guys love having some sweet young thing and playing the sugar daddy—she got *real* popular."

She lapsed into silence for a moment and then looked back at Trey. He hadn't said anything since she'd started to talk and the silence was killing her, telling him all of this was killing her. But she couldn't stop now.

* * *

Trey wanted to tell her to skip all of this.

He'd already decided he didn't give a damn.

But it was pretty clear she did—and she had to tell him. So he listened.

"Sharon's boyfriend started getting greedy. Scott started bringing in new clients, telling them that some of the girls might be willing to offer a more *personalized* service. He was careful about which of us he talked to—he didn't even let Sharon know. Hannah didn't know, I didn't . . ."

The words trailed away.

"Your cousin did."

Ressa lifted her head and met his eyes. Then she shrugged. "She says she didn't sleep with anybody for money. But she was doing other things—*they* were doing other things. Getting pictures and stuff." She stopped for a minute, then spoke again. "For blackmail."

Trey closed his eyes, dragging a hand down his face.

"One of the newer girls tried it with one of the established clients—his regular girl was sick. She'd gotten mono and he wanted a date for a business function. He was a sweet old guy, just . . . shy. A lot of these guys were harmless. He didn't like going alone and he loved having a pretty girl with him. That's what the service usually was. It was harmless," she said again. Her voice was soft, but there was an odd note under it, as if she was trying to convince him.

She turned away from him. It was a cut to the heart and he moved up behind her, curling an arm around her waist. She tensed and he thought she'd pull away. But then she sagged against him. "Marisol—that was her name—she . . . um . . . she tried to pull something in the limo and it upset him. His name was Egbert. Mr. Egbert—his regular girl always called him the Egg. He was round and pale . . . anyway. He had the driver turn around and take Marisol home and then he called Sharon, he was so upset by it. That's when she started poking around—when she realized Scott was pulling some shady shit. Marisol was an idiot—she always used a little recorder deal Scott had set her up with. It was in her purse—I don't know what all she got, but she took it to Scott, I guess to try and blackmail Egbert. He must have told her no, because she tried to do it on her own . . ." The words trailed off and she looked away.

He rested his chin on her shoulder and stroked a hand up and down her arm. She was so tense, he thought she'd break. So rigid, his own muscles ached in sympathy.

"Egbert called the police. Reported Marisol and everybody else—from what I've heard, he tried to make it clear he thought the problem was Marisol, but . . . they didn't care." She shrugged and eased away. "They started watching us. There was an investigation—it lasted for months. I'd pulled out. One of the last guys I'd gone out with, I was almost certain he was a cop and when he started pushing me for *extra services*, I shut him down, and that night I called Sharon, told her I was done. No more. Not long after that, a few of the girls—including my cousin—were arrested."

"I . . ." She stopped and swiped the back of her hand over her mouth. She shot him a look. "It turns out that guy who'd made me so nervous *was* a cop. I saw him during the trial. He was the same guy who ended up arresting my cousin. She got caught up in that because of *me*."

"No." He moved behind her and pressed his lips to her shoulder. "She made her choices. We're all responsible for the ones we make. You can't take her choices on yourself."

She turned to him then, pressing her face to his chest as silent tears spilled free.

If she could, Ressa would have let herself lean on him.

But she'd just proven to herself how badly she could fuck things up. Especially when it mattered.

Her head ached as she finally pulled away from him.

"I'm sorry," she said again. "What I said . . ."

"Stop."

His voice was weary.

The tension that filled every muscle of his body told just how much damage her careless words had done. The man had lost his wife. He was raising his child on his own. Regardless of the privileged life he'd had, he'd known more than a little heartache, more than a little loss.

"What am I supposed to do?" she asked, miserable. His gaze cut to hers and it was the hardest thing ever not to look away. "I said things to you that I didn't mean and you won't even let me apologize . . ."

"I don't need apologies." Trey just shook his head. "I came here to see you, to be with you. You're hurting. If you think I can't see that, then—"

Swearing, she shoved the heels of her hands against her eyes. "Don't be nice! You let me be a bitch to you, you won't let me apologize, and now . . ." She sputtered, reaching for the words. "After everything I've told you, you stand there and be nice! Don't do that."

"Fuck, what the hell do you want me to do?" Some sign of frustration came through in his voice.

She still didn't dare look at him.

It seemed that everything she did today was wrong, though. And her head was too messed up to handle this right.

What am I doing?

Part of her was screeching that.

But the calmer part of her, the one that was still somewhat in control, realized this was the only thing *to* do. "I . . ." Her voice cracked. "I think maybe you should leave."

Even before she said the words, Trey already knew.

Slowly, he crossed the floor to her, studying her face.

She was still, her eyes, for once, completely unreadable and her face was a blank mask.

But when he stopped in front of her, her entire body seemed to vibrate as though she had to struggle not to let any sign of anything she felt escape. He wanted to pull her up against him. No matter what she said, he didn't think she'd fight him.

Neither of them wanted to be apart from each other. But he suspected both of them needed it.

Just like he thought she was right; maybe both of them needed distance. If he touched her, everything rushing through him was going to come to the fore, and thought would melt away, lost under the need to touch. To comfort. So he kept his hands at his sides, as much as he hated it.

"I'll go," he said softly. "But first, let me tell you this. If you try to push me away because of this, then make sure you understand . . . *you* are the one doing the pushing. Not me. And I won't go away easily."

Her gaze jerked away from his.

Now he reached up and cupped her cheek. "But I can't make this work on my own, either. If you don't want to be with me, then you don't."

Dark brown eyes shot to meet his.

"I can already see that you're worried," he murmured, stroking his thumb over her lip. "It doesn't change anything for *me*. Does it change things for you?"

"Fuck, yes," she whispered.

And he felt the cut of it, deep inside.

He was bleeding, and he didn't think she even knew.

"You can't stand there and tell me that the idea of it doesn't bother you." She reached up and tugged his hand away. "You know what will happen if any of this gets out? You don't even know half of all that went down. There's more—a lot more. I'm connected to an ugly, *nasty* prostitution scandal. How is it going to affect you if that gets out? Doesn't the idea of that bother you?"

"Bother me?" He studied her, wondering just how much time she'd spent thinking about this. And here he was thinking *he* had most of the baggage. Looking away, he blew out a breath. "The idea of it pisses me off on the same level that that kind of gossip has always pissed me off. Some scumbag, sorry excuse of a reporter will push in on people's privacy and as long as there are people who want to know . . ." He stopped and shrugged.

Maybe if more people knew what it was like to have photographers hovering at your shoulder as you buried your wife, to have insinuations that you'd somehow caused her death . . . or to have lies smeared about like they'd done with Abby and her father's suicide, how that had only added to her already wrecked childhood, yeah, maybe they'd get it. Maybe they'd ease back. But this was just a part of his life. "Look, this is nothing I'm not already dealing with on some level. They'll find another way to jab at me, or Zach, or Seb. Hell, they even poke at Zane and Travis from time to time. We've lived with this our whole lives. I can deal."

Ressa just closed her eyes. Then she moved in close to him and dropped her head against his chest. He let himself hold her. Took in every nuance, every breath, every scent . . . and then, after a moment, he stepped back.

"The question is . . . can you?"

A shudder fell over her eyes. Then she backed away.

"I just don't know."

Chapter Twenty-four

The sexy car in his driveway normally would have made him smile. But at two a.m., this was the last thing he wanted to deal with.

Especially after he'd left Ressa back in her house, her words hung between them like a poisoned kiss—*I just don't know.*

He'd pulled her to him, unwilling to believe that, unwilling to accept it.

She'd let him.

Then she'd kissed him and murmured, "You should go. We both need to think. We probably should have had this talk long before now anyway."

Yeah. He guessed maybe they should have—before he went and fell halfway in love with her.

The last thing he wanted to do was *go, think.* But what was he supposed to say? *I have been thinking . . . I think I'm falling in love with you?*

That wasn't going to make things any easier. Any better. Both of them needed to breathe, and she needed to work through all of this.

What a complete mess.

His brothers spend years dragging their feet before they

actually make a move, and here he was, almost stupid about a woman he'd known weeks.

Again.

It had hit him this hard the first time . . . and he'd never expected it to happen again, but here he was, and he was faced with the prospect that she might be ready to pull out before they even got started.

Fuck it all.

Brooding, he climbed out of his car and eyed the rental—and it was a rental. It wasn't the typical rental, no doubt about that, but the sexy little convertible Ferrari was almost definitely a rental, and it was completely Sebastian's style and it was completely like his little brother to drop in unannounced.

He just hoped Sebastian would be too tired to still be up, because he was in no way ready to talk to anybody.

No, what he wanted was to grab that bottle of Glenlivet he'd bought years ago. He wanted to open it. He decided then and there he was going to have a drink. If he ended up puking his guts out, at least he'd have something else to be miserable about.

If not? Then he'd have a drink and hope he could find some way to sleep before he had to get up with Clayton.

The dark quiet of the house wrapped around him as he let himself inside. Judging by the soft snores coming from the living room, he had a feeling he might even get the silence he wanted—or close to it. A quick look into the living room confirmed the identity of his late-night crasher—Sebastian had fallen asleep on the couch, hadn't even made it to one of the guest rooms, and Trey had several, one no more than a few yards down the hall. Glancing into the darkened living room, eyes gritty, he saw his younger brother, still wearing jeans and a T-shirt that rode up over his back. His hair had grown out from the last movie, almost brushing his shoulders.

He made a grunting noise under his breath and rolled—

Trey grimaced and watched as Sebastian ended up crashing on the floor. And he didn't wake up.

The idiot had always slept like the dead.

Sighing, he moved into the room, crouching down next to the younger man. "Seb."

No response.

He reached and tapped Sebastian's cheek and then scowled when Sebastian turned his face toward him, muttering, "Not now, honey. Too tired."

"Horny son of a bitch," Trey said, amusement working in past the frustration, and the sadness that had been weighing on him ever since Ressa had unloaded on him.

"He's not going to wake up."

At the sound of the quiet voice behind him, he glanced over his shoulder.

Travis stood lost in the shadows, his eyes glinting, but Trey could make out little else other than his form as he stood in the hall.

"So I see." Resigned, he stood up and moved to the wooden chest tucked up against a wall and opened it. It was filled with the quilts Aliesha had used to keep thrown over the back of the couch, the chair. They had belonged to her grandmother, so he hadn't been able to get rid of them, but leaving them out hadn't been much of an option, either. Snagging the top one, he pulled it out and draped it over Sebastian.

That done, he rose to his feet, heading out of the room and making his way into the kitchen. He splashed some whisky into a glass and eyed his brother. "I'm tired," he said, hoping to cut off any inclination Travis might have to talk.

He was too frustrated for it. Too frustrated with himself, with Ressa—even with his brother, although his frustration with Travis had nothing to do with tonight, and everything to do with how much shit he knew Travis was holding back.

But Travis, smart man that he was, didn't seem to pick up on that subtle hint. He followed Trey up the stairs, down the hall to the big bedroom that ran almost half the length of the house.

Tossing back the whisky, Trey slammed the glass down on his dresser with enough force to break it. The strong alcohol burned all the way down and he relished every second. When it hit his stomach, he kept his eyes closed, waited. But the only thing he felt was that gnawing, restless anger . . . the frustration. The misery.

And his twin's waiting, watchful presence.

As he sat down on the edge of the bed, Trey shot Travis a look. "Maybe you didn't hear. I'm tired. I want to go to bed."

"You don't look like a man who just got laid." Travis had his thumbs hooked inside his front pockets and his head was cocked, a thoughtful look in his eyes as he studied his brother.

"You don't look like a man with a genius IQ. Appearances are deceiving. Leave me alone, Trav."

Instead of turning around and leaving, Travis did the typical brother thing. He came inside and shut the door. "What's the deal, man? You two didn't fight, did you?"

Trey focused on his shoes, giving the task of unlacing the Reeboks a lot more attention than it required. Once he was done, he kicked them off and headed into the bathroom. Aware that his brother was still watching, still waiting for an answer, he said, "No. We didn't fight."

"You . . ." Travis's voice trailed off. "There's nothing wrong between you two, is there?"

Something in his brother's voice had him pausing.

Then there was a weird, niggling sensation in his gut.

Worry—

Narrowing his eyes, he came back out of the bathroom. "What's the deal?"

Travis stared at him, dead in the eye. And fucking *lied*. "I don't know what you mean. Well, other than the fact that you obviously are pissed off. So—"

"Stop," Trey said softly, shaking his head. He moved toward his brother, watching as Travis went silent, head going back as Trey closed the distance. "You're lying. You seem to forget that weird thing, how you can always tell when I'm mad, fucked up or pissed . . . it works both ways. And you're *lying*. What is going on?"

"I don't know what you're talking about." Travis just stared at him. His eyes were level, his face blank.

And this time, there was a curious void inside Trey, the way he felt when he either worked hard to keep himself down, or when Travis was trying to do that with him.

Which only made him that much more convinced that Travis was lying.

They were as close as two brothers—as twins—could be. Or they had been. Until . . . Trey tried to pinpoint when it had started, when he'd realized his brother was keeping secrets. It hadn't been recent. He'd understood, realized there were probably things they'd just not tell each other. He hadn't told his twin how much he blamed himself over Aliesha's death, although he knew Travis suspected. He hadn't told his twin how he'd just looked at her . . . and known.

Nor had he told Travis how he'd looked at Ressa and felt a punch in the gut, something primal, possessive, even more powerful than what he'd felt with Aliesha.

No, they didn't tell each other *everything*. Even they had their secrets.

But Travis kept some dark ones.

Now, with only inches between them, Trey realized those secrets had grown into a distance and somehow, they were turning the man in front of him into somebody Trey wasn't sure he knew. "You're lying," he said again. "You think something's wrong . . . and I get the weirdest feeling you know exactly what it is."

Travis's gaze fell away, and a hard, tight knot settled in Trey's gut.

Curling one hand into a fist, he demanded, "What do you know? And how the fuck *do* you know?"

Travis's eyes glittered. The lines at the corners tightened. He opened his mouth.

The tension inside Trey gathered, mounted. Part of him felt like . . . *finally*.

But then Travis just shrugged. "Look, I don't know what you're so worked up about. It's not like Ressa and I were sitting around braiding each other's hair or anything. I don't know shit. But clearly there's something—*what the*—"

Trey shoved him back, hard. The sound of him slamming into the wall was sweet, so sweet he was tempted to do it again.

Twisted up in his own frustration, in his own worry, he didn't see the pallor that came across his twin's face.

One hand balled up into a fist and he reached up, snagged the front of Travis's shirt, half thinking that maybe what they both needed was to just pound on each other. It had helped when they were younger. Why not—

He jerked Travis forward.

The pain that split through Trey's side had him stumbling back, letting go of his brother's shirt. Travis staggered, his hand flying out as he fought for his balance. Trey caught him, steadied him.

"You son of a bitch," he said, guiding Travis over to the bed. "Don't give me this shit that you've just had a rough few weeks at work. And I don't want to hear that you've been sick, either."

Mentally, he kicked his own ass for forgetting, because he *knew* something had been wrong. He *knew* . . . and his anger, his frustration had just made him lose sight of that.

Travis didn't say anything as Trey helped him onto the bed, his face hard as stone, and when Trey straightened, his twin's eyes were unreadable. He didn't even look at Trey for long before he jerked his eyes away, staring at some point on the wall.

Trey clenched his jaw, fighting for control. It wasn't coming. He breathed in through his nose, blew it out. Tried it again, but nothing was clearing the fog from his head. There was still a dull throb of pain in his side, and he glanced at his brother, eyes instinctively going to the same area on Travis.

For the first few seconds, he wasn't even sure what he was staring at.

He figured it out about the same time Travis realized there was a problem.

Travis went to twist away at the same time Trey shot out a hand, catching the hem of his brother's faded gray T-shirt. "It's nothing—" Travis tried to say.

"Shut the *fuck* up or I'm going to put you flat on your ass," Trey warned. "And right now, I think we both know I can."

Actually, that wasn't true. Travis stared into his twin's eyes, debated on whether or not to just get the hell out of there, leave Norfolk for a while, disappear, but that wasn't the answer.

No, Trey couldn't put him on his ass.

But in his condition, he'd have to hurt his twin.

The one thing he could never do.

Swearing, he smacked Trey's hands away. "Let me up. I'll show you, as long as you keep your mouth shut."

Trey looked like he wanted to argue—no. He *did* want to argue.

"You keep it quiet," Travis warned. "I'm not in trouble. There's nothing wrong. But I know how this is going to look and I don't need everybody freaking out."

Trey's eyes narrowed. "If you think I'm not aware of the fact that you've been up to some weird shit, then you're not giving me much credit. Show me what the hell is wrong. Then we'll discuss it."

It was the best he was going to get. He'd managed to tear stitches open and he was bleeding—thanks to the hard-ass a few feet away. He forgot sometimes—they looked so much alike and shared a bond nobody could understand, and yet, they were so completely different. Except . . . not. Trey, in his own way, was every bit the same stubborn bastard Travis was.

And Travis had made the serious mistake of forgetting that.

Look where it had put him.

He needed to get the wound redressed and bandaged and he needed one of those lousy painkillers, too. With a grimace, he caught the shirt and worked it up.

Trey's low hiss had him closing his eyes.

It was a damn good thing he was getting out.

He'd never be able to keep this up now, and his brother wouldn't let it rest until he had answers.

Holding the shirt with its spotty blood stain, he looked at Trey and waited.

For the longest time, Trey just stared. Then he turned away. "I guess this is one of those things you're not going to explain to me, isn't it?"

Travis knew better than to say anything.

Trey just nodded. "Okay. Let's try this again."

Exhausted already, Travis glared at his twin's back even as he tried to figure what he *could* say. The answer was *next to nothing*. It would piss Trey off, too, but Travis didn't know how he could explain the bullet hole in his side. It didn't look so much like a bullet hole now, of course, and even if it did, it wasn't like his brother had a lot of experience with that—

"Ressa's cousin is in jail. She's had some trouble with the cops, too. I don't think I even know half of what's going on. Now . . . you want to tell me how you already know about it?"

Trey turned as he spoke and the question caught Travis off guard so he wasn't able to hide his reaction in time.

And his twin saw it on his face.

He didn't even have to say anything. They'd never been able to lie to each other, not worth shit. So instead of trying, he just lifted his shoulder—the one *not* on his injured side— but it still had that awful pain lurching through him.

"Just how do you know, Travis? Is that something a foren- sic accountant is typically going to do? Go digging around in the background of a girl his brother dates?"

Travis shrugged again.

"Nice answer. Let's try this one—does the typical forensic accountant even now where to *start* to go digging about that? You didn't even know I was dating anybody—hell, not all that long ago, I *wasn't* dating anybody."

"You've been together since I got here," Travis said softly. And he could have known within a couple hours of that vague warning. She'd all but challenged him, and because he'd known it would eat at him until he knew, he'd looked. He'd spent the past few days brooding over it, too. Brooding, debating . . . thinking. And he'd come to the exact same con- clusion he suspected his brother would.

Now he didn't have the kind of feelings for Ressa that Trey did, but if he was in Trey's shoes?

He wouldn't give a damn.

He'd seen what it was like—with his parents, with Zach and Abby—and before he'd lost her, with Trey and Aliesha. Trey *knew* what it felt like to have those kind of feelings.

"What does it matter anyway?" he asked. "It's not like it's going to change anything for you. You're already gone over on her. Anybody with eyes can see that."

"No." The ice in Trey's eyes didn't fade. "It doesn't change anything."

Then he blew out a breath and leaned back against the wall. "Complicate things? Well, yeah, that's probably going to hap- pen, but . . . no. It doesn't change what I feel." He slanted a look at his twin. "And not the issue. I just want to know how *you* know. And why you bothered to even go looking—and how the fuck you even knew *to* look . . . son of a bitch."

Trey turned away and shoved a hand through his hair.

Travis felt the tension knot inside him, while in the back of his mind, something buzzed—no. Clicked. A piece of a puzzle falling into place, a sensation he knew all too well. But he wasn't the one who'd figured something out. Lowering his gaze, he stared at the bloody bandage with its ever growing stain of red.

"You knew something that day, didn't you?" Trey murmured, turning back to look at him. "She acted . . . off. Like something was bugging her off and on half the day—it was *you*, wasn't it?"

Aw, shit. "Look, Trey—"

"Answer me!" The shout rang through the house, catching both of them off guard.

But Trey didn't back down, he came across the floor, fury in every line of his body. "How in the hell did you even know to dig up anything about her? You didn't even know her name until that day—or you shouldn't have."

"I didn't." Travis could say that much, honestly. "I didn't . . ."

He stopped, fumbling for anything he could say. He'd told too many lies, given too many half truths. Even the lies of omission—did it even *matter* that he was doing his job? Trying to . . . *trying to what*?

That small voice nagged at him, more and more. The one that had made him realize he was done.

Beyond done.

And he couldn't lie here. Not to Trey, not anymore. "Look, I didn't know anything about Ressa until you introduced me to her."

He'd thought about digging into her background, yeah. But he hadn't. And now he could tell his brother the truth. Looking Trey dead in the eye, he gave his twin what precious little honesty he could these days. "I wouldn't have gone digging around for any information but she . . ."

"What?" Trey demanded caustically. "You got a funny feeling? What the fuck are you? Hell. *Are* you with the CIA? You got that many secrets anymore."

Travis grimaced. "No. I didn't have a funny feeling. *She* did. She said something to me that afternoon . . . told me that whatever I found out, she hoped I'd remember she did care about you. And for the record, *again*, I didn't plan on digging around about her. I didn't feel like I had to—I *like* her."

"Why the fuck would she say anything to you?" Trey stared

at him, while a flicker of something—hurt, distrust—flashed through his eyes.

I should have just gone to bed, Travis thought, frustrated.

"She pegged me for a cop or something—I'm *not*—and don't ask anymore because I'm sick and fucking tired of lying, but I can't tell you." Wearily, he leaned against the wall, head falling against it. Absently, he touched his side as the pain there radiated out. Wet heat met his hand and he looked down at the blood that had already soaked through. He needed to get to his room and dig out the medical kit. He had some butterfly bandages that would help close it back up.

"Can't tell me?" Trey's voice dripped with scorn. "How about you won't tell me?"

"Oh for fuck's sake!" Snarling, he shoved off the wall and that sent another lance of pain ripping through him. Which only served to make him madder. "Would you use your damned brain? You're not an idiot. *Can't* means just that. I *can't*. There are reasons. Now put your brain to use."

Trey opened his mouth, a sneer quivering on his lips. At the same time, Travis was mentally kicking his ass. The pain, the frustration, all of it was making him stupid. Too many years of lying to people he loved, who loved him. There were reasons why most of the people in his line of work didn't have families. Slowly, he turned to the door. "If I was in trouble, I'd tell you, okay?"

No. He wouldn't. But he wouldn't come *here* if he was in any sort of trouble. No way in hell. He'd never risk his family and his family was the number one reason he was getting out.

He hadn't quite cleared the door when Trey's voice stopped him.

"So I guess this means you're really *not* a forensic accountant."

He rested a hand on the door jam, closed his eyes. "Sure I am. It says so on my tax return, doesn't it?"

"That doesn't mean jackshit." Trey was closer now and Travis glanced over his shoulder. "If you're not in trouble then why the hell are you leaking blood all over yourself?"

"I got hurt. I just tore some stitches. It will be fine."

Their gazes locked and held. Then Trey looked away. "You've been lying to us for a long time, haven't you?"

He couldn't even respond to that. Not just because it would take another lie, but because there was nothing he could say that would make it better.

But he had to say something. "It's not going to be like this much longer," he said.

And saying those words, it was like a weight fell from him. A knot loosened within him and he blew out a breath as some of the tension he'd carried for years just faded. "It won't be much longer. I just have to . . . handle some things."

With that, he headed down the hall.

He'd clean himself up. Wasn't like he hadn't done it before. Then he'd get some rest.

And next time his brother was brooding over a woman, he'd leave him to it.

Who in the hell was he to offer advice on it anyway? The last time he'd had a serious relationship had been . . .

He pushed the thought of it aside.

Yeah. It had been that long ago, and look at how *that* had ended.

Chapter Twenty-five

A week passed and every single day, she felt the absence of him.

She made plans with Mama Ang to go see Kiara the following Saturday, and each day she dreaded the trip more and more. Each day, she opened her eyes and thought about getting through another day without talking to Trey, seeing him.

They were supposed to be *thinking* about things.

The only thing she could *think* about was how much she missed him . . . and how much easier everything *wasn't* with him gone.

Oh, she *saw* him a couple of times—hard to avoid it when they both dropped the kids off at school. Trey in his gleaming truck and her all but slumping down behind the wheel of the Mustang so she didn't have to face him. They'd seen each other in the drop-off line more than once, and on her day off, she'd seen him in the pick-up line, although she doubted he'd seen her.

"Are you mad at Mr. Trey?" Neeci had asked.

"No, baby. Why?"

"Because you don't talk to him anymore."

Oh . . . but I want to.

"We've just been busy."

Busy . . . yeah, right.

She thought maybe it was just the right thing to do, let things cool off while she thought everything through.

The question is . . . can you?

Those words reverberated through her head, tying her up into knot after knot, and she was already a mess over Kiara. Mama Ang said she'd gotten a similar call from her and they made the plans.

Although Angeline hadn't said anything, Ressa knew the call had taken a toll on her.

Maybe Trey had tried to tell her it wasn't her fault, but she still carried the blame. And much of it was because she saw what it had done to the kind, gentle woman who'd changed her life—who'd *given* her a life—one worth having.

Maybe Mama Ang didn't blame her, but Ressa sure as hell blamed herself for the trouble she'd brought into the lives of her aunt and cousin.

Her aunt had ended up asking her next-door neighbor to help with Neeci. When Neeci heard she'd be spending the day with Miss Latrice, she'd sulked. *Can't we ask if I can go play with Clay? I wanna see Clay.*

That only made Ressa feel worse, because this was straining the friendship between two kids who clearly adored each other. *So I'll fix it.* She made herself that promise. But first . . . she had to get through seeing her cousin. Get that off her plate.

Saturday rolled around and although the sun gleamed golden in a clear blue sky, Ressa felt like she was trapped in a bank of thunderclouds.

She was miserable.

She missed Trey.

The question is . . . can you?

She was starting to realize she'd have to deal with it, because she didn't think she could handle anything else that didn't involve having him in her life.

There was a knock at the door and Ressa groaned, rolling her head over to stare at the clock. But first, she had to figure out why her aunt was nearly two hours early.

Because it wasn't *like* it was anybody else.

"Your fault, girl," she murmured as she climbed out of bed. "Your fault."

She grabbed her robe and tugged it on as she went to answer the door. A glance through the peephole showed it was indeed her aunt.

"Latrice is sick." Angeline sailed through the door, looking around the house. "Where's Neeci?"

"She's asleep . . . we weren't leaving for a while yet."

"Well, we need to find alternate arrangements or cancel."

"Granny?"

Mama Ang met her eyes. Angeline MacAllister was five feet four inches of softness and steel and for a moment, a thousand unsaid things passed between them.

Then Angeline looked up the steps toward the little girl.

"Hey there, baby. Come give me a hug."

Neeci plodded down the steps, her *Frozen* pj's rumpled, her hair mussed.

A few minutes later, Angeline had Neeci on her way to the kitchen, giving the two women a moment of peace.

"We can't cancel," Ressa said softly. "Kiara is up to something . . . or there's something we need to know. I have to know what it is, for Neeci's sake."

Angeline blew out a breath. "The good Lord knows I'd like to tell you that you're just being paranoid, but I know my girl too well. Okay, then. We'll have to take her with us if you don't have anybody who can watch her. I called everybody I know. Can you check with Farrah?"

"She's working today." Her heart thudded in her chest.

A sigh escaped her mother and she saw those slim shoulders slump.

Swallowing, Ressa cleared her throat. "I might be able to find somebody," she said softly. "Just let me . . ."

She turned away. "Let me get dressed."

She hadn't turned away fast enough, because a few minutes later, while she was getting dressed, her aunt slipped into her bedroom.

Ressa looked over her shoulder at her aunt. "Mama Ang, that door was closed." Closed, because she needed a few minutes to get herself together before she called Trey. "I need to shower, get dressed. Is Neeci eating?"

"You can shower and get dressed in a minute. Yes, Neeci is eating." Angeline cocked her head. "You didn't sleep again last night."

Clearly the comment about the closed door didn't matter. Closed doors, raging rivers, and the fires of hell wouldn't matter, not if she thought the happiness of her girls was at stake. She hadn't been able to help Kiara, although she'd tried. It had all but broken her heart, too, because she thought she'd failed.

Apparently hellfire, damnation, and closed doors weren't going to stop her when it came to the other young woman she loved.

"I did sleep." Ressa shrugged and looked away, moving to grab clothes from her closet since her aunt obviously wasn't leaving. "I just haven't been sleeping all that great since that last call from Kiara. Every time I think she's going to get her act together . . ." She shrugged and hoped Mama Ang would let it go at that.

"Uh-huh." The doubt was practically dripping from her aunt's voice. "I might buy that, except you're used to your cousin. You've dealt with her bullshit too well and you've never let it cost you sleep before. Now. Try again."

"I'm *fine*, Mama Ang," she said.

"Hmm." That sound was loaded with doubt. A moment passed and then Angeline said, "Neeci tells me you sorta kinda have a boyfriend. Since you're clearly so *fine*, I assume I'll meet him soon?"

The words, delivered in a laid-back, neutral tone poked a hole through the wall she'd been constructing around herself. She didn't even realize how precarious that wall was, or how brittle she felt, until the tears clogged her throat and burned her eyes.

Ressa turned away and clapped a hand over her mouth. Struggling to hold back the sniffles, she waved her aunt back when she saw her coming up in the mirror.

"Oh, don't you go pushing me away," Angeline said. She caught Ressa around the waist, oblivious to the fact that Ressa had four inches on her.

And Ressa let the older woman pull her in, dropping her head to rest it on Angeline's shoulder as she fought not to cry. "We . . . we can't do this now," she whispered.

"We can take a few minutes, baby. Now, you tell me what's wrong."

Ressa shook her head. "But . . ."

"No buts. You've been holding this in too long. You *always* hold things in too long. We can take ten minutes and you *will* tell me what is wrong."

Slowly, Ressa lifted her head and met her aunt's eyes. She was a grown woman. She could handle her own love life, right? Opening her mouth, she thought about just saying that, explaining that . . .

But that wasn't what came rushing out of her in a torrent.

"I met somebody, Mama Ang. I like him. Hell, that doesn't describe him. I think I could . . ." She pulled away to pace, unable to stay still. That gaping hole inside her seemed to spread and it just got worse if she was still. "I can't even think about it. I don't want to think about it because it can't happen. It shouldn't happen and it hurts. I never should have let myself think anything should come of it."

Dimly, she was aware of her aunt moving to settle on the edge of her bed, just as she'd done when Ressa had been struggling to adjust to a new life, a new home, a new school where she thought she'd never fit in.

"I don't know what I was thinking. I guess I wasn't thinking. It wasn't supposed to even happen, you know? Then it did, and it should have just been sex, and that was all well and good, but it ended . . ." Heat rushed up the back of her neck, but she ignored it. She'd been able to talk to her aunt about sex before—it wasn't like she hadn't already known what it was before Mama Ang had found her and brought her here.

But they were open about it. It made it easier. Still, she wasn't going to tell the woman watching her with arched brows that Trey Barnes could fuck like a dream, and that he could do something simple like kiss her hand and melt her heart.

"It ended," she finished lamely. "It was supposed to be a weekend thing. Then I ran into him again at Neeci's school and . . ." She closed her eyes, stopping once more by the dresser.

"I can't quit thinking about him. He's in my head. In my heart. Under my skin, all the time. And it can't happen. At least, I don't think it can. It shouldn't. It's too complicated, too messed up." She finally stumbled to a halt.

"Okay," Angeline said, her voice a soft, steadying presence in the uneasy silence. "Let's set aside the *it can't happen* part and focus on the rest. Does he feel the same way about you?"

She dropped her hands and looked at her mother. "Yeah. I think he does." No, she knew he did. And that made it so much harder.

"Then why *can't* it happen?" Angeline just looked curious.

"Because of who he is," she said. As her aunt continued to watch her, she turned away, shame slipping its way inside. "And . . ."

Silence was an ugly thing. She couldn't get the words now, but after a few taut, heavy seconds, she didn't have to. Her aunt did it. "How much of this is because of your past . . . and how much is because of Kiara?"

"It's all of it," she whispered, unable to swallow down the shame.

A warm hand smoothed up her arm then came to rest on her shoulder. "And here I was thinking you just needed me to boot you in the butt because you'd fallen for a white boy. Oh, Neeci told me that, too, and you oughta know I'd smack you over that—it doesn't matter who you fall for, not to me and it shouldn't matter to you. Love is love and you know that." Angeline sighed. "I'm sorry. Because it sounds like that's where you're at. Now if he's ashamed to be with you because of your cousin . . ."

"He's *not*." The words came out in a snap and she spun to stare at her aunt, the anger boiling up inside her.

Angeline inclined her head. "Oh?" She nodded. "Okay, then you've told him about your past. About the mistakes you made and he isn't okay with it?"

Ressa looked away as Angeline narrowed cool eyes on her.

Now she felt like she'd been caught sneaking out the window or something—and yes, she'd done that. More than once. Fighting the urge to fidget, she stared at her aunt, refusing to blink or look away. She was an adult, damn it.

"Please tell me that *you* are not the reason this can't work out," Angeline said quietly. "If he's the kind of guy who has accepted you, and your cousin, then you had better figure out how to make this make sense to me. You had better *not* tell me that *you* are the one standing in the way. That you're not letting your cousin or your past hold you back from a man who can make you happy."

"It's more complicated than that!" The knot that had settled inside her chest tried to take over, the emptiness inside tried to swallow her whole.

"Why? Because of who he is? Okay, then tell me *who he is* that makes this so impossible," Angeline demanded.

That caustic tone left her floundering for words. "He's . . . he's . . ."

"He's a writer."

The words came from behind them. The door, open just a crack, and as they turned their heads, Neeci slipped inside, looking at Ressa with vaguely accusatory eyes.

Fuck a duck, Ressa thought sourly. "Neeci, this doesn't concern you," she said softly.

Neeci ignored her, staring at her grandmother. "He's a writer, Granny Ang. Auntie Ressa has bunches of his book at her li'bary and his brother is famous. He's in movies and he's really hot and I might want to marry him because he's so hot."

Ressa just stared at her cousin. *Where did she learn about* hot?

Angeline made a low *hmmmm* under her breath. "It makes a little more sense now . . . I think. Although I'm curious as to who this writer and the hot brother is. By the way, Neeci, you can get married when you're fifty and after you're done with college. And no more talking about hot boys until you're twenty-five." She winked at her granddaughter and then nodded. "Now you go on back downstairs and let me deal with your cousin. I've only got about two minutes left to knock some sense into her hard head."

Neeci giggled and disappeared.

Angeline sighed.

Feeling the weight, and the command, in her aunt's stare, Ressa turned to face her.

"I don't know if I want to shake you or hug you, child."

Angeline just shook her head instead. "I take it you're concerned about what it might look like when and if things come out."

"Why wouldn't I be?" she said defensively.

"It's an understandable concern. And tell me something." Angeline gazed at the door for a long minute before looking back at Ressa. "Are you going to tell that little girl she never has the right to fall in love . . . with *whoever* she wants. That if she *ever* makes a mistake, she'd just better resign herself to an empty life? Are *you* going to be the one to tell her she better never fall for a rich man, a famous man—or any man she wants—because of what her mother did?"

Fury lit inside her and she opened her mouth—only to close it, sagging against the wall.

"I didn't think so," Angeline said, lifting an elegant black brow. "Did you explain things to him?"

"Not . . ." It came out in a rough whisper. She cleared her throat. "Not all of it. He knows about . . . me. Most of it. And he knows that Kiara's in jail, although I didn't explain all of that."

Angeline came to her then, reached up to lay a hand on her cheek. "It is hard. I think about the fool things you did, and how she was so stupid to get involved—it's not like she needed money. I think about everything that happened with Scott . . . and Sharon. Yes . . . it is hard. But *you* were the one to step up and do the right thing. She tried to hide. She made those mistakes—she did them and they are hers, hers alone. Not yours. And not mine."

"Of course they weren't yours!"

Angeline leaned in and pressed a kiss to Ressa's cheek.

Ressa breathed in the scent of White Diamonds—the only perfume Mama Ang ever wore. The familiar scent wrapped around her like a comfortable hug and impulsively, she embraced the smaller woman. Angeline caught her up in her arms and Ressa tucked her head against her aunt's shoulder.

"No," Angeline said softly. "They weren't my mistakes. We did what we could. We tried to help, not just once . . . but a hundred times. She made her choices. She has to face the consequences. Just as you've had to deal with yours. But this isn't a consequence you should have to face . . . walking away from a man you can love."

"But what if . . ."

"No." Angeline leaned back, shifting so she could grasp Ressa's arms. "No *what ifs*. You haven't given either of you a chance. Don't you deserve that? At *least* that?"

When Ressa didn't answer, Angeline smiled. "Somewhere inside, you already know the answer. Now stop being foolish and go after him. Sometimes we only get one chance in this life to be happy . . . You better not waste yours."

"But . . ."

"No *buts*. I'm not saying it will be easy. You probably already have some challenges. Shoot, we *still* don't live in a world where a black woman can marry a white man without people giving us the side eye. That's one hurdle you'll have to handle already. That he's a public figure . . . that makes another one. But if you care for him, and he cares for you, those are just details."

Just details.

"You make it sound so simple," she said, her heart twisting.

"What else is it?" Angeline shrugged and snapped the top on. "You think it was easy for me? A black woman, struggling to finish school, working two jobs, dealing with her daughter, trying to handle her no-good brother *and* take care of you, when he'd let me. Bruce took all of that on. Yes, we had people look at us—he was this rich, powerful white man and he fell in love with me, a broke, single black woman who was raising a couple of girls on her own. Yes, it happened the entire time we were married. Yes, it pissed me off. And yes . . ." She slid Ressa a slow smile. "It was worth it. Every damn night, when I came home to him, when we lay in bed together. It was all worth it, even when I had to bury him far too soon. Love is always worth it, baby. Love is what matters . . . the rest is just details. Some are bigger, and suck more than the others. But you have to ask yourself . . . do you love him?"

She paused long enough to kiss Ressa on the cheek and Ressa obediently dipped her head. "Thanks, Mama Ang."

"Think about it, baby." Angeline moved to the door. There, she paused. "I need my caffeine fix so I'm making coffee. You need to get dressed and see if whoever you had in mind can watch Neeci." She paused before she left. "And Ressa, baby?"

"Yes?"

Angeline lifted a brow. "You're too smart to do something like this . . . so sometime soon I expect to meet this man."

With a wince, Ressa said, "Well, that's going to be *really* soon. I plan on calling to see if he can help with Neeci."

"Ohhh?" Angeline drew out the word, her eyes narrowing slightly.

"Yeah." Licking her lips, she decided to get it over with. Mama Ang gobbled up his books like they were candy. *And* she was one of the people who followed that *Trey* sightings board on Pinterest. She'd recognize him in a heartbeat. "It's . . . um. It's Trey Barnes."

"Trey . . ." Her aunt's brows arched and her mouth fell open. She pressed a hand to her heart. *"Oh* . . . as in *Trey Barnes—the* Trey Barnes?"

Ressa winced at the look that flashed across Angeline's face, the way she fanned a hand in front of herself. "Hoo. It's a good thing you told me that *last* or I just might have been too busy stumbling around in shock to give you that little heart to heart."

Ressa found herself grinning as Mama Ang fumbled for the doorknob, still muttering under her breath as she closed the door behind her.

"You didn't have to fly out here because of this," Trey said, swinging between irritation toward his twin and his little brother, exhaustion, amusement, and about five hundred other emotions.

One of those emotions was longing.

It had been a week since he'd seen her, and it was killing him.

Just like that, she'd gone and made herself matter that much.

He wasn't sure if he appreciated it, especially since it seemed pretty clear she'd never really planned on letting anything serious happen between them.

Okay, true enough, they had gone from a few hot, naked sessions of twisting up the sheets to feeling like they weren't whole without the other, and it had happened fast, but she'd felt it coming on, just the same as he had.

It had also been a week since Sebastian had planted his lazy ass in Trey's house and baby brother was just *now* telling Trey why he'd come.

"Now how was I supposed to ignore that, man? I couldn't, and you know it."

Trey read through the texts—texts that clearly Clay had sent because more than a few words were either misspelled or autocorrect had been having fun—and they'd all come from Travis's phone, the night of Trey's first date with Ressa. It had taken a couple of weeks, but Sebastian had done exactly what Trey suspected he'd do.

He'd shown up on his nephew's door.

Kids at scool dont beehive your my uncle.

Beehive? Trey smiled a little even as he mentally translated the autocorrect. *Believe.*
Sebastian's response was simple.

Dude, I don't believe you're my nephew—you're too awesome for me or Trey.

Damn the idiot. He couldn't even be mad at him now.

Your funny. But they laughed at me.

The rest of the conversation went on that way and he shoved the phone back to Sebastian with a sigh. "I expect you feel about the same way I do, knowing kids are teasing him. But he also has to learn that he does have to . . ." He stopped, shaking his head.

"What?" Travis asked. "He's in kindergarten. He's got two famous uncles—and hell, his dad is an author. He's proud of you. He wants people to know. It's not like he's bragging. He was just telling the truth and kids were mean."

"People are going to be mean to him in life," Trey said, frustrated. "Sebastian and Zach can't always rush to his side to be there when somebody gives him grief."

"And I'm not going to," Sebastian said, shrugging. "But right now, he's . . . fuck. He's not even six years old. He's in kindergarten, probably nervous about school. It's gotta be hard on him, man. He—" Sebastian stopped, clamping his mouth shut and looking away.

"If it's about Aliesha, don't think I'm not aware," Trey said tiredly, shaking his head. "The first day of school, he took off out of the classroom because so many kids had their moms there."

"And that's why I wanted to come," Sebastian said softly. "He's going to have some bumps and bruises already. I had the time. I don't get to see him much anyway. What does it hurt? And if it helps him to feel better about himself? That's a good thing, right?"

"Okay." He blew out a breath and tipped his head back. "I guess I see what you mean there."

"Excellent." Sebastian gave him a wide smile. "Because I'd like to drop him off at his school on Monday."

Trey's answer was cut short by his phone ringing. Immediately, his heart did a hard and heavy slam inside of him, because that slow, lazy jazz tune was one he'd programmed for Ressa.

"What the—"

He didn't even realize he'd half lunged across the kitchen until that moment, nor did he care.

All that mattered was that she'd called.

"Hello?"

There was a faint, hesitant pause.

"Trey. It's . . . ah . . . Hi. It's Ressa."

"Hi." *Breathe. You have to breathe.* That in mind, he drew in a deep careful breath, then blew it out, slow and easy. Didn't do a damn thing to calm the sudden ragged rhythm of his heart, though.

"Are you . . . look, I feel like a heel doing this, but I need a favor. It's huge and I'm sorry, especially after . . ."

Now his heart twisted—no, he thought maybe it shriveled. "What do you need, Ressa?"

"I have to go see my cousin," she said, her voice now subdued. "I . . . she called last week and asked my aunt and me to come out. It was . . . well, I talked to her a few hours before I talked to you. There's something going on and we have to go see her. We had arrangements but they fell apart and now . . . look, I can't take Neeci out there. It messes her up too bad."

"Bring her over." He was proud to hear that he managed to keep his voice level. Completely straight. Nor did he lapse into a fit of begging. "Clay would love to see her."

Then, before she could say anything else, he disconnected.

Carefully, he put the phone down and before his brothers could say anything, he walked out.

He had probably twenty minutes—maybe a few less, because Ressa wasn't much on taking her time behind the wheel.

He would need every last one of those minutes to try to make it look like he wasn't totally falling apart inside.

Baffled, Sebastian stared at the rigid line of Trey's back as he disappeared down the hall.

"What the fuck was that?" he demanded. Then he jerked back as Travis rapped his head. "Hey!"

"Watch your mouth," Travis advised. "Clay is going to be up at any minute."

"Fu . . . yeah. Okay." Rubbing his skull, he glared at Travis through slitted eyes. "What's up? And don't tell me nothing. You two have been pissed at each other all week. He's been dragging like something tore up all his books and now . . . Son of a bitch."

This time he moved back in case Travis tried to smack him, but Travis just scowled at him. Hands on his hips, Sebastian studied Travis—the one who *used* to be the funnier twin. The lighthearted one.

"It's a woman, isn't it?"

Travis's only response was a sigh. He stared down into his coffee, brooding.

"Aaaaannnndddd there are problems." Sebastian dropped into a stool across from Travis and braced his elbows on the counter. "Who is she?"

"You should ask Trey all this," Travis pointed out. Then he

slanted a hard look at him. "Except . . . don't. They aren't in a good place right now so leave him alone."

"Well, maybe he needs to *talk* about it."

Travis rolled his eyes. "And you've been the *hey, let's talk* guy since . . . when?"

"He's my brother, too," Sebastian said quietly, rising from the stool and moving away. "Yeah, maybe I'm not as close to him as you are. But he's still my brother. I still love him."

"Damn it, Seb!"

But Sebastian just shook his head. Seemed like not a damn thing he did lately went right. He'd just go back to his room. Crash there—

"Uncle Sebastian! Hi! Wanna eat some donuts?"

Looking up, he saw the cute, sleepy eyes staring down at him from the second floor landing. He managed to smile. Well, okay. Yeah, maybe he didn't piss off everybody.

Her hands were shaking.

This is ridiculous.

She was half-afraid to even walk up to that door and she kept replaying that conversation over and over in her head. How Trey's voice had gone from warm . . . almost . . . she didn't know how to describe the low, almost intimate sound of his voice, but she knew how to describe the shift it had taken after she'd started babbling.

I'm not ready to talk relationships, honey, but hey, I need a favor . . .

He'd gone cool on her. Oh, he was polite.

And it had ripped the heart out of her, because she knew what that cool tone hid.

She'd hurt him.

As she opened the door, she looked at her aunt. "I've got . . . I've got a few minutes, don't I?"

"A few." A faint smile curved her aunt's lips. "As much as I want to get out of this car, I'm not going to. Not right now. Ressa . . . listen to your heart, okay? Not your fear and not your common sense."

She nodded and closed her hand around Neeci's. "Let's get you inside. Bet you're ready to see Clay."

They started to walk, but Neeci was dragging her feet. "But . . . but I think Granny should come. She'll wanna meet—" The girl's eyes went wide and she snapped her mouth shut.

"Meet who?" Ressa asked, frowning.

The door opened and Clayton came tumbling out—he was walking backward and he had both hands wrapped around the much larger hand of somebody else—a somebody else who *wasn't* Trey. Or his twin.

"Come on. I want you to meet my best friend."

"Okay, okay . . ." The man's voice was smooth, easy, and he laughed as Clayton dragged him along. He wasn't exactly fighting.

"Come on!" Clayton said again.

Guess he wasn't moving fast enough for the boy, Ressa mused.

"Is that who you wanted Granny to meet?" she asked, looking down at her cousin.

But Neeci had gone still, almost frozen.

"Clayton, did you finish your . . . ? Ressa."

She looked past Clayton and his hostage to see Trey standing in the door. Swallowing, she opened her mouth and a dozen things leaped into her mind. *I'm sorry. I take it back. Can we have a do-over?*

But all she said was, "Morning, Trey. Thanks for . . . helping out." It was lame and stupid and everything she didn't need to say.

"No problem." He just nodded shortly at her and then shifted his attention to Neeci, a warm easy smile on his face. "Hey, sweetie. You had breakfast yet?"

Neeci just stood there. Still frozen.

"Baby, what is wrong with you?"

"Neeci! Say hi to my Uncle Sebastian!"

Ohhhhh . . .

Shifting her attention to the man with a hat pulled down low over his face, she studied him—or what she could see. Wow.

He smiled at her. "Hello." That voice—it was rich, sinful, like liquid chocolate and rich wine, an audible stroke over bare skin. And something told her the user knew very well the power behind that voice.

That hat, too, tugged down as low as it was, didn't do a damn thing to hide the sheer male beauty of his face.

"I'll be damned," she murmured. "Sebastian Barnes."

"He's my uncle!" Clayton said, grinning with delight and obvious pride.

Amused affection flooding her heart, she looked at Clayton. "So I've heard." Then, because she had to say it, she said, "I miss seeing you, Clay."

The smile faded a little, but only for a minute, because he beamed at her. "Then you should stay and play with us. We're swimming. All day. Except Uncle Travis. He says he's still sick."

"I'd love to, baby, but I've got something I have to take care of." Because she couldn't stand the way his smile faded again, she bent down and murmured to Neeci, "You should say hi."

Neeci gave her a wide-eyed stare.

Then she looked at the man who'd moved a few feet closer. "But . . . but . . ."

"Hi there."

Sebastian crouched a short distance away, studying Neeci with solemn eyes. "I'm trying to decide if I should be jealous."

Neeci blinked at him.

Sebastian heaved out a heavy, forlorn sigh and he looked for all the world like somebody had stolen the stars from his sky. Then he slid Neeci a sad look. "Clay's been my best buddy since he was born, but now he tells me he's got a new best friend."

Neeci licked her lips. "He . . . you . . . I . . ."

"Stop it, Uncle Sebastian," Clayton said, shoving at his uncle as he wedged his smaller body between them all. With a very serious expression, he said, "I've got grown-up best friends and you're one of them, but I need a kid best friend and that's Neeci."

"Well." Sebastian frowned and then nodded. "I guess that makes sense." Then he held out his hand.

Ressa found herself charmed by him, the way he waited until Neeci slid her hand nervously into his, and apparently she wasn't the only one, because a slow, shy smile bloomed across her cousin's face in the next moment. "You're in movies."

Sebastian shrugged. "Yeah, well, I can't write books like Clayton's dad. Seemed to make sense."

Since Neeci was relaxing, Ressa straightened. Her heart lurched up in her throat as she found herself staring straight into Trey's eyes. He'd moved closer, without her realizing it. So close she could reach out and touched him, if she just took a step or two.

And she did.

But not to touch him.

Heart slamming, she watched him. Watched him watching her, but instead of the heat or the humor or the hunger she was so used to seeing, there was . . . nothing. A curious blankness like he was trying to hide everything he felt.

"Can we talk sometime? Sometime soon?" she blurted out. Her voice hitched. She couldn't do this anymore. Her aunt was right. If they could make it work, then damn it, she wanted it to work. "I . . . I messed up. I just . . ."

Her words trailed off as she felt a number of gazes swing her way.

And then, Trey's hand closed around hers and she was being pulled away from the front yard. "I have to leave," she said, resenting the fact that she *did* have to go. "My cousin—"

"I get that. Two minutes," Trey said, letting go of her wrist as soon as they rounded the corner of his house, mostly hidden from the front, thanks to the landscaping.

The scent of honeysuckle mixed with roses flooded her head as she sucked in a breath.

Two minutes.

She met his eyes. "I miss you," she said and the words came out easier than she would have thought possible. "And I can't do this. I messed up. Please . . . can we talk?"

His lashes swept down and for a moment that stretched into eternity, she felt her world crash to a halt. "Trey, please . . ." She moved closer, reaching for him, not caring in that moment if she sounded desperate—she *was*.

He caught her wrist.

She sucked in a breath.

Was it too—

And then she *couldn't* breathe.

His mouth took hers in a kiss that all but stopped her heart. His free hand came up, touched her cheek. It was a gentle touch, so at odds with the way his mouth devoured hers, his tongue pushing inside in a bold, demanding claim.

Her knees shook. Her heart rolled over. And she was about ready to wrap herself around him and beg the world to go away—for thirty minutes, or even ten—all from that one deep, devastating kiss.

They barely touched, save for that hot, hungry kiss—his hand on her cheek, the other gripping her wrist.

A growl sounded in his chest when she caught his tongue and sucked on him and then he tore away. Now, he caught her close, one hand coming up to cup the back of her neck. "*I missed you* doesn't cover what I felt," he whispered against her neck.

Then he moved away and she swallowed, her blood humming, her heart racing.

And damn him, his voice was just as cool as could be when he spoke again. "When did you have in mind?"

"I . . ." She had to clear her throat. She should also change her damn panties, she thought wryly, but that wasn't an option right now. "I don't know."

She blew out a breath and looked away. "I don't know where my head will be tonight. I don't know if I'll be pissed . . . or what . . . after I talk to Kiara."

"Why do you think you're going to be pissed off?"

"Because I know my cousin." She shrugged. "I love her, but manipulation is just what she does."

A warm hand touched her cheek and she looked up. "Are you okay?"

"I can handle it." She covered his hand with hers. "I'm used to this. Whatever happens, though . . . I need to talk with you. I *can't* handle what's going on with us . . . well, that's bullshit."

A line appeared between his brows and she turned her face into his hand, kissed him. "I can . . . I just don't want to. Being without you makes me miserable, Trey."

Something moved through his eyes, dark, fleeting, gone so fast. Then he cupped her face in both hands and brushed a quick, soft kiss against her lips, both eyes, her brow. "We'll talk. We have what matters, Ressa . . . everything else is just smoke."

Then he moved back. "You need to go." He took her elbow and escorted her around the house. Both of the kids had cornered Sebastian—and Travis, it appeared—on the porch, jabbering a mile a minute. Neeci had relaxed pretty fast.

Trey let go but before he moved away, he stroked a hand down her back. "I hope today goes okay."

A lump lodged itself in her throat. "Thanks."

She lingered only long enough to give Neeci a quick hug and then she left.

None of this was going to be any easier by taking her time.

Chapter Twenty-six

"I'm getting out soon."

Ressa studied Kiara's face across the table.

So far, the visit had gone pretty much the way they normally did.

Why didn't you bring Neeci?

Does she still remember me?

What have you told her about me?

Can you bring her next week?

That had taken up a good thirty minutes.

Now they were moving on to why Kiara wanted them there.

Ressa managed, almost, not to react. She glanced over at her aunt and then said, "I know you're up for parole. How come you're so certain you'll get out this time?"

"I've served four years. I was sentenced to seven. I know how this works." She leaned in, elbows braced on the table. A dark blue cloth wrapped around her braids, holding them back from her face. She'd slimmed down, almost too much, and her slim arms were roped with muscle. "I haven't caused any trouble and I've been taking college courses since I got in. They aren't going to keep trying to hold me in here—they're all but looking for reasons to let people out right now."

She shrugged, flicking her fingers like it was a done deal.

It might well be. Overcrowded prisons was nothing new. "Okay. Assuming you're right, what do you plan to do?"

"I'm taking Neeci back."

"No." Ressa folded her arms over her chest and met her cousin's dark, flat gaze dead on. "You signed away parental rights almost five years ago. She barely knows you. You can't provide for her the way I can. You can't give her a stable life."

Ressa didn't want to think about the shape Kiara had been in by the time everything imploded in her cousin's life. It hadn't been pretty. Ressa had been the one to focus, calm down, and get a grip on life, while Kiara lived for the next big deal, the next big score . . . the next big anything.

It was the next big *anything* that had landed her here.

"You already had one chance to prove you could straighten up," she said softly. "You couldn't do it. That's why you're here now. You can't take care of her. *I* can."

"*I* am her mother," Kiara said, her voice harsh.

"Only by blood." Ressa felt her chest constrict. Panic tried to take over. She wasn't giving Neeci up—it wasn't just love that drove her now, although that was a huge part of it. She looked at her cousin and saw a pit of chaos. Worse, she saw *herself*—she saw Neeci growing up the way *she* had, never having any stability or normalcy or even a parent who just *loved*.

How often had Neeci cried herself to sleep just after *visiting* her mother? Those short visits had done more harm than good and not because of the environment, but because Kiara couldn't stop playing head games, not even with her child.

No.

"I am the one who raised her," she said, keeping her voice calm. "I am the one who held her through every nightmare, nursed her through every cold. I'm the one who has answered all the hard questions and listened to all the crying. *I* am her mother in every way that counts, Kiara. You getting out of here doesn't mean you're entitled to jerk her around the same way you've done with everybody else."

"You selfish bitch," Kiara whispered. For a moment, it almost seemed that tears glittered, but then Kiara blinked and her eyes were just hard and cold once more. "She's my baby and I have a right to raise her."

"And *how* are you going to do that?" Ressa demanded. "You have never held a stable job in your life. You have *no* training. You don't even *like* to work—your idea of working is blackmailing lonely old men out of money or swiping credit cards from some of your johns!"

"Ressa," Angeline said, her voice firm.

"No." Ressa shot her aunt a look. "I'm not listening to this. I'm—"

"Mama." Kiara started to sob, laying her head on the table. "How can you let her talk to me like this? Talk to her. Please. Ress will listen to you. She always did. Tell her how much I need my baby. I can't face life outside this place without her . . ."

"What about what Neeci needs!" The words ripped out of her and Ressa didn't realize how loud she'd been until an odd silence rippled through the room, other inmates and their visitors going quiet as they turned to look at Ressa.

Conversation resumed after a few seconds and Ressa had to force herself to take a deep breath before she spoke again. "What about what Neeci needs, Kiara? A mother who will *be* there for her? They let you out on parole and *what* did you do but go right back to the same old thing?"

"I had a child to feed!" Kiara glared at her.

"The money Bruce gave you every year was more than *I* made in two." Ressa fisted her hands, staring at her cousin with so much rage, so much confusion. "You got a ridiculous amount of money every single *year*—"

"I should have had it all!" Kiara shouted.

The venom on her cousin's face, in her voice left Ressa shaken. Still, she shook her head. "But that's not the point. That was plenty of money to take care of a baby, Kiara. And you blew it on drugs . . . while your baby went hungry."

Kiara flinched. Then she sagged. "You . . . guys, you don't understand. I miss her. I *love* my little girl. I need her, okay? Mama, Ress, please . . ."

If Kiara had been looking at Angeline, then she might have realized she'd messed up.

As it was, it took several moments of awkward silence before she turned her head to look at the mostly silent Angeline.

When she finally did, Angeline just shook her head.

"Mama." She swallowed. "Please. Y'all don't under-stand—"

"I'm afraid you don't," Angeline said, shaking her head before Kiara could get anything else out. "You sit there and you cry about how *you* need that child. But it's not about *you*. It *can't* be about you. It's about *her.* It has to be *about* her and what she needs. She's not even six years old. Do you even have a *clue* how to take care of that little girl?"

Kiara stared at Angeline and then turned her head, looked at Ressa. With cool calculation, she reached up and swiped at the tears. "I can figure it out. You just need to get ready. My parole meeting is coming up and I *will* get out. And soon. Once I do, I want my daughter. You really want to fight me over this? You want to be the one telling her that she can't be with her mama?"

"Don't push this," Ressa said, rising from her chair. She looked at her aunt and Angeline rose. Shifting her gaze back to Kiara, she shook her head. "You signed your rights away. You might be getting out, but you aren't *capable* of giving that child the life she deserves, the life she *needs*. You're telling me not to push it, but you are the one who needs to be careful."

Kiara opened her mouth to argue, anger brimming in her eyes.

"What are you going to do, Kiara? When she asks? And she will. What are you going to do when she asks you why you went to jail? And this is going to follow you for the rest of your life."

She turned then, and headed to the door. "I'll be calling my lawyer. I suggest you be ready. I can give Neeci a real life, Kiara. You need to think about that, too."

"You just want her cuz she's *mine*!" Kiara shouted.

"No." At the door, she paused.

Mama Ang still lingered there, staring at her daughter.

"I'm sorry," Angeline said softly.

"Then don't let her do this," Kiara said, her voice pleading.

"Oh, baby. That's not what I'm apologizing for." Her mother sighed and shook her head. "I tried. I tried so hard to be a good mother to you and I still didn't do it right. I failed you some-where. Neeci, though . . . I can still help her. If you can't be the kind of parent she *needs* you to be, baby . . ."

Mama Ang shook her head and turned, walking to the door.

Kiara stared at them both.

"I love her," Ressa said softly. "But if I thought you could actually take care of her and give her a happy life, I'd give her up. I love her that much. But you *can't*, Kiara. You can't even make yourself happy. You can't even take *care* of yourself. How can you take care of a child? That's why I won't let this happen. It's because I love her that I'll fight."

She cocked a brow. "Now here's the real question. Do *you* really love her? Because I think you know which one of us can really give her a life . . . a chance."

There was a time in his life when he had been around more noise, but Trey couldn't say when.

It was almost seven o'clock, and when Sebastian managed to talk the two kids into a movie marathon, Trey could have hugged him.

He doubted there would be much of a marathon, but still, as silence fell over the house, he retreated to the front porch and collapsed on one of the rockers. He thought he may have felt this tired before.

Once.

At some point in his life.

He just didn't know when.

When Travis came out and sat down next to him, putting down a bottle of beer, he ignored it for the first ten minutes. Finally, he reached over and took it.

"I don't really want this," he said as he twisted off the cap.

"Then don't drink it." Travis shrugged.

He put the bottle to his lips, caught a hint of the smell, and took a sip anyway.

"I hate to say this, but those two kids have kicked my ass," he said.

"You did better than I did. I hid in my room half the day."

"I noticed." Trey curled his lip. "Chickenshit."

"Absolutely." Travis drained half his beer and then sighed in satisfaction. "So. How much longer . . ."

The words trailed off as the sound of a throaty engine came rolling down the street. It had them both looking up. The fatigue drained out of Trey and he almost lurched up out of his seat, had to fight the urge to leap over the railing.

Ressa, and that sexy Mustang of hers.

"Trey, you practically have a hook in your mouth—I can almost see you flopping around," Travis said, his voice wry. "It's a good look for you, man."

"Fuck off," he muttered. Ressa parked the car. A moment later, she climbed out and her aunt slid out a moment later.

It was the appearance of her aunt that kept him from rushing her.

That was it.

He couldn't care less that his brother was standing there, snickering over his beer.

But the slender, smaller woman had him freezing on the steps.

The resemblance was there. They had the same eyes, Ressa and this small, diminutive woman.

As she approached, her gaze held his and there was an appraising study there. He wasn't entirely sure how he held up, and he realized his hands were sweating.

Ressa came up the steps and stopped next to him.

"Hey."

He glanced away from her aunt. "Ah . . . hey. Hi."

She frowned and then glanced over her shoulder to her aunt. "Mama Ang, stop." She looked back at him. "She's got that *mom look* down to an art."

"I should." Her aunt smiled now. "So . . . you're the boy who has my girl all flustered."

Trey opened his mouth, closed it, then glanced at Ressa. He wasn't at all certain how to answer that. Finally, he said, "Well, she's had the same effect on me, so I figure it's only fair."

Amusement flashed through the older woman's eyes. Then she held out her hand. "I'm Angeline MacAllister. I'm also a huge fan of yours, Mr. Barnes, although I can't say I ever expected to meet you . . . and especially not like this."

"A pleasure." He shook her hand. He wasn't sure what else he could say.

She looked away from him and focused on Travis. Her gaze narrowed slightly and then she shook her head. "I bet you boys kept your mother busy."

"No, ma'am," Travis said, straight-faced. "We were too busy focusing on school."

Angeline snorted. "I just bet you were. Now . . . I think I'd like to take my grandbaby out for ice cream. Ressa, I imagine you can find your way home . . . can't you?"

Way to throw me under the bus, Mama Ang.

Nearly thirty minutes later, she stood on the porch, watching as Neeci climbed into the car with her grandmother. She'd gone somewhat reluctantly, but then as Mama Ang swept her down the steps, she'd said the magic words . . . *ice cream* and Neeci had all but dragged her granny to the car.

Now, while Clayton clung despondently to his uncle, Ressa rested her hands on the railing and stared off at the car as it backed out of the drive.

"I wish Neeci could stay here," Clayton said, his voice sullen. "Forever and ever. Nobody is as much as fun as she is."

Ressa bit the inside of her cheek to keep from laughing while both Sebastian and Travis gave the boy affronted looks. Sebastian took his hat off and put it on Clayton's head, tugging it down until the bill completely covered Clayton's face. "I'll tell you what, boy . . . I'm every bit as fun as a girl," he said, turning back toward the house.

"But you're *old*, Uncle 'Bastian."

"Your son doesn't lack for drama," Ressa said as they trailed behind.

Trey nudged the door closed and she paused to look at him. He just stared at her.

Her heart jumped, caught, racing inside her chest. She wished she could reach up. Touch him. Five minutes alone . . .

You two really do need to finish that talk.

Preferably this time without her flying off and losing her mind.

"Ah . . . so, maybe we should . . ,"

"Have you eaten?"

They both stopped, staring at each other. Then Ressa lifted a hand, laughing. "You first."

He reached out and caught her hand. "You look like you need to sit down, relax. Have you eaten?"

"I've been sitting on my ass in a car for half the day," she murmured.

"That's not the same as relaxing." His thumb stroked across the back of her hand. "Have you had anything to eat?"

She wrinkled her nose. "A burger from some fast-food joint around noon."

"Then you need to eat."

The smell of something rather delectable filled the house, and despite the fact that she wasn't hungry—or hadn't been—she could feel her belly rumbling. Maybe she could use some food, although until the past few minutes, nothing had sounded appealing.

As she roamed the house, she sipped at the wine he'd poured, wine she hadn't really wanted, but it gave her something to do, so she'd taken it.

Absently, she pushed open a door even as a voice in her mind murmured, *Don't be nosy.*

The rest of her was saying, *Nosy is better than brooding.*

Standing in the doorway, she found herself looking at a room that was clearly Clayton's.

It was easy enough to figure that out thanks to the *Star Wars* motif and toys scattered everywhere. It was a large room, bright with color. Everything a child could want for a bedroom. She moved around, picking up toys out of habit and putting them into bins or on shelves if she could see where they went.

"Hey."

She looked up and saw Trey in the door.

"Hey." She looked around. "I'm meddling. I . . . Sorry." Grimacing, she stared at the Dinobot she held and then shook her head. "I'm trying to keep my mind distracted. Today was . . . rough."

"No need to apologize." He came inside, stopped a few feet

away. Rocking back on his heels, he looked around. "I haven't ever really given you the grand tour, have I? This is Clay's room."

"Aw, man . . . and here I was thinking I found a guy who shared my obsession with Grimlock." She lifted the toy in her hand and grinned at him.

"Who says you haven't?" He took the Dinobot and easily switched it from dinosaur to robot, eying her through his lashes. "You know the best thing about buying these toys? Clayton never realizes I do it so I can play with them, too."

"Be still, my heart." She took the robot he offered and moved around him, picking up her wine as she moved past the bookshelf. "Every room in this place has a bookshelf."

"Nah. I didn't put them in the bathrooms."

She was able to laugh, she realized. Sliding him a look over her shoulder, she nodded. "Probably not a problem . . . most of us take a book in there anyway."

He grinned.

Putting the Dinobot on the bookshelf nearest the door, she headed out of the bedroom and paused in front of the next open door.

He gestured. "Just a guestroom." He reached around and flicked on a switch. "Travis is using it right now."

Ressa looked inside, saw absolutely nothing out of place and no hint of the personality of the man who was currently residing there. She doubted even Mama Ang could make a bed *that* neat.

"Did that man spend some time in the military or something? There's not a single thing out of place." She turned away, without noticing the way Trey's jaw hardened, or the tension in his shoulders as she continued her way down the hall. The next door was mostly closed but she pushed it open, glancing behind to see if he was coming.

"Hey, wa—" A guilty look flashed across his face.

It was that expression that *made* her look—it was instinct. She couldn't stop herself, or maybe she didn't try hard enough.

She thought of the ring he'd worn and some small part of her couldn't help but wonder. Did he have pictures of his wife in there? There was next to no sign of her anywhere. Was there something here?

But, no. Ressa frowned as she found herself staring into a room full of books. Not bookshelves . . . *books*.

A lot of them, and they were all his, spilling out of boxes, stacked haphazardly, and judging by the title on one of the nearest, she suspected a number of them were foreign editions. She thought that one was German.

Grimacing, she looked back at him. "Your twin has a handle on the organization thing better than you, I take it."

"Ah, yeah. Um . . ." He looked past her, a quick, almost furtive look.

"Hey, I've seen messy rooms before. And it's not exactly messy so much as disorganized." She shrugged and looked back inside.

He edged into the doorway, all but crowding her out, and his gaze once more darted to an area off to the side.

"I guess this is where you keep all your . . ." She turned, absently following his gaze. Her eyes bounced off them twice without really tracking what she was seeing. The third time, she shoved past his larger form and moved deeper into the room.

Head cocked, she stared at one shelf, jammed with books that had been carelessly double stacked. They stood out, like a spring flower among autumn leaves and winter-bare trees— that bright and sassy green, although if he hadn't kept glancing over there, she doubted she would have looked.

But yeah, now that she'd seen them, she couldn't look away. *Those* books didn't belong in here.

L. Forrester stamped the spines of those thirty-some-odd books, and piled right next to them was a stack of what might have been one of Trey's titles in French.

The title, in bright pink font, stood out, and she reached out, traced her finger down the spine

Exposing the Geek Billionaire.

Slowly, she turned her head to look at him, confused. An odd little suspicion began to form in the back of her already chaotic mind. A question hovered on the tip of her tongue, but one look at him had the question fading, while that suspicion exploded into full-on understanding.

His face was red.

The blush crept all the way down his neck and he wouldn't look at her, either.

Was it because her mind needed the release? The escape? She didn't know, but absurdly, she started to laugh. He stood there, brilliant red, half a snarl on his too beautiful face and she laughed.

"You . . ." she managed to gasp out between giggles that were edging too close to hysterical.

"What?" he demanded, hands jammed deep into his pockets, shoulders hunched.

"You are . . ." She snickered and then moved toward him, throwing her arms around him. "*You* are L. Forrester."

The red in his cheeks deepened—he blushed so hard, he looked like he'd been scalded.

"Trey, you dirty devil." Ressa laughed harder, completely delighted. The book he'd signed to her. The way he'd acted in the bookstore at Chillers. She pressed a smacking kiss to his lips.

His hands came up and gripped her waist while she continued to laugh.

He still didn't say anything and she finally managed to get that half-desperate laughter under control. Once she did, she lifted her face and met his gaze. Those blue eyes glittered and his hands flexed on her waist. "Glad you find this amusing," he said gruffly.

"Oh, it's not *amusing*," she said, a smile still twisting at her lips. "I think it's perfect . . . but you're busted, pal. Sorry, but I got your number now."

"Yeah?" He slid a hand up her back, tangled his fingers in her hair. "Well, there's a problem with you knowing my secret. I have to keep you. Make sure it stays between us."

She cocked an eyebrow at him and he leaned down, nipped her lower lip.

"I have to go check on the food," he said, his voice still oddly strained.

"Oh, I'm not done talking to you about this." Especially not now that she'd managed to find something else to think about, even if only for a few minutes.

She caught up with him in the hall and he shot her an exasperated look. "What's to talk about? You do realize that a lot of authors write under a second name, right? Plenty of them try to keep it quiet when the material is that different."

"Oh, hey." She bit her inner cheek to keep from smiling. If she did that, she might tip back over into that laughter and the rest of her emotions were fighting to boil out of control, everything kiting back and forth, with her anger still at a keen edge. But now, just now, the brightness of this moment overshadowed everything. "Don't go getting defensive on me. I think it's fantastic that you're so . . . flexible."

That mischievous glint in her eyes had him torn. Okay, he was hugely embarrassed now, but there was something in her eyes.

Something dark.

Something dark and edgy. That he understood.

Distraction could prove vital for sanity. That was why he'd buried himself in stories, in books . . . wrapped himself in Clayton for so long after Aliesha had died.

"Why are you blushing?" she asked.

Mortified, he realized his face was still hot and probably burning red. Turning away, he checked the pasta and then turned off the water. "I'm not," he lied.

"Okay. Then how did you suddenly become so sunburned?"

Sighing, he braced his hands on the counter. "You're getting a kick out of this, aren't you?"

"Why are you so worked up over it?"

Aggravated, he shrugged. "The hell if I know."

"You know, I think it's wonderful you can write like that."

Grabbing a colander from the cabinet, he slanted a look at her. He opened his mouth, closed it, then finally just shook his head.

She drew closer, and the self-consciousness he felt now only added to his discomfort. When she settled her hips against the counter next to him, he couldn't really keep avoiding her gaze, either.

"You're weren't this gun-shy talking about your other stuff."

Shows what you know. He just hid it better—because he'd been prepared. But he kept those words behind his teeth. Jerking a shoulder in a shrug, he said, "That was . . . different."

"Different how?" Her tone was tart. "Let me guess . . . you're fine with pushing the dark and the dismal and the intellectual, but bring something fun and sexy to the table and *that* is a problem?"

"Hell, no." Aggravated all over again, he shot her a look. "Have you *seen* my bookshelves downstairs? Those are my books, Ressa, and you know what kind of books I read. They are *mine*. There's everything from *The Story of O* to Jules Verne to *The Iliad* to Grisham and J.D. Robb. If I can read about sex, then I can damn well write about it."

"Then what's your problem?" she asked, lifting a brow. "Why do you look like you got caught sneaking your dad's *Playboy* magazine? Why do you look so embarrassed?"

He snorted. "First of all, assuming my dad *had* them, I never would have found them—and I doubt he had them. The only time I ever got my hands on them was when I found Zach's old stash. Second of all . . ." His mind went blank. Once more, he found himself floundering for words, because he was absolutely incapable of figuring out how to put it into words. "It's not about . . ."

Trey sighed and gave himself a minute as he mixed up some olive oil with garlic, red pepper, and salt. After his mind settled a little, he glanced at her. "It's not about being embarrassed, okay? I write. It's what I do. It's what I've always done. It's like . . . I've always breathed. I was able to learn how to walk well enough, too, although I don't remember doing that. I've always been able to write. I'm good at it—I know that, and I work hard at it, but . . . I've always done . . . . It's . . ." Lowering his hands, he scowled at her. "It's weird having the woman I'm sleeping with making a big deal out of it. Especially with those books, because I saw that ARC I gave you in your bedroom. You've already practically read that L. Forrester book to pieces."

Ressa had never realized how appealing it could be to see a man look that flustered. Although she realized she'd been off target—embarrassed wasn't quite right.

Self-conscious was the term she needed.

He focused on the food he was putting together with a single-minded intensity, although considering how easily he had done everything, she suspected being in the kitchen came about as easily as everything—well, everything that didn't involve anything public. "It's done," he said less than a minute later, while she was still pondering her next step. "They ate earlier. I ordered pizza, but I didn't eat much and I'm starving now."

She moved to block him.

"So . . . what? You think this is just a regular, old, everyday job and people shouldn't be interested?" she asked, her eyes narrowed on his face.

"It *is* a job. It's one I'm just suited for better than some others—like any one of my brothers." A wide grin split his face as he said it, and then, as it faded, he turned toward the glossy blue refrigerator and opened it up. A line formed between his brows as he looked at her. "It's a job. Some people are born to be soldiers, some are born to be cops. Zach was born to act—for a while, and then he lost touch with it. He found what made him happy. Others are good with kids and they go on to teach or be counselors or that kind of thing. I've got stories in my head. I didn't *ask* for them to be there, although I won't complain that I have them. It's a job, Ressa."

"It's a damn good job, most of the time," he said softly. Turning away, he got plates from a cabinet, focusing on that simple task. "People pay me to do the one thing I have to do if I want to sleep at night . . . but yeah, it's a job."

"It's a job you're brilliant at." She slid a hand up his back. "I don't see why you feel so self-conscious about it."

"Yeah, well, I'd probably feel just as weird if I was into roofing and you discovered I secretly did plumbing and were all excited about that, too." He pushed the plates into her hands. "Here. You can do this part."

Thirty minutes later, she sat outside curled up on a lounge watching the fire dance in the fire pit in front of her. It was gas and it had only taken her a few seconds of fiddling with it to get it going.

She heard a door open but she didn't move.

She had managed to keep her mind off everything that had happened with Kiara earlier, but now, in the quiet of the night, it was harder.

Kiara.

She thought she was getting out.

And she just might be right.

She'd done four years. This was her second offense and yeah, it had been one hell of an offense, but she'd been on the straight and narrow ever since.

Kiara had stayed out of trouble, kept her nose clean, taken college courses, all the things a parole board would look for.

Trey sat down beside her and Ressa still continued to stare out over the yard. The pool sparkled, the blue light glowing faintly in the darkness. There was something soothing about it, the way the water flowed and rippled in the night.

"Tell me something," she said after a long time had passed. A car pulled up nearby and they listened as the engine cut off, as a door shut.

"What do you want to know?" he murmured.

"I don't know. I just want you to talk." Then she frowned and lifted her head. "Tell me about the books . . . the Forrester ones. How did that happen?"

"What, you couldn't ask me about how me and Travis would talk Zach into ganging up on Zane?" he asked, his voice grouchy. Then he sighed. "That's *fun* to talk about."

"Yes," she said, her voice dry. "I've gotten the point . . . you kind of hate to talk about the books. But I'm curious."

"I've noticed." He slid her a look from the corner of his eye. "Look, the Forrester thing . . . nobody knows."

"Yeah?" Curious, she studied him. Firelight danced over his face, casting him into ever changing slivers of light and shadow.

"Yeah." He shrugged. "I mean my editor. Some of the people in house. My agent. Travis does. My assistant, although she's been on leave . . . sorta . . . for a while. But that's it. None of my other brothers know, my parents don't. You know now. I want to keep it quiet."

"Okay." She laid a hand on his cheek, studying his eyes. "But can I ask why? I mean, it's your call and everything, but I don't see why you don't want people to know or anything."

"I . . ." He rolled his eyes and rose to his feet. She watched as he moved to the fire pit, crouching down to fiddle with the controls. "I get nervous in front of people. I always have. I'm fine if I'm talking about my brothers and even better if I'm not the only one up there—growing up, there was almost always a couple of us together anyway, so I had to learn to deal with that." He grimaced and shot her a look. "I had to or I might as well become a recluse. But when it comes to me? I don't know. I tend to half panic and I have to spend days—sometimes weeks—psyching myself up for it. It's stressful enough to do it for one. I don't know if I can handle doing it for two."

As he slowly straightened from his crouch, he shot her a caustic look. "And it's even more nerve-wracking thinking about doing it in front of a bunch of women."

"Whatever."

"Yeah, you roll your eyes." He scraped his nails down the five o'clock shadow that had darkened his face. "You're not the one who damn near had panic attacks every time an essay or a project was due in high school. Shit, I even bribed Travis into doing it for me a few times—until we got caught."

"You bribed . . . you mean you had your *twin* giving your reports in class?"

"I wrote them," he said defensively. "He just read them."

A smile twitched at her lips and he had to clench his jaw not to smile back. Okay, yeah, that had been this side of desperate, the two of them swapping out classes, just so Trey didn't have to give those damn reports. Getting caught—thanks to a teacher who had figured out he couldn't go from panicked and ready to puke, to suave and cool within the span of a month or two—had probably been the kick in the pants he needed to actually *learn* how to handle getting up in front of people on his own.

And it had gotten *better*. Most of the time, other than a few twitches in his gut, he'd learned how to deal.

But he just wasn't certain if he was ready to handle it for *both* faces he seemed to be wearing these days. Especially not yet. He was just now learning how to function in this world again. He didn't need to juggle more on top.

"How did you get started writing them anyway?" Ressa asked. "I mean, *Absence* is a huge leap away from *Exposing the Geek Billionaire*."

There were still shadows in her eyes. He wanted to carry her up to his bedroom and hold her until she slept—okay, other things *first*—but she needed sleep.

"Well." He settled on the foot of the lounger and caught her hand. Her nails were wicked red, a slim ring of twisted copper on her right middle finger. He wished he could draw worth a damn, because he loved her hands. Elegant and beautiful and strong.

Aware she was still watching him, he finally looked up and met her eyes. "It was Aliesha," he said. "She kept pushing at me to do it. After she died, I couldn't write—not anything—for a year."

Ressa's eyes fell away.

He continued to hold her hand as he talked. "Then on the anniversary of the day she died, I woke up, and this idea—the idea she kept teasing me about, was just there." Toying with her fingers, he thought about that morning—it was weird. He still couldn't clearly recall Aliesha's face, but that morning, when he'd taken those first steps toward saying good-bye, he remembered in stark, vivid detail. "I'd talked about wanting to try something different and she wanted me to do it, told me I could. So . . . I tried. I finished—and then I bawled like a baby, because the day I finished was the day I really let myself admit she was gone."

"So this was some sort of closure for you," she murmured.

"The first one was." He shrugged. "Yeah. The second one? There was another idea . . . and it was fun. *I* had fun with it and I hadn't had fun with writing for a long time. So . . . I wrote the third one. I'll keep doing it as long as I have fun with it."

"And when you stop having fun?"

"I'll try another kind of story." He gazed into the fire. The firelight danced over his skin and she was struck anew by how beautiful he was.

The question hovered in the back of her throat.

Ressa told herself not to ask.

Now wasn't the time.

She didn't need to do this right now. She opened her mouth, then closed it, feeling like a fool. Before her internal debate could be solved, there was a crashing sound and they both went silent, turning to follow the noise that had come from beyond the hedge that ran along Trey's yard.

There was no way to see beyond it, not with the fence and the thick, lush green that rose above it.

The odd sensation of being watched settled over her. "What was that?"

"Probably Nadine's dog," Trey said. "She's got an old bull-dog that's blind as a bat."

The night was quiet, save for the lapping of the water in the pool.

He brushed his fingers down her cheek. "You worry too much."

Forcing herself to look up, she met his gaze.

"What?"

He cupped her cheek, stroked his thumb over her lip. Tucked there in the corner of his backyard, she felt like it was just the two of them in the world.

He lifted his eyes to hers but they were practically lost in the shadows.

"You wear every thought, right there for people to see," he said. "Instead of worrying, why don't you just ask?"

Ressa's heart lodged up in her throat. She licked her lips, opened her mouth. But the words wouldn't come.

Trey just shook his head, a faint smile twitching on his lips. "I loved Aliesha. She was Clayton's mother, was the love of my life . . . while I had her. But she's gone and I'm not the man I used to be."

Reaching up, she lay a hand against his cheek. Stubble scraped against her palm. "And who are you now?"

"In this very moment?" He turned his face into her touch. "I'm the man who wants to take you to bed."

Her heart jumped up into her throat.

She thought of Neeci, thought of Clayton, thought of a hundred reasons why maybe this wasn't the smart thing to do.

But she could argue with herself for hours.

For once, she was going to listen to what her heart said.

"I like that man . . . a lot."

Chapter Twenty-seven

Ressa didn't know why she felt so nervous.

It had seemed so easy, so right, outside a few minutes ago.

She'd called her aunt and Angeline had acted so casual, taken it completely in stride when Ressa said she was thinking about staying the night with Trey.

Shoot, the woman had already *planned* for that.

"I've already got clothes for Neeci here, baby. We'll work out plans to meet tomorrow for you to get your car."

So simple, so easy.

Except it wasn't.

Now, lingering by the French doors in Trey's room, she tried to calm the crazy knots in her belly. She heard a door open—the bathroom, she assumed, and she shivered, opened her mouth to say something. *Stall . . . say something, you need to think . . .*

But then she was in his arms.

"I missed you," he whispered against her mouth.

Think.

Yeah, she was going to be doing a *lot* of that.

Trey moved—she had the dizzying impression of the room

spinning and then she was pressed up between him and the wall. "You sure about this?" he asked, his mouth sliding along her cheekbone to nuzzle at her neck.

"Shut up." She dragged his mouth back to her, nipped his lower lip.

"Yes, ma'am." Trey stripped her shirt away and then he leaned in, his mouth seeking out the curve of her neck while he reached behind her for the catch on her bra.

"You, too," she demanded, tugging at the plain white button-down.

She laughed when he pulled it off with a force that sent buttons flying.

"I hope that wasn't one of your favorites," she said as he boosted her up.

"Wouldn't matter. It was in the way." He braced her against the wall, leaning in to press his mouth to her neck, then go lower, brushing soft, light kisses along her collarbone, and then he moved back up, claiming her mouth with his.

His tongue stabbed into her mouth as he popped the button on her jeans, undid the zipper. He seemed to have a thousand hands, because the jeans were gone in a blink. Then he boosted her up, braced her against the wall so he could rock against her. He was only wearing a pair of jeans now—and other than her panties, rough denim was all that separated him from her. His cock pulsed and she whimpered, feeling that sensation all the way down to her toes. Wrapping her legs around his hips, she clung tight, almost delirious with the pleasure.

He caught her tongue and sucked it into his mouth and then rubbed against her again.

Was it really possible to see sparks? Maybe even *feel* them? Because in that moment, she thought she was seeing, feeling . . . tasting—

Tearing her mouth away, she shoved him back. "Stop."

He went still. "Stop?" His voice was harsh, uneasy, his breathing as ragged as her own.

"I can't . . ." She had to wait a second to catch her breath. "I can't breathe."

The slow, wicked smile that curled his lips sent fire sizzling through her veins and she thought maybe, just maybe, she'd learn what it felt like to combust. "Good." He leaned back in, but instead of covering her mouth with his, he pressed his lips to the curve where neck and shoulder met. She hissed out a breath, the heat of him scalding her, and the sensation of him raking his teeth down her skin sent shivers racing through every part of her.

She shivered as he trailed his lips in a downward path. His thumb caught one nipple and rolled it while he used his mouth, his tongue to trace the edge of the triquetra on her chest. "I love this," he whispered against her flesh, and that was another caress all its own. "And this . . ." His fingers trailed up the unfinished tattoo on her side as he sank to his knees.

"There's no tattoo there, Trey," she murmured as he pressed a kiss to her hip.

The molten hot look he slid her all but sent her to *her* knees. This so was *not* going to help her get her breath back.

His lips skimmed along the lace edging the waistband of her panties.

Head falling back against the door, she felt the air in her lungs start to rasp in and out as he went lower, nuzzling her through the cotton of her panties. Anticipation sizzled, burned inside and broken, strange noises lifted in the air around her.

Me . . . that's me . . . She figured it out only when he went to pull back and a harsh cry of denial escaped her.

Twisting her fingers in his short, dark hair, she stared at him, rolled her hips.

He followed the waistband of her panties to her hipbone and she shivered as he brushed a kiss to the new tattoo she'd started working on when she'd gotten back from Trenton. A butterfly kiss to the book inked on her flesh, then another, just a little higher—how many damn books did she have on that tattoo?

She thought she might die until he muttered something under his breath and caught the waistband of her panties, dragged them down. She stepped out of them, but he kept her from doing anything else merely by putting a hand on her belly.

The brush of his hair against her inner thighs was soft.

His mouth was hot, wet.

The scrape of his teeth over her clit was a white-hot pleasure that had her arching closer while a broken moan ripped from her.

He growled against her and she felt the vibration all the way to the soul of her. Pressing him closer, she unconsciously curled one leg around his upper body, opening herself.

He stabbed his tongue inside and the sensation was intense, all consuming. Panting out his name, she forced herself to look down and then she jolted, because he was watching her. Through his lashes, eyes rolled up so that he could see over the plane of her body, he stared at her.

That intimate connection lit her up even more thoroughly than the way he slid one hand up her thigh in the next moment, placing two fingers against the swollen entrance to her pussy as he started to push in.

Her hands went to his shoulders and she clutched at him, feeling the orgasm gathering inside—gathering *her*—like everything inside her waited on this. Just this—

He twisted his wrist as he screwed his fingers in and she came with a hoarse, unintelligible cry. If he hadn't been right there, ready to brace her, catch her, she would have fallen.

And damn if she would have cared.

She was still shaking, still shuddering, when Trey rose to his feet. He leaned against her, his cock pulsating, the need a monster inside him.

Settling his hips against hers, he waited until her lashes lifted, until the sleepy, almost drugged look started to fade. She closed her hands around his hips, a smile flirting with the corners of her mouth.

He wanted—*needed*—to kiss her. The taste of her was still heavy in his mouth and he wanted to share that with her, join it with the taste of her kiss as he sank inside. Catching one of her wrists, he guided it down, pressed her hand to his cock, rigid behind the confining material of his jeans. She molded her fingers around his cock, squeezed.

"My condoms are in the truck," he said, his voice flat. "I didn't think about it until a couple of minutes ago."

She blinked, her lashes flickering down to shield her eyes.

Then she tightened her hand around him, gave his cock another taunting, teasing squeeze. "I'm on the pill." She stroked her hand up, then down. "I can wait, though. If you need to go get them . . ."

"Do I?" he asked as their gazes locked, held.

Instead of answering, she freed his cock and the feel of her fingers, cool and strong on his flesh, was almost too much. He jerked in her hand, the need to close her fingers around him, rock into her touch almost overpowering.

"Not on my account," she said softly.

Watching her, he nudged her hands out of the way and shoved the jeans, his boxers, down, kicking them out of the way. Eyes still on hers, he boosted her up, steadying her against the door. Hooking her knees over his elbows, he looked down, staring at her—her sleek, golden brown thighs, the heart of her—so wet, her flesh pink and ready for him. "Put me inside you," he said, his voice barely more than a growl.

She shivered and he shot a quick look up, saw the glassy look in her eyes as she stared down—watching them as well. Too much. It was—

Bliss—

"Oh. . . ." She arched, as best as she could, as the first few inches of him slid inside. Swollen and thick, his skin silken, but ridged, the sensation of him bare inside her was an erotic, seductive pleasure.

His fingers bit almost brutally into her as he pulled out, his cock rasping over swollen, sensitive tissue and then he sank back inside, tugging her against him as he moved. Not all the way inside—no, about halfway he stopped, and then retreated, using that same, mind-blowingly slow pace.

After a third, then fourth time when he still hadn't filled her all the way, she cried out and twisted, tried to close herself around him, and his entire body went rigid. "Please," she gasped out.

He tensed, so still against her. She could see the pulse throbbing within his neck, see the searing, intense blue of his eyes—

He drove in, deep, so deep, it ripped a scream out of her as she arched her back. It was like she felt him in every part of her—body and soul.

He let go of her knees to lock his arms around her and Ressa twined her legs around him, desperate to be as close as she could.

Her name was a snarl on his lips and she turned her mouth to meet his, breathless before he'd even kissed her.

His cock, already bruising, seemed to swell, and she moaned under the onslaught—his cock driving inside, his kisses dominating her mouth, his entire being overwhelming—taking her in.

The orgasm grabbed her by the throat, all but slammed her to the ground with its ferocity. Nearly knocked unconscious from the power of it, she was only vaguely aware of him still moving against her—then he tensed, groaning her name.

As he slumped against her, she tightened her grip on him, afraid to let go.

Afraid to let go . . . but at the same time, she was still scared to really grab on.

Chapter Twenty-eight

Ressa came to awareness to feel Trey's mouth on her back.

She was in a bed. With Trey. A moment of pure, insane happiness washed over her. She'd spent the entire night with him . . .

But then her brain kicked in, and she remembered the way the day had played out.

Trey sighed and shifted his body up, resting his chin on her shoulder.

"You're thinking hard and I haven't even had coffee," he said. "This could be a major problem in our relationship, Ressa."

With a lump in her throat, she wiggled over onto her back and stared up at him. "If only that was the biggest problem we had."

Lifting a hand, she pressed it against his cheek. "I never did tell you everything," she said quietly. "And I think I need to."

For a moment, Trey just studied her and then he nodded. "Give me a minute," he said, bending down to brush his lips over her cheek.

As he rolled out of bed, she was overcome by the urge to haul him back to her. Cling to him. Never let go.

But this had to be done.

Consequences, she thought. Mama Ang had talked about consequences and how Kiara was suffering the consequences of her actions. Maybe Mama Ang didn't blame her, but Ressa was suffering some consequences of her own.

If she'd pushed harder, if she'd tried harder, she could have done something more to help her cousin. If she'd just never gotten involved herself . . .

Those troubled thoughts chased her until the door opened back up and Trey came in. He'd gotten dressed—sort of. He had on the white shirt from last night, although it wasn't buttoned and a pair of jeans. With his sleepy eyes and the stubble on his face, he looked like a beautiful dream. And he carried two cups of coffee.

Maybe he was a dream. One that just didn't belong in her life. She'd find out, sometime here soon.

"I told you I was arrested on suspicion of prostitution," she said as she wrapped her hands around the thick mug he'd given her.

"Yeah." Eyes narrowed, Trey lifted his mug to his lips. "And I already told you, I'm not walking."

"Yeah." She took a sip and then blew out a sigh. "You do know that it could get ugly . . . you, your brothers . . . your family. I see what happens when people get hooked up with anybody with some sort of scandal."

"Look . . . just stop. I know my family. If I like you, they're going to like you. Besides, you must not be paying attention to the gossip rags." Trey shrugged. "Seb gives them more than enough to talk about and when *he* isn't making their tongues wag, then Zach is telling nosy producers he has a freezer full of bodies in his house. I'm too boring for them to mess with the majority of the time. I live in Norfolk, I'm a widowed dad and I write books . . . I'm boring compared to Sebastian and Zach."

"You could never be boring." A watery laugh escaped her. "Your family . . . they sound . . ."

"Crazy?" Trey offered.

"No." She flicked him a look. "I was thinking they sounded wonderful."

She put the coffee down, staring into it. But no answers appeared there.

Climbing from the bed, she grabbed the sheet and wrapped it around herself. "It was a few weeks after I'd told Sharon I was quitting. She asked me to at least see through the commitments I'd made for that month and I felt bad, so I said yes. One of the guys was somebody Scott had brought in. I'd never liked him, but it wasn't my job to like him. We were out at dinner and he had his hand on my back, was whispering in my ear about how much better the night could be if I'd give him one of those little extras Scott had suggested. That was when the cop showed up—he'd been following us. Listening."

She looked back at him. "It was the same cop who'd tried to catch me and I knew right away I was in trouble. The dickhead with me starts saying he hadn't done anything—I was the one who suggested we exchange *favors*."

"The cop, though . . . Detective Moritz, he'd heard. He was . . ." She paused, reaching for a word to describe a man who'd been a part of the worst time of her life. "He was fair. I hated him for a long time, but he was fair. I spent that one night in jail—had a PD come talk to me and the next morning, Hank Moritz was there. He told me they weren't going to hold me, no charges would be pressed." She sighed and rubbed one hand down her arm, chilled. The sun coming through the window did nothing to warm her. "He showed up at the bus stop. I tried to just walk away but he walked with me. Told me he knew just about everything there was to know about me— all the bad shit."

She laughed bitterly. "*All* the bad shit. I thought he was going to pull some crap bit and try to get me to sleep with *him* . . . but then he smiled at me and said, *I know the good shit, too, kid.* He knew about the scholarship, how Mama Ang had helped me catch up with school . . . I read fine when she found me, had always enjoyed it, but while the rest of the kids were doing geometry and trig, I struggled with multiplication and fractions. Algebra—*that* was hell. She got me a tutor and I was working at grade level within a year. He knew—all of it. Somehow, he knew. He told me I was smart, that I had a chance at a real life . . . if I'd just try to take it."

Look at what you could have—you could be almost any-

thing. Now look at what you came from. You're too close to going back— what you need to do is go forward, he'd said. *You got a chance at a real life. You're too smart not to take it.*

Gazing into the backyard, she found herself thinking of that grizzled, hard face and eyes that had seemed like granite. She'd hated him. Then . . . and after.

But those words had been lingered, echoed in the back of her mind for weeks, months. Even now. Years later.

"I got out of it. I was ready to go back to the fast-food thing, even, but I'd met Farrah." Looking back at Trey, she said, "My best friend. You haven't met her, but she's amazing. I was always at the library whenever I had time, and she'd been working here a while, mentioned they were looking for volunteers. I couldn't do volunteer work—I needed a real job, but she kept bugging me so I did it, started helping out once a month—I did it when I wasn't flipping burgers. And found . . . something. I changed my major that summer, focused on becoming a librarian. I hadn't even had a goal at that point—I was in school to make Mama Ang happy. I did it just to shut her up. The next summer, I was offered a part-time job. And I took it. A for-real job . . . something respectable even. I quit the fast-food place . . ." She laughed. "I still hate Big Macs, you know. *Hate* them."

Turning from the window, she moved over to the sitting area, tucked just beneath the bay window. Trey held out a hand, and for a moment she just stared, and then she put her hand in his, let him draw her close. She ended up settled between his legs, one of his hands rubbing the small of her back while she talked.

"Kiara was getting into more trouble, though. The cops pretty much blew the entire thing wide open. Sharon wasn't charged, but she moved out of the state. Hannah, a few others and me—we just kind of watched from the sidelines, had to talk to the cops a few times. But Kiara, two other girls . . . and Scott—the guy who'd started hooking some of the girls out, they were all arrested and charged. Scott was the only one who went to trial and he ended up copping a plea bargain before it ended. He'll be getting out of jail soon. He got hit hard because of all the evidence they found of him blackmailing people. Kiara and the others, they were given a deal—six months and probation if they testified against Scott. They all took it. The other two straightened up. Kiara . . . I swear, she can't find herself for nothing."

"Some people don't want to straighten up," Trey murmured, his lips against her brow. "That's not on you."

"Maybe not . . . Hannah's death is."

Trey went still.

Ressa closed her eyes. He cupped her cheek but she wouldn't look at him. After a moment, he stopped trying to make her and just held her.

"Kiara kept getting in trouble, more and more, all the time. She fell in with this guy who'd known Scott—Christo. He knew what had been going down—I think he might have been one of her johns at some point. And she . . ." Ressa shrugged. "She went right back to it. We'd get into fights and I'd tell her to get a clue and she'd tell me to mind my own business . . . sex was the easiest way to make money ever—and it was fun. Fun. She ended up having a little girl—Neeci—and she had no idea who the dad was. I told her she was lucky she hadn't ended up sick or worse . . . It was the same thing. Over and *over* again. I was *sick* of it. I was the one taking care of Neeci at that point and I was tired from working and taking care of a baby— Neeci was only two months old and she didn't sleep well . . . there were . . ." She swallowed, fighting the anger she always had to fight when she talked about this. "Neeci was in pretty bad shape the first few months—Kiara hadn't taken care of herself and Neeci came early, couldn't eat well . . . had other problems. She's okay now, but that first year was hard. I was just *tired*."

My fault—

Trying to silence that voice, she twisted in Trey's arms, sitting with her back against his chest. Part of her wanted to move away, but the rest of her, it needed this. He still held her.

"It was six years ago . . . almost to the day. Next Saturday, as a matter of fact."

Trey tensed, unable to stop it. Next Saturday—it was the anniversary of the worst day of his life.

Ressa looked at him, her eyes bruised. "What happened six years ago?" he asked, focusing on her and not the past.

"She got in trouble." Ressa sighed, the sound tired and strained, like the things she was telling him just wore down on her. "I was at home when she called. It was probably around eleven. She'd been out with Christo—she told me she'd been *working*—that's what she called it. And this guy . . . she was ranting about how he messed everything up and made Christo mad at her. There was a fight and the cops were called and Christo acted like it was her fault . . . It took me forever to figure out what she was talking about. But she'd tried to . . ."

She stopped, closing one hand into a fist. A moment later, she surged off his lap and he watched as she went over to her clothes. They lay in a tangle and his heart broke a little as she fought with them.

He went to his closet and grabbed the first thing that came to hand. "Here," he said, kneeling in front of her.

She went still as he settled the black cotton on her shoulders, tucking her arms into the sleeves like she was a child. "I don't know why you have to be so wonderful," she said softly. "I just . . . I don't get it. Why are some men like Christo and others like you?"

Uncomfortable with the way she was watching him, Trey shrugged. "I don't know this Christo jerk, but if he's the kind of slug I think he is, he doesn't sound like much of a man."

"No." Ressa shook her head. "He's really not."

She reached up and closed a hand around his wrist and Trey sank down on the floor in front of her.

"She made money by sleeping with other men," she said softly. "Sometimes they knew they'd be paying her. Sometimes . . ."

She looked away. "Sometimes they didn't. Christo was a dealer. She got drugs from him, would slip it into a guy's drink. He'd forget her—and everything else—by the time he woke up. That night, it didn't go the way they planned. Christo hit her. He'd hit her before and she always went back to him. This time it was because she'd fucked up the *job*."

She smoothed her hands back over her hair and locked them at the base of her neck, staring at nothing. "The *job*—

she picks up men, drugs them, steals from them and it's a *job*. This time, the guy she tried to pick up in this bar hadn't been into her. Christo said she must have fucked up—fucked up. Yeah, that covers it." She bit her lip, her gaze skittering off to the side before she looked back at him. "They looked for marks who looked like they had it pretty good. Nice cars, nice clothes . . ."

Trey's gut started to churn.

Fuck.

"This guy, she'd given him something and he'd been drinking, but he wasn't going for it. Christo was determined, though. He was in trouble himself, owed people some money and I guess this guy looked like he was doing pretty well and each time Kiara tried to find somebody else there, he'd push her back to this one guy. Then the guy up and leaves the bar . . . there was some kind of fight, though. She took off and Christo caught up with her at their place. Hurt her pretty bad. She . . ." Ressa's voice tripped. "She came to me. My cousin came to me, all battered and bloody and bruised. She had some stranger's credit cards, his cash. She told me she just needed to stay there that night—she'd pay me. She offered to *pay* me. The idiot. Then . . ."

The words came out hard, flinty. "Christo showed up at my door. Banging on it, yelling at me. I told Kiara to never tell that son of a bitch where I lived, but she'd done it anyway. He kept banging . . . I called the cops. Kiara saw me do it and she hit me. There I am, trying to report somebody who'd beat her, somebody who was practically trying to knock my door down while a little baby slept in the bedroom upstairs and Kiara *hit* me. I almost hit her back. But . . ."

Trey waited. Her hands clenched and unclenched, her jaw went tight. Finally, she shook her head. "It wouldn't have done any good. I told her that son of a bitch was not getting in my house—that the police would be there and I hoped like hell they arrested him. And she went to the door. I told her if she left with him, she'd better not keep dragging me back into her life—told her I was trying to take care of her baby, trying to take care of myself—I couldn't take care of her, too. I was mad, I was scared . . . I . . . I shouldn't have said it."

"You were thinking about Neeci, it sounds like. About

yourself and your safety and the fact that you had to take care of both of you. Kiara wasn't going to worry about her daughter—somebody had to," Trey said.

He didn't think she even heard him.

"I don't know much of what happened between the time she left and the next phone call. Kiara said he hit her again and she thought she passed out. When she woke up, he was gone and she was alone in a motel where they'd ended up. She called Hannah. She was scared and alone and I'd told her not to keep dragging me into it, so she called Hannah."

Ressa tried to think of the first time she'd met Hannah. A pretty girl who had just come fresh from the farm— and she looked liked it, too—all golden hair and blue eyes and sunshine. She'd been a hot mess half the time they'd known each other. Hannah had dropped out of college and ended up the mistress of one of the men she'd met through Sharon.

Ressa rarely saw her friend after she left school, but sometimes they'd have coffee and Hannah had seemed happy. *We never did . . . you know . . . while I was one of Sharon's girls,* Hannah had said, blushing the entire time. *But I needed the money and I called him, asked if he'd still like to have me go to dinner and stuff when he was in town . . . this is just how it ended up.*

Hannah had been at home, a cute little cottage where a fifty-nine-year-old married banker kept her in the kind of style she'd always wanted. She was pampered and spoiled and she had a sweet heart.

"She told Kiara to come over. Promised she'd help her. Give her money . . . whatever. Kiara went over. A couple hours later, Christo came looking for her. It turns out he'd put a GPS thing on her phone—she never went anywhere that he didn't know about. He went over there, broke in. Had Kiara by the hair and was dragging her out when Hannah went after him with a baseball bat. She hit him once . . . and he got it away from her. Killed her. Kiara was there—saw the whole thing. And when he was done and said they had to get away, get rid of the evidence, Kiara just went along with it."

Trey thought he might be sick. For so many reasons—the

mark. The fucking *mark*. A girl dead. His head pounded. *Son of a bitch.*

"Somebody heard the screams, saw them leaving," Ressa said, her voice faint. "They released a sketch. I saw it on the news the next day. And I knew. I wanted to be wrong. But I knew. She came over that night, crying. She begged me to be quiet, said she hadn't meant for anything bad to happen. Christo was sorry and he hadn't touched her since and they were just going to leave . . ."

Her fingers twisted with his, clung tight.

He doubted she even realized how desperately she held on in that moment.

"She was going to just *run away*. It was like Hannah's death meant nothing—just a sad accident, and if she left it would make everything better. She'd come that night to tell me that she wanted me to get things together for Neeci. So she could take the baby with her . . ." Her eyes searched his. "I couldn't do it. I lied and said, *Okay. I'll be quiet . . . I'll get it ready.* I told her exactly what she wanted to hear and I made her believe it . . . and then I called the cops. I turned my cousin in, Trey."

Chapter Twenty-nine

For the longest time, he didn't speak.

Then, just when Ressa was ready to pull away—no, *run* away—Trey cupped her face in his hands.

He pressed a kiss to her brow, one to each eye and then brushed his lips over her cheeks. When he pressed his mouth to hers, she almost choked on the sob.

"You did the only thing you could have done," he said softly.

"I—"

"You *did* the *only* thing you could have done."

When he looked at her, his eyes were intense, that surreal blue green all consuming. "I can understand that she was probably scared of this guy. He probably had her convinced that she had to lie. I can't imagine how she felt, or what she went through. But he'd killed somebody. She wanted to take her baby and run off with this guy. What else were you going to do?"

She grabbed at his wrists. "I didn't even try to look for another way out. I just called them. *All* I could think about was Neeci. I didn't think about Kiara or what might happen. What does that make me?" she demanded.

"I think it makes you a mom," he said softly.

She sucked in a breath.

His thumb brushed over her mouth. "You reacted out of a need to take care of a baby you loved."

"I'm *not* her mother," she said. "What I did caused Neeci to *lose* her mother."

"What you did protected her—her mother, or at least the woman who gave birth to her—sounds like she's already lost."

"I . . ." She stopped. Slowly untangling her hands from his wrists, her legs from his, she stood up. "I'd do it again. In a heartbeat. I told Mama Ang what I did and I lied to her face when I said I was sorry, but I'd do it again."

"I wouldn't expect anything less. Honestly, Ressa . . . do you think that little girl would have been happy with Kiara? Shit, we can set that aside completely—would she have been *safe*?"

"No." She didn't even have to think it through.

"Then I'll say it again—you did the only thing you could do."

He got up and rubbed his hands over his face before he tipped his head back.

"*Fuck*," he snarled.

"Trey, I . . ."

He just shook his head and held up a hand. "Nothing's changed," he said softly. "Not for me. But . . ."

He blew out a breath and moved to the closet.

She stared at the black raven that stretched out over his back, watched the wings flex as he reached up to grab a box down from the shelf.

"Your sister . . ." When he looked back at her, his face was grim. "Her last name isn't MacAllister or Bliss, is it?"

"What?" Confused, she shook her head. "No, it's . . ."

"Oxford," they said it at the same time.

Ressa sucked in a breath. "How do you . . . ?"

She stopped as he moved to the bed. He took the lid off the box.

"The night of my wife's funeral, I couldn't come home," he said, taking out a folder and flipping it open, then closing it. "I couldn't stand the thought of sleeping in the bed I'd shared with Aliesha—not without her."

Ressa's gaze involuntarily moved to the bed they'd shared. "It's new."

She looked back at him.

"I donated the old bedroom suite a few years ago. I wasn't even able to sleep in here for almost a year—used a guest bedroom. Then I decided I'd avoided the truth long enough . . . it was hard. I had to go through it twice . . ."

He found something—a letter. When he opened it, something fell out.

"Twice?" she asked, distracted by whatever it was he held.

"Yeah." He looked over at her now. "I'd gone out. Went to a hotel and rented a room, then hit the closest bar. Got shit-faced drunk. I don't remember much. Much—shit. I don't remember *any* of it. The next day . . ."

He paused and looked away. "I woke up in the hospital. Travis was there. I'd forgotten. For a few minutes, I'd forgotten that Aliesha was dead."

"Why—" She stopped the question when her voice cracked. Holding up a hand, she took a deep breath and then forced the question out. "Why were you in the hospital?"

"I think you already know, Ressa."

Ice replaced the blood in her veins. Turning away, Ressa shoved her fists up by her temples, shaking her head. "No."

"I'm sorry," he said softly.

"You—" She spun around, questions and denials and rage choking her.

And he held out the letter.

She almost dropped it when she caught sight of a name on it.

Mr. Barnes
   My partner and I understand that you didn't want
to file a report regarding the events of . . .

Her heart lurched as they landed on the date.

Most of the letter turned into a blur but her heart froze as she read her cousin's name and read a brief, concise version of the charges that were placed against Kiara for the thefts she'd been involved in—thefts, and several sexual assaults.

A few of the victims had filed reports.

And Christo had kept more than a few pieces of evidence . . . souvenirs that had ended up weighing very heavily against him and Kiara.

> *Your wallet was found among the items recovered.*
> *As it had a picture of you and your wife and was*
> *monogrammed with your initials, I feel fairly*
> *confident it's yours.*
>   *Kiara Oxford and Christo Klemons were both*
> *found guilty in separate trials. Christo matches the*
> *description of the man you were seen to be fighting*
> *with the evening of the events.*
>   *I realize this happened at an awful time for you.*
> *I hope this doesn't add to your grief, but offers some*
> *closure. If you'd like to claim your belongings, please*
> *contact me.*

It was signed Detective Julie Maynard.

Julie . . . She barely remembered her, but she knew her.

Julie had been Hank Moritz's partner.

Two of the detectives involved in the case against her cousin.

The letter fell.

She didn't even notice.

"It was you," she said, the words a flat monotone. It didn't even sound like her voice.

"Looks like."

She rubbed at her mouth, her fingertips feeling oddly numb. "How . . . I . . . I don't . . . why are you telling me this?" she whispered.

"Why?"

The haunted look in her eyes would haunt him.

She wanted to know *why*.

It was now or never, he realized. Either what they had was strong enough, or it wasn't.

He closed the distance between them and didn't know if it was a good sign or not when she didn't move. She looked trapped, frozen in place.

Wrapping her in his arms, he pulled her up against him.

"The why is easy." There, he pressed his brow to hers, held her gaze. "I love you. It started months ago . . . seeing you with Clayton, watching you act like you weren't trying to watch me even while I was doing the same. I think I was already half in love with you the first night we were together."

"You . . . What . . ."

She twisted away and he had no choice but to let her.

"You can't be serious."

"Why not?" He kept his voice level, stayed where he was, although what he wanted was to grab her, hold her.

She spun back around and stared at him, eyes half wild. "Don't do that don't sound all reasonable right now. I'm terrified. I'm confused . . . and I'm mad at her all over again. Don't sound . . ."

She blinked and shook her head. "You make it sound like that's all that matters."

"It is." He reached out, traced his fingers along the bow of her upper lip. "I love you. For me, *that* is what matters. And I don't know about you, but if the two of us can work through this? I'd say we can handle just about anything else life throws at us."

Chapter Thirty

Ressa stared at him, her eyes wide and he thought he almost saw a flicker of hope in them. A flicker of . . . everything.

"So . . . can we work through this?"

She sucked in a deep breath and looked away, but he caught her chin and guided her face back to his. "I'm not asking for a declaration of undying love, but if you care—"

"If I *care*?" she interrupted. Her voice cracked. "You stupid idiot. I love you—if I didn't *care*—"

I love you—that was all he heard. All he needed to hear. Pulling her up against him, he slanted his mouth across hers. When she didn't open right away, he nibbled on her lower lip and whispered her name.

Her lips parted as she curled one arm around his neck.

A fist banged on the door.

"Not now!" Trey was going to hurt whoever was at the door. That was all there was to it.

The knock came again. "I said, not *now*!"

"Yes, now." Travis's voice sounded grim. "Your agent has been calling half the morning. Your editor just started calling.

A hell of a lot of other people who shouldn't even have your number are calling, too."

"Tell them to go to hell." Trey didn't looked away from Ressa's face. He cupped her chin and angled her head back. "Tell my agent to call back in two hours. Unless the world is ending. Then call back in one."

"Unless the world is ending?" she asked, laughing weakly.

"I figure if the world is ending, there's not much I can do to help anyway." He shrugged, and then he hooked his arms over her shoulders. "We can't undo the past. Any of it. And hell, the past—your past, Kiara's past—all of that gave you Neeci. Would you undo that?"

Ressa closed her eyes and then buried her face against his neck. "No." It was a soft, barely audible whisper. "And I feel awful for saying that. I mean . . . Hannah . . ."

"Don't." He pressed his lips to her temple. "You didn't cause her death, baby. You didn't."

"Trey!" Travis. *Again.* "Two seconds warning! I'm coming in."

That two-second warning was literally all they got because the door opened and Travis filled the doorway. He looked at the two of them standing there half-dressed and cocked a brow. "Damn. I was hoping that two-second warning wouldn't be enough."

"Travis." Trey kept his voice level. "Didn't I just tell you to come back? Do you want to die?"

"It's going to happen sooner or later." Travis shrugged and then held out the phone in his hand. "You need to talk to your damn agent and don't give me this shit about the world ending. He's already tried to rip me a new one and I was in a bad mood to begin with."

"Shit." Frustrated, he looked at Ressa and then snatched the phone from his twin's hand.

From the corner of his eye, he saw Ressa duck into the bathroom.

"What the hell is so important that I had to be dragged out of bed?" He almost sagged in relief when Ressa appeared back in the doorway a moment later, tying his robe around her waist.

"It's almost noon, son. I take it you haven't been online." Reuben's voice had that brusque, clipped tone—a sure sign that his temper was edging near the boiling point.

"No. It's Sunday. I kind of take that day off—also, if I want to stay in bed until almost noon, well, bully for me."

He slid Ressa a look then glanced at his brother, saw that Travis was slouched in the doorway. Travis had his own phone out and there was a muscle pulsing in his twin's jaw.

Shit.

"What is going on?"

Reuben said, "You'd be better off seeing for yourself." He named a popular publishing blog and said, "Pull it up. I'll wait."

Trey sighed. "I'm not in front of my computer right now, man."

Travis just held out his phone.

Trepidation filled Trey as he took it. "Never mind . . . I got it."

"Are you reading?" Reuben asked.

"I am now." Something that started out as fury brewed in his gut. Only to give away to disbelief and then settle down into something cold and tight.

He kind of hates to talk about his writing in any way.

He did it for his wife, you see . . . Started them on the anniversary of the day she died.

He still loves her. It's going to take a long time before he gets over her.

Each book is written for her.

Every sentence made that knot of cold fury draw tighter. And every time he saw the name the so-called article was attributed to, he wanted to hit something.

Sebastian appeared in the doorway and either the youngest Barnes was too tired or too senseless to realize the stupidity of it, because he stood there for a long moment, just staring at Ressa, gaze roaming over her with a little too much leisure.

Travis smacked him across the head.

"Fu . . ." He rubbed his head and then looked down the hall with a grimace. "Ah, sorry. Sorry. Ah, Ressa? Your phone has been vibrating non-stop for the past ten minutes. Clayton

almost answered it, too. The kids are getting restless downstairs, too."

"The kids?"

"Yeah." Sebastian gave them both a look. "Angeline
brought Neeci over not that long ago."

Sebastian's gaze drifted once more to Ressa, his eyes lingering on legs left bare by the robe she'd tied around her waist.
Trey bared his teeth at his younger brother. Sebastian held out
her phone and when she accepted, Sebastian gave Trey an un-
abashed grin.

"Trey, damn it, son, are you even awake?" an irate voice
bellowed from the phone.

He lowered the phone he still held to his ear, glanced at it.
Then sighed an answered, "I'm here, Reuben."

"Who is this Bliss woman? Did you pick up some crazed
stalker?"

Trey managed to keep his voice neutral through sheer will.
"No, Reuben. She's my girlfriend."

There was a faint pause and then Reuben said, "Part of
me is glad to hear that. The other part is wondering what the
hell?"

"Stick with the first part. Somebody is messing with me."

Then he hung up.

He tossed the cordless to his brother and turned to find
Ressa staring at her phone, ashen. Her hands were shaking and
he reached out to the electronic device. She clung to it but he
persisted and finally, she let go.

She sagged back onto the bed and lifted her eyes to his. "I
didn't do this," she said, her voice a low rasp.

He held her gaze for just a moment. "That was never even
a question for me."

Then he started to read. It was a different blog, one geared
more for readers and the blogger had taken a different slant;
the post was filled with more than a little speculative doubt.
The comments, though, they ran the gamut from scathing to
outright cruel, and most of the condemnation was directed at
Ressa.

His vision went red because a few had already dug up information about her cousin's trial. In that moment, more than

ever, he was glad he hadn't decided to take any kind of legal action for what happened that night.

Right there, in the comments, people were already laying her cousin's crimes at her feet—*testified against her own blood . . . what kind of woman does that*?

He did see more than a few snide comments about how naturally he'd hidden behind a name because he was too embarrassed to claim the romances.

Bite me, he thought. He scrolled down to read more but before he could, a text popped up.

> *Girl, I am not kidding. You need to call me and now. Thompkins is on my ass and they are talking about firing you over this. Call me. Now.*

He stared at the name, frowned. Farrah. Tapping on it took him to the contact and he found himself staring at a woman that was vaguely familiar. He'd seen her a time or two at the library where Ressa used to work, he thought.

Sliding Ressa a look from under his lashes, he asked, "Who is Thompkins?"

"What?" She stared at him. Her eyes looked too dark, almost stunned.

"Who is Thompkins?"

She blinked and then rubbed the back of her hand over her mouth. "Technically, my boss. Or one of them. He's in administration, but I never really see him."

Staring at the phone Trey still held, Ressa rose.

At some point, Sebastian and Travis had left the room, but she didn't know when.

She couldn't think.

Every time she tried to get a concrete thought in her head, her mind spun right back to that headline.

The secret side to one of America's most popular authors.

She didn't even have to read the article to get it. The L. Forrester book was side by side with Trey's latest, the two covers so completely at odds with each other.

"Hello . . . would this be Farrah?"

The sound of Trey's voice, hard and flat, dragged her attention back to the present and she jumped up, gaping at him.

He stared at her.

She made a grab for the phone.

He moved out of her reach, evading her with an ease that was almost pathetic. Steaming, she tried again while listening to one side of the conversation. "I understand somebody wants to talk with Ressa. . . . yes, I assume it's about the article that went live earlier today . . . ? Yeah, thought so. So, there's a problem . . . , no. No. That's not the problem. Here's the thing—you're *talking* to Trey Barnes and there's no way Ressa did that interview."

She gaped at him. "Give me my damn phone. This is *my* problem."

"No." He lifted his phone away from his ear for a minute. "You got pulled into something because of me. I don't know why but that makes it *my* problem, too."

"This is *not* how people make relationships work." She glared at him, chin raised. She wanted to punch him.

He caught her chin in his hand and then, while she continued to glare at him, he kissed her.

"Okay, so we *are* in a relationship? Good." He broke away long enough to ask that question and then he kissed her again—hard and fast.

She was balling up her hand to punch him when he moved away. "We also don't make relationships work while letting one person handle a problem that the other person *somehow* caused. You're not getting fired because of me, Ressa, and I'm not going to watch somebody drag you through the dirt, either. Deal with it."

Then he turned his back on her.

"Arrrghhh!" She grabbed a pillow from the bed and swung it at his head.

He caught it halfway through the next swing, approaching her with a glint sparking in his eyes.

"Yes, I'm aware of what the article says, but there's a problem with all of that, because Ressa has spent pretty much every second of the past thirty-six hours either with me or traveling. She hasn't had time to do any sort of interview on this."

Another pause and Ressa held out her hand. He cocked a

brow. "No . . . but I'll find out," he said. "You can pass *that* on to whoever wants to talk to her. She didn't do shit so don't try to pass this off on her."

Then he ended the call and tossed it on the bed.

"You still wanna fight?"

She grab another pillow and threw it at him. "I would have handled it!"

As she reached for another pillow, he tackled her and took her to the bed.

Breathless, trapped under one hundred eighty pounds of hard, lean male, she tried to hold onto the anger. Tried not to think about the fact that a robe, her panties, the shirt he'd all but tucked her into earlier and his jeans were the only things separating them.

"What was I supposed to do . . . let you get raked over the coals because somebody was screwing with me?" he asked. He dipped his head and pressed a kiss to the skin bared by the open vee of his robe. "Let somebody try to fire you? I don't think so."

"I don't believe in having a guy fight my battles."

"But this wasn't *your* battle—it involves both of us so that makes it *ours*," he said, dragging his lips up. "Also . . . you said relationship. Ressa, does that mean we still have one?"

She froze.

She had said that.

He stared down at her.

Neither of them spoke and he sighed, lowered his head back to hers, rubbed his lips over her cheek. "Ressa, have I ever told you how much I love the way you smell?" He went to kiss her and she bit his lip. *"Ouch!"*

Jerking his head back, he glared at her and touched his throbbing lip with his tongue.

"Stop trying to distract me."

"You're distracting me." He gave her a quick kiss and then rolled off. Drawing his knees up, he hooked his elbows around them. "It's not just *your* fight. It's about both of us and I figure there were two ways to handle that and you wouldn't like either of them. I could either tell whoever that was that you didn't have shit to do with that so-called interview, or I could go with you when you leave. You'd bellow at me about either one."

"Damn straight."

He shrugged and looked away. "So you're mad either way. But I'm not going to say I'm sorry. If you *had* been involved, this would be a different discussion, but you weren't. That means it has to do with me. Why should you bear the brunt of it?"

She opened her mouth, then snapped it shut with an audible click of her jaw. "I don't much like the fact that you're being logical about this."

"Yeah. It always pissed my brothers off, too."

With a withering stare, she climbed off the bed and started to get dressed.

He was moderately mollified by the fact that she pulled the black button-down back on over her bra. Watching her fingers dance over the buttons, covering up all that lovely skin seemed to be a crime. "What are you going to do?" he asked, dragging his gaze up to meet hers.

She narrowed her eyes. "Men," she muttered.

He grinned at her. "Yeah. Well." Then he shrugged and repeated the question.

"I don't even know how to answer that." She sighed and caught her hair, dragged it out of the collar of the shirt, then looked for her jeans.

He snagged them from the floor by the bed and tossed them to her, watched as she shimmied into them.

"Trey!"

The sound of Travis shouting his name up the steps had him flopping back on the bed and throwing his elbow over his eyes.

"What?" he bellowed back, the habit of shouting back and forth across a house something he'd never really forgotten.

There wasn't an immediate answer and he shook his head. "You know, it's a beautiful morning. I've got a beautiful woman with me. I'd really like to be in my bed making love to her . . . but *nooooo*. . . ."

Travis appeared in the doorway. "Your neighbor is at the door," he said, his voice curiously flat.

Trey stared at him, puzzled. "I don't have time for this," he said, shaking his head.

"Make time," Travis suggested.

Trey headed out the door, muttering under his breath.

But when Ressa went to follow, Travis caught her elbow and held her back.

"Trey . . ."

He opened the door and wasn't surprised when Nadine slid inside, moving past him as though he'd flung it opened and welcomed her with open arms.

The sight behind her was a little more disturbing—and it had him gritting his teeth. Two news vans. One reporter was all set up, the other still fumbling with her equipment, but the second they saw him, they both started shouting questions.

He slammed the door shut and put his back to it.

Not again. He'd never been as good at this as his brothers. He could handle it, yeah. But he *hated* it.

"I'm so sorry," Nadine said, her voice soft. Sympathy filled her voice and she twisted the pearls at her neck.

"Sorry . . . ?" he asked. "For what?"

She waved a hand. "This. That . . . this woman you're dating. Whoever she is. What she's done. We never really met, but it's awful what she did to you. I can't imagine how you feel."

"Hmm."

Her gaze skipped to his, then away.

"Yeah, I bet you can't." He folded his arms over his chest, chewed on the inside of his lip for a second. There was an odd look in her eyes. It wasn't *guilt*—not exactly. But it was something.

Going with his gut, he asked, "How long were you listening to us the other night?"

Blood rushed to her face. "I was—" A nervous laugh escaped. "I don't know what you're talking about."

"You."

Ressa's voice came from the top of the steps.

Nadine jerked her head around, her jaw dropping at the sight of Ressa there, descending slowly.

"What . . . Trey, why is *she* here?" Nadine demanded.

He didn't even have a chance to respond before Ressa came between them and none too subtly pushed him back. "Not what you need to be worrying about," Ressa said, her voice sharp enough to cut. "Worry about *me*."

Nadine backed up a step.

"Ressa, hold up a min—"

She whirled on him, her hair flying around her shoulders. "Oh, *no*. I don't think so. You remember that little chat upstairs? You're not letting me fight this all on my own because it involves you? Well, guess what? She did this because she's *jealous*. I'm with you and she's not. So that means it's every bit as much about *me* as it is about *you*."

Trey studied her and then slowly, backed away. He tucked his hands into his pockets and settled back against the door.

"Trey." His name was a tremulous plea on Nadine's lips. It scraped over his nerves like steel wool on an open wound. "You can't think I had anything to do with this. All the interviews say it was her . . . they talked about her and her blog and everything. She could be doing this for publicity. It makes sense."

"In what *world*?" Ressa snapped. "This is *not* the kind of publicity I want. *Ever*."

Nadine's green gaze bounced away, not connecting with Ressa's. "She could be doing it just to toy with you. Who knows?"

"*I* know," Trey said. He shoved away from the door. He laid a hand on Ressa's shoulder. "This isn't the kind of thing she'd do—she cares about me too much."

Ressa felt some of the knots inside her dissolve. It was like he'd never even had any doubts.

Nadine's porcelain skin went even whiter, though, and her mouth drew tighter. "But there's *proof*—"

"I wonder how the proof will hold up if Trey decides to pursue any kind of legal action," Travis asked, jogging down the stairs. "Ressa, I'm good on computers. You willing to let me access your laptop? We can clear that up right here. Seeing as how you've been with either your aunt or here with Trey—and us—for the past thirty-six hours, shouldn't take much to figure out if you really did do that interview—since naturally, it was *requested* that everything be done via e-mail."

He smiled thinly at Nadine. "Might have been harder to

pull off if you'd done a live interview, I'm thinking." Planting himself at Trey's side, Travis glanced over at Ressa. "So . . . laptop?"

Ressa frowned. "I didn't bring my laptop. It's back at my house."

"Hmmm. Okay. That simplifies it." Travis shrugged. "Trey, that means if she did that online interview, it was from here. They said it was an exclusive online interview, obtained early yesterday . . . although, damn . . ."

Travis tsked. "You and your aunt were on the road, right? Were you typing and driving or what? Those are some hellaciously *long* interview questions."

"Trav." Trey bared his teeth. "Please feel free to check my computers. Ressa, would you let him check your phone?"

"That doesn't prove—" Nadine stopped, sucked in a breath.

"Come off it," Ressa suggested. "We all know. Thanks for almost costing me my job, by the way. I *really* appreciate that."

Nadine shot a look to the left, then the right, before looking at Trey. "You really think I could do this?" she whispered.

"I didn't want to. But the answer is pretty clear. What I don't know is why?"

Nadine sniffed and moved to the door. "I can't believe you think I'd . . ." Abruptly, she froze and her voice went tight. Slowly, she turned and the uncertain, nervous female just . . . faded. "I did it because *I* waited. All this time. I waited for you to see me and you never did."

Then she spun back around and jerked the door open, half falling out in her determination to leave.

Travis sighed and shook his head. "I'll make sure she gets home okay."

"Behave," Trey warned.

"I always do." He shot them a wicked grin. "But for your sake, I'll behave *nicely*."

He slid out the door.

Trey went to shut it and the rush of voices caught his attention. Wincing, he glanced outside and saw that in the past few minutes, the two vans had multiplied to five.

"And here I was thinking *I* would be the one catching their attention," Sebastian said from the living room, glancing around the arched doorway.

"Shut up or I'll drag your scrawny ass out there." Sighing, Trey reached down and caught Ressa's hand. "You trust me?"

Her eyes flew wide.

"You aren't serious."

"I'm just going to address it, real quick," he said. "They won't go away until I give them something."

She winced, look down at herself. "I'm a mess. I don't have makeup on. My hair is probably a wreck. I'm wearing *your* shirt . . . *I don't have makeup on*. I barely remembered to put a bra on!"

"You didn't have to do that on my account," Sebastian offered.

"I'm killing you when I'm done," Trey warned. Then he reached up, smoothed her hair down. "They aren't going to focus on any of that. You look beautiful."

He pressed a kiss to her lips, remained there. "Trust me?"

"I might kill you for this," she whispered against his mouth. "Fine."

Ressa gulped at the sudden flash of cameras, the rush of questions. There were only a few people, she'd *thought*. Now it seemed like dozens.

Stunned into silence, she gripped Trey's hand and held tight.

"Mr. Barnes! Mr. Barnes! Is it true that you're also writing erotic sexy stories under another name? What does your family think about this?"

"They are romance books," he said. How could he sound so calm. "And knowing my mom? She's probably going to be mad I didn't let her know already so she could read them. She loves romance."

There was a faint pause and then the next rush of questions, most of them running over each other.

One finally distinguished itself from another. "Is this Ressa Bliss? Your former girlfriend? Why do you think she gave that interview?"

"Does she *look* like a former girlfriend?" He laughed. "This is Ms. Bliss but let me make it clear. We are still dating. I can't explain what happened with that interview but the in-

terviewer didn't bother to verify their source. Ressa didn't give
the interview. She's spent the past few days with me or traveling with family. She hasn't had time to give an interview."

Now there was another flurry, but when Trey opened his
mouth to answer, Ressa squeezed his hand and answered herself. "No, we are not *claiming* that I didn't give the interview,"
she said, her voice like ice. "We are *stating* that. Whoever did
that interview wasn't talking to me."

The reporters paused, but it was so brief, it couldn't even
be measured by breaths.

"Are things serious between you two?"

Instead of answering that, Trey turned to Ressa and cupped
her face in his hands. She stood there as he closed his mouth
over hers, but slowly, she relaxed against him, her hands gripping his waist.

He broke away after a moment and hooked his arm around
her neck. As he led her into the house, he said over his shoulder, "No comment."

"You didn't even pause when you read that." Ressa
stood in his office, staring at bookshelf after bookshelf. Trey
sat at his desk, pounding furiously away at his keyboard. "You
believed in me. Just like that."

He paused at her words and looked up. "Of course I did."

Of course I did.

She thought about everything that had unfolded over the
span of the past day—all the secrets she'd been afraid to tell
him . . . and the one *huge* fear that had lingered over her head.
All of it was out in the open.

Of course I did.

"You're doing it again."

She opened her eyes and turned her head to meet his gaze.
"Doing what?"

"Worrying." He looked back at his computer.

"No." She moved to him then, coming around the desk. She
stared at the headline on his monitor. It was yet another prom-
inent blog, one that focused on books and authors. It read:

BUSTED!

It referenced the news about Trey and his alter ego, but it

also included snippets from that so-called interview. There was also a link to the trial. She skimmed some of the e-mail he was writing and caught his wrists. "Dial it back, baby. They didn't do anything—and hell, the woman is just re-posting some of what she read. She didn't do anything."

He flexed his hands, stared at the computer. "I'm pissed off."

"So am I. But not at anybody online . . . well, except the person who didn't bother to make sure she was actually talking to me." She pressed her lips to his temple. "You already talked to your publicist. The site in question has already pulled it and a retraction will be up this afternoon. Although . . . the horror . . . you now have to give a real interview."

He slid her a narrow look. "I think I should give it to you. What better place to put it than *Blissed Out On Books*. People are tanking you and your blog."

"Better idea." She nodded to the monitor. "Give it to them. Start your e-mail over, give the bloggers enough info to explain what *mostly* happened without getting personal and ask if they'd like to help you with a real interview. They're bigger than I am. You want the word out? Do it that way."

He blew out a breath, then shrugged. "If I do it that way, will you quit worrying so much?"

"I'm not worrying. I'm thinking." She draped her arms around his shoulders and pressed a kiss to the sensitive spot below his ear. His body tensed.

"If you want me doing anything besides pressing you up against a wall, you shouldn't do that."

Things in her belly went low and tight, but despite the temptation, she went still and read the e-mail. Once he sent it off, he spun in the chair. He pulled her into his lap and she wiggled, tried to adjust to the confines of the chair. "I'm thinking," she said again. "This is all so simple to you. I called Farrah back. She spoke with Thompkins—he's still furious, but he's agreed to give it a few days and see what happens."

Studying Trey's face, she smoothed a finger across his mouth. "Farrah apologized—she was—is—sorry but *she* thought I'd done it . . . for a few minutes at least. Trey, you would have had every right to at least *ask*."

"No." He hooked his arm around her neck and pulled her

in against him. "No, I wouldn't. Because the woman I fell in love with isn't the woman who would do that. I knew it, without even thinking about it."

"Details." She remembered what her aunt had told her. Okay, yeah, she and Trey had some crazy . . . *details*, but he'd just proven to her, beyond a shadow of a doubt that he had faith. Not just in her, but in them.

"What?"

Tipping her head back, she pressed a kiss to the corner of his mouth. "Mama Ang told me that if we had love, everything else was just details. She was right. When I'm with you, I forget about all the crazy things, the complicated things. I forget about Kiara and every reason why this is a bad idea."

She laughed wryly. "*This* . . . today . . . that's exactly why I've been so afraid to try anything with you because this would happen. People would find out. And . . ."

"And the world didn't end." He wrapped his arms around her. "We're still here. The world can't mess us up unless we let it. I think we've already proven we've got what matters."

"Yeah." That solid, warm weight of her had his entire body sighing in satisfaction. As he brushed his lips against her brow, she said, "They're all just details."

Twisting her head, she caught his mouth. "We just might be crazy, going after this."

"We'd be crazier not to. Life doesn't always give you a second chance to be happy, Ressa." He angled the chair back and she yelped as she ended up sprawled against his chest. He took her mouth in a slow, leisurely kiss. It was the first time all over again, slow and gentle, tasting her, learning every hollow, every crevice of her mouth.

When it ended, Trey pressed to her and murmured, "Crazy or not, I haven't felt whole like this in . . . too long. It may be crazy, but it's right. You feel it, too."

"I feel it, too."

He lifted his head, studied her eyes. "Then the rest is just details. We'll handle them."

"Yeah." Ressa smiled then, leaning in to rub her lips against his. "I never really thought about it, but I'm pretty good at handling details."

Discover Romance

berkleyjoveauthors.com

See what's coming up next from your favorite romance authors and explore all the latest Berkley, Jove, and Sensation selections.

See what's new

~

Find author appearances

~

Win fantastic prizes

~

Get reading recommendations

~

Chat with authors and other fans

~

Read interviews with authors you love